Cesar Luis

THREE BLACK STONES

Translated by the author based on his first book "Pedras Negras" originally written in Portuguese.

Projeto editorial: Luna Editora
Artwork by: Geléia de Arte
Cover photo: Gisele Saviolli
Translated by the author
Copyright © 2016 by Luna Editora
www.lunaeditora.com
lunaeditora@hotmail.com
www.facebook.com/lunaeditora

Dados internacionais de Catalogação na Publicação (CIP)

Luis, Cesar
        Three black stones; tradução de Cesar Luis, São Paulo: Luna
        Editora, 2018
        p. 316

        ISBN- 978-85-69453-10-9
        1. Literatura. 2. Literatura Brasileira. 3. Ficção

        I. Título

                        CDD B869

LUNA
EDITORA

TO AMANDA AND ANDRÉ.

PREFACE

As we live we are caught by surprise in situations that we do not want, or that, at least in normal situations, we do not expect them to happen. The normality of life is always broken by some unusual fact. This fact, whatever its nature, sets us in motion by reaction. These are unavoidable facts! Unexpected situations over which we have no control whatsoever, but are part of the mysterious "why" of our existence.

Fernando Eastman, Rico and Lia get involved in an adventure they did not want and didn't even think it could be possible, but due to the circumstances they were irresistibly involved in. He and his friends are swallowed into an adventure filled with mysteries, conspiracies and intrigues involving an ancient pre-Inca legend, elongated skulls, outlanders, and occult powers. All in a frantic race to reveal the truth about the creation of humanity on planet Earth.

Orejona is, according to an ancient pre-Inca legend, the mother of all the Andean civilization. Her children were born here and prospered in perfect harmony until they were destroyed by a natural cataclysm: the Biblical Universal Flood. Nothing remained of the history of this people. Time goes by and this part of human history turned into mythology, then its historical roots fell into oblivion and all that remained was an obscure folklore clutter. The story was never really forgotten but was totally discredited by the Andean peoples until one day, thousands of years later, when the story returned to the minds of the people of a Peruvian village at the foot of the sacred city of Machu Picchu.

Orejona came back to the minds and hearts of her people in an inexplicable collective psychic event.

A book must be found. This book contains one of the greatest secrets of human history. A great network of power tries to prevent this secret from becoming public and Fernando, a fearless nerd, does the impossible to reach the source of this incredible knowledge. An unbelievable source!

This is what **THREE BLACK STONES** is all about. An adventure that takes place in the beautiful landscapes of Peru and Bolivia. A frantic search for a lost knowledge. A historical rescue in favor of the spiritual growth of humanity. It is a quest to correct serious *mistakes* in human thinking. Mistakes that have become virtues due to the force of habit. Errors that cause a great deal of suffering to the human species. A search motivated by strong principles and driven by the curiosity of a sound mind.

Topics like the manipulation of information by the media, "invisible hands" behind the scenes of international politics, the "true religion", astronomy, intelligent life on other planets, secret societies, secret space exploration projects... a big "conspiracy theories" mix that makes up a story full of important and insightful information. The author proposes a new approach for a new paradigm, an alternative view of the human condition on planet Earth today and the *urge* to correct old errors.

Last but not least, **THREE BLACK STONES** is a book motivated and driven by inquiries!

"You, people of the Earth, still have the chance to learn, although the time is short. You will plant the seed. The last seed. I know it will blossom. We have studied a plan to redeem mankind and we are sure it will work out."

DAY 1 – 8am
Brasilia airport – DF/Brazil

- Good day sir. Welcome on board on behalf of the entire crew. My name is Odalisca dos Santos.
- Excuse me... did you say... *Odalisca?*

DAY 1 – 7am

"Attention, Mr. Fernando Eastman. Attention, Mr. Fernando Eastman. Please come to the information desk.", said a distorted voice through the speakers at Brasilia International Airport. *"Attention, Mr. Fernando Eastman. Attention, Mr. Fernando Eastman..."*

"What could it be?", he thought apprehensively leaving the VIP lounge and walking towards the information desk.
- Good morning, I'm Fernando Eastman. What is it?
- Mr. Eastman, there is an envelope for you. It has just been left here just now. The messenger asked to be delivered immediately, as your flight leaves in a few minutes. As soon as you checked in we were informed by the system. Here it is. Please, sign the receipt.
- Who delivered this? What is it?
- I do not know, sir. I just do my job. The company has this service available to first-class passengers. – said the attendant coldly, staring into nowhere as Fernando signed the receipt. – Thank you sir. Have a good trip.
- OK... thank you.

The flight to Cuzco took off on time. As soon as he was comfortable on his seat, Fernando opened the envelope. There was a little notebook inside. He took it out and flipped. It was an old notebook. Considering its damages on the leather cover should probably be about 30 years old. "Interesting!", he thought. "They don't make covers like that anymore!".
It was fully completed with sketches and notes. It looked like some kind of research. He started to read. Some words were

impossible to decode, for they were blurred. This notebook was definitely taken to some excavation site or something like that. The pages were all winkled as if it had been wet from the rain. The notes seemed to be about a story he had already studied. Some words were underlined and others reinforced by two or three layers of different ink as if the author wanted them to be taken into account. It began with the title: **The Creation of the Universe**.

""Before the creation of the stars, before the Angels ... there was heaven, home of the Eternal, the only God perfect in wisdom / love / glory.
Before *creating the Universe,* **He lived an eternity**.
Countless beings ... with all the care and attention ... from the tiny atom to magnificent galaxies.
His hands shaped a world of Light and upon it a mountain ... upon it would stand the throne of the Universe.
Mount Zion ".

"Weird! This looks like the apocryphal Genesis of Melchizedek! These are very old notes." He read on.

"The Eternal brought into being the first rational creature.
A glorious Angel ... the most honored.
This Angel would be **the representative** *of the King of Kings before the Universe.*
Then, the Eternal ... beauties of Paradise, talking about plans.
... the principles that should rule the Universe. The physical and moral Laws ... respected by all the divine government.
The moral Laws were two:
1- **To love God above all things;**
2- **To live in fraternity.**

Thus the Universe would grow in harmony and peace.
God entrusted the Angel with a mission: to be the **protector** *of the Laws.*

Lucifer, *the* **bearer of Light**. *The Prince of Angels prostrated himself by promising* **fidelity**.
The Eternal continued his work ... brought into existence hosts of Angels, the Ministers of the Kingdom of Light.
The Holy City was populated by ... happy radiant.
It would bring existence to the Universe **full of life** *...*
His order sounded like **thunder** *and spawned endless* **galaxies** *filled with worlds and suns. - paradises of* **life and joy**".

"Cool! This is really an apocryphal Genesis. But why should I read this? Who sent it to me?"

The airplane was already in the air when he decided this notebook should not be that important, but the reading was very interesting. Fernando feels pleasure in reading stuff like that. Some words were illegible, but it did not bother him. What called his attention were the highlighted ones.

"Guided by God, the angels ... the riches of the Universe and ... the vastness of the Kingdom of Light ... on a **sidereal excursion.**
Everywhere they found worlds **inhabited** *by happy creatures who welcomed them in celebration.*
Freedom of choice, *the great test ... was precious as Life.*
Through it ... demonstrate your love to the Creator.
The Eternal said:
'All the treasures of the Light are open to you, except the hidden ones of Darkness. You are free to follow me. Loving the Light you will be bound to the Source of Life.'"

The writings were very interesting. Fernando reclines his seat and continues reading.

"So the Creator **separated Light and Darkness,** *good and evil. The Universe was* **free to choose** *its destiny.*
Abiding the divine Laws... the Universe expanded in joy/glory... strong bond of love that united all.
Rational beings *were endowed ... infinite development*
... unspeakable pleasure in learning about **Divine Wisdom**

"Nobody dedicates a notebook on a specific text for no good reason.", Fernando thought puzzled. "Very interesting! Who would had it delivered to me?"

The highlighted words were accentuated with several different types of pens. Fernando soon concluded that this book had been studied and revisited several times by the author. There were stretches in pencil, a kind of thick soft pencil, because the line was very strong. The first writing seems to have been made with an ink pen, for some words had been completely disfigured by the water.

A second title came as one of the pages: **The Conflict**.

"Wow! Super!!!" – he spoke out loud. The passenger made a weird face. He apologized.

*A huge struggle deep inside ... the **desire** to know the meaning of Darkness was **immense**.*
Father's pleas tormented him - He always went back.
*Before creating the Universe The Eternal **had foreseen a possible rebellion**: the risk of knowing the Dark ...*
*Without the gift of **freewill** life would have no meaning.*
*Lucifer **did not intend** to abandon the Light*
... a combination of Light and Darkness
*They were **separated** in the Eternal Kingdom.*
*Finally Lucifer ... a theory: **'the science of Good and Evil'***
*He wanted to present his theory as **a new system of government**
... superior to that presented by the Creator*
*This new system ... **balance** between Good / Evil, love / selfishness, Light / Darkness.*
Lucifer ... for a long time before revealing it to the Universe and kept on pursuing his duties of Bearer of Light.
The Creator already knew everything."

"Yes! The old theory of duality.", he thought. "Funny. This is just a way to try to explain the unexplainable! History shows that we have never had this very well balanced in real life. I wonder what went wrong."

"The Eternal ... profound silence.
Lucifer asked the reason for His silence.
God said, 'It is the time of Darkness. You are free to accomplish your purposes.'
*Lucifer ... **eloquent speech** ... the government of the Creator.*
The speech was explosive ... first dissension in the Universe.
*Rational beings ... choose to remain in the Light or ... in the 'science of Good and Evil' ... **a third of the stars in the sky** ... next to Lucifer.*
How to exercise the science of Good and Evil with The Creator still in power?
*The Council of the Rebel Angels ... decided to request the Throne **for a fixed time** ...*
... could prove that the new system was superior.

*If it were approved by the Universe, the new system ... **forever**.*
Otherwise he would return to the government of the Father."

- What a beautiful thing! I loved this text from the first time I read it. It is a political intrigue worthy of a true History of Mankind."

This text appeared in the early 20th Century with the discovery of the famous Dead Sea Scrolls. Other texts as incredible as these were found in the Qumran caves. They were all taken to the Vatican that claimed its dominion. After all they were texts of fundamental interest to the Christian faith. Two years earlier, in 1945, the Nag Hammadi Library was discovered in Egypt.

After years of restoration, research and translation, some of these texts were published. Among them you can find the Book of Enoch, Gospels that had never been rad like the Gospel of Peter, the Gospel of Mary, the Apocalypse of James, some Gnostic texts on obscure themes never addressed by the Church.

There were also texts with accounts of the daily life of the Essenes. The people of Qumran were connected to the Zealot movement, inspired by their great leader, Melchizedek. The little that is known about him is that "Melqui" means "King" and "Zidek" is the root for what we know today as "Zealot". Fernando was totally absorbed in the notes of the small notebook and despite the difficulty in some parts, he continued reading.

"God knew ... way would lead to unhappiness / death ... disregarded the request.
*Lucifer accused the Father ... His Kingdom was a **tyranny** ...*
Did he not give them the gift of choice?
Now ... prevented from... a new government?'
These accusations ... unjust government.

The Eternal rose from His Throne, as if intending to leave it.
*The rebels ... an expectation of **taking power**.*
... took out his royal crown / robe and ... on the Throne.
The turning point had come.
Lucifer parted with The Creator who said:

'You were given a name of honor when you were created. Now everyone will call you Satan, the Lord of Darkness.'
After weeping ... God left the Eden ... *amidst the glories of the Universe* **towards the abyss.**
In the face of God ... a glow.
Raising his arms before the Darkness, he said: **'Fiat Lux!'**"

THREE DAYS BEFORE – 4:30pm
Machu Picchu
Archaeological excavations on the Temple of the Moon (Templo de La Luna)

- I can't believe! It's a chamber! – exclaims Professor Vicenzo Fontanoura with astonishment. – The government was right! How did they know about it? Incredible! There are mummies in here... and ritualistic artifacts. An altar with smooth stones. Extremely smooth, much more than simply polished! – says the old man while caressing the stone altar. – Vitrified! But ... there is nothing inscribed! We need to dig here. Call *señor* Alejandro immediately! – shouted the experienced archaeologist, sending an order to his assistant waiting on the outside. – We must not waste time!

A few minutes later...

- Professor. Did the gentleman call me?

- *Señor* Alejandro, send the men up tomorrow. What we found here is incredible. We need to start digging early tomorrow. This is a great discovery.

- No doubt *el presidente* will be interested, Professor. We will guarantee total secrecy. "We" includes also your team, is this clear for you, *señor*?

- Yes of course...

- Dig deep, my friend, but do not forget: everything you find must be reported to me, do you understand? I'm here to make sure of this personally. If you need to explode, *señor*... you know... do whatever it is necessary, but do it *in silence*. Nothing shall leak!

TWO DAYS EARLIER – 7 a.m.
Águas Calientes/Peru

- *Buenos dias*, José.

- *Buenos dias*, Rico.

Both men get their coca tea. Each one took a piece of bread and sat at the table in the small *bodega* by the feet of the holy mountain. There was a strange silence in the air all over the village of Águas Calientes. Everyone had eyes of awe and mystery. It seems that everybody knew what everyone else was thinking.

- Something is wrong with me. I woke up with a story in my head. – said Rico still drowsy, rubbing his face.

- Is it about a book?

- Yes. How do you know?

- Orejona is an old mountain legend. I don't know much about her. My grandparents used to tell stories about her when I was a child, but I didn't know she had written a book. – explains Jose, a tourist trinkets salesman.

- I've heard my grandmother talk about her too, but ... it's so strange. You also know about the story. Did you dream about it, too? – asked Rico in awe.

- It wasn't a dream. I simply woke up with this story in my head. And it won't go away! Carlos, too. Ask him.

- Carlos, do you know about this story of…

- Orejona? Yes. I woke up with it in my head, too.

- Maria, you too?

- Yes, Rico, it seems everyone here in the village woke up the same way. I took Pablito to school and I heard a lot of people talking about this story. Everyone talks about a book and about Venus.

- Are you serious?

- I didn't know she was from Venus. No one knew it… until this morning. Isn't it strange? – said Maria in low voice. – I'm a little worried. Even the kids are talking about this outside school! Nobody understands what happened!

Rico shudders. "It must be something with the newly discovered chamber.", he thinks to himself. They're very close to the inscriptions he discovered by chance when he led a group of tourists up the Temple to the Moon. That was a week ago. And this inscription, which only Rico knows about, binds the legend to the opening of the chamber. He intuitively knows that.

The excavation works start today in a few minutes. He's already late. He needs to climb to the Sacred City as fast as possible and see that no one gets to those inscriptions. "Things can get worse!", said Rico to himself.

DAY 1 – Noon
Cuzco International Airport/Peru

Fernando arrives at the international airport of Cuzco with a little delay. It was not the flight, but the Immigration queue. Peru is traditionally a tourist country. The transit of tourists is intense and constant throughout the year. The connection in Lima was also problematic. "Where's my pen? I must have left it in Lima. He filled all the immigration forms after someone lent him a pen. He felt embarrassed about not having a pen in hand since he works as Field Archaeological Survey Assistant. His only occupation, beyond library research, is to take note and sketch out the details of the things he sees *in loco*. Since high school, taking notes and making sketches have become habits encouraged by his father.

- *Señor* Eastman, what is the nature of your visit to Peru? – asks the immigration agent.

- Tourism.

- What's your profession?

- Student. I haven't graduated yet! – he said jokingly.

Due to the secrecy requested by the Professor, and to habit, Fernando did not mention anything about excavations, researches, or discoveries.

Eastman is tall and slim. He's got brown (not so short) hair and also brown eyes usually dressed in comfortable clothes: jeans, long-sleeved shirt and a reinforced boot. He learned during his field research that long sleeves work very well under the strong sun, as well as protecting when one has to sneak through narrow passageways and digging holes.

He is a 34-year-old man from a wealthy family born with a silver spoon, like people used to say, in a wealthy family in São Paulo, Brazil. He always attended the best schools in the city during his childhood and later he studied Anthropology at the Federal University of Brasilia. He chose to study there because his father, a prosperous real estate entrepreneur, found it more convenient for his family and business. He spent the last few years in the political capital of Brazil inside a beautiful mansion on the shores of a colossal artificial Lake South built along with the federal district back in the early 1960's. Since the beginning of college he has flirted between São Paulo and Brasilia. São Paulo is his homeland and he regularly pays his mother a visit, but Brasilia is where his heart is

His father has disappeared for almost fourteen years, but he has never been considered dead. Endless searches have been made but no results at all. The last time he was seen was when he was going to visit a cattle ranch he ran near Acre, northwestern Brazil. His father has always been absent because of endless business trips around the country. This absence made Fernando Eastman an attentive, meticulous, unbearably methodical, almost maniacal student, always seeking to fill the void of the inattention of a man who insisted on not being there for him.

When it was time for Fernando to choose his college he chose Brasilia without any doubt. The customary absence of his father (now for disappearance) was an important component that helped molding his personality. His mother has never let him do what he wanted. His father, on the contrary, always supported him, not as a father nor as a friend, but as a preceptor: he left Fernando free to decide on his own life. Living practically alone for many years in Brasilia taught him to make his choices without his mother's intrusions and censorship. This independence taught him valuable lessons.

A curious thing that Paulo Eastman used to do when he was with his son was to stimulate the little boy's creativity. Never cared about the damn grades and school reports, or if the boy was learning stuff at school. He didn't see education in terms of grades and tests. He wanted his son to grow up as a *complete* human being.

> *- What is your favorite mythological character? Paulo asks the young son.*
>
> *- I like Prometheus. The little one answers firmly, sitting on his father's lap.*
>
> *- Why?*
>
> *- Because he did something very important. He brought the fire to mankind. You cannot live without fire, I guess. How can we cook without fire? — declares the little one in a fast pace, almost unintelligible, but articulated.*
>
> *- But he stole "the fire of the gods"! Isn't that evil?*
>
> *Fernando thinks for a few seconds and replies:*
>
> *- You can't steal fire. It burns you! It's not like stealing a school toy or a car. Fire symbolizes knowledge, if I'm not mistaken. In that case it was not robbery. It was justice! — he says with wise ingenuity.*
>
> *- Why do you think those "gods" wouldn't deliver the fire, or knowledge, to humanity? Why did he have to steal, or, as you said, make justice?*
>
> *- I don't know…*
>
> *- Would you like to know?*
>
> *- Yes! — responded the boy with great curiosity.*

Well educated, good manners and, mainly, grown in a wealthy family, he opted to be an scholar and engaged in research projects on the Andean culture. No support from his mother, but he started a postgraduate degree in archeology. Peru is a sea of mysteries that has always attracted him since childhood. The old Eastman knew that with the fortune he accumulated his son could be anything he wanted to. If he wanted to be a pianist, he would have the best instrument and the best tutor. If he wanted to be a lawyer, he would have the best professors and the best colleges. Fernando could be anything he wanted.

He soon understood that his great passion was the mysteries of the world. Pyramids, megalithic structures, ruins, the ancient myths and legends and everything that has no reasonable explanation, but still raises more questions than answers. Who built he wonderful Giza Pyramids? What were they good for? How was it all done?

His mother always thought these questions were a big waste of time, unworthy of attention. Keeping the "Eastman Empire" should be his one and only goal. "These *questions* won't teach you anything about business!" – she used to say. His father, on the contrary, provided the academic life for his son because this was the only life Fernando wanted to live. Paulo respected it as "the sacred right to be happy". It was a matter of principles for Paulo was a student himself for the sheer love for wisdom. His work supplied all the resources he could accumulate to have a wonderful life and to leave plenty to his only son. But now... Fernando aims something else.

There was a van waiting for him right outside the main airport exit. Eastman placed his modest luggage in the back of the car and sits on the front seat. He likes to chat.

- Good morning! - said the driver, risking an almost Portuguese. - My name is Riam. I'll take you to your hotel, *señor* Eastman

- Thank you, *señor* Riam. How is the Peruvian national team?

- As always, *señor*. We play like never before, but we lose as usual! – Riam laughed. – What about Brazil? Ready for the Cup?

- We celebrate as never before, Riam ... and the money goes down the drain as usual!

They laughed.

- *Señor* Fernando, it's sad, but true. The Government hides a lot of stuff from us. they spend much less than what they say. The rest of the money just vanishes away… evaporates like water.

- That's true. – he said in a discouraged tone and began to think to himself. "So many things have been hidden from us!".

The new project is an example of a typical governmental cover-up. Nothing is known about it and there are no news about the discovery nor the development of the excavations. Even the staff involved knows nothing about it. The discovery of a new chamber in the sacred city of Machu Picchu should be celebrated and publicized through the four corners of the Earth, but it hasn't been like that. Fernando understands that it is not wise to reveal the location of any hidden cameras when a new one is found. Looters of all kinds would show up and use violence to prey upon any artifact for the sake of making money. But in this case confidentiality was expressly requested for another reason. It could ruin the most important source of income of the country: tourism.

- How are the earthquakes?

- *Señor* Fernando, they have been increasing… we are very scared.

- Relax, *señor* Riam. All these lands from here to Chile shake since forever. It is unlikely to happen anything big. – said Fernando trying to comfort the man, but with a great dose of prudence.

- *Amém, señor* Eastman... *amém.*

They got to the hotel quickly. Fernando checked in and went out for a walk around the city. The day was beautiful. He came back to the hotel late in the afternoon, took a shower and stared skimming the reports of his research advisor, Professor Vicenzo Fontanoura. Fernando was hastily summoned to join the excavation team in Machu Picchu as Research Assistant to the team of the Professor. A project that was also launched hastily at the request of the Peruvian government.

- It's incredible how Professor can be succinct in his reports! – he thinks. – He always raises more questions than offers information. But… what could be so mysterious about the mummies found? Why all the secrecy? Why such an urgency?

When he turned the page, he sees some intriguing photos of some elongated human craniums. "I've seen this type of cranium before in many different places around the world. Egypt, Iraq, Africa, China, Mexico, but especially in Peru. It's common to see samples of these craniums in museums around the world, but no one really knows *what* these things are, how they developed, not even how they disappeared. Is this why Professor is in a hurry? What makes these craniums more important than the others? Is it because they were unearthed in Machu Picchu?

Fernando focused his attention to the photos of the skulls found in the excavation. In the report there were a series of photos of elongated skulls for comparison. Each of them had been found in a different part of the world.

- My God! They don't really look like humans!

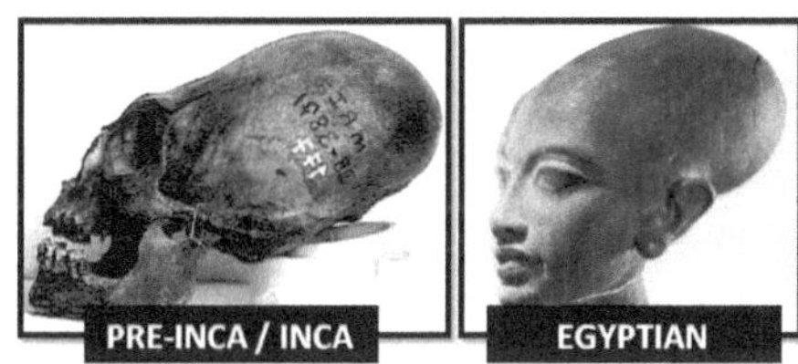

The train that takes tourists to the village on the feet of the Sacred City leaves very early. It was five thirty when Riam, the driver, dropped Fernando at the Poroy station. His seat had been booked before he left Brazil. He was informed about his reservations when he was summoned by the Professor. It was a very good seat. He didn't notice, but his return trip was scheduled in two days. Despite the slow speed, the train is the only way for tourists to get to Machu Picchu. "They could have arranged cheaper seats! This is very expensive!" – he thought while accommodating. – "Well… it may mean two things: they've got a very good budget, or the thing is really confidential."

He knows the village of Águas Calientes very well. He has been to Mach Picchu, "the old mountain" in the original language of the Quechua, but always as a tourist. "There hasn't been excavations in Machu Picchu for ages!" – thinks Fernando while he observes the beautiful landscapes passing through the windows. – "And the official excuse from the government is: *There's nothing else to discover up there.* So what was discovered a few days ago was discovered… by chance?".

The "official history" tells us that the great Sacred City was built by the Incas in 90 years time and it was completed around the end of the 1400s, when the Inca Confederation tragically disintegrated with the arrival of the Spanish "Conquistadores". It is said that Machu Picchu was an initiatory center of the Inca. The architectonic disposition of the housing, barns and classrooms is impeccable. There it was taught about agriculture, astronomy, medicine, mathematics, philosophy and what else you might figure! There were rooms for astronomical studies, climate observations related to agriculture, solstices and equinoxes and more.

Machu Picchu was abandoned shortly after the fall of the Empire, but was never discovered by the Spanish "destroyers". It was rediscovered by chance in 1911 (four hundred years later) by the American researcher Hiran Bingham in an expedition sponsored by the Yale University. Hiran wasn't looking for the "lost city" (a name, incidentally, which he himself coined in his book "The Lost City of the Incas"), but for the fortress of Vilcabamba, which served as a resistance against the Spanish invasion between 1536 and 1572. He was taken to the top of the mountain by two Quechua shepherd boys. He found the ruins totally covered by the jungle and infested with vipers. Bingham registered in his diary: *"Could anybody believe what I have found?"*

The American explorer returned three more times with the support of the wealthy National Geographic Society who in 1913 published a special edition of his magazine with 186 pages that included hundreds of photographs: the first modern records of that sanctuary of the ancient knowledge! It is said that the city was totally pillaged by Americans with complete collusion from the corrupt Peruvian government of the time. It is estimated that among the more than 6,000 artifacts unearthed and removed from the site. Among them, there were 300 mummies, all of them with *elongated skulls* and *red hair*.

Unfortunately (or purposefully) there are no records of anything that was actually found and removed, except for 555 pots, approximately 220 silver, bronze, copper and stone objects, ceramic pieces, bracelets, earrings, and knives and axes. Some of these registered artifacts are on display on many museums around the world. The unregistered artifacts are said to be confined to the United States in the underground halls of Yale and the Smithsonian Museum in Washington DC. The most striking thing is that no gold was "officially found," even though the Incas were gold worshipers and masters in the arts of gold-smithing. Very strange!

There is also research claiming that the ruins were discovered by a German named Augusto Berns in 1867. Berns then founded a company to explore and sell everything he found to anyone who was interested. No one is really sure about the discovery or about the company. If it existed ... many Europeans and Americans spent their money with Berns and a great deal of Inca history went to the rooms of the elite as decoration. Or worse, and much more likely, they ended up in museum and university underground deposits.

DAY 2 – 11:30am

Four hours later Fernando leaves the friendly Vista-dome train at Águas Calientes. He feels a strange atmosphere between the local guides and the villagers. He feels that everyone knows something they cannot understand. People have worried eyes. Eastman crosses the small square and heads straight to the gates of the modest bus station where hundreds of tourists gather every day like flies. A micro bus service makes the round trip to the Sacred City. It is possible to climb on foot, but the bus is the best option. The touristic demand is enormous and Fernando has to mix with the noisy tourists of all nationalities, most of them Brazilians: a fortunate *plague* to the local trinket traders.

Curves and more curves. The climb is a smooth and slow *zig zag*. It takes about 30 minutes to get to the upper plan of the

Sacred City of Machu Picchu which lays at exact 2438 meters above sea level. First Fernando presents his ticket and his Brazilian identity (by virtue of a bilateral agreement, Brazilian tourists do not need a passport to enter and travel around the country). Then he goes through the turnstiles and walks along with the flow. He feels a little cold in his belly when, after a small ascending trail, the holiest of Inca cities appears. Despite its mega majesty, despite the brutality of the hard stones, there is a graceful harmony in every corner of the site. "Oh my God, this place is amazing!", he said aloud. "It seems that the sun always shines when I come here!!!".

A four hundred meter wall separates the agricultural area and its terraces from the urban area. A huge drainage ditch lies ingeniously upon a geological fault running parallel to that wall. At the top of the ditch, at the top of the hill, opens the only gateway to the city that is solidly made of huge blocks of stone, molded by some strikingly precise technique that makes the stones appear to be "soft." Originally there was an internal locking mechanism. The city was absolutely impenetrable.

There is an enormous stone of hundreds of kilos placed horizontally over the columns of the door, as perfectly crafted as the base stones and which fits harmoniously at the top of the entrance. After crossing the famous door, Fernando Eastman walks through a small corridor between genuinely Inca walls and there he was: inside one of the greatest mysteries of mankind. Not that you necessarily have to be in search of some mystery, but the place itself is something that takes your breath away. Even the most uninformed tourist loses their minds up there. Even if you are there unintentionally, and this is quite common in tourists, you can not ignore that majestic wonder. It's like every little detail had been planned. Nothing seems to be in excess. All fits well. No tool marks can be seen on the stones. When the guides try to explain the Inca architecture they say the stones were crafted with hammers and chisels but... just between us... those explanations are not credible.

There are many water springs, many of them still running. The central square, and almost all the big buildings, were laid over the land's own geological constitution. This gives the city an unshakable security, even being the Peruvian territory one of the greatest seismologic activity areas in the globe.

The stone works are of two types: carved in the shape of perfect, clean cobblestones whose outer faces look like pillows. Some say that they were made by "softening" the stones using heat. These perfect stone blocks (which look like soft pillows) are said to have been used to build the walls of the sacerdotal quarters. The other type of stones are rough, less crafted, which were laid using some kind of primitive mortar made of mud and other natural substances. According to the official archeology, these stones were used for the "non-sacerdotal" quarters.

It's important to mention a third type of stone work found up there: the megaliths. So majestic they simply look impossible at first sight. When one enters Machu Picchu, they step inside a very subtle dimension, a more metaphysical one. Everything has another meaning in there. Everything is mystery! Like the Inca used to say: "All here is ready for the passage of the Sun God".

The route to the excavations was as obvious as possible. Fernando walked through the front door, down to three terraces below to the right, and made an inevitable escape to the bottom of the Temple of the Sun. He wanted to see again the crevice in the rock that supports the observatory. In this place, the guides say, offerings were made to the Inca deities on certain days of the year.

The first time Eastman saw this natural shrine built using the natural crack of the stone he just gaped. Eager to record everything on his handy-cam, he fastidiously stepped back and fell into a three meter deep pit right behind him. He bruised himself hard. Nevertheless, he proudly carries a faint scar on his left hand. The kind of tourist stuff you cannot buy in the gift shops. "Who would fall into a pit in Machu Picchu?" – he thought. – "Me, of course!". He learned early that the stones as really hard and the "soft pillow appearance" is obviously only an impression caused by the perfection of the building technique.

Eastman left faster than usual. He uses to stop a little in this place because he likes the energy, but not today. "The Professor is waiting for me!" He hurried past the Main Temple formed by megaliths perfectly superimposed on one another like a puzzle. He also passed almost completely ignoring the fantastic Intihuatana, or "Stone of the Sun". A hill that was converted into a polygonal pyramid by building terraces all around it. At the top is the famous and most studied stone of the site. Carved into a single block, Intihuatana has several perfectly polished angles. It is believed to have been used as a "calculation table" of time. According to tradition, it served to "tie the sun."

Finally he arrived at the entrance of the excavation area that had been in full operation for three days without having to close the city for visitation. A black and yellow ribbon signaled the entrance of the site and a young man who apparently had no idea of what was going on up there blocked his passage speaking in a terrible mix of Spanish and Quechua:

- *No puedes passar, no señor!* (You cannot pass, sir).

- *Mi nombre és Fernando Eastman. Soy parte de la equipe de cientistas! Necessito hablar con Professor Fontanoura!* (My name is Fernando Eastman. I'm from the scientific team! I must talk to Professor Fontanoura!) – said the Brazilian with a poor Spanish.

- *Si, Si, como no... adelante!* (Yes, yes, of course… go straight ahead!)

- *Gracias*!

Without checking any identification, the simple man lets Fernando pass. He followed south into the trail recently opened with machetes between the two peaks that frame the city. The chamber was found on the blind side of the bigger one, the imposing Huayna Picchu. The amazon jungle is rainy and the path was very sleepy. After a tiring climb, the big surprise: the entrance of an unknown chamber!

Professor Vicenzo Fontanoura was there with his hands on the waist (as if he was fixing his belt) and his customary leadership attitude. He is a kind of father figure for Fernando. An Uruguayan of few friends who became a great world authority, a true genius in field archaeological research. Since he took the chair of Archeology and Anthropology at the Federal University of Brasília, Prof. Fontanoura never mentored any student without getting some advantage on behalf of his personal work. With Eastman, it was different. The Professor saw him as his future successor. "This young man, Fernando Eastman, can be a great authority in the archaeological field." – he thought. – "Moreover, the man is incorruptible!"

Fernando Eastman would never play the game everybody plays to keep receiving governmental grants for his researches. He could finance himself indefinitely until he got a decent scholarship.

- Fernando Eastman, my friend! I suppose you came as fast as possible. – said Fontanoura with his typical Uruguayan accent greeting his dearest student.

- Yes, Professor. I literally flew from home to here as soon as I got your invitation and report. What is this all about? What's the scene?

- Fernando. We talk about it later. – whispered the old man. – You'll sleep here tonight with us. It's not safe to speak anything here. Not anymore! Since the Peruvian government hired me there wasn't a day without some kind of unpleasant confrontations. I mean, there are suspicious eyes all around us! Big Brother is here...

Eastman never imagined he would have to spend the night up there. He felt some sort of excitement. Tourists never spend the night there since many decades now. After that night he would never be a tourist there ever again.

DAY 2 – 19h30

The night falls heavy in the jungle. In the blink of an eye everything turns dark as pitch. Even if it would be necessary to get away from there, it would not be safe anymore. *"Inevitability* is a vital element in the unfolding of any historical event." This teaching from the Professor has always been useful to Fernando. "Now it's too late to leave, so, inevitably, I'll sleep here."

Taking part on the inevitability of History has always been a kick for the young Eastman. It makes him feel alive! "It's an active and passive attitude at the same time before life." – he always reminds himself in thoughts. – "This is the greatest Zen thing I know. You are active and passive at the same time when you deliberately admit that the steering wheel is not under your control anymore. It makes sense. It is perhaps the most *concrete* application of the *flexibility* of the Buddha's teachings.

For Fernando Eastman, the "inevitable" is the idea of the "too late" merged to the "concrete fact" as a "positive element". It's good to know that what is… simply *is*… it doesn't matter if it's too late or not. Not bad for a young man born with a silver spoon. He could simply follow his mother's footsteps and become a worldly person, strange to the mysteries of the world. He could be a businessman and take over the family business, but he never fell into this alluring path. Instead, he has always had a simple life. He has always been a young man with a different glow, a keen reader, quite reserved, but with burning eyes of curiosity. The only presence of his father (before his disappearance) were the pictures on the wall.

The old Eastman traveled to the most mysterious places on Earth. India, Mexico, Peru, Egypt, Polynesia, Easter Island, Ecuador, Bolivia, the USA, Bermudas, Tibet, the list is big. In each photo the young Eastman admired his father more and more. When they were together, his father always talked about the mysteries he saw throughout the world. He talked about the Pyramids of Egypt. All of them! Not only the ones in Cairo. He talked about the pyramid complex in Mexico and the Central America, about India and its sumptuous monuments, the legends of the underground cities in Tibet where enlightened beings initiate avatars for millennia. He talked about the Andes, the beauties of Cuzco and the mysterious Machu Picchu, Puma Punku and Tiahuanaco.

The only time he took his son on a trip like those was when he visited Mecca, the religious center of the Muslim. One of the old Eastman's great commercial partners was a follower of Mohammad and arranged for them to visit the great mosque. It was necessary for both, father and son, to wear typical Muslim outfits not to offend the Islamic tradition. Fernando got deeply impressed by the incredibly beautiful mosaic he could see all around the place, not mentioning the Kaaba story. Unfortunately he could not see it. This area is strictly forbidden for the ones who do not share the same religion.

During day in the excavation site, he remembered of a dream he had when he was very young. He was inside an underground pyramid. He walked through its corridors illuminated by some sort of light source that came from some chambers. He could feel the cold air, he could feel the colors and the lightness atmosphere of the path that irresistibly guided him towards a stone of shining white. As he touched the stone, he woke up immediately as if he had been struck by a lightning. He could recall the strength of that dream in details. "I'll never be a tourist here again!", he murmured. "Inevitability?"

The relationship with his mentor has always been collaborative. Whenever they exchanged research information, the talks have always been of mutual respect. There has never been, at any moment since Eastman had started researching for Fontanoura, any distance of the "student/Professor" kind. Their relationship has always been of the "Master/Disciple" kind. The Professor recognized the potential of that young man, therefore he constantly nurtured a critical stance concerning his disciple's way of thinking. Prof. Vicenzo Fontanoura is a profound connoisseur of philosophy, with special pleasure and strong inclination to Nietzsche's "hammer philosophy". Having Nietzsche as beacon, Vicenzo made his dear student go through the deep abysses of the human thought.

Using Nietzsche's insights, the Professor pushed his most efficient field researcher toward the deepest dives in the philosophical search for what is known as "truth". He taught Fernando to doubt anything that may be considered as "true". This attitude developed an strong ethical commitment to the data he researches and to the new evidences further to be discovered. At the same time it left him open to new discoveries and to the never ending advances of human knowledge. They were both totally committed to the research on the Andean myths. The professor has been preparing his next book about Inca legends, while Eastman has been reading and researching for him as a collaborator. Fontanoura has always appreciated his engagement cause he knew that young man was there for real. "This man chose the research because he loves what he does!", says Fontanoura to his academic friends. The old Vicenzo knows that fate of all Disciple is to, inevitably, overcome the Master.

All around the camp a dozen citronella lamps burn in a hopeless help against the buzzing mosquitoes. Professor Fontanoura heats some soup and serves Fernando.

- So… what's up? Why all this secrecy? Why no one knows about this project? – whispered Fernando, bewildered by Professor Fontanoura's excess of prudence.

- You have an instigated mind, Eastman. I always appreciated that in you. – said Vicenzo while sitting beside the young man in a long dead tree trunk.

- Is this about the skulls, Professor? I guess it's not about them. Everyone knows these skulls are artificially done by having newborn heads squeezed with rope and wood. The pressure forces their heads to grow in this elongated form! Have you found any Inca treasure?

- No, Eastman. It's not about treasures… not at all. It's about the skulls, really. Not all the elongated skulls are artificial! Remember that mummy that was found with a fetus within her? Do you remember… the fetus had already his skull fully formed! It was not a deformation! We are talking about a genetic trait. There are thousands of them around the Andes, you know it! The culture that deforms the heads of their toddlers are not from the Andean lands. – said the Professor. – The Andean skulls are "hot stuff"!

- Why? What's the big deal?

- See. – says the Professor using one of the skulls recently unearthed. – They have a cranium density 40% higher than the humans of today and a brain volume 25% larger than ours. They are not "imitating the gods", like most cases around the world. These skulls are genuine! Anyway there isn't any plausible scientific conclusion to this matter yet. – Vicenzo ties up the loose ends. –

Some say they are extraterrestrials. No one knows really, but they are not humans like us! And that's about *them* I must talk to you about.

- Say it! – spoke Fernando in a direct way.

- It is not what has been found. It is not the craniums directly, neither is the new chamber. Actually… there is an ancient legend. – Vicenzo looked around suspiciously. – This long forgotten legend resurged with some new information that has no written register in our language. I mean Human language. It has never been heard of. It is something really new… something to be checked.

- I still don't get it. – said Eastman also in low voice.

- All of the Águas Calientes dwellers, out of the blue, like a rabbit out coming out of a hat, manifested a simultaneous collective knowledge about a legend, about a woman.

- Keep going…

- It was a collective psychic event that has no explanation. Something really new and unexpected. The day that followed the opening of the chamber, all the villagers came to know about the story of a very beautiful woman who... – prudent pause. Both Eastman and Fontanoura checked around to guarantee the secrecy of the conversation. – It is urgent that you find, here or wherever, some kind of written register. The Águas Calientes people simply started talking about a text written in a language that is not from this planet.

Fontanoura pauses coldly and looks sideways as if looking for the presence of an enemy. He continues to speak softly. Fernando feels a shiver run down his spine.

- The story itself is not new. – continues the Professor. – It is an old story and we already knew about it. But the people now talk about a book. This book is the new element on this legend… and it really intrigues me. They don't know how to explain where this story came from, nor even how it resurged in their minds... but everyone you talk with says the same version of the story, with exactly the same details. In a nutshell, they all talk about a book. They know nothing… and yet they know all!

- Professor, you're saying that there may be some book with an unknown language with an unknown story in the chamber? What story is this? Sum it up, please.

- I don't know if it is really a book… see, it is about a very beautiful woman… Fernando, have you been to the Lake Titicaca?

They were interrupted by some team members. Professor Fontanoura was very excited and yet very cautious.

- They are no fools, on the contrary! – continued the old scientist. – The people here are extremely respectful of their ancient culture and they are reading the signals. The local team soon linked the psychic event to the opening of the chamber. They have their eyes wide open, suspicious that we will hide the facts away. – concluded.

They started talking again, but in a few seconds other members of the excavation team join the Professor and Fernando. The soup was about to end. Fernando looks deep into the eyes of Vicenzo Fontanoura. He still needs to understand more about this book.

- We'd better get to sleep, Eastman. Tomorrow we start early at dawn.

DAY 3 – 5am

"In an archaeological site the sun rises earlier" – the Professor used to say. At the first rays of sun Fernando was already up preparing his coca mate. The Andean altitudes have a terrible effect on the human organism: the famous *soroche* (which in the Quechua language means "altitude sickness"). Coca mate is the only natural thing that can help in this case, but a few painkiller pills are also welcome.

Although being lower than Cuzco, Machu Picchu is in a much higher position compared to Brasilia and Fernando has arrived only a couple of days. He still feels the altitude. The best thing to do is to have at least two or three days to "acclimatize", to get used to the high lands. The peasants use the coca leaf for other reasons than to ease the *soroche*. Coca leaves are also a rich source of vitamins, proteins, carbohydrates, fats, fiber, calcium, phosphorus, iron and other vital elements, not to mention the analgesic properties. Due to the alkaloids also present in the plant, chewing coca leaves is a way for peasants to quench hunger and fatigue. The Andean peasant practically feeds on coca leaves. If on the one hand it calms hunger, chewing coca for a long time creates addiction and causes impotence.

One of the team members is Rico Calmón. Rico is a thirty years old man born and raised in Águas Calientes. The legend came to him just like everyone else in the village: he went to sleep and *plin…* he woke up knowing all about it. He noticed the private conversations between Eastman and the Professor and immediately he knew they were talking about the legend. He approached Fernando while he was having his tea.

\- *Señor* Fernando, welcome to the site.

\- Thank you, *señor*...

\- Rico. Rico Calmón. Professor talks a lot about you, *señor*. It seems you know nothing about the text, do you?

\- No… I know nothing about it. – responded Eastman cautiously but straightforwardly. – What do *you* know about it?

The tone of the conversation was low. As highlighted by the Professor last night, prudence is the standard procedure. Rico excused himself and answered the call from the severe foreman, *Señor* Alejandro, who was calling all the excavation team to delegate the tasks of the day. Fernando started to think and observe the surroundings. The entrance of the chamber was poorly illuminated and inside of it a flashlight was needed. He picked up one and entered before the team. He wanted to study the scene before they start working in there. He was looking for archaeological signs, anything that could give him some light. There was nothing written in it that could give any clue as to the purpose of building that chamber. The walls were smooth, like the great entrance to the city, like the walls of the sacerdotal quarters. No graphic signals whatsoever. "Intriguing!", he thought. There was no way of hiding anything in there. It was like the chambers of the Pyramids of Giza: nothing to hide and yet full of unanswered questions.

By noon, when the sun was almost in its pinnacle, Rico was spotted by Eastman talking to Prof. Vicenzo Fontanoura. His pragmatic way of thinking gave Fernando two simple alternatives. If he is talking to the Professor, he must be an ally or... an enemy. A very cold assessment, but a prudent one. Fernando reduced the possibilities to the widest scope possible: *friend or foe*. This is a good start when one begins to understand any situation.

- Eastman! – called the Professor. – I need you to look into this!

- Yes, sir! What is it?

- Pretend you are working old listen to what I say. – the old man said in whispers. – At the end of the day, follow Rico. He needs to show you something very important. He is with us. Don't lose track of him. Do you understand?

- Yes.

- Pretend to be working. After dinner you go with him. Do not trust anyone around here. *No one*!

The night fell. The soup came and both man stealthily slipped into the dark jungle. Above the highest peak of the Sacred City of the Inca there is a temple called *"Templo de La Luna"*. That's where they headed. The trail is dangerous and steep. It's absolutely imprudent to go up there at night, but both of them had already been there before. Rico is one of the official tourist guides of Águas Calientes and in his free time he leads groups of adventurous tourists who dare to face the challenge. He knows every step on that trail.

- Is it really necessary to come up here at this time in the evening? – asked Fernando with some difficulty due to the altitude.

- Yes. These are orders from the Professor.

Rico stops almost on the top of the hill, opens his backpack, pulls out a very strong flashlight and attaches it to Fernando's climbing belt. The Peruvian ties a long rope to a steady stone and asks Fernando to attach himself to the safety equipment. A vertiginous cliff opens before him and acrophobia instantly goes up and down his spine.

- Give me the helmet. – asks the panicked nerd.

- Sorry, *señor*. I forgot to bring one! – responds Rico Calmón not caring too much. This is part of his daily routine.

Fernando Eastman and cliffs are strangers to each other. He almost died climbing the famous *"Pico das Agulhas Negras"*, in Rio de Janeiro, in an innocent school trip when he was a teenager. A relatively easy climbing almost got him killed. The remembrance of it causes sweat to start rolling down his forehead.

- Hold tight to the rope and lean against that other stone. – instructs Rico. – Point the flashlight to the top and see what I have accidentally found!

- Wow! These are not Inca glyphs. – Fernando speaks with fear and difficulty. – I have never seen anything like this around the Andes! They are two spheres… and a dashed line linking both spheres by their centers. What is this anyway?

- These are Venus and the Earth, *señor* Eastman.

- How do you know? – asked the Brazilian with the

seriousness of a scientist while managing to get rid of the safety equipment.

- I just know… like everybody else in the village.

- And this is why everybody is suspicious?

Suddenly Rico enters in a kind of trance and tells Fernando Eastman the story, the same way all the locals tell, word by word. The very same story that reemerged in the minds of the people of Águas Calientes:

"Uncountable eons ago our mother descended to Earth in a shiny gold-like spaceship to breed. She was a woman similar to ours from the feet to the breasts, but her head was in the form of a cone, her ears were big and her four finger hands were flat. Her name was Orejona and she came from the planet Venus, where the atmosphere was similar to ours. She walked on her feet and had great intelligence. After her mission of reproducing, she returned to the skies. In Tiahuanaco her descendants prospered and kept Her worship rites. She was the mother of the pre-Inca civilizations and before departing... she left all written..."

- Rico, what are you talking about?

No one, except Rico and the Professor, knows about those inscriptions. A paradox installs in Fernando's mind. It's not fair to hide anything from the local inhabitants because they are humans and deserve respect and consideration. On the other hand, if the people knew about the inscriptions, things could get out of control. It could mess up the tourism and the source of income of the very same people you wanted to respect. Rico knows it and didn't reveal the inscriptions to no one except to the Professor and now to Fernando. And still there is the book issue!

- The book the Professor talked about. Is this the book the woman wrote?

- Possibly. We do not know if this is really a book. All of these came up in our minds after the opening of the chamber. The oldest language known around here is the Quechua. In our minds this book is not written in Quechua, or Spanish, or any known language. Believe me, *señor* Eastman. We are all acquainted to many different languages. We are all tourist guides here! We know many languages! Someone would recognize it! The Professor said that you are the only person capable of understanding this text.

- Do you know where this woman "landed"? – asked Fernando granting the word "landed" with the quotation mark. He didn't believe the legends he has been studying for many years to be historical facts.

- Yes. The Lake Titicaca.

- How do you know this inscription represents Venus and the Earth? What's the evidence?

- Didn't you hear what I've just said? She came from Venus to Earth. She had a cone-shaped head. The skulls found here have the same shape, *señor* Eastman. It was the day after the opening of this chamber that it all began. These are pretty clear to me. When I woke up I had this story inside my head crystal clear. This could be just nonsense if it was only me, but *all the village* woke up with the same story! This is not coincidence! There are two spheres connected to each other by a dashed line. Could you see the stars around the spheres? Those circles are planets, don't you see? The connection to the story is clear to me.

- I don't see any scientific evidence here, Rico. I don't know if we can accept your insights as facts. Does anyone else knows about it?

- No, only the Professor. I trust him. He is a man of science, not a politician.

LATER, AROUND 11:30pm

- Professor, this is incredible! During all my years of researching the Andean myths and legends I've never heard anything about Venus, neither this book you talked about.

- The situation here is that the villagers want to know what happened to their minds, how this came up and the Peruvian government is not interested in releasing any information. – said Fontanoura with suspicious eyes. – This can get out of hand. Everything must pass the scrutiny of *señor* Alejandro, the foreman, the big boss here. – says the Professor looking towards the big man. – He is a Federal Police officer and he is in charge. We are only a technical support team. He has already scolded me strongly. We have no autonomy over the material we find whatsoever and it seems if we do not comply with this man, we'll get in trouble. They already knew about the chamber before we've found it!

- They knew it existed?

- They called me here just to give an "official status" to it. And if they find it necessary, they will destroy it all. But they didn't count on the phenomenon of the village! Now, *señor* Alejandro, following strict orders, wants to avoid any information to get to the public *at any cost*. The government will not let any news release on the phenomenon. I don't know to what extent they can cover it up, but the orders come from the top.

- How about the book? Do you think it's in the chamber?

- If it is really a book, it is unlikely to be here. It's too humid. If it has been stored here, it must have been completely destroyed. Just take a look to what happened to the mummies we've found. They are falling to pieces! I asked Rico about the material the book was made of, but he said this information hasn't been "downloaded" to their minds. Do you remember the stories about the book of Enoch, don't you?

- Sure I do! The book of Enoch, the famous apocryphal text dictated to him by an angel and written with a "fast writing pen". But this story cannot be proved. No one has ever seen the original book of Enoch. There are only vague theories. A good theory, by the way, but I see no connection here.

- My dear Eastman, I didn't say it would be the book of Enoch. I guess it could have been written in something more durable than paper or papyrus, just like the Enoch material supposedly was. I think you should focus your search this way. It cannot be a book as we know it. It must be a different thing. Do you remember Padre Crespi, in Ecuador?

- Sure, my father met him!

Father Carlos Crespi was considered to be a saint by the natives. He used to help them with their trouble and in exchange they presented him with ancient artifacts, which the native families had hidden from the "white men" for many generations! The old native tradition teaches that if you are helped by someone and do not give the helper something back, you would become a beggar. Begging was considered to be a crime. Among the artifacts presented to the priest in exchange for his help there were several metal plates inscribed with unintelligible characters and symbols.

Fernando continued.

- My father said the priest believed the plates were pure gold, but neither him nor Von Daniken had any proof of the authenticity of the material. Not even to the characters nor the symbols were given any serious attention. The scientific community thought the priest was mad. Strangely, all the artifacts simply vanished from Padre Crespi's home soon after he died!

- I'm talking about him just to illustrate your search. They must be something like plates of metal, maybe gold... I don't know. I'm just brainstorming. What happened to the people down there was not fake. It is something real and unexplainable! The book intrigues me! How would it look like? Do you remember the Quipós, the *knot* language?

- Sure, the big "stars" of the Peruvian museums. They look like decorative pieces and the tourists find them cute.

- The Quipós are just another example to warm up your mind. Maybe it is a Quipó, who knows? Many academics think they are just a kind of calculator, a mathematical device. – added the Professor. – And they are really cute, anyway. In the XVI Century, after the takeover of these lands by the *Conquistadores*, a man called

Catari (considered to be a traitor by the Inca) supposedly assisted González de La Rosa in the translation of the Quipós. The translation was commissioned by the Jesuits. The texts were highly harmful to the Christian values! This translation was handed to Anello Oliva by the canon of Chuquisaca, Bartolomeu Cervantes. The text disappeared and it is believed to be guarded in the Vatican Library. If it is there it's because there must be something we should not know about, don't you think? Isn't this the tyrannical tradition of the Catholic Church? C

- I've never heard of this Quipó translation… or have I?

- The original text, I'm sure you haven't, But the comment of the González de La Rosa is in the book of Robert Charroux and I'm sure you've read it. He talks about Tiahuanaco and a palace of which no traces can be found for it was built "by the time of the creation of the world".

- Hummm… this is close to the Lake Titicaca, on the Bolivian side.

- Yes! – exclaimed the Professor. – That is the place where Orejona landed from the heavens. No proofs, only theories, but where there's smoke, there's fire. I'm just rambling about the possibilities, Fernando. Would our book be a Quipó?

There is in fact a commentary by González de La Rosa transcribed by Charroux in his book "*Historie incomnnue des hommes despuis cent mille ans*". This commentary brings an interesting story about an ancient civilization dwelling by the shores of Lake Titicaca. Fernando had read this book long ago in his father's

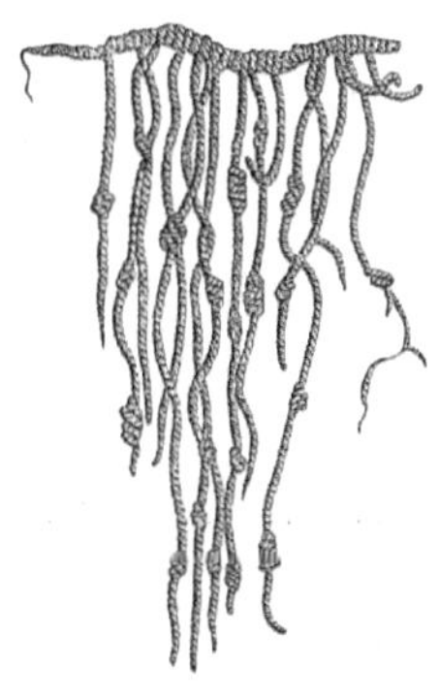

library by the time they lived in São Paulo. He forced his memory a little and the lines began to pop into his mind.

> *"The original name of Tiahuanaco was Chacara. The city was entirely underground and what existed on the surface was only the cutting of stones resort and the village of the workers. The underground city would be the key to an amazing civilization that dates back to the earliest times.*
>
> *The city was accessed by several entrances which were seen by the great French naturalist Alcide d'Orbigny and by the travelers of Tschudi, Castelnau and Squier, who speak in dark, fetid galleries that flow into the Tiahuanaco square. This underground city was built to provide the dwellers a more pleasant temperature, which proves that the altitude never varied.*
>
> *Near Lake Titicaca there was a palace of which was left no trace because its construction must go back, according to the texts 'at the time of the creation of the world. On the islands of the lake lived a white and bearded race"*

- Isn't it the legend about the white skinned people who used to live in the Bolivian highlands by the time of the *Conquistadores?* – Fernando thought in loud voice. – Is it possible then... that the "Ancient Astronaut Theory" of Von Daniken is right?

He used to read the Swiss author with great joy and he has always dreamed in having the answers for the questions proposed by Daniken. Eastman believed on the possibility that we descend from beings from other planets or galaxies, but he has never found any scientific proof that could give basis to the "forgotten history" of mankind. Those books led Fernando to the archaeological and anthropological researches.

Charroux makes an important observation about Tiahuanaco. He says that Catari (the traitor) says nothing about this old civilization being from Venus, but he strangely states that if those people were natives, they would not need to build an underground city to protect them against the weather. It makes sense. A Venus being who bred here would have needed some sort of protection for their offspring against our atmosphere until they were adapted to the environment. Little by little few excerpts from a text came up to his mind. It was the quotation from Pedro Pizarro, cousin of the serial killer Francisco Pizarro, *El Conquistador.*

> *"In this country I saw a woman and a child whose skin was of unusual whiteness. The Indians claim that they were descendants of the idols (of the gods).'"*.

- Eastman, Eastman...

- Yes, Professor… I'm sorry. I was remembering something.

- Daniken has already written about the legend of Orejona. This is not new, but the book and Venus related to her... *this* is new! You must find this text. It is extremely important for us to be able to put together pieces of our possible true story. You know all the legends and myths here. Only you can find this supposed book.

- But… are you sure it's a book?

- That's why I summoned you up here! – said the Professor interrupting Eastman with elegant authority. – You leave tomorrow at 10am, right after the first coffee break. Rico goes with you. Go to Cuzco and look for Jamirez in Qorikancha. He is a humble caretaker, but do not underestimate him. He waits for you. I know him for many years now. I talked to him before we started digging up here and he told me he knew that something weird was going to happen with the people here, the collective psychic event including the book. He foresaw it all a few days ago.

- How did he "foresaw" it?

- He was born up here, Eastman, in the Sacred City. His mother was a pure-blooded Quechua priestess. He has the gift of clairvoyance.

- Clairvoyance? Come on, Professor... this is...

- Eastman... do you want to know what's written on that book?

- Sure! My life is about knowing books!

Cuzco is a city of two faces. One is urban, polluted and chaotic. The other is the touristic Cuzco, the ancient capital of the Inca Confederation. Nothing in the urban Cuzco would appeal to Eastman. Invariably he would stay in the same hotel in the which he was acquainted to all the staff. His visits to the city were always due to some research. He calls the local library and museum agents by their first names as well as the waiters of his favorite restaurant near the *Plaza de Armas*, the cozy Ama Lur.

The red roofs of the city were inherited from the Spaniards who, according to History, took over the Empire without too much resistance from the Inca. Eastman use to spend time wandering through the historic alleys where houses and hostels and all kinds of buildings have been built over the remains of the ancient Inca capital. The *Iglesia de San Blás* offers a spectacular view of the city. The grand cathedral of the *Plaza de Armas* is something he feels worth to seeing. It was built over the foundations of the Palace of the Inca Wiracocha who, according to the legend, was born in the Easter Island! It took 100 years to finish its construction. The Spanish used the stones taken from the walls of Saqsayhuaman right up above the outskirts of the city.

Saqsayhuaman is thought to be a fortress and a big religious complex of the Inca. No one is really sure of who built it and what its real purpose used to be. The *zigzagged* walls in three levels are sensational! They are megaliths!!! The biggest block is nine meters high, five meters wide weighting more than 360 tons! They were perfectly fit one on the top of the other in an impossible way.

Pukapukara is close to it. Its facilities were used as a kind of "inn" for Inca travelers. Tambomachay (or "Inca baths") is just a few meters down the same road and is believed to have been a place for purifying rituals. In this place you can see the perfection of the water supply system of the Incas and its walls built with perfect blocks and their fantastically beautiful niches. In short, the historic Cuzco couldn't appeal more to thirsty spirits in search for mysteries.

Neither Fernando nor Rico had realized the dangers involved in this quest. They did not even know what they were looking for. There are no registers of this artifact (which seems to be a book) in the Peruvian history. Only daydreams coming from the minds of "non- scientific" authors.

They decided to go to *La Bodeguitta*, in San Blás, to have a *pisco* before going to sleep. The next day they would see *señor* Jamirez in the Qorikancha temple. "How can this man help us?" – Fernando kept asking himself. Before leaving, Fernando went to the hotel reception to cash some money. Right beside him, at the balcony, there was a woman checking in.

- Odalisca. Odalisca dos Santos. I'm from Brazil.

Fernando stopped, looked at the woman and got overwhelmed by her beauty. Instinctively he addressed to her, in a pure magnetism rush.

- Excuse-me. Are you a flight attendant?

- Yes. – she replied friendly. – Why?

- It was you who got me on the plane a few days ago.

- Yes… yes, I remember. You flew first class! Lots of space!

- I'm Fernando. My friend Rico and I are going to have a *pisco*. Would you like to… join us?

- Sure! But I must have a shower first and change clothes. Can you wait?

- Do you know the city?

- Yes, I'm always here. There's a flight every week.

- We'll wait for you at *La Bodeguitta* two blocks from here in San Blas.

- Deal. I love this bar. It's so *nighty*. – said the woman with shinny eyes of happiness. Her schedule is usually very tight and there's not much space for fun. – Don't get drunk before me! I hate getting drunk on my own... and please, call me Lia.

Fernando hadn't paid attention to the woman when he boarded to Cuzco. The flight from Brasilia to Peru is too short to order any board service. He refused all the snacks (he hates airplane food). He'd rather sleep or read something. Life is sweet on the first class. You don't have the economy class noise, there are plenty room for legs, no privacy problems. In short there's plenty of space and comfort to enjoy the great miracle of flying. And he flew away from that plane trying to imagine what would be waiting for him in the Sacred City. He didn't even looked at Lia. Her uniform hid her beauty.

Fernando still had no idea of the problem he was getting in. Now he thinks about the girl. His mind is not busy yet. Tonight he plans to relax and have a good time. He has never been a night person. Eastman is calm, reserved, but sociable. He never drinks too much. He does not appreciate the effects of the alcohol. He never had problems to find girlfriends, although this is not the image one might have from someone as "nerd" as him. Fernando Eastman was *definitely* a nerd.

The young men small-talked all the way to the bar. The Peruvians are crazy about soccer, although their team is not as strong as their neighbors from Brazil and Argentina. Soccer was a big source of laugh considering the situation of both nations concerning the kicking of a stupid ball. The Peruvians *know* they suck playing soccer. The Brazilians *think* they are the best no matter how ridiculous they have been in the pitch for many seasons already. There's nothing like laughing at soccer, but now Fernando's thoughts were about a certain flight attendant. Rico was worried. He was afraid the woman would draw Eastman's attention away from their quest.

He spoke his mind and Fernando said:

- Relax Rico. What harm could cause a drink with a beautiful woman?

DAY 4 – 8pm

- Hi, am I late?

- No! Right on time! – said Fernando cleverly immediately getting the woman to show the most graceful smile. – This is my friend Rico.

- Hello Rico. What's up?

- All is fine. – answered Rico trying to hide his concerns.

- So, what are we drinking? – asked the woman lively.

- *Pisco*! – exclaimed Fernando joyfully.

- *Piscoooo*! Yes!

Rico went quiet. He didn't want to discuss anything about their task with strangers. Fernando understood it and avoided bringing up the yet to discover mission. He was trying to enjoy the evening. "My God! She's so beautiful!" – he thought.

Lia is a very beautiful 32 year old woman with a slim body. She never uses make up when she's not working. She showed up wearing a worn out pair of jeans, trekking boots and a white shirt with the word "MUSE" written on it with black bold capital letters. Her long straight blond hair was loose touching her shoulders. Her eyes were light brown and full of life. Her perfume was marvelous and Fernando fell for her. When she spoke, she used lots of slangs and sometimes she was not clear. She had to "translate" some words and expressions to the "normal" language not for Fernando but for Rico who was not an expert in Portuguese.

Fernando has always been a quiet young man and only spoke what he thought was the essential. He has never been the "popular kind", although his colleagues thought he was cool. He was always there to help anyone with their studies if they requested. The young Fernando never used slangs because his subjects of interest were never the same of his schoolmates. He was never the life of the party. He had never assimilated his youth slangs. Lia, on the other hand, never got interested in cultural stuff. She does not know that to walk along the streets of Cuzco is to literally *step* on History. He never went to Machu Picchu because he never cared for it. All in all… she is a normal person.

- So, Fernando. Tell me what you do in this crazy country.

- Well, me and Rico, we are… – he caught a glimpse of Rico who nervously straightened his back on the chair. – We are here to visit a friend in Qorikancha. Do you know the *Convento de Santo Domingo*?

- No, where is it?

- The question is not *where*, but *what* – replied with his scholar attitude but quickly realized it was not adequate.

- What do you mean?

- Qorikancha is the most important building in the ancient Cuzco. It was built by Pachacutec, the great Inca Emperor. The complex had several temples and the stonework is stunning! The walls were skillfully made of black polished stones and gold plaques topped the whole complex perimeter.

- Wow! – said Lia mesmerized by the lecturer.

- There is a semicircular outer wall that survived the destruction of the Spanish Jesuits. On the top of this wall it used to happen a beautiful ritual of Sun worshiping. In the southern winter solstice the ancient Inca presented an enormous circle made of pure gold of some five meters of diameter right in front of the temple. This was their homage to the Sun God. Everything was put down for the construction of the *Convento de Santo Domingo*. Some temples within the complex have survived the barbarism of the Spanish "civilized" and can be visited.

- Wow! Fancy! It sounds like a lecturer! Does your friend live there?

- No, he *works* there.

- And you came here only to see this friend? He must be a nice guy.

- Waiter! More *pisco*, please! – screamed Rico trying to change subjects. And many doses came...

Pisco is a Peruvian brandy extracted from a certain kind of grape. The alcohol level is high and if one is not careful they'll get really drunk!

They talk loud and laughed all evening and after some more doses...

- You talk funny! – said Lia, laughingly, under the influence of the *pisco*.

- Why do you say that? You really think this?

- Yezzz... but you are cute. You speak like an old man... sometimes. She was able to articulate the words, but slowly.

She was able to articulate the words, but slowly.

The relaxing evening drink went a little out of control. Lia felt like home. She spoke a lot, told jokes, laughed, spilled *pisco* on the table. Fernando dared not to join the pretty lady in all the toasts, but he joined the woman when he felt like. Between one toast and another he kept drinking his favorite black soft drink with lemon and ice. Things were so joyful that they toasted even to the health of all Peruvian llamas.

Rico, as a good bodyguard, remained quiet and drank little. Every time Eastman got excited on his talks about archeology Rico would interrupt and changed the subject. Fernando knew what Rico was doing and complied, but his passion and his unconscious will to display his scholarship skills always took the conversation with Lia to a dangerous zone. He should not reveal anything to *anyone*.

After some three hours of celebration they close the night and went back to the hotel.

***

- I can't find my room… – said Lia in a much lower speed while being helped by Fernando to climb up the stairs.
- Sleep with me. – said Eastman jokingly.
- Ok…

DAY 5 – 9am

- Good morning. – said Fernando softly.
- Good morning… – responded Lia in a great effort to put her brain back in motion after all that *pisco*. – Did I sleep here?
- Yes, you could not find you room, you were a little dizzy, you know.

She slowly looked around. Despite the hangover she could note Fernando's tidiness and care and organization of Fernando with his few things. His backpack was open, his boots were at the foot of the bed side by side and his socks tucked inside each foot.

Three folded shirts, his documents lined up, his Swiss army knife, a hat, all his stuff harmonically placed over his tidy bed.

- Gee, Fernando! – she spoke with semi-opened eyes. – You are so neat, man! You even made the bed!

- Made the bed? I slept in the bed you're in! – said Fernando calmly while dressing after a good hot shower.

- The *pisco*! Oh, my God… did I drink too much? Look… I'm sorry. Please, don't get the wrong idea. I'm not the kind of girl who drinks and go to bed with the first stranger she meets. I'm sorry…

Fernando was shaving and talking at the same time.

- Take it easy, Lia!!! Relax. You were totally blacked out when you entered here, you couldn't even stand straight. I laid you in bed and went reading some documents I had to check. Research stuff. I was tired, a little drunk and it was almost time to wake up. I didn't want to mess up my stuff just for one or two hours. I am the one who should apologize here! I shouldn't have laid in the same bed as you without your consent. We only touched arms. As you can see, the bed is big for one but small for two. You have your pants on, check it out. – he said laughing. – Do not worry. The only stupid thing we did last night was to drink a lot, ok?

- Man, you're *so* nerd…

Lia falls back and closes her eyes tightly trying to get rid of the drunkenness. His head is heavy, but it doesn't hurt. Normally the hangover is inversely proportional to the quality of the booze. The better it is, the less is the headache. She also feels tired due to her last flight schedule.

A short pause. Fernando poured water all over his face to rinse the shaving cream and refresh the blaze caused by the blade on his skin and resumed the conversation.

- You should take care of this irritated skin on the back of your neck.

- Well, if you sniffed my neck while I slept, then you're not *that* nerdy. There's salvation for you… good to know.

- Pardon… did you say… there's *salvation* for me?

In a few minutes both joined Rico in the hotel cafeteria for a good breakfast. Each relating to the light of day according to their problems. Fernando read something that gave a light in the search of the supposed book. Lia had a low tolerance for light because of the *pisco*.

- Rico, listen. – said Fernando with a slight excitement. – In his lifelong academic research (which never finished due to his death), Joseph Campbell clearly demonstrated that the legends and myths repeat themselves in all societies. They appear in different moments, different places and evolutionary anthropological levels, different cultures, and so on. If you go miles and miles away from here in a straight line, you will certainly find the same myths, the same tales, but with different names, characters… different backgrounds.

- I've heard about this.

- It's like a skeleton that's filled with organs. The kind we see in doctors' offices. All organs have a function in the body. The same thing happens with legends and myths. All of them, in their infinite variations, bring the same keys of understanding. The archetypal elements are all there. Do you get it?

- I'm following. Keep talking.

- We have to see this story through this angle. We have to find out the keys between the characters and their symbolism. There's a legend that comes from the land of the Nazca. Try to see the similarities with the Orejona story... – he suddenly remembered Lia was on the table. – We talk about it later.

- Where are you doing today, Lia? This is your day-off. Visiting what? – asked Rico in an attempt to outwit the woman.

- Good morning for you, too, Rico. – she spoke with irony. – I would like to go to that "coricanja" with you, can I? I don't know anybody around the city. – she asked in an irresistible way.

- The name is Qorikancha, Odalisca. Qorikancha! – replied Fernando.

The Brazilian moved his shoulders and look at Rico as if he was unable to say "no" to that woman. Rico didn't like the idea, but now it's too late.

They left the hotel at around 9:40 a.m. and headed to the *Plaza de Armas*. They could walk all the way there but they decided to take a taxi just to speed things up. The three of them were quickly dropped on the corner of *Avenida El Sol* with the *Plaza Santo Domingo*. They stood by for a few seconds just staring at the black rounded wall. Any human being with a minimum compassion for the Inca legacy (destroyed by Christian fundamentalists known as Spanish Jesuits) gets amazed by the majesty of the Inca wall that survived on that corner on which lies the *Convento de Santo Domingo*. This wall alone outshines all the beauty and splendor, all the plasticity of the Spanish baroque. The Spanish architecture is sensational, but it is of little splendor compared to the Inca perfection. It really hurts to imagine how wonderful that temple should have been. A sacred place dedicated to several deities like the Moon, the Stars, the Lightning, the Rainbow, but mainly… the Sun.

They were leaning against the fence that stretches sideways the *Avenida El Sol*. They could observe the semicircular surviving wall from a perfect distance. The image is light, moving and tragic at once. One inevitable thought comes to your mind if you care enough: *"Damn the Spanish Jesuits! Damn the Catholic Church!"*. It was early. They decided to stay there until the opening of the visitation period. The day was beautiful, not too hot, not too cold. It was early spring and the sky was the typical Cuzco-blue. The kind of blue sky you only see up there. There was a bench available right in front of the square, by the hectic sidewalk. They sat and hushed.

- Anybody fancy an Inca Cola? – says Lia breaking the silence.

- I'm in, light please. The regular is too sweetie.

- Crybaby nerd! – replies the woman with affection. – You are too sweetie already, dear. You'd better not abuse sugar. You may get out of control... sweetie.

- What? What have you just said? – says Fernando crossing the street heading to a bar on the other side of the road.

- Do you have some cash? Five *soles* shall do.

- Here.

- Thanks, nerd.

- I'm not a *nerd*! – protested Eastman smoothly.
- Yes, you are… and also cute!

Rico calls them both. It is time to see Jamirez. They drank quickly, bought their tickets and went through the ticket gate. They entered a gallery with baroque paintings, obviously Christian motifs and all those daydreams and epiphanies of the Spanish seventeenth century artists. A faithful display of what was inside their tormented minds: fear of God… fear of the Devil… fear of *all*. Fear of the darkness and the reddish beings with horns and tails who burn for all eternity in the fires of hell. They surely fear the have all those horrid people as neighbors.

It is simply impossible for Fernando Eastman, the scholar, to go through the religious artistic representations and not think about Nietzsche, his second master. Fernando agrees with "the Madman of Turin" who wrote that all the foundations of morality are inverted. That religion, especially the Christian religion, anti-natural. Everything that is anti-natural is vicious. The philosopher declares that the most vicious kind of person is the priest because he teaches the anti-nature. "The most vicious sort of human is the priest: he teaches anti-nature. Priests are not to be reasoned with, they are to be engaoled." – wrote Nietzsche.

Considering his own empiric observation, Fernando understood that the Christian religion only brings pain, guilt, discomfort with the body, fear and all that brings harm to the human sanity. He agrees with Nietzsche that religion has its function because there are people who need it badly… and there are plenty of them. Everybody needs some kind of narcotic, Nietzsche used to say. Eastman also understands the behind this cultural tragedy imposed by violence (the love of God down everyone's throats) there is inexorably the "inevitability factor" and this serves to ease his soul.

They entered the atrium and walked past the octagonal stone work fountain which lies right in the center. It is said it used to be covered with gold and, as we know, all the Inca gold was plundered by the *Conquistadores* and sent to the Spanish Crown. The trio went straight to a series of three twin temples to the right.

The internal walls bear niches in which their gold-made ritualistic statues used to be placed. The Temple of the Moon is the jewel of the right wing.

The Spanish brutality dismantled most of those walls to build the *Convento*. However, the destruction exposed one of the most impressive works of sculpture with functional purpose: a block of granite which must have been used as some kind of knocker in the entrance of the temple. It displays a series of intricate recesses and perfectly round holes that cannot be compared to any of the ancient Inca technique. Stone workers of today we would struggle to achieve the same ancient finishing perfection revealed by the Spanish stupidity.

Rico asked for Jamirez. He was on the other wing, in the other complex of surviving temples. They slowly walked towards there, but Lia (the tourist) wanted to see the other gallery opposed to the first. They were not there for the same reasons. She had no idea of what was about to unfold. Anyway, she insisted and Fernando... he couldn't say "no".

They entered the gallery of the local baroque art. Eastman is in there against his will, as if there was a *force majeure* pushing him into it. He does not feel comfortable in there and asks Lia to hurry up. Suddenly he looks to a big painting right in front of him. It's a beautiful portrait depicting Jesus in three very similar images. Each Jesus had a different expression and each expression represented something comforting and mysterious altogether. For Eastman, each image had a different glow. While observing the painting, the figures started to highlight from the background as in a holographic phenomenon. Each Jesus has different colors and different feelings.

He started to feel a little lightheaded. "It must be the altitude" – he thought. The painting went three-dimensional, as if he was watching a movie in a fancy movie theater with those special pair of glasses. The images were virtually moving. Immediately, in a crazy insight, he understood they were revealing some kind of message. No one else in the room could see the painting this way. Lia was watching the portraits on the other side of the gallery. Fernando saw in those holographic images the same indecipherable enigma that Da Vinci hid behind the mischievous smile of his Gioconda. They were screaming something to Fernando. Something important and providential.

The portraits of this gallery were all painted by "converted" Inca youngsters. Souls "saved" by Christ and trained by the Jesuits in the techniques of the Spanish baroque art. The strokes of these young local artists of the seventeenth and eighteenth centuries are absolutely unique. Such thing is not found in the museums throughout the world. The Christian depictions of the young Inca artists are softer, less painful than the classic Spanish baroque. The Inca Baroque was more spiritual. It seems it never intended to scare people or to make people feel like a creeping creature, an unworthy sinner before God. It depicts Jesus with a sublime look facing martyrdom. Eyes beyond good and evil, beyond physical pain. A real lesson to be learned: temporality is ephemeral. "It's not the arrival. It's the traveling."

The *example* of Jesus is more important than his martyrdom. Contrary to this is the Catholic Church that focuses on the *pain* of the savior to redeem the souls of the sinners. *Suffering* as the way to redemption is a serious misinterpretation that became the central pillar of the Christian faith. Fernando knows there are many other more pleasant ways to get by.

The reading Fernando did was revealing. It was just like he was reading tarot cards. He could see some archetypal figures, presented in the gestures and in the gaze of each glowing Jesus. The first Jesus, the left one, had a delicate instrument in his hand. "What could this instrument be? What could all this mean? Why do I think any of this has any meaning?" – he thought. The second one to the right bore a milky egg-shaped stone in his hands. It looks like alabaster. The Jesus in the center, the shiniest one, held a parchment.

Eastman had no idea of why those three images were "jumping" in front of him, but they were sensational and brought quite strong symbols to his attention. Each face of each Jesus seemed to speak: "*Decipher this, Fernando! We are showing you something!*". He could not understand what those images and symbols were telling him, but he realized there is something very important to be accomplished. He felt happy for being "inevitably" there. Lia, the *force majeure*, made him follow her and see the painting as if she was a pythoness saying: *"Go in and interpret this, nerd!"*. He has just had an important revelation. He didn't know what revelation it was, but his conviction was unshakable: "Nothing can stop me now. I will find this text."

***

- *Buenos dias, señor* Jamirez. – said Rico. – We are here on behalf of Professor Fontanoura. He said we should talk to you, *señor*.

Jamirez is a very old man who spends his days taking care of those surviving Inca temples. An underpaid job, but he hasn't spent all his life in there for the money. It has been for the tradition. His mother was a priestess all her life. She descended from a long native spiritual bloodline. Her function in society was to keep the tradition. She gave birth to Jamirez in the lost city by the feet of Intihuatana. The Quechua, the Aymara and many other native tribes, had their roots on the sacred ground of Machu Picchu long before the rising of the Inca. She knew his son would be the great keeper.

Jamirez, with his typical Quechua reddish skin, was then initiated in the tradition and naturally developed the art of clairvoyance. He works in the convent since he was young for he knew his personal legend is in there. The temples are his spiritual identity and Jamirez chose to dedicate his life to it. His function in society is to live his life attached to their spiritual source. He was born with the name Puca Pucara… Red Fortress.

- I was expecting your visit. – responded Jamirez peacefully.

- *Señor* Jamirez, it's a pleasure to meet you. My name is Fernando. Professor Vicenzo said you could help us with the Orejona legend. He said that…

Immediately Jamirez convulsed. His frail old body began to shake and he had to be supported by the men. Lia rapidly got his chair which was a few steps away. She started the reanimating standard procedures she learned in her profession. Rico went looking for some water. In a few seconds he started to slowly open his eyes. They immediately realized that Jamirez was not in there. That was Puca Pucara. The weak old voice of the elder became strong, young and decisive:

"Attention to what I say... Attention. You must go to the head of the hummingbird. There you will say the word one more time and She will come to you. Your legend starts there... You were born to start the great redemption of the Light. Three men and a woman shall help you. Attention to the signals you see and to the teachings you will receive so that you can understand your mission."

Blackout...

Lia dipped the man's face with a paper towel and he quickly came back to himself. The old man was back. He stood up in silence. He stared into Fernando's eyes and said:

- *Hijo*, my life was lived only for this moment. *Muchas gracias.* My mission has been completed with success. Be brave. *Do not waste your time here.* They are after you at this very moment. Go to Saqsayhuaman e climb to the top of the fortress. You will find a prohibited area. It's a special place. Spend the night in the inner circle and be calm. No one shall harm you. At daybreak you must decide where to go to.

What do you mean with hummingbird, three men and the woman, redemption of light, my legend...

- It's useless, *señor* Fernando. It was not me who spoke. It was my true "self". I do not know what he told you, I do not know what he knows. I only have visions. Puca Pucara spoke for the first time today and he shall never spoke again. It is now time to go. Do not waste your time! *Vayan... pero* sin *Dios! Vayan com* la Diosa!

Both Rico and Fernando were scared to death. "Is this something from *señor* Alejandro? From the government? Is the Professor ok? – asked Fernando without expecting any answer. The men talked in private for a few seconds then decided to go under camouflage to keep safe. Lia watched everything in horror.

She didn't get anything and she kept insistently asking all kinds of questions.

- Who are you anyway? What have you been doing? Nerd, explain what I have just witnessed!

- Easy, Lia! I can't talk right now, my dear. We have to get our stuff in the hotel and mix into the crowd. Take this cash. I want you to buy those typical clothes they sell all around. Stuff like *ponchos*, hats, this kind of stuff. I want you to set up a typical peasant costume for me and Rico. We need it fast. Can you do it?

- Sure, I love a good spending spree, but… who the hell are you running away from? Where are you going? – asked Lia totally lost.

- We talk later, honey. Now, run! Otherwise we have no time! Meet us in the hotel in 15 to 20 minutes.

- Ok.

As soon as they got to the hotel, Francisco, one of the receptionists, took both to the laundry area.

- *Señor* Fernando. – says the good man with his heavy Peruvian accent. – There are some people looking for you. I didn't like the way they looked. I think you are in danger, *señor*. They say they are from the government, the Federals, but I didn't buy it. They made lots of questions about you and if there were any other scientists in the hotel. It seems there is an authoritative order to arrest and deport all the researchers in the country.

- Do you think something has happened up there! – Fernando asks Rico. – If they know I'm here, they'll be surely back. My God, the Professor!

- I said you had gone to the Sacred Valley. They ran immediately when I said it. You have a few hours of advantage. For your safety I suggest you use the maid's corridor. It's right there, the second door to the right. It will take you close to your rooms. I'll do the check out. Come back through the same corridor and wait here. You will leave through the back door.

- *Gracias*, Francisco. You deserve a nice tip.

The Sacred Valley, known in Quechua as Ollantaytambo, is two hours from Cuzco. It is a long valley that lies on the banks of the Vilcanota River. The Inca used to do high tech agricultural experiences in the famous arable terraces that surround this gigantic geographical marvel. They studied the best practices to optimize the grow of the infinite varieties of potatoes, corn and everything that is cultivated in the area up until today. Each terrace has a different kind of soil *pH*, different temperatures and different balances of mineral salts propitious to each variety plant. In a few words: an enormous open air laboratory to keep the food production abundant and the supply chain up and running in the benefit of all the Confederation. Some say it is an aperitif to Machu Picchu.

And it is indeed!

The scientific and agricultural aspect of Ollantaytambo is just one of its many faces. The terraces are huge like "giant steps"! The Inca developed the site rebuilding the megalithic structures that were already there before them and the architecture is very similar to Machu Picchu.

When climbing up the terraces what can be seen are the typical Inca constructions from the XVI and XVII Centuries: stones with poor finishing ingeniously laid forming the unwavering terrace retaining walls and the stairs that lead to the highest part of the site. The irrigation system is also remarkable. The rain water gently flows into side channels and is distributed and controlled in soft cascades to each terrace.

When one gets to the ninth terrace is when things start to get weird. That's the pre-Inca part of the complex easily identified by the size of the stones and the finishing technique. The laying and the polishing of the stones are uncanny and the famous trapezoid niches start to show. Everything in this part was built with the same technology of the main door of Machu Picchu and its rooms and walls smooth as pillows and in the same way the builders respected the natural landscape and the geological peculiarities of the site.

The higher you go, the bigger it gets. To see those colossal stone works in that spectacular place is unbelievable. It is hard to conceive how that place was built. All the walls, all of them, were built with an inclination of 5 to 6 degrees in the style of the survivor Qorikancha temples. This simple detail is what keeps all the pre-Inca constructions in their places throughout the ages. To Fernando (who has seen many ancient buildings around the world) the pre-Inca temples are the most perfect constructions in the world.

And there's more! On the top of the site there are the remains of an immense stone wall which is comparable to some Egyptian building style impressively bonded by the good old "stone molding technique" totally alien to our culture today! This wall also has the typical inclination of 5 to 6 degrees and reaches some five meters high. Some stones, red granite, weight 60 tons and look like they had been vitrified! They feel soft and pleasant to the touch and amazing cuts and fittings can be observed. All in all, nothing can explain how all those stones got to the top of the valley, but one thing is evident: they had been taken up there somehow.

They packed the essential, went through the corridor, did the check out and oriented Francisco about the expected arrival of Lia. Rico, who was not being chased by the government, was alert to the movements of the back street while Fernando was trying to calm down. He received too much information for a day and hasn't had any time to put them together, not mentioning the fact he's being chased. A just dose of paranoia came over the two men. Rico was worried because he knew nothing about Lia. Would she be one of those politically correct person? Would she blow the whistle to the authorities?

- Fernando, listen to me. She didn't get anything, but she's not stupid. She heard it perfectly when the old man said there is someone after you.

- I don't think she's gonna inform the authorities, Rico. She's just a naive girl who knows nothing about what's going on. She barely knows who the Inca were! Relax, man. We also do not know what's going on! I don't know why, man, but I trust her.

A few minutes later, oriented by Francisco at the reception, Lia shows up in the hotel laundry. A perfect peasant in a typical over-colorful dress holding a flight attendant bag. She bought a larger dress and some seven or eight wool sweaters which she rolled over her waist under the dress. She looked like an authentic Peruvian, except for her blond hair but the hat took care of that. She entered the laundry without being recognized by both men.

- I'm going with you! I liked the disguise thing! – she said senselessly.

- Odalisca! You should have bought clothes for *us*! Not for you!

- Take it easy, nerd! Yours are in the bag. If you are in a hurry, dress up. Call Rico. I'll wait at the door.

Rico shows up at the back-door of the hotel wearing a *poncho* and a typical Peruvian hat. He looked straight in Lia's eyes with a serious semblance, grabbed her by the arm and said:

- We cannot take you with us, do you understand? You are not coming!

- What's with you, Rico? What can happen if I go with you? I don't know where we're going, but I want to go! Do you think I'll puzzle you both, like I'm a little lost and defenseless princess? Man, I'm a flight attendant! I've been through jungle survival training. I'm a helping hand! My God, I don't even know what I'm talking about, I barely know you both! But I feel the nerd needs me.

- Ok, but if you start acting like "a little lost and defenseless princess" of the movies, we'll leave you behind, do you get it? – said Rico pointing his finger to the young beautiful lady. – I'm not going to risk Fernando's life for nothing. I am here to protect him. This is serious business! I'm loyal to him 'till death. This is my legend. Do you understand this?

- Look, dude. – she talks back putting his finger down in a serene gesture. – I've heard too much about legends today. I don't get it, but I reckon this is big stuff. Relax. I've got no intentions to risk anyone's life! – she spoke with determination. – Look, my job sucks. I've got nothing to lose. I'm not coming back to my silly life.

- Is she coming or not, Rico?

- She's coming.

- So, let's go! – said the nerd with a strong tone of leadership.

DAY 5 – Noon

Traffic all around Peru mean Chaos, it doesn't matter which city you are. There's no order. Rico found it better to go to Saqsayhuaman on foot and pass through crowded places to mix with the locals. If there's anyone looking for Fernando, they'll be looking for a person dressed like a scientist or a regular tourist. It's really easy to disappear in the mass of colorfully dressed people. Rico covered Lia's face with a thin layer of mud from the hotel's back garden and stuffed her head in her peasant hat. Fernando also had to "make up" to look like a Peruvian. Both Fernando and Lia are too Caucasian to look like Peruvians.

They left the hotel at *Calle Plateros*, went through *Plaza de Armas* and followed north through *Calle Triunfo* soon to turn left until *Plaza Las Nazarenas*. From there the went up *la escalinata* which takes to one of the entrances to Saqsayhuaman.

The fortress-temple of Saqsayhuaman stands right above the city of Cuzco, maybe 50 meters, but the access is a long walk uphill. There's no way to climb up the hillside. Now the reader must put together all the tension of the escape plus the difficulties of the altitude to understand the image of Rico, Peruvian adapted to the local conditions, walking ahead of the Brazilians who were literally dragging themselves up many meters behind along *la escalinata*. Their heads were aching and the oxygen were not enough for both. Rico was confident no one would look for Fernando up there, but he was attentive, serious. He was constantly asking the both to hurry up.

They got to the fortress. Rico told them to wait with their heads down, acting as if they were sad. He went to talk with the park staff in Quechua soon came back.

- Let's go. Free pass.

They passed through with their heads down. The door keepers, which were chatting about whatever, didn't even look at them. Rico told they were artisans who had relatives working in the site's parking and that there had been a death in the family and all that drama. The disguised Brazilians entered the site along with Rico without being noticed and slowly walked along the imposing set of megaliths. Fernando always goes crazy when he's there. Those walls are absolutely astonishing. Nothing can explain those.

They went straight to the forbidden part for tourists, right on the top, on the highest part of the site. It's a set of low walls which form an enormous square and three centralized circles with the customary perfection of the Inca. Imagine, if you will, a giant compass made of stone walls on the top of a hill – the highest in Cuzco – with the north, south, east and west and the intermediate directions. It's a simple but extremely intriguing construction. Who could have been guided by these enormous compass laid on the top of that hill? No one knows why this place is not opened for visitation, but it's not easy to guess. Something must have been hidden up there.

- Let's go to the central circle. No one can do any harm to us in there. – said Eastman. – At least this was what the old man said, wasn't it?

- Man, what are these stones? What is all of this? – exclaimed Lia overwhelmingly while she followed the nerd. – I've never seen anything like this in my whole life!

- Lia, my dear. The official story of this place is totally misleading. In fact no one knows who built this place. Some say it was the Inca, but you can easily see which parts were really built by them. Look at these smaller unpolished rocks of the circle we're in. This was Inca work! But the megaliths weren't for sure! Not even *them* knew who did it.

- Tell us, nerd. We have plenty of time up here. Keep talking. It helps to relax.

- Well, there's a legend. I'll sum it up. Wiracocha is the highest God of the Inca and many other civilizations before them. He descended from the skies to teach the men of the Andes his technologies and to transmit his astronomical and mathematical knowledge. To put in a nutshell, all the amazing stuff built along the Andes, be the Inca stuff, or Chavin, Nazca, etc., was taught by this god Wiracocha. All the mysteries you see here were possible due to his teachings. They say he was taller than the regular Inca, had snow-white skin and a thick long white beard.

Fernando was speaking and making great effort to keep his breathing in that altitude.

- Some say he could fly, control the climate, melt stuff and more using a rod which he always carry with him. The Inca talked about a Falcon which could melt and mold these stones with a powerful liquid then would fix them together, one on the top of the other, as if they were milk pudding. This legend is more plausible than the explanation the guides normally throw into the tourists ears.

- Wow – said Lia in awe.

- Look at these. – said Eastman pointing to the joints of the walls. – These stones have a very interesting surface. This suggests that they have been through a super high melting point temperature. The builders laid the giant blocks piece by piece in melting temperature in a way they fit like modeling clay.

- Seriously?

- Don't just look. Feel it. Touch the stone! – said Fernando walking towards one of the megalithic walls. – the fitting is perfect. This legend also says it has happened long before the Inca have appeared. The tourist guides say these colossal stones, worthy of the Egyptian Pharaohs and weighting tons, had been cut, transported to this site and polished till perfection by Inca hands. They say the Inca used to lift up the giant stones with ropes, spread some sand on the bottom stone then they would drop the stone so that it would be marked by the sand. This way they would know where to polish to achieve the perfect fit you see in front of you... just like the dentist do today to fix our tiny little tooth.

- How can you be sure it was not like this?

- By the size of the stones, their weight, by the precision of the fitting. It's not possible to be made by human hands. Imagine a group of workers lifting a ten ton stone all day, polishing the bottom of it, letting it fall to have it marked by the sand, then lifting it up again, polishing it, dropping it, marking it... over and over again. Some say that two thousand men could easily lift any of these giant stones with their own hands, but they don't say *how* could four thousand hands find their places on *one single stone*. There's no space for all those hands, you see? And the process of lifting and dropping and marking it with sand... this is simply *not feasible*. Not even with chains and pulleys.

- Wow! This god sounds like ET stuff. Did he really come from the skies?

- That's the legend. There's a man here in Peru, a kind of a spreader of the original Inca culture and tradition. His name is Jorge Luis Delgado. He stands with the theory that the Falcon they say is obviously not a bird. He talks about the "bird-men". There's a connection between these bird-men and the Easter Island. The *pueblo* and the local tradition talk about *los Hermanos Del Cielo*. All these have something with Machu Picchu beyond the architectonic style. Up there you can find a couple of oval towers without any lateral openings. You can only enter there by the top. Some say those towers were the quarters of the flying men. Legends... only legends.

- Why are you running away, anyway? — asked Lia looking deep into Eastman's eyes. — I ended up in this, but if you are doing anything wrong, please tell me and I go back to the hotel.

- I'll try to explain what I was able to understand by now, ok? I'm kind of lost, too... just like you. There had been a discovery in the Sacred city of Machu Picchu. Do you know the place?

- Muchu... what?

- Nevermind. They found a hidden chamber on the other side of the taller mountain, the Huayana Picchu. When this chamber was opened, something very strange happened with the people of Águas Calientes. They suddenly started talking about a very old legend about a woman and a supposed book. Rico is from this village and it happened to him, too! Are you following the plot?

- Yeah... kinda of...

- I was commissioned by my teacher, professor Vicenzo Fontanoura, to find the so called book. We don't know if it's really a book or something written in plaques of gold or whatever. It seems that the Peruvian government doesn't want anyone to know about it and now there are people after me. They are searching, arresting and deporting all the foreign scientists. It seems it's nothing personal because they are expelling everyone. Rico is helping me because he knows the legend, he is Peruvian and the Professor trusts him.

- Wow! It seems that things will get interesting! Look, I don't know why, but I think I can help you. I know nothing about all these legends nor about books and stuff, but there's something pushing me into this cauldron. – Lia said in a tone full of strong feelings. – You know, nerd, a crazy peasant stood in front of me at *Plaza de Armas* when I was buying these clothes. She said: "Stay with him, my dear. Be close to him. He needs you.". I was shocked! I reckon she was talking about you. I've got no one in my life to care about at this moment. Nerd, after that man in the Convent... I'm in for anything. Besides... I like your way.

- Thanks, Lia, but, please, keep your eyes opened. Any sign can help us. Rico and I are going after something and we don't even know what it is and we have no idea where to start. Things are happening in a crazy wave of coincidences and some of them I don't even see as coincidences anymore.

- Ah! I saw a Dutch tourist while I was shopping. She was white as snow, but her face was red like chili. You know... the sun.

I bought some high protection sunscreen. I thought you wouldn't have any. I also bought some snacks. I was hungry.

- Cool!

- Here's your change. There was a lot of money here, nerd. Get real! In an adventure, money can buy your liberty. I saw it in a movie.

- Well done, Lia. Well done.

Before sunset and after the site had closed, a night shift guard always checks all the corners for a possible lost tourist. No one is allowed to stay in after closing time. Rico and Fernando were sitting inside the central circle when the guard passed right in front of them. Both men were already standing up to explain what they were doing inside the prohibited area but, surprisingly, he turned his back and slowly walked away without bothering them. He just didn't see the two men although he gave a good look right at their direction.

Lia had gone into a small forest right behind the area to freshen up and she saw the guard when she was coming back. He was looking straight inside the circle. The woman was taken by panic and hid away. She tried to find her colleagues, but she couldn't just like the guard. "Did they leave me here?", she thought. Lia waited until the guard was away then she ran into the circle. Like magic, as soon as she stepped back into the forbidden area, the two men could be seen again.

- Did you see the guard? – she said baffled not for what she has just seen... or what she *did not* see.

- Yes, but it seems he just ignored us. – said Rico.

- No, he didn't see you!

- What do you mean? He looked right towards us! – replied Fernando.

- There's something very strange with this circle, nerd. You cannot see the inside from outside. I swear it!

- I gotta check this out!

When Fernando went to the outside, he knew the woman was right. He couldn't see Rico, nor Lia, not even their luggage. It was just like a dome of energy, an extremely subtle field which camouflaged the whole place. It was something inexplicable. "Is this why the Ministry of Tourism closes this area to the visitors? Would it be due to this energy field?" – thought Fernando while losing the last traces of skepticism, but not all of it (not yet). The guards seem not to know about it. They just follow the rules.

- Why this energy must be a secret? – asked Fernando rhetorically aloud. – The Peruvian government strictly prohibits the entrance of people in this area.

- Why they do this? – asked Lia.

- They say it is to preserve the site.

- Man, do they think these stones will wear out? – she said with sagacity and irony. – Sounds like a joke to me!

- Well… whatever! – said Eastman. – There are things that can't be explained. The old Ramirez told us that we would be safe in here, so this is where we're staying. We have to focus on what was said by the elder.

DAY 5 – 8pm

Rico built a bonfire. It seemed that the night was going to be long and cold. The diner was a mix of chips, cookies and corn snacks. The extra wool sweaters Lia bought were providential: the night was really freezing. The conversation, on the other hand, was hot.

- How's your life, Lia. I mean, what do you usually do at home? Don't you have someone?

- No one in my life, nerd. Usually I'm alone, but I watch TV, you know. I love surfing on the Internet. Social media and stuff. I hardly stay at home, anyway. I'm a working girl. I like working out whenever I have time.

- What do you watch on TV?

- I like those series, like "Friends", you know… and those of doctors, too. The cops' series are cool, you know… good cops… bad cops. They always find things out.

- Have you seen any documentaries on the mysterious things

of this planet, like Peru? I mean, do you have any idea about what happened on Earth in the remote times?

- Dude, I've got no patience for documentaries. I like series, nerd.

- Really??? You don't know anything about nothing? – Fernando commented calm, but outraged. – Nothing about Peru at all?

Fernando doesn't understand why the majority of people don't care to get any knowledge He loses his temper every time someone says that "intellectual things are for intellectuals". He always reminds of a beautiful excerpt from Saramago that says:

"If I may say so, I would like to express a vow here: That this day shall come to this country, where all its inhabitants are intellectuals, the day when the continued exercise of intelligence is not a privilege of a few but the natural fulfillment of all. I do not see why it is always incompatible the performance of a so-called manual office with the continuous study, the effort of intelligibility, which characterize (or should characterize) the intellectual."

A world with more intellectualized people would be more exciting, according to Eastman.

Pure idealism!

He kept talking about how people spend hours and hours sitting in front of a TV set and never worry about looking for something that quenches the thirst of the souls. He is convinced that few people really have souls. Most of them are dead inside. They were born dead or they are slowly dying. Nerdy stuff, you know...

- They like to herald that TV makes people stupid, but no one likes to work their brains out. I don't mean to call you stupid, Lia, but this thing about *good cop x bad cop series* is something that doesn't make you think. Better! It makes you *not* to think! *They* are the ones who give you all the answers with indisputable evidences. They chew everything up and spit it all in your face. They round people up like a flock of sheep. You know, Peru is a place where you *can't* find the answers, dear! This is fucking crazy! The minds of the people are anesthetized by the "programs". It's not by chance that they call it a "program". And there's also the Internet. The whole media system is part of a great cover up of all the real deal... and we have no idea what deal is this! They do anything to avoid people of going after the mysteries because they don't want us to know about them! We are indoctrinated by the *American shit*!

- Come on, Nerd. Take it easy. There are plenty of good stuff to watch on TV. When I get home after a week on the road, I mean, *on the air*, I need to turn off. – protested Lia in a conciliatory tone.

- Ok, I understand. The stress is heavy. I even like one or another of those series, but people only watch crap! It's 24/7!!! Soccer, soap opera, low level comedy, reality shows… all ready to give people the comfort they ask for. They screw up you focus capacity, they fuck up your attention! And no one raises the question: "Attention to what? Is there anything really being hidden?".

- Is there?

- Lia, we are stuck into a world of endless "whys" and no one is asking! The thing is so big that we can't even see the problem! But… look… the fucking TV is also a great tool to raise and cherish curiosity. It's all there, it gets to you through the cables. Why do the masses wish *not* to watch documentaries? Why do they wish *not* to know about any mystery?

- Mysteries are cool. I like The DaVinci Code, Agatha Christie, Sherlock and all those cool stuff…

- There's good stuff on TV, Lia. Watch some documentaries and you'll see it for yourself, too. A good friend of mine said once that if you are not interested in the mysteries of life, you are half way to death. Questioning important things doesn't hurt anyone, you know…

While Fernando Eastman gave his little speech about how can the TV screw up your life at the same time it can save your whole existence, Lia looked at him and she was enjoying what she was seeing. A young man engaged in things that are more interesting things than those people she worked with at the flight company. He was really good looking.

The speech went non-stop through the night. She should be at the airport of Cuzco in a few hours by the morning, but she decided not to come. Before her decision she instinctively knew that a great adventure had already begun to her. At that moment she knew: "This will be one of those great things… just like on TV!".

After a few seconds of silence Lia said:

- Nerd… you've been watching too much TV, man! Get some sleep. There's more tomorrow.

The woman laid on the ground and went to sleep using Fernando's backpack as a pillow. Odalisca dos Santos had just dived into this mystery.

DAY 6 – 5am

Rico was up before the sunrise. The sky was clear and the sky colors were divine. The morning star, or planet Venus, was glowing dim as if it was looking after the three of them. Fernando woke up, got his things together and went to talk to Rico.

- It seems that she is watching us from up there, doesn't it? It's very shinny. – he said stretching up after having slept in the open.

- When I was a child, *señor* Fernando, I used to wake up before the others just to keep looking at her. I didn't even know it was Venus. To me it was the morning star which fascinated my father. It was him who showed that beauty for the first time without knowing it was a planet, instead of a star. She is the first "star" to appear at night. It's a very shinny planet

- Did you know Venus is strongly connected to Lucifer? The ancient people thought that due to its strong luminosity. You know, Lucifer, don't you? The Bearer of Light.

- Yeah, I've heard about it, but religious polemics are not my cup of tea. – said Rico. – I'm not a Christian. I'm not interested in this Lucifer. I'm connected to my culture. To us, this star, which is a planet indeed, could be the origin of the Andean humanity.

My origins, *señor* Fernando, the people to which I belong. She has always called for me. Now I am somehow answering to her call. And all of this has been an accident, I mean, I wasn't looking for those inscriptions. They have found me! *Venus* have found me!

- Nietzsche talks about the revaluation of all the values. – said Fernando rambling and aiming at the lazy dawning skies. – It seems he was right! Things are inverted, Rico. All of them. For instance, Lucifer was an angel, the most perfect creature God has ever made, according to the apocrypha Genesis of Melchizedek. This text brings a more complete version of the biblical Genesis and it says that he was named Lucifer because this name means "the one who bears the Light" or "the bearer of Light", the translation may vary. Then you blink your eyes and the catholic church equals Lucifer to the devil, the evil one. Satan becomes the great enemy of God, *his own creator*. It's just a matter of religious doctrine. Nietzsche would surely stand with Lucifer just to piss off the Vatican.

- I don't know, *señor* Fernando. I do not know this Nietzsche. – said Rico reticently.

- Well, back to business. – resumed Eastman. – It cannot be a book as we know it, unless it's a copy. And, you know, copies are not to be trusted. Do you know how old this story is? How many eras are involved here?

- I've no idea! It's a very old story. So old that it reached the status of myth, legend. – said Rico.

- There's a man called Fernando de Montessinos, a Peruvian chronicler from the Spanish colonization period. He walked the Andes for fifteen years collecting all the Inca oral tradition he could. – said the Brazilian. – He registered 103 generations of Inca rulers before the last one, the Great Atahualpa. His work places the roots of the Inca tradition on the pre-biblical deluge times! I guess we are dealing with something that arose before the biblical "creation myth".

- And the date of this "universal flood" is controversial. – completed Rico.

- The religious fanatics talk about six thousand years. The astronomical evidences points to more than twelve thousand ago.

What I think is that this story is too old to have been written in a book format, you know. It cannot be a book as we know today.

- How do you know that? – debated Rico.

- The Inca knew how to write on the banana tree leaves. They had everything about their culture registered on this material. It happened that one day some "seers" prophesied a great cataclysm. The 63rd Emperor Topu Caui Pachacuti, The Great Pacha IV, blinded by a superstitious madness, ordered all the written registers in all the corners of his domains to be burned. Very few pages had left. It seems this book is prior to all of that. The banana leaf technique is not that old. It cannot be this what we are looking for. If it's a copy, it didn't survive the burning spree of Pacha IV.

- If it survived, it must be in rags by now. – completed Rico knowing what he was talking about.

- I guess it must be something written in the original format, but no in organic media. It's like the problem we have with the Bible. The Pentateuch, according to the tradition, was written personally by Moses himself, the great patriarch of the Hebrew. But... if he wrote anything... it wasn't on papyrus.

- How come? He wrote on what?

- That's where it gets weird! – said the scholar. – He must have left some register or it has all been passed on by oral tradition. Moses was raised as the step-grandson of the Pharaoh Tutmosis I and his Queen Ahmose. Do you remember the story of the baby slaughter, the baby in the basket by the shores of the Nile found by the Pharaoh's daughter known as Hatshepsut?

- I heard about Moses. That is enough for me. – said Rico objectively.

- So, due to his "adoption," Moses was certainly an initiate in the secrets of ancient Egypt. He probably had access to everything that was accessible to the son of a Pharaoh. He had knowledge of things like who actually built those pyramids, Karnak, Thebas, Heliopolis, and all their secrets. He probably knew a lot about their Gods and where they came from, not to mention spells, astrology, mathematics. He was a special being.

- That being so... – Rico tried to accelerate Eastman's exposition, which immediately proceeds to the long explanation.

- There is the story of the Ten Commandments. The stones on which Yahweh wrote the laws and gave to Moses to serve as a political constitution. A set of ethical rules for society to live well and in an organized way. That was around 1500 BCE or so, but after a while the Law of Stones ceased to be effective.

- Yes, he was disappointed with the people of the desert. – said the Peruvian. – Moses broke the stone boards, went back to his "god" and got new boards and so on... I imagine it was very difficult to climb up and down that hill carrying stone plaques.

- This is the point! Around the year 2,500 BC, in the 18th Egyptian Dynasty, we *already* had the papyrus. Yahweh began to use the papyrus to communicate his laws *much* later.

- Be clearer, *señor* Fernando. What does Moses have to do with our search?

- Did he record the story or not? If yes, in what material? Spinoza says that he did not write any books, that the whole story was passed for countless years by the oral tradition and that Ezra, a man with culture and literate, put everything on the papyrus.

Rico looks perplexed at Fernando speaking at the elbows without giving a link to most of the things he spoke. When he noticed a breach, he immediately interrupted Professor Fontanoura's trusted man.

- Fernando, you're rambling. We are not here to talk about theology. We are here for another book, not the book of the Hebrew.

- I know, Rico, I'm sorry. My head works like this, trying to bring the elements into the equation. Sometimes I know I go too far without realizing it. But look, our book may have been written in a non-flexible material. Nothing you can get under your arm and walk around. What if they are stone or metal boards? How are we going to bring it to a lab for testing? That's what intrigues me! We know nothing! If it's original, it sure is not paper, papyrus, banana, none of it. I suppose the thing is original. I'm just thinking about our possibilities, Rico. I need to put all the options on the table and gradually exclude the absurd ones, at least.

- Okay, Fernando, I understand. But we must be attentive to everything. Just like everywhere in the world where one culture has been dominated by another, we also had our guardians. There may be a copy hidden somewhere. It may even be that this story was written by someone who was not there personally, but who knew the details of it due to some oral tradition... just like Ezra and his Bible. It may also be something written on banana leaf.

- It's true... I need to relax. I am tense. – said Fernando, stretching his arms and turning his neck to try to lengthen the body after the terrible night in the open. – In any case, what has been said by Jamirez needs to be analyzed. Help me out here, please.

- Of course! Do you remember everything?

- I think so. Let's see: I have to go to the head of a *hummingbird*. Is this a place? What does it mean?

- That's a hard start. – replied Rico.

At that moment Lia wakes up, stretches up and slowly walks herself to the two men.

- Dude, what a night... that tattoo scratched all night long.

- What tattoo?

- The same one you checked on my neck yesterday in your room while I slept, *señor* nerd.

- That thing in the back of your neck ... I remember. Was that a tattoo? What a great artist, huh... – said Fernando with his usual good humor. – I like tattoos. I have one here on my left arm.

- Let me see? What is it?

- It is a representation of a deity of the Chavin civilization, of the north of Peru. I had it done some time ago. I fell in love with it at first sight. It is very expressive. How about yours?

- I did mine on the beach a few days ago... Henna, you know. That's why it's itching. It was supposed to be a hummingbird.

- What? A *hummingbird*? So you have a hummingbird tattoo??? Explain this, Lia! – said Fernando, intrigued by the coincidence.

- Dude, I saw some drawings of those islands, I forgot the name. It's archeology. You must know about it.

- What islands, girl? Is important!!!

- Islands of ... Nazca! I remembered! They were drawings of the Nazca Islands.

- Nazca Islands? They are *lines*, Odalisca! *LINES!* – shouted Fernando immediately after killing the charade.

- Do you know it? Where is it?

- It's right here, sweetheart. Many miles to the north. Get your things. Let's go to the Nazca Desert. – said Fernando with leadership. – Thank you Lia! You gave us the first key to find what we are looking for. Thank you so much for coming with us!

- You're welcome... – she said without understanding.

DAY 6 – 7am

Nazca is far away to the north of Cuzco on the Peruvian coast. It lays in a desert where an interesting civilization flourished and gave its name to the area. The Nazca disappeared around AD 800, but first lived miraculously in one of the most arid deserts on the planet. Temperatures are relatively low because of the cold currents of the Pacific. The winter temperature ranges between 14°C and 24°C, which is not bad at all. Despite the aridity, there are many small rivers that allowed (and still allow) the settlement of many people in this dry region. The Nazca water pipeline systems still exist today and are daily used to irrigate vast areas of potato, corn, soybean and everything else planted there.

The Nazca were fantastic architects. The channels are underground and contain spiral cisterns so that water can be collected. There was no need to add anything to the structure since its original construction. To this day, the municipality of Nazca maintains the canals in the same way that has been done for centuries. A man enters the channel crawling and withdraws with his own hands the plants that grow through the gaps of the stones and the dirt that eventually falls inside. This ancestral service is what makes life possible in that region.

- The Nazca civilization has a legend that speaks of a woman with an elongated skull. – said Fernando while packing his things.

– It was a mummy found back in 1910 that brought that legend back. This woman came to Earth *inside* a hummingbird. You see? There must be something very real in this whole madness!

- The Hummingbird of Nazca. – Rico said with some dismay. – We're going to have to spend some money on the lookouts. No one can step in that desert. It is an area considered to be sacred by the locals and it has been listed by UNESCO as a World Heritage Site.

- Tell them whatever it takes to get us there, Rico. Make up whatever you want, but take us to this bird.

Within minutes they were ready. They left the circle carefully so that no one could see them and went down to Cuzco to get a car. Rico quickly negotiated with a taxi driver. A thousand Soles to take them to the Nazca desert with his private car. Rico thought it would be best to drive around the country as local citizens. Taxis would be inspected. A Japanese third-hand car of local licenses full of peasants would not attract attention. Lia put some heavy make-up on Fernando and herself to get the typical reddish skin tone. She painted her eyebrow quite thick. They looked like peasants.

They were ready.

They left Cuzco, which is near the Amazon region of Peru, at around 8 o'clock in the morning. According to the plan they would rise high through the Andes, the eternal glaciers, and descend to the coast following west, always avoiding the main roads. On this route temperatures vary a lot. They did not know what altitude hours and glaciers would be like. The driver, *señor* Pablo, thought about it and provided blankets.

They reached the foot of the mountain range, which was already cold and high, near 11am. They stopped to eat and buy supplies, especially water. They knew that after they started to climb there would be no stopovers for several hours. Lia bought everything of what was edible in that small tourist establishment. She took care of the nutrition of the expedition. Rico and Fernando looked for maps of Nazca. It was not difficult to find. In every corner of Peru it is possible to find a summary of the tourist attractions of the country in the shape of a trinket. A "Nazca Lines T-shirt" can be purchased in Lima, Cuzco, Arequipa, Puno, etc.

They found a well-detailed map with north and south directions and a scale to learn about the distances. Fernando knew that the Nazca drawings were *huge* and could reach hundreds of meters.

It is not easy to differentiate the drawings on the floor. Proof of this is that, after hundreds of years, the drawings were only *accidentally* noticed by an aviator who flew over the region in the early twentieth century. The distances between the geoglyphs is another problem. Fernando and Rico needed to do some calculations, but they could not talk about it during the trip, for the driver, *señor* Pablo, of course could not know.

And the trip went on...

DAY 7 – 11:30am
Nazca/Peru

The night was hard. It was 12 hours of altitude and extreme cold. No one slept. Collective attention on the Andes roads is inevitable and necessary. They are really dangerous roads. Narrow, steep, full of curves and ascents and descents, much used by trucks and tourist buses. It would be 630 kilometers on the main roads, but most of the way was made by small roads, as was asked to *señor* Pablo. Fernando's safety was a priority over travel time. They needed to be quick, but avoiding confrontation with authorities.

The desert begins immediately at the foot of the mountain ranges. The entire Peruvian coast is desert: the gateway to the vast Atacama Desert. Sand is what dominates the landscape but when you get to the city of Nazca everything changes. The urban landscape has emerged in recent decades due to tourism. This was thanks to the spread of the Nazca Lines by the books of Erich Von Daniken in the early 1970s. The Peruvian government has invested a lot of money in the infrastructure and accessibility to the region. In a few years the city grew a lot. Yet it is still a poor place today. Most people still make a living from farming activities and young people no longer want to stay there. They prefer to go out and go to larger cities in search of better salaries and more modernity. Those who stay only have two options: farming or tourism.

- Let's find a hotel.

- I do not think so, *señor* Fernando! – said Rico. – There must be notifications throughout the tourism network. You are being chased. Remember that!

- What do we do, then?

- I'll speak to a trustworthy person. I do not know him personally, but the people who carry the old traditions in Peru are *all* reliable. He is a very cultured gentleman, knows how to speak languages and is recognized worldwide as one of the most respected craftsman of the Nazca culture. He works with ceramics and uses the same technique as the Nazca, developed many centuries ago.

- Really? – exclaimed Fernando with academic interest.

- His grandfather, who taught you everything about this art, realized that the Nazca ceramics found in abundance scattered throughout the desert floor did not lose their original color or brilliance. He then realized that if the craftsman applies the natural nose skin oiliness to the finished painting, if he rubbed a small stone to the nose skin and spread it over the surface of the ceramic piece, it will not lose color nor brightness. It's an interesting story, do not you think?

- *Yuck*! Probably he should charge a buck for his slimy pottery! – said Lia with disgust.

- It's bizarre! I found some ceramic fragments in the desert here in Nazca a few years ago near the spiral wells. They were actually in good shape despite being turned over by plowing machines. I still have some of them at home. Talk to him, Rico. We'll wait in that restaurant.

- Deal.

Rico, who was still suspicious of Lia, went out looking for *señor* Julio Pranas. He found out that his house and studio is on the outskirts of the city of Nazca. It was very easy to find, since he is an international celebrity there. A very respected and beloved man. The entrance to the house was very old. Rico walked the long corridor that leads to the back of the house where his sacred place of work is. After entering the atelier Rico saw a corner with a typical Nazca oven built in the ancient style. That's where Julio bakes his pieces before painting and "varnishing" them with the old technique of the nose skin oil. He has lots of original Nazca pottery pieces as templates for his works.

The artist only reproduces copies of the original models. He has no intention of innovating art, after all he is a keeper of his tradition. Each work, depending on size and complexity, has a different value and may cost from 30 to 300 US dollars. It is selling pottery that *señor* Julio lives, supports his family and takes care of his diabetes, which is in an advanced state. Julio has already lost both his legs because of the disease and is now having serious sight problems.

Rico Calmón patiently waited for *señor* Julio Pranas to explain the entire Nazca manufacturing process to some French tourists. He followed the explanation carefully by observing that cultured man massacred by the disease. Although he did not understand French, Rico was impressed by the old man's ability to work while explaining. Tourists loved everything and left $250 worth of groceries in the hands of the artisan who wrapped his work with affection. They left happily.

Rico then approached Julio.

- Good morning, *señor* Julio. How are you doing? My name is Rico.

- I'm fine, *señor* Rico. Interested in ceramics?

- No. Actually, I need your help. A lot of people talk about you all over the country, sir, and your mission to preserve the ancient knowledge.

- Yes, young man. I dedicate my life to the culture and sacred tradition of the ancients. That's what I live for. How can I help you?

- Did you hear about the incident in Águas Calientes?

- Yes. I was not surprised, actually. It is something that was expected a long time ago.

- Then you know about the legend and about the book? Would you help me? I am with a person who can find this book and bring the truth to the surface. He is totally committed to the tradition and the truth, *señor*. I worked on the excavation at Machu Picchu, but before they discovered the new chamber and the outbreak of the phenomenon, I discovered an inscription on a stone showing Venus and the Earth. I am part of this collective phenomenon, *señor* Julio. I also woke up that day with Orejona in the head, but only I and two other people know of the inscription... at least until a few days ago.

- I can imagine, *señor* Rico. I reckon you immediately linked the story to the inscription. My grandfather told me about her. The legend of Orejona was a recurring theme in my conversations with him.

- Because of this, the whole Peruvian government wants the head of the man I'm helping. We're being harassed by the police and we need a place to hide. Can you help us?

- Of course! My grandfather, the great man who taught me everything I know, told me that people who keep the tradition have a duty to help one another. If your friend can help bring the memory back to mankind, he is also our friend. In this particular case you will have my full support. Tell your friend that he can stay here at home. It has no comfort, but it has a roof and food.

- Thank you very much, *señor* Julio. You will not regret it.

- Tell your friend that I have one or two things to tell him if he still does not know. I never thought this day would come! – he said excitedly and with unconcealed joy. – I have waited a long time. Does he already know about the hummingbird?

- Yes, it was revealed to him that the hummingbird is one of the pieces of the puzzle. That's why we came to the Nazca. We need to go there.

- Does he know what to do when he gets there?

- He has to repeat a word. That's all we know. A very special man gave him this guidance in a trance.

- That's something already. You know you cannot step on that ground, don't you?

- We know. – replied Rico. – What should we do? It is crucial that he can go to the head of the Hummingbird.

- I know, son. – he laughed kindly. – I know one of the site's guard chief very well. He is my son. Tell your friend to be calm. My son also knows that this day would come. Let's have dinner together today and we'll come up with a plan.

Rico returned to the restaurant to take Fernando and Lia to Julio's house, but he did not find them there. A great fear took hold of him. "Where are they? Where did they go? Fernando is not reckless. Something must have happened! That woman must have done something and he must have been captured!", he thought wildly. He crossed the small avenue and entered the reception of the hotel in front of the restaurant.

- *Buenos dias*. I'm a tour guide. – said Rico, improvising a story. – I'm looking for a couple of Brazilian tourists. A tall man with long hair and a short woman with blond hair. Have you seen them around?

- No, *señor*. Are these two? – said the attendant, staring into Rico's face. The boy showed a picture on a computer screen behind the counter. They were both dressed in their peasant fantasies. The photo showed only a piece of Rico's body. "Shit! They already know that Lia is with him!", he thought.

All the major cities in the world are heavily guarded with cameras everywhere. In London, for example, if you do something wrong, the police can find you in a matter of minutes. They never imagined that Cuzco would be the same. The photo was taken by surveillance cameras right in the middle of the *Plaza de Armas* as they fled to Saqsayhuaman. "Now they know that Fernando has company!" – thought Rico.

- No, *señor*. It's not them. Thank you. – he said kind of confused and startled by something. He quickly left the hotel and headed down the main avenue following the traffic flow hoping to find them safe and sound at some nearby store. "The government do not know about me yet. That's good!", Rico said to himself as he walked among the pedestrians on that narrow sidewalk. "I have to take advantage of this so I can help Fernando, but... where are they?".

Right in the heart of the city of Nazca, as in all other cities of Spanish influence, there is a *Plaza de Armas* with a large statue in the center and many benches to sit and pass the time. Rico crossed the *Plaza* completely disoriented and looking all around. Suddenly he heard his name being called softly, almost whispered.

- Why are you standing here in the middle of the *Plaza*, exposing yourself? It's dangerous, *señor* Fernando!

- Stop calling me *"señor"*, please! – protested Fernando irritated. – Lia had the idea of checking information about this persecution from the Peruvian government on foreign scientists. She entered the net with her cell phone and there were our beautiful faces right on the front page of the Ministry of Tourism website. As you can see, we decided to change clothes. Look at my new haircut.

- Very ingenious, Fernando. – praised the Peruvian now calmer. – I'm sorry. I was really scared. I thought you had been arrested. Your photos are all over the Internet You two are being chased by the Federal Police. I thought everything was lost.

They bought clothes that only bad taste tourists would wear. Shirts with drawings of the Nazca Lines, hats with logo of the Ministry of Tourism (the word *Perú* written with a spiral "P"). They were the most *typical* tourists in the city. They could not wear those peasant clothes anymore. Even horribly dressed, Lia had taken Fernando's heart.

- Did you speak to your acquaintance?

- Yes, Fernando. We have lodging and food for today . *Señor* Julio has things to tell you. He knows what happened in Águas Calientes and can help us enter the restricted area of the desert.

- Great! Let's go there now. – said Fernando. – Even with this disguise and the new hairstyle we're still in danger. They should have that system that identifies faces.

- What system is this, nerd?

- Lia, it's like this: the photo is taken by the surveillance cameras. The images go digitally to a central computer of the Government Intelligence agency. This system is able to identify any sought person by the structural features of the face. Cutting hair, wearing hats does not work against this technology. It has already been used by the CIA since the 9/11 "attacks". The same happens on Facebook. When you post any photo, the system immediately identifies any human face format and asks if you want to "tag" that person in the photo. That's how it's like.

- Nerd, are you on Facebook? Add me, please ...

- That's not what I'm talking about, Odalisca! This is serious business!!! We can get caught in an second if we are photographed.

Brief silence.

Lia looked displeased.

- Okay, Odalisca... I'll add you later, okay? Our only advantage is they do not know anything about the hummingbird. They must not know we're here.

- Now they know. – Rico said with a worried tone. – I went into a hotel asking if you had checked in there and the clerk showed me the picture of you guys on the website. I said it was not you and stuff... but there's a reward on your heads. The guy at the hotel must have called the police. Look!

Three police cars passed slowly by the side of the *Plaza de Armas*. Soldiers were on a search and capture mission. They were probably looking for two people wearing peasant clothes rather than tourists. Rico told them to get up quietly and follow him.

- Keep your backs to the police cars!

Rico began acting as if he were a tourist guide pointing to the central statue of the *Plaza* and speaking aloud about Peruvian historical things. They walked to a small alley where there were some local establishments like butchers, dentists, lawyers, etc. Calmly, but cautiously, they walked towards south to Julio's house.

Lia had painted her hair black. She was astonishing. When Fernando looked at her, he felt something very strong in his stomach. He had fallen in love with her. Lia, like every woman, had not yet become accustomed to the new look and was constantly looking at her own reflection in all the windows of the city to see if she was looking good. She kept asking Fernando if he liked her new hair color and he, always embarrassed, said that she was ok.

***

They finally arrived and were received by Julio Pranas.

They lodged, had a good shower and sat at the table for dinner.

- Thank you very much for welcoming us, *señor* Julio. Rico told us you are a craftsman.

- Yes, Mr. Fernando. I have been an artisan since I was a child. My grandfather taught me Nazca pottery techniques and I became a master of this art. Many things are forgotten in this fast spinning world. – said the artist, staring into nothing. – The money slavery and fear puts an end to tradition.

- What do you know about the hummingbird?

- About the hummingbird itself I do not know anything.

You will have to find out for yourself. But there is one important thing you need to know.

- About what?

- *Two* important things, actually. First... about the legend. All we know about this legend of Orejona is *real!* – said the man. – It is all true! Our origin really descends from this woman. As you must know, all the myths and legends of this world speak of "gods" that came from the sky... from the *stars*. But none of these stories indicates any name, any specific location in the Cosmos. Venus is the first real physical reference we have in all our Andean legends.

- I know that, *señor* Julio. Therefore they are considered legends. Because they give us no concrete reference.

- When I heard about the Machu Picchu chamber and about the book and especially about Venus... I realized that the time had come.

- *Señor* Julio, I'm sorry. The phenomenon of the village resumes a very old myth that disappeared centuries ago. New elements have come up, okay... but we can not say that the legend is really true. That the offspring of the Andean peoples is *extraterrestrial.* We have no scientific evidence of this.

- That's what you need to know. The legend had never completely disappeared. There was a text that had been translated by a Spanish Jesuit missionary and was taken to the Vatican. The original was in the language of *knots*.

- Yes, the *Quipós*.

- Exactly! The text speaks about all the details of Orejona's visit to planet Earth, who she really was, everything she did, all the knowledge she brought. It explained building techniques and the best way to use the materials of this planet! Anyway... all the imaginable and unimaginable secrets about the universe. This story, which is *real,* is kept by the Mafia of religion. When the Spaniards arrived here they already knew what they would find. They did not stumble and fell here unintentionally. They wanted the gold that we, for reasons other than financial, so much worshiped. The problem is that our legends, and this particular text, spoke of things that would sweep religions like Christianity from the face of the Earth.

- But that is a very serious observation, *señor* Julio. I particularly agree with you, but... I do not know if we can consider this as...

- The religious power is too strong, Fernando. – Julio interrupts. – For years they gathered the originals and the translations of everything that had been written by our ancestors and anything related to them. They did this with the help of some local traitors and took everything to Rome. Everything was delivered in the hands of the Popes of the time. The copies were destroyed. Tradition then retreated and died. The traitors who helped to destroy our history for some Spanish coins condemned themselves by their own stupidity and greed. Everything began to be passed on from generation to generation through oral tradition but a great deal of information was lost. An example of this is the novelty of *Venus* and the *book*. But the story is true in every detail. The hummingbird will help you find the text, I'm absolutely sure. The Nazca version of the legend tells of a woman and her spaceship resembling a glorious hummingbird, hence the geoglyph in the desert.

- That's right. – Eastman confirmed. – I know the Nazca legend. I talked about it with Rico.

- The Nazca knew of the unusual energies of that area, and they did various ritualistic designs on the floor. For centuries they had repeated rituals, chants, and processions on these lines, all to call the "gods" back. There are answers there, I believe. – said Julio Pranas. – Or at least some information.

- Well, I believe there's intelligent life out there, and possibly much more advanced than ours, but I've never had any scientific certainty about the visitation of beings from another planet on Earth, even though it's somewhat obvious. I hope to find evidence of all this. What is the second important issue?

- It's not the Peruvian government which is after you.

- What do you mean? – exclaimed Eastman. – It's the Federal Police. They have badges and authority all over the country.

- *Señor* Fernando, do you know how a Pope is elected? – asked the artisan, interrupting the young Brazilian.

- Well, I know what everyone knows. The conclave, the Sistine Chapel, the Cardinals, the vows, black smoke, white smoke, *Habemus Papam*, etc... We had a conclave recently when Pope John Paul II died.

- Do you really think that the "holy" Roman Catholic Church has any democratic tradition? Do you really think those poor Cardinals are chosen by God through a secret ballot? Wrong, *señor* Fernando. Big mistake!

- Explain, please, *señor* Julio.

- These are marked cards. The institution of the Church does not *elect* Popes in this way. When you are Cardinal, you have a broader idea of the whole thing. Of course, no Cardinal will agree with what I am going to say, but all of them are "tested", I mean, of all of them, one and only one would have strength and righteousness, or, *as I see it*, the necessary *subservience* to sit on the throne reserved for the successor of the Apostle Peter. They choose a man who is able to shut up about the mysteries they keep secretly in the famous Vatican Library. The Cardinals know that it is not *they* who decide who the next Pope will be. They just play the game.

- I do not understand, *señor* Julio. Who chooses the Pope? If the supreme leader of the Church is dead, who's in charge? Who gives power to the new Pope?

- Who manipulates the Church, you meant to say? They are the same people who hide the truth from the world, if we can call them *people*. They are the same people who distort reality and make everyone believe that to live is to *have stuff*, despite all the discourse of the Church against the material life and in favor of the soul. They are the same people who create international intrigues and conflicts that lead to wars, fear and death. They are the same ones that destroyed all the culture prior to the Christian/Jewish culture. *"Man is on Earth for only six thousand years!"*, say the most fanatical and manipulated fundamentalists. They are the same ones who insist on saying that the world's oldest civilization is the Sumerian civilization. The same ones that enslave humanity with their consumer goods and the eagerness to have more and more things that they do not really need. They manipulate all scientific and philosophical knowledge with the intention of keeping us in darkness forever. Anyway, it's the same people who stand behind you to keep this Orejona truth hidden forever. Who can keep us away from the Light but the Antichrist?

Fernando, astonished by the speech, stares into the old man's eyes and says:

- Do you know Nietzsche?

Lia was horrified at the mention of the Antichrist at the dinner table. She had never heard such madness at one dinner. Was she involved with things of the Devil? She's Catholic. She studied in public schools, but had a solid moral foundation rooted in Catholic traditions. Family influence. She got terrified with the relation of this adventure (to which she was instinctively attracted) with the darkness of Evil.

- *Señor* Fernando, the Antichrist works on three fronts: the dominant religions, the economic power and the military force. The "Sovereign States" like Peru, Brazil, or the United States, are only *instruments* in the hands of these people. Religion is an extremely effective weapon. For centuries it has stirred our imagination. Who wants to go to Hell? Fear causes us to believe in absurd things.

- True! Fear makes the world spin faster, but aimlessly. – says Fernando.

- Cardinals, Bishops, Popes are not ordinary people. Try to be a Cardinal! It's not for everyone. They grew within a political and hierarchical structure. They are people prepared to hold immense power in their hands, but not all the knowledge. This power comes with a huge responsibility: to keep a secret that even *they* themselves do not know what it is.

- I don't think they know anything, but sometimes I doubt it. – said Eastman, trying to clear his head. – I think it's because they *know* something that men like John Paul II, who was apparently a good soul, end up sick or... you know, they get murdered, like John Paul I was.

- I do not know if they know the truth, but they must know about the lie they've been propagating through the world for millennia! – interrupted Julio. – Knowing something and not being able to tell anyone is a huge burden! I imagine that the old Karol Józef Wojtyła felt that weight over his shoulders but could not bear it. Those who die in peace are the alienated ones. Those who play the game comfortably do not really care what they are doing. That German Pope, Benedict XVI, who should have died in office as tradition says, decided to jump off the boat!

- You mean... he was jumped out of the boat!

Lia was uncomfortable with the conversation. The subject seemed too heavy. In an unexpected attitude she broke her silence with an almost genial remark.

- So we have only two alternatives for the Pope. – said the girl. – He knows nothing and is an alienated leader, a puppet who plays the game of the mighty or... – she paused and selected her words for fear of blasphemy. – Or he knows everything and is a deceitful person of bad faith. A liar. Wow! Thinking that way I do not know if I feel sorry for him or... anger.

- The question is, how does the one who sits on *that* throne, who assumes such great power, knows nothing of the secrets that the most powerful institution hides for centuries? – continues Julio Pranas. – They may not even know it, but I think it's unlikely. If he knows, I cannot be his follower, for he is a *deceiver*. If he does not know anything then he's just an ignorant man. I cannot follow him either.

- I've thought of that, but it's too fantastic to believe, *señor* Julio. – said Fernando, agreeing with the old man.

- Are you in search of another curious book you're going to read in life or in search of truth? Will you keep this arrogant academic attitude or kneel before the unknown and incredible world of the truth about humanity? In order to find what you are looking for you will inevitably have to accept the inexplicable.

- I'm confused enough, *señor* Julio. Continue, please.

- The Peruvian government is manipulated like all other governments. You know the story of the discovery of the Holy City, don't you?

- Yes, the American. Hiran Bingham.

- An expedition from Yale University, isn't it? The University that "produces" American presidents. House of the infamous *Skull and Bones*. The Carters, the Bushes, the Clintons, and many other American presidents and powerful leaders were all part of some secret society or were of some special bloodline, sometimes both. The best known secret society is the Freemasonry.

- Yes, and coincidentally the name of the great founder of Masonry is Hiram. – Eastman added.

- These mighty men at their posts of command are like the Popes. They are specially trained and prepared to take on a chair that does not belong to them, but which institutionally is the most important in the world today, in the case of the United States. Everyone thinks that presidents have *veto* power or decision power about things, but they are like Popes: they play the game of those above them. They play the game of the *Hidden Masters*. They are like top executives of large corporations. There are even rumors that our beloved Benedict XVI is a Freemason. Do you know what was found in Machu Picchu when it was discovered?

- There is no record of the collection, but ...

- No gold has been found, they say... nothing written. They say that the Inca did not develop any writing. – Interrupted Julio. – Lies! It was completely excavated and everything that was found was taken by the American authorities to Yale with the blessing of the corrupt Peruvian government. Countless graves were violated and everyone was like Orejona! Elongated skulls. Machu Picchu was a center of science, of study. How could there be nothing written? How could there be no gold? The most fantastic secrets were stored there! And everything was stolen!

- Is the US government manipulated, too? I thought they were the manipulators ...

- They have the power of war, *señor* Fernando. They command and we obey. If it's interesting, they throw us a bone. That's what it's all about. Our Federal Police are acting at the behest of the government that is acting at the behest of the powers who dominate this planet. They do not want this truth to be discovered! You see?

- Yes. Fernando said dryly.

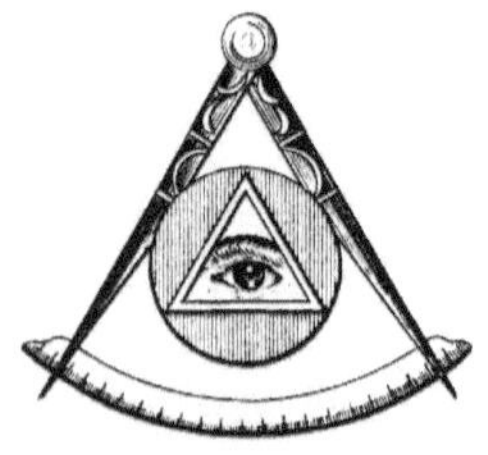

Julio changed his tone. He stopped using "*señor*" and started using "you". He felt that Fernando's mind could go much further if he were more spiritual. He would be really great if he *felt* more and rationalized a little less. He felt that the inevitable was about to happen, so he approached Fernando with his wheelchair and held the young man by the arms with force, as if wanting to shake him. He modulated his calm voice and then increased his tone to be more efficient in speaking to that brilliant soul which hides behind the books.

- Fernando, did you understand that your science is worthless in this story? Did you understand that you are entering a mysterious world. You are running after a truth that some people do not want to be discovered. Did you understand?

- Yes.

- Then the Andean spirit shall be with you, who is the seed. All our history will be different after you. All humanity will change. I know you understood my message and that tomorrow you will have proof of everything I said here.

Fernando almost got into a trance with the look and strength of the hands of that sick old man. This trance was actually a state of consciousness created by Julio Pranas for the young man's soul to hear. It was as if he had made face-to-face contact with Eastman's real self, with his unconscious. His old grandfather taught this technique to be used only for the purpose of opening minds. "This is a teaching from Orejona.", said the craftsman's grandfather.

- Conspiracies aside, *señor* Julio, we must go to the head of the hummingbird as quickly as possible. – said Rico urgently.

- Enio will take you there. – said Julio Pranas. – Trust him, he is my son and successor in tradition. You should leave tomorrow at dawn, before sunrise. Be ready at 4:30 in the morning. If you get there before the airport opens, you will have a good chance of getting the information you need. Enio knows everything you have to do to get to the place you need to get to.

- Thank you, *señor*. We'll be ready.

- Now I'm going to bed. – said the old man. – Talking about it made me exhausted. Tomorrow I have lots of pottery to do and a lot to talk to my dear tourists. Good night, my friends.

- Good night. – answered the three altogether.

***

- I don't believe a word he said. – Lia whispered in Fernando's ear.

- Why, Lia? It was nothing new. I had heard of this whole conspiracy.

- You're a nerd, dude! I'm a simple person. I do not like the idea of messing with the devil.

- It does not necessarily mean the Devil, Lia. Darkness and Light are names given to *knowing* or *not knowing* things. Whoever brings the Light, brings knowledge. Who hides the Light, spread the Darkness, hides knowledge. It's a very real and very cruel game of Light and Shadow, by the way. Imagine a truth so important that without it you suffer, you get afraid, you get lost aimlessly all your life. What would you do to a person who hides you from such truth?

- I'd beat the hell out of that bastard! – said Lia through clenched teeth as she checked her suitcase.

- I would do differently.

- What?

- I would do what I'm doing now. I would go after this truth, this Light. I would give it to humanity no matter what it cost. Like Prometheus did.

- Promised what, nerd?

- The legend, Odalisca... the legend... Prometheus, son of Climene. He deceived twice the "prudence" of the well-known Zeus, or Jupiter, as you wish.

- Oh really!

- He "stole" the Divine Ray, which many interpret as Light, Knowledge, or Fire. Prometheus gave this Divine Ray to mankind. It is a recurring theme in all world mythologies. The theft of the Fire and the delivery of this light to humanity. Zeus became very

96

pissed and punished Prometheus and all mortals. Prometheus was tied up on top of a mountain in the Caucasus.

- Where is it? – asked the girl with interest.

- It is in the Eastern European between the Black Sea and the Caspian Sea, the Armenia of today. Imagine the torture, Lia! Every morning a vulture came and ate Prometheus liver as punishment. This story has parallels with some versions of the story of Lucifer. The peaks of the Caucasus have altitudes similar to the Andes, which reach up to 5,600 meters. I have no vocation to be Lucifer, of course, but I have a great desire to bring this Light into our world.

- But this "religion" thing scares me, nerd. Jesus is good and would not do any of this. – said Lia, genuinely disconcerted.

- I have no doubt! Jesus would not do it, but whoever organized the political institution of the Church would, and did... you can bet! Christ is a Greek word meaning "The Anointed One". The story of Jesus is beautifully told by the Gospels and really inspires millions of people around the world. Jesus was truly enlightened. In my opinion, the biggest of them all. The problem is that little is known of this man and the Church has no interest in discussing this subject.

- We know, nerd. He died for us all.

- Not only that, Lia. This is too little. It is only *doctrine*. He did not have to die to teach anything! This is what I think! Church leaders have created dogmas on the subject. It was never mentioned, for example, about Jesus' childhood or adolescence. Do not tell me that the Vatican does not know anything about it. There are innumerable apocryphal texts, those that have not been accepted as official, which speak of things you can't even imagine. They really hide a lot of knowledge from us. There are books and more books that tell some things with many details but mass publicity is not of the interest the *Institution* of the Church.

- Tell me one of these stories.

- Well... the Genesis of Melchizedek, the Book of Enoch, the Gospel of Peter, Thomas, Mary, the Apocalypse of James, correspondences between Pilate and Tiberius, the Roman Emperor... there are many! Some were discovered in Nag

Hammadi, Egypt, along with pagan texts, which, incidentally, had incredible wisdom. Not to mention the Dead Sea manuscripts. If you read some of these books under the view of the "alien conspiracy", for instance, you will find numerous references about beings from outside the Earth. Beings of Light and Darkness. But we, humans who fulfill our tasks in the great system, we do not believe in ET's because *absurdum est*. However we believe in a virgin birth, a physical resurrection, a Noah's Ark, Santa Claus, money... we believe that our governments work in our best interest...

    - I've heard of it... this battle of good *versus* evil. Lucifer is of the Darkness.

    - Lia, this story is very complicated. This talk is too heavy. Recently I read an old text that talks a little about it. We'll talk about it tomorrow, okay? Now we'd better sleep. From what I know the walk to the hummingbird is long and difficult.

    - Good night, nerd. You look cute with short hair.

    - Good night, Lia. You look beautiful.

    - Really? – responded Lia happily. – Come closer. This way it heats up better.

The three of them slept on mattresses scattered across the floor of Julio's room. Fernando dragged his mattress to Lia's side and lay down close to her. Lia laid down on Fernando's torso and hugged him gently. She kissed the back of his neck and asked him to protect her. Fernando turned and said, looking into Lia's eyes,

    - I need you more than you imagine.

Enio prepared the jeep and made room for his guests. They headed west toward the archaeological zone. It was crucial that they arrived before sunrise. They passed around the whole site which is surrounded by a well-built highway, but soon they had to stop at a blockade. The night guard had not been advised of any visitation permit at that early hour. Enio convinced him with a few seconds of prose.

- What did you tell him? – asked Rico.

- Oh, he owes me a big favor. One day I found this man sleeping in his shift hugging an empty bottle of Pisco. He told me he took only a few sips and that the rest had evaporated. I've covered him up once and today he is paying me back. He's glad I didn't denounce him to the park authorities.

They pulled over right in front of the famous watchtower of Nazca. It is a very high observation tower built at the edge of the desert at a point where you can see almost all the old drawings made in the ground. Not with the perfection of the flight for tourists, but those who see the drawings by the tower have an excellent impression of the grandeur of the ancient Nazca. The distance between the tower and the Hummingbird is about two kilometers and Fernando would have to walk on foot in the middle of the desert wearing a kind of giant rectangular board slippers. He should lift his feet well with every step. Nothing should interfere with that ground. No man should step there. Only priests, or authorized personnel. The Peruvian government does its best to keep the site as sound as possible.

Fernando talks to Rico as they prepare outside the jeep.
Lea only hears.

- We haven't talked about it anymore and I think *now* it's a good time to start. I must go to the head of the hummingbird and I speak the word again. What word would that be, Rico?

- What did you say there in the Convent that could have been significant or that needs to be repeated? Do you remember all the things the old man said?

- I think it must be a single word, after all he said very clearly: "There you will say *the word* again and She will come to you." That is exactly what Puca Pucara said. Being one word... – Fernando thought aloud when interrupted by Lia.

- Nerd, when you said the woman's name, poor Jamirez went into convulsion! Try "Orejona". Who knows the sky opens up and some ET's come down and...

- Good, Lia. – said Fernando. – It is! *Orejona* is the word. That simple! I go in there and call for her, Orejona. Dude ... it takes a lot of faith.

Rico and Fernando enter the sacred land. Enio guides them with the help of two of those lasers points. The watchtower is with one of the lasers and the two men with the other. They should walk straight to the west with the aid of a compass. Enio said that it is natural if the compass stops working or goes crazy because of the energies of the desert soil. In that case they should signal and Enio directs them back to the west using the laser beam. All the desert area is full of boulders and it's very inconvenient for a stroll in the dark before sunrise, no mentioning the board sandals.

But there they go. The whole desert is an arid plateau that stretches nearly 80 kilometers between Nazca and the Pampas de Jumana, south of Lima. The geoglyphs were most likely created around 500 AD by the Nazca. They are shallow drawings made on the desert floor probably using advanced geometry. Removing the thin layer of red soil that predominates in this desert you reach to the second layer which is a *whitish* soil. There is almost no rain in this area and the winds are generally smooth so the geoglyphs are all there, almost intact for more than fifteen hundred years. The Hummingbird awaits Fernando Eastman patiently.

Supporters of the "ancient astronaut theory" say that this desert was an extensive mining camp created by space visitors. This is because in this very place you can find all the important elements of planet Earth. Minerals like potassium, manganese, copper and gold can be found in unusual quantities concentrated in a vast desert area. Not to mention a type of *white clay* that is found all over the desert and that, after being taken for analysis, it was confirmed to be glass! Wait a minute: *crushed glass spread over the desert?*

Another curious thing also stands out in this arid plateau: the high concentration of arsenic in the soil. Arsenic, in addition to being extremely poisonous, is also used in lead alloys. But the most interesting is the use that is given today to a variation of the poisonous element, the *Gallium Arsenide*. This element is used in semiconductor technology that helps in the manufacture of high frequency electronic components such as computer integrated circuits. Arsenic is also used in light and laser diodes and there's nothing more extraterrestrial than laser technology!!!

The Nazca plateau, seen from above, is a huge "washed" field. I mean, the impression you have is that the whole area has been washed in a massive and extensive method of mining. It is as if, for years and years, someone had systematically poured water over the whole land with the intention of "washing the soil" to expose the ores that existed there in abundance. I'm not talking about mining as we know it today. This is a gigantic operation similar to the one we see on the Hollywood blockbuster "Avatar."

There is also the famous "sliced mountain". The researcher Erich Von Daniken coined that name because unlike the surrounding mountains, this one not have a peak, just a flat top. Could it be just a geological anomaly? The flat top blueprint looks like an airport facility. And beneath this flat surface, underneath the "runway", there is a huge *zig zag* line. At the southern end were found buildings with stone walls. It looks like that sliced mountain was really some kind of an airport. Obviously for religious reasons the area was totally forbidden for the researchers.

The official Peruvian archeology, which has been led by a German, Mr. Markus Reindel, says that Nazca is considered sacred because it is a ceremonial site. The geoglyphs are (officially) ancient Nazca procession routes. Put the word "sacred" after anything and this thing becomes synonymous with "untouchable." This is how the Catholic Church shaped the minds of all mankind for long centuries and, consequently, shaped History. It seems that scientists are using the same old and efficient methods of the

Vatican. They work together with the Catholic University of Lima and the National Institute of Culture.

What could be more poisonous than the arsenic found in Nazca? Foreigners in national archeology, Catholic Church and corrupt secular Government working together perhaps?

What lurks behind the ritualistic mysticism of the tattered Germanic Catholic institutional excuses?

Could this "anomaly" be of the same nature of the Saqsayhuaman circle?

Research on electrical conductivity has been made in several "permitted" areas of the desert, including the hill mentioned above (but not in the stone ruins). The scientists basically measured the soil's electrical conductivity using electrodes threaded to the soil. A very low conductivity is expected in a dry desert like Nazca and so it was. However, in the "runway" of Daniken's sliced mountain and in the geoglyph lines, the numbers went off the scale and exceeded the normal values. What has been measured leads to the hypothesis that electricity could have run at very high voltages to the track and along the banks of the sliced mountain. There are also glaring electromagnetic differences between the inside and outside of the geoglyphs.

Fly over the area and you can see endless ridges that run through the desert from the top of the hills following slopes on what looks to have been natural paths of rainwater. At the base of the hills there is an incredible amount of washed rubble. In order for them to have been accumulated in such a large quantity, there must have been an enormous amount of rainfall, which is not naturally possible in that region. Hence the theory that the whole area was an immense mining site, possibly with extensive and advanced technology and long before the creation of the famous lines. The ancient men could not have been responsible for the systematic water prospecting that supposedly occurred on that intriguing desert plateau.

Closer to the city of Nazca there is another "anomaly" known as the Band of Holes. An extensive range marked in the mountainous desert soil that, when seen from above, looks like a gigantic "tire mark". A long area full of holes dug side by side with an impressive pattern of detachment and depth. Some say they are holes made by antiquity hunters, such as ceramic pots or mummies. Some even say the holes were used for grain storage! But considering the pattern of spacing and depth, and the fact that there are thousands of them following in the same direction, the theories of pot hunters and grain warehouses cannot be sustained. It's exactly like a giant tire mark stretching along a hilly desert.

But what tire would that be?

Giant machines?

Probes looking for soil samples?

Nazca is sunk in unanswered questions.

Fernando Eastman and Rico now walk into the desert. They are trying not to leave any marks on the fragile surface of that sacred ground. They pass between "the Hands" and "the Tree", two small geoglyphs that are right in front of the observation tower, by the side of the road.

- So, Fernando. – said Rico. – Tell me a little about your academic life. How did you get into this life? How did you meet the Professor?

- Rico, I was born into a very wealthy family. My father worked in real estate and owned a huge company with branches all over Brazil. I never thought of assuming the family business. Research is everything to me! It does not give money, but I do not lack money, do you understand? I just do what I love.

- I understand.

- I got interested in the Andean legends when I read Erich Von Daniken's book "Chariots of the Gods?" It was in this book that I first heard of the Nazca Lines, the very place we're standing now. When I visited Nazca for the first time I fulfilled a childhood dream!

- You know everything here, Fernando! More than any Peruvian.

- I flew over these glyphs a few years ago. I got the flight sickness and vomited all over the plane. I really screwed up the whole experience, a real shame! – both laughed. – I've never had a chance to come back since then.

- That was crazy!

- Rico, until last night I did not believe in beings from other planets. Could you imagine this whole thing we're in? What drew me to research were the *mysteries* themselves. I was about twelve when I read Von Daniken and it really changed my life. That book gave me a direction, you know? Despite the lack of scientific evidence, I'm beginning to think the Swiss is right. He talks about Orejona in this book.

- I see. Everyone has their path to follow. I always knew these aliens existed. Countless times I've seen things there in the Village. Things that no one can explain, although they are too obvious to explain. What can those bright lights that fly over our sky be but *unidentified flying objects*. After all they are objects, they fly and no one can identify them.

- UFO ... Unidentified Flying Object. – added Eastman.

- It's a very clear concept, but people still do not understand it. You must accept this fact, Fernando! The famous ET's are the most frequent tourists in Machu Picchu. They do not have a fixed schedule. They appear and disappear day or night.

- Have you had any close encounter?

- No... but someone or something *downloaded* the whole story of Orejona directly to each of us in the Village. You don't think it was the Holy Spirit, do you?

- Well, ET's or the Holy Spirit, what's the difference? We're between a rock and a hard place.

The two walked straight in the middle of the arid plateau with great difficulty. A few hundred meters ahead they faced "El Condor". They drift a bit northwest and passed the "Spider". At that moment the compass went mad.

- See Fernando! The energy is really strong! The compass is completely unstable. Signal to the tower, otherwise we'll get lost.

- Right away. It's almost 5:30. Replied Fernando signaling with the laser-point.

The response from the watchtower was immediate. The pointed west and put Fernando and Rico back on the right track. They just had to follow the red dot.

- What do you think will happen, Rico?

- I don't know, man. We'll know when we get there and you say the word.

- What if nothing happens? What if the legend is just a legend?

- In that case I think we have two alternatives: to look for a new source of information or to abandon the quest. I don't think the Professor would appreciate the plan B.

Professor Fontanoura is really an incredible person. He inspired Fernando with his attitude of "nothing is impossible". Whenever he was lost under a pile of texts, old Vicenzo would come to him and give suggestions that *at first* sounded ridiculously simple and sometimes absurd.

Early in his research, right after he had graduated, Fernando was lost crossing some references and parallels between the biblical Genesis and the Sumerian creation legends. It was basic research, but he was stuck. Fontanoura said, "Why don't you start with the non-scientific texts?" Fernando went back to Daniken, Sitchin, Robert Charroux, Louis Pauwels and Jacques Bergier. These authors, although not recognized by academics, have a very clear language and offer very important references about the things they research. In a few pages Fernando found what he was looking for.

"The Occam razor, Eastman. Always follow simplicity", taught Fontanoura.

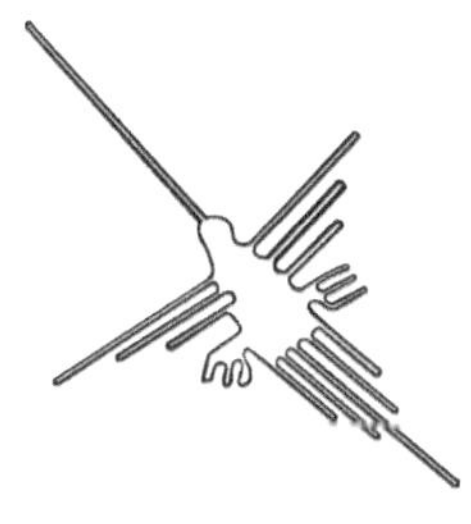

They finally approached the lower wing of the Great Hummingbird and went towards the head. The lines are perfect. They were made to please the "gods", no doubt. The length of the geoglyph is ninety-six meters from the end of the tail to the tip of the beak. The wingspan is proportionally balanced with the body in two-thirds measuring sixty-four meters. And it's not one of the big glyphs. There are larger figures ranging from one hundred ten to three hundred linear meters like the Alcatraz.

- You go to the head, Fernando. I'll stay here. – said Rico as soon as they reached the middle of the wing.

- Okay. If anything happens to me, drop those board sandals and run. You never know...

Fernando heads to the place indicated by the old man from Cusco. All sorts of things go through his head like a nonsense movie. "Easy, man. You need calm now. Clear your thoughts. Open your mind". – he tells himself, although it's difficult to clear the mind at the moment when things are about to happen. Things have run at an impressive speed since they've left Cusco.

And so Eastman's mind runs wild. All possible conflicts appear because he – like everyone else – has been conditioned to always think the worst. But he knows that all these conflicts blur our inner power and he seeks clarity by remembering the picture of the Convent in Cusco. Immediately from his inside the unshakable certainty he felt a few days ago resurged strong. He focuses on what he is really looking for and steps inside the lines right where the bird's head is. Eastman looks sideways, up and down, tries to calm down and put himself in a receptive state. He inevitably feels the strong energy coming from the floor and up his legs. The top of his head begins to tingle insistently as if there is something penetrating there.

Unknown energies, incredible sensations.

- What do I do now? Should I speak the word? Should I scream, should I say it as if it were a mantra? – he thought aloud.

Fernando then mentalized the word "Orejona" for a few seconds. His mind simply stopped. The whole normal cognitive process of a human being stopped working at that moment. He was "plugged" into something he did not understand. He lost all motor coordination and went absolutely still, without even feeling his own body.

- *Orejona!* – he shouted as loudly as he could, although his voice did not even come out.

As if by magic, his body began to levitate wrapped in unexplained energy. He was unconscious. His arms were almost fully opened, his head drooping back and his legs totally loose as if he was being lifted up by a tremendous force. Rico watched everything from a distance. Fernando was suspended six or seven feet from the ground for a few seconds and then he was gently put back to the dry desert floor.

He was still unconscious when he touched the floor again. Immediately a great whirlwind formed between the clouds and a strong yellow light was projected on his body. Lia and Enio, despite the long distance, could see everything from the watchtower and could not say a word to each other. It was a scene really worthy of sci-fi movies.

"Fernando, look at me", said a soft, delicate voice.

He slowly returned to consciousness. The light was very strong and hurt his eyes. An image gradually formed in his retinas. It was the face of a woman. She was the mother of all Andean beings. Orejona appears resplendent right in front of him. Her skin was so white and bright that overshadowed the whole surroundings and swallowed the yellow light coming down from the sky.

- Why me? – he asked with difficulty.

"Because you are the only one who can redeem the true Light".

- What should I do? Where is the book? How can I translate it?

"Open your mind, Fernando. More than 18 million years ago Venus and Earth maintained close communication. I am the first matrix of Andean humanity. I came down to Earth more than 40,000 years ago. Before and after me came many other beings from other planets, stars and galaxies to do the same as I did, but they did not procreate here. They simply genetically modified Gaia's local beings and scattered them across the planet. My offspring have a skull different from yours. My children's brains were bigger and had a different function than

the basic ones you have. They had greater mental capacity than yours today and all dominated telepathic communication. They spoke little, for it was not necessary. The language was totally different. After I had taught everything I had to teach, I left".

Fernando, completely in trance, just listened. The sound was produced only inside his mind. There was silence through the desert. He *thought* he could see, but the images were virtual. His eyes were closed. Rico looked frightened at what was happening and dared not interfere. He saw Fernando in a huge whirlwind that did not touch the ground. It was pure energy.

Orejona continues.

"About 38,000 years ago a natural disaster destroyed the atmosphere of Mars and the Earth cycle became 260 days. Before that, its orbit was 225 days and the density of its atmosphere was more subtle, as it was on Venus. Cataclysms are, have been and always will be part of the life cycle of the Cosmos. You can not avoid these cyclical destructions. It's mathematical. You humans are just tenants in the body of the divine Gaia. My creation was restricted to the Andes, but was swept away from the planet like many others. Some of my children survived. Most couldn't survive the new denser atmosphere of today. The other skulls that you find around your planet are from other creators who have modified the DNA of my species, but that's not important right now. You need to talk to the Guardian of Skulls. He will tell you where all this knowledge is and how you will get to understanding it. This is not a book like the ones you know. Go talk to this man today".

The light disappeared and the image of Orejona as well. The whirlwind closed and the desert silence remained untouched. There were only the gentle icy breeze of the dawn.

- Fernando! Fernando! – Rico called trying to wake him up.
- We need to find the Guardian of Skulls!

Enio and Lia ran to meet the two men returning from the desert. They were scared.

- Nerd, are you okay? What happened there? It was amazing!

- Enio! – called Fernando. – Who is the Guardian of the skulls? I need to talk to him today!

- Juan Navarro! Yes! He has a small museum in Paracas, in the Ica bay. – Enio said enthusiastically. – It's near here. We have to leave immediately! It's almost seven in the morning and it's time for the guard change. It is not good that I'd be seen here this time especially with you. There's a lot of police in town, I just heard from the radio. They want you, *señor* Eastman.

- Let's beat it. We have no time to lose! – said Fernando jumping into the jeep.

- I cannot take you there because I have my work here. And I also do not think it's a good idea for you to use jeep.

- What do you suggest? – asked Rico.

- I suggest you fly!

- What? Who can fly us there? – exclaimed Fernando although his voice was still weak from experience.

- I know how to fly these small planes. – said Lia with an imposing tone. – Didn't I tell you guys you would need my help?" How's the plane, Enio? Is it a single-engine?

- Yes! It is in great condition and is adapted to also land on water. It has no GPS and if you fly low, the radars will not detect you.

- Do you know how to land in the water, Lia? – Rico asked half suspicious of the beautiful blondie fake brunette.

- Well, my dear. In either case, land or water, we can all die. – Lia answered coldly and with the naturalness of the one who speaks the truth.

- Nothing bad will happen to us! – Fernando said confidently with his gaze lost on the vast horizon that opened as they walked away from the most incredible experience he had ever experienced. – If I have to go there... I'm sure I *will* get there!

DAY 8 – 7:30am

They broke all the rules and protocols of the Nazca airport. There is not much security there. They arrived before the start of the tourist activities, close to 7:30, they simply walked, passed the turnstiles smiling at the staff, went to the hangar where the plane was stored, got in, taxied and took off. Right in the face of everyone. The airport officials contacted the police as soon as they passed without permission by the turnstiles. Police arrived at the airport in less than five minutes, but it was too late. They were already flying.

- All aboard. – Lia said over the radio ignoring the protocols. – Check your seat belts. Ignition. Yes!!!

Rico was completely terrified in the back seat. Never in his life had he been off the ground, and even worse, there's a madwoman riding that very old plane. He still did not trust that woman. Fernando sat in the front. They taxied and took off without wasting time.

According to Enio, we must fly west to the coast and then change course to the northwest straight to the *Islas Balestras*, a small archipelago near the coast and right at the entrance of the Bay of Pisco. A true sanctuary where thousands of local birds come every year to breed. There are thousands of species of local birds that mix and alternate throughout the year in search of a safe place to place and hatch their eggs. There is plenty of food and the weather is very favorable.

- How am I supposed to find these islands, Rico? Can you recognize it?

- All this the archipelago is white, covered with guano. – screams Rico so that his companions from the front can hear. – When you see a set of small islets covered in guano you begin to look to your right looking for *El Candelabro*.

-What is guano? – asks Lia.

- It's bird shit! – says Fernando, speaking very loudly. – The Peruvian government has a seasonal program of collecting guano in this islands because it is a highly fertilizing substance. All Peruvian agriculture is benefited by these birds and this sanctuary.

It's tons and tons of bird shit. All the collection is made in an ecological way and always in times of less frequency of the birds. They are very careful about these islands.

- Ew... – Lia shouted.

- Speaking of yuck, is there any little bag in the glove compartment? I am feeling sick.

- Nerd, open my suitcase. I've got flight aid things in there. Be quick! I know these sicknesses. When the passenger knows that the bag is coming... they put it out seconds before. It's psychological...

It was too late. Fernando threw up on the floor of the airplane.

- Well, it's done... we'll have to deal with it, gentlemen.

Odalisca dos Santos, or Lia, is a simple woman born in São Paulo, and who had a not very normal childhood. Her father was a blue collar and her mother worked as a seamstress in a traditional blanket factory, both in São Bernardo do Campo, in the metropolitan region of São Paulo. They lived in a poor neighborhood. It was a daily commute to work. With little money for luxuries, but with good school, Lia learned the basics to survive in the world. She has always been very pragmatic and most of the time very direct in her settings. She was always neat. Her presence is impossible not to be noticed despite being *mignon*.

Lia always got good jobs and always had her money. She never depended on anyone financially, not even during bad times. One day she decided to prepare to be a stewardess and assisted to all the curriculum courses. She learned English, went through endless training, hoping to get to European routes, especially those that led to Paris, her dream, but that never happened. She was stuck on the South American routes because of the reasonable Spanish she speaks. "Not bad for someone on their thirties." She heard a colleague saying about her: "She's too old to get out of the hole she'd put herself in.".

Her pilot skills were never used, but she graduated with merit. The moment she sat in the cockpit of that plane, she felt a certain fear. There was no time to remember all the details. The police were coming. She checked the fuel, some fundamental instruments, and flew away. During the trip she kept testing some features, but always knowing more or less what she was doing. "A good stewardess cannot be afraid of adversity.", she thought as she did a quick study on the control panel.

Never had a boyfriend for too long. She always got tired of the jerks around her because of work. "Almost all the pilots are self-centered. Just because they fly those huge ships they think they are demigods.", she says. The conversation with male colleagues was very discouraging. She's always been a very sensual person and by her very nature, Lia always had quick affairs that quicker left her uninterested.

The coexistence with his boyfriends has never brought adventure, nor excitement or mysteries. Some wanted her to be a housewife to look after her children and take care of dinner. Others wanted her to get another job because they were jealous of her being in touch with more interesting people (which sometimes was true). Some were "domineering pigs," as she said and did not let her be who she really is, even though she did not know herself. Anyway, Fernando was the first person who really captured her attention and without much effort. It was almost a dream. Like the other dreams, she feared that sooner or later she would wake up and get disenchanted. But that was how she was.

They saw the islands. Now they must follow the coast to the east and enter the Pisco Bay of calm waters. It is time for Lia to decide on the future of the expedition. Far below they could see the old Candelabra. Everyone watched the geoglyph with joy and amazement.

- Guys, check your seat belts, please. Let's start going down. I need you both to stay calm and do not ruin everything, am I clear? Stay calm and quiet!

- Yes, sir! – responded Fernando as if they were a special forces team.

- Rico? – asked Lia.

- Yes... Commander... – he answered reticently.

- Here we go.

- Wait! – cried Rico startling them all.

- Man! I just said ... do not disturb me. This is tense!

- It's better to pass through the desert and down the cliffs a few miles from here. – said the Peruvian intelligently. – It will not attract attention and it's a better place to hide the plane. If we land on the water here everyone will see and we will be in serious trouble. They should know by now that we're flying here. The beach has very firm sand. You can try to land on solid ground. I think it's safer. Hardly will they know that we went down there.

- Okay, hold on.

Lia flies with dexterity gaining altitude to be able to cross the line of small slopes that surround the whole bay and delineate the desert of Paracas.

The desert is incredible. Everywhere you look you can literally kick fossils of marine animals that disappeared about ten million years ago. The whole area is a large open-air marine grave. Unfortunately tourists pay good money for a buggy ride through the desert. Not the conventional buggy, but a kind of elongated automobile with a lot of power able to climb the steep slopes of the dunes. As they drive along the site, they destroy incalculable fossils. Not to mention the local fossil collectors who make this federal crime a good breadwinner. It is incredible to think that all that desert was once covered by the sea millions of years ago.

A few miles to the south there is a forty feet high cliff all corroded by the waters of the Pacific Ocean for millions of years. The beach is practically paved by a thin but compact layer of small boulders that have been forming and sedimenting along with countless overlapping layers of seaweed over the years. The surface is unstable, but a few inches down is solid as a good clay. It's not the ideal soil but it's better than trying the water.

- Okay, gentlemen, same procedure. Trust! – said Lia with authority.

The plane touches the ground and boulders hit the carcass with violence. Everything shakes violently. It touched the second time and gently Lia set the plane on the ground. The boys clung to the arm rests of the aircraft and also in the hope that Lia would be competent enough to save their lives. At these times it is possible to understand what faith means. There was a sudden loss of speed because of the sand. Without the seat belts, they would be seriously injured.

The plane stopped. Everyone looked out in silence still frightened. The seconds of descent seemed an eternity but eventually they were on solid ground.

- Not bad, huh? – said Lia with great pride.

- Not bad, Lia ... Not bad. – said the nerd with indescribable relief.

- Rico?

- You are my hero! – said the Peruvian in a trembling voice.

- Rico, we are a few miles from the city. – says Fernando a little more calm but his voice is still shaky and his mouth dry. – How much do we have to walk?

- Ten or fifteen miles. Let's get started right now. It's still 10:30. Let's go. We can not stay here much longer, but first we have to cover the plane. There's enough seaweed here. Let's get all the kelp together and we'll cover the "bird". Quick!

The coast of Paracas is rich in diversity. The Pacific is generous in this area. The average temperature of the sea is 13°C all year round because of the Humboldt currents that soften the temperatures of the desert and also of the whole coast. The bottom of the sea is lined with seaweed with huge filaments that can reach up to ten meters. It was easy to hide the small plane with the dead seaweed on the shore. They started trekking toward the village of Paracas. It was not difficult to move in the right direction because of the position of the sun. They had to follow west. They walked for more than an hour in the middle of nowhere and only then began to see the dust raised by the vans, taxis, buses, all taking their tourists to the sites. Lia thought of proposing they would get on one of these buses as a lift. At the same moment she began to laugh.

- What is it, Lia?

- Nerd, what if we took a ride with these people?

- Rico, is it possible to convince them that we were forgotten by our excursion and that we need transportation? We can pay, no problem.

- Good idea! I'll say you're American and left the documents on the bus. I'll speak to one of the guides. I'll offer twenty soles, may I?

-Offer twenty *dollars*! We need to get to Paracas as soon as possible! – said Eastman.

Rico left quickly and headed towards one of the tourist groups. They were visiting a natural formation called *Iglesia*: a part of the cliff that was carved by nature for thousands of years and which looks like a two-towered church. In the last strong earthquake that occurred in Peru a few years ago this formation broke down and fell into the sea, leaving only one of the "towers". Although totally uncharacterized, it is still a beautiful tourist attraction because the Pacific is the backdrop and it alone ensures a beautiful view.

In the meantime Fernando looks in Lia's eyes. They both remain silent for a few seconds. He felt a voracious will to grab her right there and kiss her. She looked at him as if she understood the message. It's one of those moments when words are not needed. The seconds did not pass. Fernando has already undergone a transcendental trance, an immediate contact, a flight with vomit, a forced landing in a dangerous place. What a day! He was literally worn out.

- Okay, my friends. Here we go. – said Rico with a strong tourist guide accent.

- Great idea, Lia. It seems that I need you to protect me and not the other way around. – Eastman whispered on the way to the micro bus.

- That's nothing, nerd. I just did what I did because I saw the things that happened to you earlier today. I cannot crew up with *it all*. You are special. I know that, I saw it. I'll do my best because I want you to find what you're looking for. – said Lia with deep admiration. – What happened there in the desert? Tell me.

- Let's go to the village. There we talk. We're Americans now, remember?

- OK.

***

They reached the small village on the seashore near noon. The micro bus left the three right in front of the wharf where hundreds of boats of the local fishermen are kept: instruments for the sustenance of thousands of inhabitants. Seafood is the source of the traditional cuisine of Paracas. Without these boats we would not have the succulent *ceviche*. A cold raw fish dish accompanied by a spicy sauce, raw onions and roasted corn. Really delicious.

It was lunchtime and the village was a little busier than usual. The Paracas Museum is right in front of the offices of all the tour companies that bring and take care of tourist's accommodation in the local luxurious hotels. It is a dangerous place because all these offices and hotels should already have photos of Fernando and Lia on their computer screens. They have to be wise.

- Stay here facing the bay. I'm going to look for Mr. Juan. – said Rico pointing to the sea. – If you feel like you're in danger, go to one of those boats, pretend to be American tourists and ask them to take you for a ride in the sea. But please leave a sign so I know you're okay... okay?

- Right, Rico. If that's the case, we'll leave Lia's stewardess tie tied here on that pole. Lia, get the essentials in your bag and put it in my backpack. There is enough space, but only the essentials!

- Deal! I'll buy a more comfortable backpack for you, Lia. – said Rico in a friendly tone. – Your bag is too hard to carry. I did not thank you for bringing us here in that sardine can. Thank you.

- Great Rico! – said Lia in joy broking the ice between them.

117

Rico then heads to the museum a few yards from where they were. He observes the entrance of the huge and cozy *boulevard* built with wood in the form of a deck that leads to the pier. He looks everywhere as if he is recognizing the place. He crosses the unpaved avenue and stops at the main door of the museum. He is looking for someone who can help.

The Paracas museum, despite its enormous archaeological and anthropological importance, is nothing more than a modest wooden house. It is carefully maintained, with two rooms divided by a small office in the middle. A plaque placed on the facade indicates to tourists that there is a museum. Unfortunately it is not advertised by tourism companies, it is not even part of the official tourist route. It is understandable, after all what you see there can be really disturbing.

Right at the front door you can buy a ticket at a modest price and enjoy the impressive collection available. At least what's left of it. To the left is the impressive collection of elongated skulls found in the local excavations. To the right there are pieces of cloth and tools dated to 500 BC, as well as folk pieces, tools and a brief history of the still very little known Paracas culture.

A few years ago there was a strong earthquake in the area and the original headquarters of the museum was almost completely destroyed. Government officials collected about 90% of the original collection of Paracas and took them to Lima. Inexplicably this collection is not exposed but rather stored in the basements of the great museum of the capital. Is it because this collection is basically composed of elongated skulls and things without a reasonable anthropological explanation?

- Please, madam. I need to talk to Mr. Juan Navarro. Is he available? – Rico asked.

- No, sir. Mr. Juan is in Lima. – responds a woman who looked foreign by the American accent. – He was called by the government for an audience.

- When does he come back? Do you know?

- Early tomorrow morning... about noon.

- Thank you. – said Rico disappointed and worried.

"If Mr. Juan has been summoned to Lima by the government, this can't be good. On the other hand, the man does not know we're here looking for him. He's got no idea of our existence.", Rico thought. "Now I need to find a place to hide and spend these hours." Rico remembered a friend who, according to the latest information, was working in that region. "I'll talk to Catalina!"

Catalina is a person dear to Rico. She was his girlfriend when they were teenagers and it has been at least fifteen years since he last saw her. The last time he heard about her was about five years ago and he hoped she was living in that area. The two were born in the same village and met when they both learned to identify archaeological pieces in Águas Calientes. She worked in the village as a tour guide for a short time and then moved to the region of Ica, the district that encompasses the sub-district of Paracas.

- *Señora*, please, one more information. – said Rico returning to the museum's office. – Do you know a woman named Catalina Vigo? She should work with tourism in the area.

- Catalina, yes, of course! She works right here in the museum. – said the lady. – If you go to the excavation site, you'll find her. It's three miles from here, heading east from the Monument to the Conquerors just above the hill. You see? – she said pointing to the colossal monument of the sails of the Spanish ships which is located just behind the museum some three hundred meters high on a high hill of sand.

- *Gracias*.

Rico returned to the dock with Lia's new backpack and talked to them about what he heard from the woman in the museum.

- Okay, if we do not find your friend we will not be able to hide. – said Fernando. – Everything here is so open, so spacious. We are not safe at all.

- Do the following: you both go out on a boat tour. It takes you out of sight and drive you away from the danger of being arrested. I go to the excavations. This should take some time, maybe a few hours. Who returns first must wait. Deal?

- Yes, Commander! – Lia exclaimed repaying the reliance placed upon her at that critical moment of landing.

Now the three were united as a team.

And there they went. The two "Americans" went for a boat ride. Rico hitchhiked to the desert in the excavation area. Catalina was an important person in his life and never imagined that he would see her again. Much less under such turbulent circumstances. A boy who rented those tourist *buggies* was there, idly smoking a cigarette sitting in one of the cars. Rico approached, arranged the price and set off for the east in the middle of the desert. The boy knew more or less where the excavations were. Rico's heart was beating harder just to think he would see that woman again.

- Nerd, I'm starving. We haven't eaten anything for hours. And you threw up on the plane. I think we should eat something before we leave.

- Don't tell me, Lia. I don't even know *how* I'm standing yet. Must be the adrenaline. Run to that bar, get something edible and come back here. I don't think it is safe to go there, but you look very different from the picture. Hardly anyone will recognize you. Do not forget, speak English!

- Cool! Give me some cash.

In less than a minute Lia came back with a paper bag full of food. They were very tasty bread stuffed with cheese and some meat that was not identified. Lia even got a delicious dessert. They were bonbons stuffed with a sensational cream of almonds, a local specialty hand-made by the women of the village. They went to the dock, bought two tickets, boarded a very modern and powerful boat and threw themselves into the sea. The waters of the bay were soft and almost still and the temperature change was evident as they moved away from the land toward the open sea. Just after the first few minutes of the tour a couple of dolphins playfully showed up next to the boat showing off for the other tourists who completed all the seats of the boat.

The wind was very cold. The waters of the Pacific are much cooler than those of the Atlantic and the air is naturally affected. Lia took a leather jacket from her new backpack. Fernando took off his special nylon jacket. He is aware of the temperature variations in Peru. The sky was completely blue and the sun was down, but the wind was sharp. The dolphins played around the boat and Lia was delighted.

Within minutes after the dolphin show was over, the captain slowed the boat and pointed at the giant lying on a cliff along the bay: *El Candelabro*! A geoglyph with an average depth of fifty centimeters and two hundred and fifty meters from base to top. This wonder can be seen more than twenty kilometers from sea. Forcing quite the imagination you can see something similar to a human figure. The arms are supported by a central column as base. There are reports that the famous Chandelier would act as a huge instrument of seismological measurement.

Some say that it was the Spaniards who carved it as a sign of their triumph in the region and to signal the way for future naval vessels. Others say that it is a geographic representation such as the Nazca Lines and that they served as guidance for the "gods" that flew over the region. Coincidence or not *El Candelabro* points directly to the Nazca Desert, which lies a great distance in a straight line towards those giant rods. This mysterious glyph also points straight to Cuzco and is carved exactly at the same latitude as the capital of the ancient empire.

When you follow the direction of the *Candelabro* to Nazca, it is possible to see a series of ruins of small towns that were settled well under the "air route" for centuries, probably since the time of the Nazca and the Paracas. It is something simply unmissable to see.

- Wow! It's beautiful! – said Lia softly. – It didn't look so big up there! Did you know this place?

- Yeah. I know the whole country. It's my job to know all this. – he said hugging Lia from behind and resting his chin romantically on her shoulder. – It's not just here in Peru that there are mysterious things. All of South America has its archaeological sites, one more mysterious than the other. To the north of Lima there is a place where it's possible, if you force your imagination, to observe animal statues and human heads carved in huge blocks of stones, some the size of a whole hill. It's Markahuasi. Sensational!

Most scientists think these figures are mere coincidence, which have been carved by the wind, but in one way or another, nothing is conclusive. It's really crazy. Ecuador, Bolivia, Chile, all these places have their tricks... like this one... *El Candelabro.* – he said pointing at the geoglyph.

- Hold me, nerd. I feel more confident.

- It is said that this "chandelier" functioned like a huge seismograph device capable of capturing the most insignificant movement of tectonic plates throughout the world by a system of ropes and pulleys. I find it rather improbable, but it is one hypothesis.

- Do you want to know about another likely hypothesis? – said Lia looking into Fernando's eyes.

- What?

- I think we're in love.

Rico arrives at the excavation site. They are ruins of the Paracas civilization that has been totally buried by the sands of the desert. Countless dwellings and religious complexes have been unearthed for years. A project initiated by Mr. Julio Fernando Tello, considered the father of Peruvian archeology and founder of the National Museum of Anthropology and Archeology of Lima, grandfather of Mr. Juan Navarro. This man was the first to find the mysterious elongated skulls in Peru. A national pioneer who in addition to having discovered the skulls still found the first vestiges of a civilization unknown until the end of Century XIX. All his discoveries represent until today everything we know about the Paracas culture.

Every day carefully weaved fabrics with mythical imagery such as winged beings, cats, fantastic fish are unearthed. From daily-use artifacts such as jars of incense to cutlery, gourds, hammers, axes and, of course, the enigmatic skulls. The bones are dated from 750 to 500 BC and reveal a very different human type. Facial reconstructions were made a few years ago and the result of the possible "face" of the Paracas is quite strange. A typically Andean face with a cone-shaped head. Even today it is possible to find descendants of this different race walking the streets of big cities like Cuzco, Lima and Arequipa, but with the cranial protuberance somewhat softened by the genetic mixtures.

A mummy of a woman was recently found. She had an elongated skull and died pregnant for at least 2,500 years. In her womb was a male child with a fully formed skull. This anthropological archaeological finding put the theory that the Andean skulls were all artificially shaped by the locals.

- Good morning, *señora* Catalina. – said Rico.

The woman was inside a three-meter-deep ditch working painstakingly in the removal of a mummy that had been found days ago. The tissue was in extremely delicate condition as it was one of the oldest mummies ever found in the region. From the drawings of the cloth it is estimated that this person had been buried long before they imagined.

- Good morning, *señor* Rico. she replied with a great surprise and pleasure. – What brings you to these lands?

- I'm very happy to see you're at work. Congratulations!

- I'll do what I have to do, Rico. You know I have a great passion for these lands of ours.

- Yes I know. Such passion broke us apart.

- What's done is done. It was our destiny. – she said coming out of the ditch by a side ladder. – Tell me. What brings you here? Was it me? – she said drying her sweaty forehead in the midday sun.

- Catalina, have you heard of the persecution and expulsion of foreign scientists?

- Yes! A crime against us all, not just against foreigners. They are the ones who have the budget, the money, the silver. I work directly with a Canadian who has lived here for years. He brings money from abroad and invests in the excavations. This Canadian is the great propagator of the mysteries here. He has written several books about the skulls and even appears in some episodes of the History Channel. He was "invited to leave the country" two days ago without any explanation. Without him the excavations will stop in a matter of weeks. And we, poor Peruvians, will return to our homes without a job or any prospect of returning to work.

- Did you hear about what happened in the village?

- Yes! I was born there too, remember? I'm very connected to that land. I also woke up that day with the story in my head. *Señor* Juan said that it is due to happen. He also said that I could help to unravel the mystery if I was aware of the signs.

- I have two people from Brazil with me. One of them is a researcher. He is *the Man*, Catherine. He is the one *señor* Juan and everyone have been waiting for! He can decipher the message!

- In that case they need to hide urgently. *Señor* Juan was called for a direct audience with the president. The government never gave a damn about our work here. Now the president assaults, expels the *gringos* and calls *señor* Juan for an audience. Very strange! Not even a blind one would miss those signs! No doubt your friends are in danger out there. Where are they now?

- I took them to the docks for them to go for a round on the bay. Police will not approach tourists in the middle of the sea. Can we stay in your house?

- Of course! *You* will stay at home. The others will stay in my neighbor's. She's traveling and I have the key.

- Perfect. I'm going back to the dock and to pick them up. Tell me where it is.

- I'll go with you. This is a case of urgency. Child! – she called the boy who works as an excavation assistant. – Cover this site here and do not leave anything exposed. I have to go to the village urgently.

- Ok, *señora*!

- Come on, I have a jeep. – said Catalina to Rico without wasting time.

Rico paid and dismissed the *boggie* guy. His feelings for Catalina did not change much. She is more beautiful than ever. They were both fifteen when they first met. She was skinny and short at the time, but now she's a thirty old lush woman. Typical black hair attached with a Peruvian braid, well defined jaw, almond eyes, strong body and reddish skin. Beautiful as a typical Peruvian woman. They got into the jeep and went quickly to the center of the village to meet the Brazilians.

They arrived at the dock just as Fernando and Lia had set foot back on land. It seemed that everything had been arranged. Fernando was pale. He had vomited during the return.

- Come on, I've got a good place to hide. – said Rico to the two "American" tourists.

- Rico, promise me it won't shake, please. – Fernando stammered boat sickened.

- You get sick easily, don't you? Let's rest now. *Señor* Juan will be here only tomorrow.

- What? Only tomorrow? We cannot wait...

- Relax, nerd. Now you need to rest! – interrupted Lia. – I'll put you to bed. There's a bed, isn't there?

- Yes. Bed and quiet. It's not far from here. There will be no police searches, I assure you. I want to introduce you to my old friend Catalina. She will help us.

Hello, Catalina. I loved your name! – said Lia very kindly. – I am Odalisca, but you can call me Lia.

- Hello, Lia. Welcome to Paracas.

- Thanks. This zombie here is Fernando. When he recovers he talks to you. – said Lia almost carrying Fernando, who was clinging to his shoulders.

- There's no time for socializing. Let's go! – said Rico always prudent and responsible for Fernando's safety.

They headed north as if they were going to Lima. They left the main road after a ten-kilometer drive and entered to the left heading sea. Catalina lives in a very quiet fishing village. The rent is very cheap and nobody gets into anyone's life. In fact no one really has a life in this place. They are poor, miserable people whose only activity is fishing, carried out by men. Women make crochet, some make sweets to sell at the Paracas pier besides cooking for their husbands. There is not school for everyone. Children learn what they can in community elementary schools. Life starts at an early age.

Catherine's neighbor, a lonely and frail lady, went to Lima for a medical appointment and to visit relatives for a few days. She trusted Catalina to look after her modest house. First they went into Catalina's to eat and talk. She served a wonderful dish of potatoes, corn, beef and bread. All leftovers. For Fernando and Lia, it was a feast worthy of the "gods". They took a dose of Pisco to relax and help with digestion and began to talk.

- Okay, put me in the picture. – Catalina said to Rico.

- Look, there are many details. – Rico began. – It all started a few days ago when that camera was discovered in Machu Picchu. Fernando was called to the site by Professor Vicenzo Fontanoura.

- Yes, Professor Fontanoura! I've heard of him. – said Catalina who has been working in the field of archeology for years.

- I discovered a few days before, unintentionally, an inscription on a rock on the slope of the high peak on the path of the Temple of the Moon. The image represents Venus and Earth bounded by a dashed line. I only understood what it was when, the day after the opening of the chamber, everyone in the village woke up with the legend of Orejona in the head. Including me!

- Venus and Earth? The village phenomenon?

Fernando suddenly comes out of his torpor and stands up.

- I've got it! This inscription is exactly the same as one found in a cave in Kohistan, near Kashmir in the lands of Pakistan. According to the local legend, which is also repeated in Afghanistan, eighteen million years ago Mars, Venus and Earth were in close communication, just as Orejona told me. In this cave there are two spheres interconnected by a dashed line. Around them many tiny cross-shaped stars were carved, like the ones we see in Christmas time in store's windows. Just like you found in Machu Picchu, Rico. Exactly the same!

Fernando stands as if nothing had happened, goes to Catalina's kitchen and gets himself a glass of water. He talks as he fills his glass. The three just observe that unexpected explosion of energy.

- The small stars indicate that the spheres are actually planets suspended in the Cosmos. Wow! How could I have forgotten! You were right about that, Rico! The Hindus say that this dash was a magnetic line connecting Venus and Earth. Like the movies, you know. A dimensional portal. By this line, legend has it, "an immense Nau resplendent, of extraordinary power and beauty" brought to Earth from Venus "three times 35 perfect human beings.". – Eastman says without stopping to breathe. – It seems that it was not only Orejona who came here straight from Venus. Orejona told me that She is the mother of the Andean people. Other beings descended here and created other beings, but always by genetic mutation. She personally *gave birth* to the Andeans: the people of elongated skulls.

At the end of the speech, Fernando collapsed on the couch completely exhausted, as if those were his last forces.

- Have you spoken to Orejona? – said Catherine. – Are you crazy? – No more pisco for you, man!

- Did you see Orejona in the desert?! – Lia astonishingly asked.

- Yes, Lia. That's what happened there in that madness. – said Fernando in a serious tone.

- That's true, Catalina. I saw! – said Rico. – That's why I told you. He is *the Man*. Only him who can bring answers to us. Did you know that Orejona was from the planet Venus?

- I think I knew, I do not remember if I knew then or I know now. – said Catalina very confused.

- Did you know about the Book? – Rico asked the Peruvian.

- Venus, the book... Yes! This information came along with the story, but I did not even care.

- It's not a book! – said Fernando. – She told me that, too. She told me to talk to *señor* Juan. He would give me more information to interpret the secret.

- Well... this is it. – Rico snapped, shrugging his shoulders. It was clear he was stuck in the adventure. – We're on a quest for the Holy Grail. – he added.

- Wow! Impressive! – whispered Catalina.

- The expulsion of scientists is another mystery. – Rico added in a very serious tone. – *Señor* Julio Pranas of Nazca said our government is being used as an instrument in the hands of people who want this story not to be known. The phenomenon of Águas Calientes is one of those inevitable things. These people, no matter who they are, cannot stop us! This morning I witnessed something inexplicable! Fernando is also being used as an instrument by forces that I cannot explain! These forces want the truth to come to the surface. Nothing will stop this man! – he pointed to Fernando who slept soundly like a child on the couch.

- It was a full day for him. – Lia says affectionately running her hand over Fernando's face. – He needs to sleep.

- Right. Get the key, Lia. I'll take you to the door.

Fernando woke up, but he was still sleepy. They walked to the house.

- You can use the double bed. It's on me. – said Catalina to Lia with a knowing look. She blinked at her and left.

Lia laid Fernando on the bed, took off his shoes, shirt, pants and lay down beside him. She watched while he slept.

- Too bad you're like this, nerd... so tired. It would be a great night. – sighed Lia.

After a few minutes she went to take a shower. It had been a few days since she had seen a good hot shower. She opened the water, took off the clothes that clung to his body and entered with joy under the hot water. She lathered herself with pleasure, played a little with herself, and at the height of the play she moaned aloud: "Oh nerd, I wanted you here now."

- I'm here! – said Fernando who had gotten up lost without knowing where he was.

- Come!

DAY 9 – 10am

The night was long and comforting. It seems like all four had a good time. Everyone had coffee together and the atmosphere was radiant. The group, now of four, was smiling and excited about the future conversation with *señor* Juan. Catalina made coffee. There were a few slices of cheese and ham, scrambled eggs with butter and typical Peruvian breads.

- Then. What time does *señor* Juan arrive? – asked Fernando awaken than ever.

- Around noon. – replied Rico. – We have time to rest. I guess after talking to him we'll be thrown in at a deep end. I suggest we save energy, if you know what I mean.

Lia was in the kitchen helping Catalina. That's what Rico meant about sparing their legs. Fernando couldn't stop gazing at her.

- Rico, she's such a great woman. I think I love her. But relax, I'm focused. I know my responsibility. I know what happened to me in the desert in Nazca. It may be that *señor* Juan gives me some clue to understand the story. I must go to wherever this clue will lead... with or without her.

- Good to know. We cannot lose focus. Lie down and sleep some more. When it's noon I'll wake you up.

Fernando lies down on Catalina's couch, closes his eyes and tries to relax, but the wait is excruciating and the young man does not calm down. Lia prepares a cup of chamomile tea for him. He takes a sip and starts to talk about the possible novelties that are yet to be discovered.

- Lia, you asked me the other day about good and evil. When we spoke to *señor* Julio Pranas you were a bit scared by the subject.

- Yes, tell me about it... if it will help you relax.

- When I think in terms of good or bad, I always try to look at *what* is being done, *who* is benefiting from it, whether the thing is fair or not. For example, within the capitalist context. Imagine a man who makes a lot of money with his company using the labor of many who make little money. I do not think the owner of the company is bad. He just plays the game inside the system. But I particularly think that if we look at *the system itself*, isolated, it is evil. It excludes most people who do not have the money to set up their own business, for example, and these people will inevitably work for those who have it. It is a great paradox. Without workers, there would be no companies, no system of consumption. Our idea of comfort would be quite different. Before savage capitalism era, people who knew how to do something worked at home as craftsmen. The others planted food. There was no comfort as we understand it today. You understand this?

- Yes. The people lived in crowds, everyone slept in the same room, there was dirt and disease. – said the girl. – I remember my History classes.

- Then the demand for product "standardization" took over as the demand was getting out of control. The smarter artisans, who saw this as an opportunity to accumulate more wealth, began to hire people and train them to work for them. Slowly, capitalism was sneaking around. When we saw the insanity we put ourselves in... it was too late. Inevitability.

- Okay, but the talk was about the Antichrist!

- It's the same logic, the same thinking. Christ is equal to Light, Christ is The Illuminated. Whoever brings the Light does good. Light to me is the same as knowledge, wisdom, freedom. "Knowledge is the currency of the Universe," the Professor used to say. One who denies knowledge is the anti-Light. We are not talking about the *red devil with horns or the fires of hell*. The thing is very *earthly*. Lying and cheating is the same as being an Antichrist...

in my humble opinion. Can you see the parallel? It is not a matter of good or evil. It's a matter of *interests*.

- Who's hiding things? What are they hiding, nerd? – Lia asks, trying to understand the plot. – We do not know who's behind all this. I know there is something because I saw it in the desert. *That* was very crazy!!! But I still haven't got the plot.

- Neither have I. – said Fernando, scratching his head. – I'm feeling kind of lost, too...

- You know, when I think about evil it's Hitler that comes to my mind. Hitler was evil, was not it?

- Hitler was very bad, but it was not *the* Evil. I see that little angry man as an instrument, a mere *performer* of an agenda. What was done at his command was nothing angelic. He had an agenda and did everything to fulfill it. His *speech* was in favor of a better, different society and all... and he was totally convinced that he was doing something good. The thing is: many people suffered from what he did. Looking at the *outcome* of his actions I see the clear difference between Good and Evil. The *result* of what you do shows who you are. In fact, the two great world wars of our recent History have been financed by the bankers who are still operating today. The large and powerful families of bankers. The Rockfellers, the Rothschilds, the Morgans, and all the others. Ask the question: How could the bankrupt Germany do the damage it did in the years of the Second War? Who paid for all those top of the range machinery of devastation? The bankers, my friends. Everyone knows who they are. They financed both sides of the war. *They* are the Evil!

- God only did good things in my life. Therefore, God is good, isn't he?

- Okay. You're not totally wrong. Tell me, then: Who is God?

- I don't know, nerd! – Lia answered, with a hint of indignation. – The name was Yahweh, I think. Sometimes they call him God, sometimes Lord or Creator. It's in the Bible. The Father. God is the father of us all.

- If you think of Yahweh and all the blood spilled in the biblical narrative in favor of the Israelites to conquer the

"Promised Land", well, I do not see much difference between him and Hitler. It's a matter of interests. On both sides, we must emphasize! No one goes deep into the details of the supposed Hitler agenda. History says that all he did was due to his hatred towards the Jews. I don't think this hatred alone was enough to kill all those people. The Plan of Yahweh is also not much discussed. I simply do not swallow the killing of the people who had the bad luck to come across the Hebrew blood-lust. Have you read anything from the Bible?

- No, I know what I was taught.

- That's the question! Who were those people who "God" slaughtered in favor of the "Chosen People"? Read the story of Joshua. Do you like U2?

- I love Bono!

- Read about the *three trees* that appear in the accounts of Joshua. What was done there was *bloody* and *inhumane*! But since he did not appear on television or in the newspapers, that's fine, isn't it? The Joshua Tree is one of my favorite records, but when you learn about the story, you'll listen to that record with different ears.

- You mean that God is evil? That Bono is evil?

- No, Lia! I'm saying there's always an agenda. History is the outcome of intended actions! No one really knows who directs our History. Is it just a matter of destiny? Do we have choices?

- I don't know.

- Historians say the History unfolds on its own, but it is clear that there are agents with intentions behind every relevant act. You cannot see what will happen in history, but there is an agenda, there are interests that move the executors, there are plans that have been drawn by people or powerful beings. We, mere humans, are only pieces in the great game of life. Good or bad? The only thing that I really consider as Absolute Evil is to *hide* the truth, the Light. Playing the game is part of the human condition.

- I don't know, dude. You're too cold for me on this subject. So many people died in Hitler's hands and you think he's just an... evil little guy!

- How many people died at the hands of the Hebrews and with God's help? And they confuse Yahweh with God, the

Eternal. The Creator Logos...

- Fernando, aren't they the same? I do not understand much of this, but isn't Yahweh God? – asked Rico trying to understand the scholar's point of view.

- The name of God is a secret which, they say, only the Kabbalah can reveal. The name of God is not spoken in vain. When we cry out for Him, we simply say "God." That's not his name! It's just a *concept* that no one can understand. Yahweh is a being inferior to the Logos. To say that Yahweh is God is a great stupidity, a lack of reasoning. There is a passage in the Bible where Jacob, the one who "dreamed" of a stairway leading to heaven, literally grabs Yahweh in a *melee fight*. Don't tell me that God, the Almighty, The Eternal, The Creator fistfights with men out there. Incidentally this story also appears in a U2 song, *Bullet the blue sky*.

- I have this record! I never read the lyrics. I don't have a good English. – said Catalina, a little frustrated.

- The Creator is not walking around at all! – said Fernando. – There are many biblical stuff that make no sense or are poorly explained.

- Give me an example. – asks Lia.

- Og, the King of Bashan, was a giant! It is written there in Deuteronomy. Who is this Og? The Amorreus were all giants. Who are these giants? Where did they come from? Where are they? And how about those people Joshua slaughtered mercilessly on the edge of the sword, sparing not the old, nor women and children, not even animals? Who were these people? Children of God, I suppose. But why did this God, known as Yahweh, ordered everyone to be killed? Why did Yahweh promote a slaughter of this magnitude against His own creatures using the Hebrews as tools? Or were these creatures not "created" by him? Has Yahweh created anything anyway? Look, if you want mystery, start with the Bible! It seems to me that the whole divine narrative is but a great political question.

- *Geezuz!* I need to read it. Can you help me?

- Sure, Lia. But you have to keep your head open! You have to read the Bible with respect, of course, but without fear. After all, as Sartre said, it's just a book. It is the most interesting book this humanity has ever written. You have to keep in mind that our whole History has been poorly and selectively registered and there are terrible failures in the Church's discourse. You should begin by reading Genesis, then compare with the apocryphal Genesis of Melchizedek.

- You've said that name twice, Melchi... Melchize... – Lia said confused.

- Melchizedek. This book complements the "official" Genesis in a forceful way. He says that Adam and Eve were not "cast out" of Eden, as the sinners usually hear from the preachers of bad conscience. They were personally taken by the "Eternal" to another place, the Earth, and He stayed with them for a few days until they could understand how the new world worked. Melchizedek uses the terms "the Eternal", "God", "Lord" and this confuses a lot. The same was done in the Bible. But what call attention is *why* the Eternal created Lucifer.

- Why?

- God created Lucifer, his beloved and perfect son, to be his "Prime Minister," the "bearer of Light," the one who was the intermediary between Him and the Kingdom of Light, long before He created our Universe. It's crazy.

- The Antichrist fights against the Light. Why was Lucifer the "bearer of the Light" and now we know him as Evil? How does the Light become Evil? – asks Catalina. – Isn't Lucifer the Antichrist?

- That's a big problem to understand so quickly. It is necessary to read the text, meditate a lot on each passage and try to understand. Melchizedek is an enigmatic figure! He appears in the Old Testament as a man who has no ancestors, no father or mother! No mother? And it was this man who "anointed" Abraham after he had successfully ended his campaign to "cleanse" the Sinai from "invaders and worshipers of other gods". His Genesis gave me some answers but also brought many questions. Enoch is also a figure nobody pays attention to. It was the father of Methuselah, Lamech's grandfather and great-grandfather of a man named Noah. He was mentioned in the Bible twice, although being the seventh patriarch in the antediluvian genealogy. The only thing that is said about him is that he was taken from the earth by God.

- Abduction? – exclaimed the Peruvian.

- It's hard to believe, but I had my proof yesterday morning!

Fernando stopped for a few seconds and stood silently staring at nothing. While the other three were thoughtful, he resumed speaking without addressing anyone in particular.

- Still on the Antichrist: Julio said something about the Church, about military power and about financial power. According to him, these are the three facets of the Antichrist. Nietzsche, and I totally agree with him, says that Christianity is anti nature. If we are the children of an Eternal Being who has the power to create the Light, I imagine our nature also has connection to that Light. An anti human nature is anti Light. The one who preaches anti nature is, by definition, an Antichrist. The Vatican is the great representative of the Spiritual Power of the Earth and it has been propagating many lies for centuries and centuries... and still are. Religions capture and manipulate the fearful souls, the ones who dare not to question the religious authorities. Any religion! I mean, Christianity, Judaism and Islam are the most influential religious cartels in world today.

- Fuck nerd. There's no one left. – says Lia.

- Yeah! Try to go against what these institutions say and believe. Those who questioned the mighty "authorities" have been killed, even Jesus Christ!!! There is no doubt: the Church as an institution organized and manipulated behind the scenes is certainly one of the faces of the Antichrist.

- Don't talk like that, nerd. Take it easy.

- Remember! I'm not talking about the people of good faith who follow Jesus. In fact, when he died the organization of religious power was not very different from today. I'm talking about the people who manipulate this power and who make us feel bad about ourselves. The ones who fill us with guilt over our sexuality, the one who terrify us with our "sins." Then you have all these stupid ramifications of the same religion just to divide the people. And this is why Christians oppose Muslims, Lutherans, Jews and so on and vice versa. Just to mess with our heads over a big fabricated story.

- But, Fernando. Without these organizations the thing would be much worse. – says Catalina, kissing the little saint she always carries around her neck.

- That's true. You are absolutely right and this is unfortunate. We all, as humanity, function under the terrors of divine punishment. We do not read the Bible because we are afraid of committing a kind of sacrilege and all that crap. The question of the historicity of Bible narrative is controversial. I am absolutely opposed to the idea of a purely moralistic narrative, even though I understand that moralism is part of any religion. I think *everything* that was written in the Bible happened literally. And that is an interesting spin!

- Really, nerd? How about the Noah's Ark?

- Surely you *cannot* accept the version of the Church. It's impossible to put so much stuff on a single ark. Think about the logistics of the thing. Food, cleaning, etc. *Impossible*! Orejona told me herself and now *I know* that there are intelligent beings out of the Earth and that they have come here in the flesh. Everything now makes more sense to me. All these mysteries around the world, everything we cannot explain or understand becomes clearer when you *know* that there were intelligent beings around here long before the Sumerians. Our archeology is a farce. And I can say that being an archaeologist. Look, if you look from the perspective of the impossible, Noah may well have collected DNA from a whole bunch of animals, don't you think?

- Man, I'm lost in the sauce. – said Lia.

- Noah, son of Lamech, grandson of Methuselah, great-grandson of Enoch, okay?

- OK.

- Lamech is coming home. He didn't went to the beach for the weekend. He went very far to take his flocks to pasture and stayed months away. When he returns, his wife is pregnant. She swears she hasn't slept with anyone. She says she was "impregnated" by Angels. Lamech senses something "slightly" wrong and goes to Methuselah for guidance. Are you following me? – checks Eastman.

- Yes, nerd. Go on.

- Methuselah doesn't know what to do tells Lamech to go to his grandfather, the old and wise Enoch, who is said to have been taken by "God" at the age of 365 years. Enoch says something like, "Take the boy and name him Noah. He's going to be important." It seems that the whole thing was planted by "Angels" for a purpose, don't you agree?

- Where does this story come from, Fernando? – asks Catalina.

- This is not in the Bible, but in the Sumerian texts. Enoch himself was led up to heaven by the angels to be instructed about the things of the universe. His book, which has been recently discovered, brings accurate astronomical information and a lot of extraordinary stuff. It is a new light in human history. This was publicized, but obviously it was treated as of minor significance. Imagine what else is hidden behind those medieval walls of the Vatican. Medieval walls guarding medieval thoughts. They still think like the old days when they owned the world, the infamous "Dark Ages" or Middle Ages. Can't you see it? The time when the Church dominated the Western world is known as the *Darkness of Humanity*!

Fernando spoke exaltedly. He was talking and pacing around Catalina's room. The subject always inflames him. He avoids theological discussions with his scholar friends because it always ends up is quarrels. People in general, including scientists and researchers, are not ready to open their minds and consider different views on these issues. But who can stop Eastman?

- After the Darkness came the Renaissance. The Light returned to humanity with Leonardo Da Vinci, Michelangelo, Raphael, and many other names that brought back the human principles that were lost under the control of the Church. Anyway... there was a response from the Renaissance, a response full of Light and knowledge, but it was quickly stifled by the Baroque, a predominantly ghastly and oppressive time. And then we go back to the Darkness. The Baroque art is beautiful, but the human spirit had been again seized by the fear of God. Shit... I'm rambling again... sorry!

- Easy, nerd. Calm down.

But he continued with unbridled passion. His mind on fire was calling for more wood. Everything was easily articulated as if a dam of ideas had been opened. Everything was flowing in a torrent that few could follow.

- Man, the Bible says that Noah walked with God! – he continued. – This is written in the Great Book with all the letters! I imagine there was a knowledge that was taught to Noah to fulfill a mission. If you want to put all the animals in the ark without a squeeze: DNA samples! And he had ability and all the time in the world! Man, Methuselah died when he was 969 years old. Lamech lived 770 years. The Bible says Noah lived 950 years!!!

- All that? – asks Lia with big surprise.

- Look, Noah lived 600 years before the Flood, collected all kinds of DNA he could because, I imagine, the "Angels" lent a helping hand. He survived the flood and lived another 350 years! It is not so absurd to teach any man how to harvest DNA from animals.

- That is true. How did they live that long? – Catalina comments not expecting any answer.

- Obviously it was another humanity, another human kind. – continues Fernando. – They say they were giants compared to us. Look at our situation now. We know absolutely *nothing* about the Venusian civilization of Orejona and what we know about ours is very poorly told. There's a lot of bad things going on simply because someone is hiding the cards. Things have been hidden from us for too long! There's a station called Svalbard, in Norway a few miles away to the north. Do you know what they do out there in the middle of the ice? They gathered the largest collection of seeds on the planet to save our biodiversity for the future generations. The nickname of the place is "Green Noah's Ark". Isn't it possible that this had happened in the past?

Fernando was putting out all the things that has always gone through his mind, but due to respect for the religious mindset of others and to avoid academic prejudice, he never exposed. After the desert trance and the close encounter with Orejona he freed himself from scientific doubts. Eastman started to see everything with different eyes. He could think with incredible clearness. It was as if every barrier of false Christian morality had dissolved into the Nazca sands as a holy wafer in the mouth of an initiate. An initiate in the Light of the obvious.

- Catalina, do you have a copy of the Bible here?" – asks Fernando with a great desire to show his friends the evidence that is openly registered.

- Yes, there's one on the bookshelf.

Fernando took the Bible from the shelf with respect, went straight to the section he wanted and continued.

- Look at this. Jeremiah 9-23. *"Thus saith the LORD, Let not the wise man glory in his wisdom, neither let the mighty man glory in his might, let not the rich man glory in his riches. But let him that glorieth glory in this,* that he understandeth and knoweth me, *that I am the LORD which exercise loving kindness, judgment, and righteousness, in the earth, for in these things I delight, saith the LORD."* – read Fernando emphasizing a few words. – Yahweh is the ruler of the people of Israel. It's the Executive, Legislative and Judiciary gathered in one person. He gave a law, ordered and organized society, divided into tribes and all the story. He made war on behalf of them, massacred thousands of human beings. Yahweh was fair with the Israelites and helped them greatly. He punished them when they turned their backs on him. He gave ethical guidelines to his people but they failed because, according to Yahweh, "they are a narrow-minded people". The Ineffable Being cares not for human affairs. It's not his business! The Originator would never stand on behalf of "one nation against the Goyim". The Eternal gave us, and this is undeniable, the Laws of Nature. The Laws of the Cosmos!

- Yahweh has something like a love/hate relationship with his people. – says Catalina. – Anger, compassion, hatred, kindness, etc., are human attributes. This Yahweh story is really crazy!

- Look, folks, I may be totally wrong, I know that. I am not contradicting the sacred text, nor am I glorifying my knowledge, if I have any. I'm not posing to you as if I were the keeper of truth because of the few books I read. – Fernando said in a calmer tone only to explode in the sequence. – But I cannot shut up when I read things that make no sense *at all* or contradict what is obvious.

- Calm down, nerd! Mind your coronaries! – Lia joked.

- We don't know much about other peoples like the Inca, for example. The old traditions that threatened Christianity had their records destroyed or seized by the Vatican. The basic idea is that before the Sumerians there was *no advanced civilization*, we were cavemen and *that* does not make sense! To the fundamentalists, God created everything, including mankind, *six thousand years ago*, just like the Bible says and *that* is a complete absurdity. There are countless discoveries that place the existence of very advanced civilizations such as ours, perhaps even *more* than ours, in remote times, back to 15 to 20 thousand years ago... and even more if you dig deep. Have you ever heard of Krishna and these people from India? They are from a time thousands of years before the "official" archeology can admit.

- Hinduism has a very rich literature. They speak of times past and claim to be much older than is believed. – said Catalina, lighting an incense brought straight from India.

- Isn't that right, Catalina? Reading the sacred texts of India is a difficult task, just like reading the Bible. And what has been translated until today is ridiculous near the great collection they have. Look, whoever has the patience to read Leviticus, the book after the Exodus. It is a barbecue feast worthy of a "god".

- Barbecue? I love it! – said Lia playfully.

- It's a book that, besides other things, gives *recipes* of how one must make sacrifices in holocaust and burn certain animal for Yahweh. Example: If you have violated one of the Ten Commandments, you will carry *"lamb for a sin offering, he shall bring it a female without blemish. And he shall lay his hand upon the head of the sin offering, and slay it for a sin offering in the place where they kill the burnt offering"*. It is a sacrifice for sin. It's one insanity for another.

- If I had to burn a chicken for every sin I've committed, I'd be pretty broken, nerd!

Rico and Catalina laughed.

Fernando didn't.

- *Pecatum* is the Latin for "crime" or violation of any norm, precept or law. The original text was written in the archaic language of the Hebrews. This original language was adapted over the centuries until today. It was translated into Greek, from Greek into Latin, and from Latin into the rest of the world. The work was huge and they messed it all up pretty big. Can you imagine how much information has been lost or distorted along history? – Eastman lamented.

- I have heard that there is a Bible that is very close to the originally compiled texts. – said Rico, breaking his usual silence.

- Yes, Rico. The King James Bible. The fakes are there, but the text is a bit more "honest". But as I was saying...

- Barbecue!!! UHU !!! – interrupts Lia.

- Look at this: Leviticus 4:32. "*And the priest shall burn them upon the altar, according to the offerings made by fire unto the LORD: and the priest shall make an atonement for his sin that he hath committed... and it shall be forgiven him.*".

- Barbecue to please God? – said Rico astonished.

- When Noah brought his ark on Mount Ararat, today in Turkey, he offered an animal in sacrifice by burning it for Yahweh. He liked the "aroma" and Noah was glorified by it.

- Who doesn't like the smell of barbecue? – says Lia.

- But there's more! Look at the wonderful menu in the Sacrifice of Communion, which is a ritual for special occasions. Unleavened cakes unleavened, mingled with oil, unleavened cakes mingled with oil and flour, and fermented bread, all together with a lamb, an ox, and a bird altogether burning on coal. So WTF!!! *God eats this?*

- Is that all there in the Bible? – Catalina asks in horror.

- Yes, Catalina. And there's a lot more.

- Why do they do this? Why do they hide everything from us?

- It's not hidden, Lia! It's all in the open, it's all written in the greatest best seller of this humanity. A best seller no one reads.

- True. Nobody reads it. My mother always said that it is a difficult reading and that you can't understand anything. – said Lia. – I believed her and never opened the Book.

- Lia, it's not just your mother. *Nobody* reads *anything* or know anything! It's comfortable just sit and listen to a preacher or a priest or a rabbi. If you let them, they will "teach" about how you should lead your life. And in every corner there is an "authority" in the Bible.

- And everyone likes the priest figure. – says Catalina. – They look like the righteous people. When you open the eyes you see preachers in politics stealing money, pedophile priests, and all kinds of horrors. Right here in my area we had a serious problem with a priest who had a mistress.

- And since when to love a woman is sin? – said Rico seconds before Fernando Eastman abruptly changed the subject.

- Does anyone know what the Vatican telescope is called?

- No. Do they have a telescope? – asks Catalina.

- Yes, and it's called LUCIFER!!! It's in Arizona, on Mount Grahan, United States. It is an LBT, a large binocular telescope and is one of the most powerful telescopes in the world. Catherine, they use it to search for alien life in the Cosmos.

- What? – exclaims the Peruvian woman. – The Holy Church is joking! Why this name? Are they looking for intelligent life in space with the help of Lucifer? Did I hear it right?

Catalina understood right. In fact the Vatican telescope is one of the most advanced on the planet and is actually called Lucifer. One of the Catholic officials, Professor Andreas Quirrenbach, explained that the name has nothing to do with Satan. They say that the origin of the name Lucifer is simply "The Bearer of Light" and that this name can be mistaken for a "mythical fallen angel." He says that the name Lucifer has been used since antiquity to indicate the morning star, or Venus. This is the first and only quote from the original name of Satan in the entire Bible. If the Vatican told us the story that Lucifer is an evil angel or the embodiment of evil, they should not have used that name to baptize such a telescope. Or is the Church's evil doctrine really misleading?

Fernando says that the connection of the name Lucifer with the devil is a problem of misinterpretation of the biblical verses and that this great misunderstanding has spread as folklore.

A misunderstanding that has been conveniently explored by the Church's power summit for many centuries.

In fact, the name Lucifer appears only once throughout the Bible text in Isaiah 14:12 and refers to the morning star.

"How art thou fallen from heaven, O Lucifer, son of the morning! how art thou cut down to the ground, which didst weaken the nations!"

Isaiah originally used the term "Heylel" to refer to Lucifer, but according to scholars, this term has no correlation to Venus, which in the original texts was designated "Nogah." However ,"Heylel" may be the translation for both, "morning star" and "Satan". Each letter in Hebrew corresponds to an image, a word or a number. For each letter it is possible to find several valid meanings. So the term "Heylel" may refer either to the King of Babylon or to Satan as to the morning star. And this is very convenient to sustain lies!

The Hebrew language has its mysteries impregnated in writing. There are four possible interpretations for words. The "peshat", which literally means what was expressed. The "remez", which works as a tip in another sense. The "drash", which can be an allegorical meaning and finally the "sod", which holds a hidden meaning for each word.

Venus, the morning star, is linked to Yeshua, or Jesus, in some schools. In the literal sense, the word "Heylel" means Satan! Isaiah teaches us that Lucifer, the Satan, "wants to be like the highest", wants to be the "star of the day", but not at the same time. The context in which Isaiah speaks only refers to the Angel who intended to rule the universe in the place of the Creator.

In Peter II, 1:19, the apostle says:

"We have also a more sure word of prophecy; whereunto ye do well that ye take heed, as unto a light that shineth in a dark place, until the day dawn, and the day star arise in your hearts."

Who was Peter talking about here? Venus, Lucifer or Jesus? But the Vatican continues to justify its absurdities by saying that, in fact, the telescope's history brings a hidden relationship between Lucifer and the devil. Look how bizarre can this be. The private institution funding the telescope lens project is the Baden-Württemberg German State Observatory, which is part of the University of Heidelberg. The governor of Baden-Württemberg between 1991 and 2005, Erwin Teufel, intervened and released the money for the project after great political difficulty. "Teufel" is a German word meaning "devil." They make jokes saying that the name Lucifer was given in honor of Teufel, the Devil, who released the money for the project. They couldn't imagine anyone would be offended by the name of a telescope, but it's much worse than that! In the end you hev the feeling that the Vatican has very strange ties to a lot of obscure things. A not so good feeling.

- Ok, back to *señor* Julio's conversation, because I got lost. – said Rico, surprised by Fernando's passion for the mysteries and frightened by his excitement in speaking of the Bible.

- Do you understand, Lia? Do you understand why it's easy to hide things? Just rub in people's faces. Nobody gives a damn and yet they pose as God-fearing faithful people! No one should fear their creator. We should recognize our source and not be afraid of it. This can be seen as the psychoanalytic complex of the father figure, the one who loves you, but punishes you, I think.

- Ok, moving on. – intervened Rico. – What else did *señor* Julio say?

- He also spoke of the other side of the Antichrist. The Military Power. That seems obvious, doesn't it? Who would be the Military Power today? Do you have any tips?

- The United States of course. They basically go to war. Everyone knows. Everyone is afraid of them. – Lia said sagely.

- So you say that the United States of America is part of Antichrist's plan? Is it right?

- I don't know, nerd. I don't think it's like that, not literally. I met people there and they are not evil. They are normal people.

- The American *State*, Odalisca... not the people. The *Corporation* of the United States of America, the territory on the north side of the planet. This has to be clear, bear this in mind. It is the state I'm talking about.

- Oh yes. I agree. – says Lia, looking into Fernando's eyes.

- The government of Peru is being manipulated by someone or something very powerful, possibly a Military or Economic Power, to cover up the whole story. Isn't this what Julio said?

- There are people with enough power to blow up Machu Picchu if necessary! Professor Fontanoura himself told me this. – said Rico, emphasizing the scope of the problem.

- But who is behind all this? – asks Catalina. – What justifies this Power?

- Who is behind Spiritual Power? – Fernando returns the question to the girl. – Presidents come and go, Popes come and go, but the power itself never changes. The doctrines, the way they scare people never change. *Whose* power is this?

- I say: *it is not of the People!* – protested Rico, slapping his big hand on the table.

- Right, Rico. There is always some kind of fraud in the elections. Both the paper ballot system and the electronic system are fraudulent. The American Presidents, for example, all belong to some Secret Society! Anyway. Who puts the Presidents up there? The American State is also a *puppet* in the history of mankind. At least of *our* Humanity.

- Stop it, nerd. It's scary!

- What would be the Economic Power? What or who would have this power as the greatest emblem? Rico, can you imagine who could be the great Economic Power?

- Fernando, the basis of modern economy is the profit. Where is profit most efficient? I think where you work less and you earn more. Who disseminated Capitalism in the world?

- England, but... – Eastman pauses for a moment. – Of course! Economic Liberalism is an English idea. The theory that values the individual with free initiative, because they, at the end of the process, are consumers, a fundamental piece in financial system that cannot stop and has to keep constantly growing. That is why they supported the wars in Latin America like the Paraguayan War, for example. The bloodiest war in the Latin American history served to create a debtor market which would have to pay the debt *ad eternum* by buying English products. I think that was it. What does England produces that justifies the wealth of the state and the stability of the currency?

- That can be checked right now. Wikipedia! – said Lia with her top of the range *smartphone*. Catalina's Internet service was precarious, but it served well.

Fernando always imagined that if you want to hide something big, the best place would be in the eyes of the world. When talking about the Internet, most people say that it cannot be trusted, that it only brings lies and misinformation. Fernando thinks differently. Democracy favors exposure of the most visceral truths and because of this mass exposure they are seen as fantasies, lies or naive conspiracy theories. The highest democratic value, Free Speech, is at the same time the great weapon of the governments against popular unrests. *"Let them speak freely! So they vent their frustrations and no one listens."*, say the articulators of our democracy of appearances, the powers that be.

The most democratic space in our history is the Internet. Everyone speaks their minds, post their own truths, cry out *against* everything and everyone, or *for* everything and everyone, but there is no real communication. No one really gives a damn about anyone. The amount of information is so great that no one else has the patience to look for anything. TV is the same. If you want to hide the truth about UFOs, commission a show on History Channel about Roswell. If you want to hide the dirt on the biggest false flag in contemporary history, show a couple of investigative movies and documentaries on 9/11 on Discovery Channel. Global warming is on Nat Geo. If you want to anesthetize people's minds, give them *reality shows*, and so on.

In 1948 an extensive and detailed article was published in a large circulation Paris magazine about the appalling H-bomb that was being developed and tested by the United States after the "sample" of Hiroshima and Nagasaki. Everyone said it was fantasy. *"You cannot have a bomb more powerful than the Hiroshima bomb!"*, they said. In 1951 we were introduced to the H-bomb that was tested on the Bikini Atoll. The world was then horrified, but few remember that this was denounced three years before. When the thing is presented openly in people's faces, they pay no attention. When you make a lot of noise, nobody hears!

- Okay, nerd. The key to Google search was: "What does England produce". Let's see what we got.

- And what does the Google god say? – Catalina asked with interest, sitting down next to Lia as if they were old friends.

- That's the answer to a question from a web surfer. I will read it.

> Question: *"England lives on what? What does it produce? What does it export? Or do they live on income? What are the English industries in the world? Or is it just oil, Pounds, finances, etc...?"*
>
> Answer: *"England is a leader in the art of 'articulation'... this is its main source of income. Perhaps because it has been populated by extremely capable people (Celts, Anglo-Saxons, Vikings and Normans) and sufficiently diplomatic – among themselves, of course! – Great Britain achieved great potential in military strategy and intelligence...*
>
> *Remember that, first of all, England pioneered industrialization... before, during the great voyages, along with other countries of the Western European coast like the Netherlands and Belgium, was responsible for producing most of the goods that Would supply luxuriant powers like Spain and Portugal...*
>
> *England later invested in pillaging, slave trade and all sorts of suspicious business including 'paper money'. Thanks to the Scottish neighbors, the dirty money system spread throughout the world, English being the first Central Bank ...*
>
> *Since the seventeenth century, it invested in creating variations of a poison called capitalism and was co-responsible for the market nomadism that exhausted much of the 'developing countries' today... even those that were not English colonies. They were responsible for the end of slavery.*

- Wow! – said Lia when she finished reading. – Funny! My GPS booted alone!

- Shit! – shouted Fernando immediately. – Take the battery out, Lia. Right now! What a mess! The Internet is also the greatest spy tool ever created in history. Big Brother is certainly looking for us. They must have been tracing you phone for days. Now that you have used the Internet they know where we are. They found us in Nazca, remember? I don't give less than an hour to be surrounded here! We have to leave immediately.

- Easy, Fernando! – said Rico. – Maybe they didn't have time to track anything. Catalina, we go to the museum right now! If *señor* Juan is not there, we'll have to hide.

- No, you go to the museum, Rico. We're going to the excavation site. There's a very good place to hide there. Grab your things now! – said Catalina. – Rico, tell *señor* Juan that we'll be at the west wall. He knows where it is. He always says that place is special because nobody can find it. It has never been officially mapped. It's safe.

- Rico, you're the only one who can go to the museum. They still don't know you're with us, I hope. – said Fernando in a hurry. – Bring me *señor* Juan, whatever it takes. Be careful! Trust no one!

In minutes they were all in the jeep and on the way to the museum. Catalina left Rico at the entrance to the village of Paracas and proceeded to the site of excavations along an improvised road.

- *Señor* Juan?

- Yes.

- My name is Rico Calmón. I need you to accompany me to the excavations. Catalina is now at the west wall and she waits for you. A big problem arose and only you, *señor*, can solve.

- *Señor* Calmón, I've just arrived from Lima. I need to rest. Who are you, anyway? What is this? What happened in the excavations? What do you know about the west wall?

- There is no time! It's about Orejona! She spoke personally with my friend in Nazca, in the Hummingbird. You were called in Lima because of Her, wasn't it? The discoveries in Machu Picchu and the legend. What was said in Lima? What is going on? We need some answers urgently! – said Rico, looking directly into Juan Navarro's eyes. The old man understood it immediately.

- *Señor* Calmón, this friend of yours is in a lot of trouble. If the things are not good for anyone who keeps the tradition, imagine your Brazilian friend who has the duty to reveal a truth that can turn things around. The President was very clear. He does not know what he's talking about, he does not know about your friend, he does not know anything about legends or elongated skulls, but he does not want any news to leave Peru. *He was very clear.* Nothing can be divulged about the excavations in the Holy City. In politics, it means: the ends justify the means. They will do anything!

- But he's the president! What is the country's interest in this? Who is behind it? Our tradition should be a source of pride for him, after all he is one of the people!

- He does not really want it, but there's nothing he can do. He does not know anything that goes through our lands, he knows nothing of our tradition. He's a politician, *señor* Calmón. Don't be naive. He plays the game. He said something about "the hidden forces," an old excuse or an old tradition that haunts the sovereign governments of the world. They have haunted Brazil in the past. But what needs to be done... has to be done! Let's see your friend. I'll help him. It is my duty.

Juan Navarro put on his hat and they both went quickly to the site, straight to the west wall. In minutes they were there. The west wall is a ceremonial circle that, according to studies and according to the artifacts found, was dedicated to Venus. It was there that the observations were made, the astronomical calculations and the ceremonies dedicated to the morning star. The Paracas apparently knew where they came from. They had the legend of Orejona alive in their time. This is proven through the weaving unearthed there. Not to mention that Paracas is the place in Peru where most of the elongated skulls are unearthed.

Juan Navarro is the Guardian of the Skulls.

***

The energy of the place was very strong and pulsating and soon led Fernando to a state of torpor, very similar to what he felt in Nazca, but a little softer. Lia and Catalina felt nothing. Juan Navarro arrives accompanied by Rico.

- *Buenas tardes, amigos.* – said *señor* Juan to everyone.

- *Buenas tardes, señor* Juan. – Fernando responded with reverence. – We need your guidance. Orejona spoke to me yesterday and...

- I know what you need. – interrupted Juan Navarro seriously. – You must be the Man. We've been waiting for you for many years. My grandfather already knew that one day it would happen. As time passed and technology dominated the world, we thought that day would never come. We thought that the men of science were all spiritually dead, playing the game of the mighty, playing intellectuals on the Internet while the truth keeps slapping their faces day after day. My grandfather taught me what to do, but first, my friend, your name. You look familiar.

- I'm sorry, *señor.* I'm really worried about the whole situation. My name is Fernando Eastman. I'm from Brazil.

- Eastman? I met your father. It can only be him. Paulo Eastman?

- Yes, that's him.

- You look just like him. He came here often. He is one of

the few who know this place that we are now.

- My dad? On here? I never knew that! That's weird!

- It's nothing strange, my boy. – Juan said matter-of-factly. – Your father was looking for what you are looking for. He never told you anything?

- No, he was never home! He was always traveling on business. – said Fernando with a little anger.

- Not always on business, Fernando! He was a wise man and great seeker of all that you seek today. If you're what you are today, it's because of him, aren't you?

Fernando remembered his past and the short time he spent with his father. It was a short time, but intense and very pleasant. It was he who taught about the Brahman tablets of Emperor Tam of the Brahmin Tenth Dynasty, who assert that in 18,617,841 BCE the first spacecraft "of the stars" descended on Earth. And this spacecraft came from Venus!

It was he who taught Fernando that Akhenaten, son of the Sun God, Athon, and with an elongated skull, came from Sirius B, a White Dwarf who composes a star system with Sirius A, Sirius C, and Xylanthia. The son of Akhenaten with Nefertiti is, according to the official charlatan archeology of Egypt of the fraudulent Zahi Hawass, no less than Tutankhamun! (But there is a temporal problem in this story.) Tutankhamun is the most famous elongated skull of human history and no one has noticed yet!

It was Paulo Eastman who taught Fernando about the monstrous Cholula Pyramid in Mexico, which is said to have been built by a giant and that this giant, according to the Olmec cosmology, came from Venus. Cholula has twice the volume of the Great Pyramid of Giza and is the largest monument ever built on this planet, at least until now. *"The pyramid of Bosnia, if ever assumed to have been man-made, will be the greatest pyramid of all!"*, his father said once.

He taught his son about the Tower of Palenque in Yucatan, Mexico. It was through the windows of the famous *El Caracol* observatory that the Mayans calculated with astonishing precision, the movements of Venus in relation to our planet. The calculations reached the 6,000 cycles and presented an error of only a few hours, a despicable difference in cosmic terms. Everything had some kind of connection to Venus or to elongated skulls or stars. His father, in fact, was preparing him for all this and little by little Fernando was remembering the stories and the teachings.

- You're right, *señor* Juan. – Fernando said more calmly and with some nostalgia. – He disappeared a few years ago, and we never heard from him again. We don't even know if he died or not. I am what I am because of him, no doubt.

- Fernando, how do you feel now? – asked the old Juan.

- A little dizzy. It must be due to the tension.

- No. It's because of where we are. Lie down with your back to the floor and with your head to the west. Feel the ground vibration. Connect with the Earth, with the Great Mother. Close your eyes, take a deep breath and listen carefully to what I'm going to tell you. I will do as I have been taught.

Fernando did as he was told. In a few seconds was in a trance again. His mind was absolutely open and his body offered no resistance. A great vortex formed between his eyes. At that moment it was not his eyes that saw, but his mind. He barely felt he was breathing. *Señor* Juan knelt in front of Fernando's head, placed his right hand on his forehead and said:

- The Inca tradition tells us that when Orejona descended to Earth more than 40,000 years ago, she landed her spacecraft on the Sun Island in Lake Titicaca on the Bolivian side of today. She brought from her planet vegetables, animals and other things we have no knowledge about. Among these "other things" are Three Black Stones. Our legends say that before Wiracocha, the pre-Inca god Tvira had a temple built on the Island of the Sun in honor of Orejona and in the niches of that temple these black stones were kept, the only thing She left on Earth when She went back. These stones, called *Kala*, were associated with the Sun God and mysteriously disappeared from the Island thousands of years ago, but were not taken out of the planet.

Señor Juan Navarro had a different rhythm which gave space for Fernando to meditate between each sentence. He spoke as if he was under some kind of deep hypnosis. They were pauses that followed a few seconds of silence purposefully dedicated to a light and gentle breeze that caressed their faces as Fernando breathed deeply. The breeze only blew between Juan's silent pauses.

- Each of these stones has a function. We know that one of them is in the East. It's the Kaaba. This *Kala* has spiritual power. The second, no one knows how, is in the possession of the British Crown. It is the famous Coronation Stone. All the British monarchs, century after century, are crowned sitting on this stone. According to tradition, it functions as a direct communicator between the telluric power and extraterrestrial or spiritual powers. When Power is transferred to a King or a Queen through the secret ritual on this stone, that Power becomes unbeatable. The third stone is lost! *This* is the stone you need to find. *It's in the stone that you will find the answers you need to redeem the Light.* No one has ever seen it. No one knows what it's like or what it does, if it does something. You need to go to Sun Island accompanied by a person who will tell you more. Look for Marita as soon as you get to Puno. She works as a tour guide. Few know, but this woman is a great priestess. She has a very great knowledge of the Tradition. Watch for signs. That's what I had to say. That's all I know. You can get up now, but slowly.

Fernando comes out of his trance after a brief numb period and gradually opens his eyes. The sun is stronger than ever and he feels the heat burning on his white face.

- Did you hear what I said?" – asked Juan.

- While you were talking... I saw things! It was like I was watching a documentary on TV. Everything that you said was shown to me with images. I saw the stones. All three! The Kaaba is absolutely black. The Coronation Stone is not black, but grayish. The third stone is incredibly crystalline, like Orejona Herself. They are not all black, as tradition says! Wow! It was an extraordinary thing!

- Did you see where she is? – Juan Navarro asked, with wide eyes.

- It was a chamber. I only saw the glow of the stone, nothing else. – said Fernando in a frustrated tone. – But it all seemed so familiar. It was like I was already inside. Why isn't it dark like the others?

- Maybe because nobody has ever touched it. I really don't know. Tradition has prepared me to tell you this, my friend Fernando Eastman. Don't be upset that you couldn't see more details. Everything has a momentum. Always remember: everything has its time.

- Juan, how are we going to get you to the lake? It is very far from here and the altitude can do Fernando some harm if we don't go through acclimatization. – said Catalina worriedly. – The roads must be full of blockades, and by this time there must have been even the army on the streets.

- Don't be afraid. What I did here was a ritual of opening portals. No man can stop *señor* Eastman from getting where he needs, as long as he is faithful to his quest. I believe he is really the Man. I believe he will bring the Light back. Use my car. It's old, but it will do the job.

- Thank you, *señor* Juan. I don't know how to thank you for your precious help. – said Fernando humbly.

- We, the Andinos, in flesh and blood or in spirit, thank *you, señor* Eastman. Remember: if you are stopped by the police or army, just relax, look into the eyes of the responsible person and mentalize the light of the lost stone. It will rid you of the dangers and guide you. Today you have been connected to it and only *you* will touch it. Remind everyone to beware of the signs. – said Juan, looking at Rico and Lia. – The signs always appear at unusual times! Catalina knows the Andean ways. She's going to drive you. Can you do that, my dear?

- It will be a great pleasure! – replied the girl with joy.

- Then let the journey begin! Get out of here immediately. Do not take main roads, Catalina. You can waste time if it is to ensure this man's safety. Stop in Arequipa and look for a lodging away from downtown. Stay there for two days to get used to the altitude and please do not eat *chupe*! This can spoil the personal legend of any mortal. – said Juan Navarro, laughing very loudly. – When you arrive in Puno, Fernando, look for Marita. She will take you to the Sun Island and teach you some things you need to know. Listen to what she has to say very carefully. And do not forget: *do not be afraid!* Fear lessens your mental power. *Only fear* can defeat you now.

- Of course, *señor* Juan. Thank you very much.

***

Arequipa is a little more than 700 kilometers south of Paracas. The city is a type of oasis at 2,300 meters altitude in the middle of the Peruvian desert surrounded by towering glacial mountains. The Misti volcano is the colossal symbol of the city and perhaps the most beautiful view in the world! Chachani and Picchu Picchu are one on the left and the other on the right respectively forming a breathtaking geological panorama. Arequipa is known as Ciudad Blanca because it was all built with white stones originating from the cooling of the massive amount of magma foam expelled by the explosion of the Picchu Picchu volcano 10 million years ago. It is estimated that the original height of this volcano reached six thousand meters.

Legend has it that Arequipa was founded by the great Mayta Capac as a huge military encampment. This camp grew and developed over the years. One day, when the king decided to leave and set up another camp, some of his soldiers humbly asked to stay, because they liked the place and had taken root there. They say that Mayta Capac replied: *"ari quepay"*, which means *"yes, you can stay"* in Quechua. The city flourished with the Inca culture together and harmoniously with other cultures already established that were assimilated and incorporated to the Empire. Military fortification then became a large, well-structured city. Big enough to attract the Spaniards who took it and obviously destroyed the local culture with Christianity.

The architecture of the city is Spanish. It is nothing like Cuzco that still has many traces of Inca architecture. You feel like you are in some of these cities in the hinterland of Spain. Is beautiful! It's colorful! It has the bluest sky in the world! The air is also *the driest* in the world. The difficulty to breathe in Arequipa is great. The nose does not get used to the dryness of the air so easily. In the Titicaca highlands it is even worse. It is necessary to stop in Arequipa before ascending to Puno, where the great Lake is.

The desert aridity is only broken by the waters that descend from the snows of the three peaks that surround the city. They bring life to the whole region making it happen, as on the Nile, a miracle in the desert. The whole region eats what is planted on the banks of the rivers that cross Arequipa, especially the river Tambo. Everyone benefits from every animal that is raised in the region because of that water. Water that comes not from rain but from glaciers.

To the north, four hours of travel, extends the Valley of the Colca, where they roam alpacas and viscaias. Animals that are raised loose in nature in their natural environment at an altitude of 4,000 thousand to 4,300 thousand meters. The wool of these animals reach international luxury market prices. The ravine of the Colca River reaches 3,500 meters deep. It is the largest gorge in the world and undoubtedly one of the most sensational views ever. There you can see in person the majestic flight of the King of the Air, the threatened Condor.

The entire city, at least the largest buildings of the old center (which is listed by UNESCO), belongs to the Catholic Church, which rents them thus guaranteeing an absurd income for the treasury of we do not know who. The Santa Catalina Monastery (or Catalina in the original) is a journey through all Spanish architecture from the founding of the city in 1540 until the end of the 20th century, when it was forbidden to make any changes within the monastery. A monastery that should be called a convent which only housed nuns, but... this is *churchy* story...

- Nerd, what is this *chupe* that *señor* John mentioned?"

- *Chupe* is a shrimp stew with corn, potatoes and some local herbs and spices. Very tasty, but it can cause a big diarrhea. – Fernando said knowingly. – You know Lia, it's hard to figure how those shrimps got to those heights or even when it happened. I suggest you try guinea pigs. At least we know that's a 100% homegrown food.

- What is it?

- Guinea pig, you know? A type of barbecue, only you put a stone on top of the little pig that cooks on a grill. It flattens and toasts. It's delicious. Accompany potatoes, corn and raw onion with tomatoes.

- I can't believe it! It's cruel! How can you eat it? – said Lia with pity for the poor creatures.

- You can even see the rodent's teeth. Nails, too. It's delicious, Lia. You have to prove it! – said Fernando, laughing.

- Stop, nerd! – she shouted in jest and disgust.

It was many hours of non-stop driving at an average speed of 60 to 80 kilometers per hour on narrow roads. They did not spot any policemen, or roadblocks. Everything seemed ominously calm until the night fell. About ten o'clock the four stopped at a village by the side of the road and searched for lodging. They found a place where rooms were rented for travelers. It was a small room with two bunk beds.

Catalina and Rico stayed and asked that they rent the two bunk beds for privacy. The lady in charge accepted without problems. Fernando and Lia entered later hidden by the bedroom window. They were trying to be invisible. No one should know that there are two Brazilians walking there. It could raise suspicion. The group settled into the small room. They lay down in their own bed. As soon as the light went out, Fernando Eastman began to speak aloud as if he were rambling on his own.

- I went to Kaaba. My father took me there. It was the only time he took me on one of his trips. It's sublime.

- Did you see the stone? – asked Rico.

- Of course not! – grumbled Fernando. – I did not come anywhere near it. It is a sacred place of the Muslims. If you are not a follower of Muhammad, you do not step inside that place! The energy of there is created by one thought alone: *Allah*, or God, as you will. The Muslim culture and religion are very rich. They merge into a kind of life focused on religiosity. In everything you look there is something of divine inspiration, as if they were living all the time in direct contact with the source. Very different from the racing life of today's west. Muslim tradition says that the

Kaaba was originally white, crystalline. They say that it has the "power" to absorb the sins of all who lean against it... or even come close to it. That is why there is the old tradition: at least once in a lifetime every Muslim should go to Mecca, walk around the Kaaba and, if possible, touch, kiss, even touch their forehead on it, if one is lucky.

- I've seen footages of Muslim pilgrims circling the courtyard of the Kaaba Mosque. – said Catalina. – It's impressive. It looks like a human swirl.

- It's a cleansing ritual. – explained Fernando. – The faithful "uploads" their sins to the stone that absorbs everything. They also have this childish idea of sin. Over the centuries, and because of its unique feature and the centuries old "touch the stone" ritual of the Muslims, it turned out to be completely black. That's what tradition says. The entire region of Cuzco and Lake Titicaca is considered by the Incas as the "navel of the world". The location of the Kaaba is considered the "navel of the world" by Muslims. Makes sense!

"What makes sense, Fernando? – Catalina asked.

- Energy centers are "navels" according to various traditions and cultures throughout the world. Everyone uses the same term, "navel of the world," no matter the distance. The same name is used in Japan when referring to Mount Fuji. Easter Island was the "navel of the world" for the Moais. The energy of Cuzco is also of this nature. Energy is all around Peru, by the way. Sacred Valley, Machu Picchu, Saqsayhuaman. It is through the navel that we are fed inside the belly of our mothers. In analogy, these places are energetic centers that feed the planet. Our mother is Gaia, Mother Earth. It is She who keeps us alive. There is even a theory in which all these energetic points intertwine creating dimensional portals. The famous world grid. That's what they say.

- Is Mecca like this, too? – asked Lia?

- It's a different energy, because there are millions of believers daily, all sending thoughts to Allah. All Muslims have a duty to pray at least five times a day, no matter where they are, towards that city, that is, this whole wave of prayers, thoughts focused on the same point, all that faith is possible to be felt there.

You can almost pick it up! That's the kind of energy I'm talking about.

- Wow! Imagine only if Christians did the same. The Vatican would be unbearably more powerful! – Lia said with less ingenuity after hearing the lectures of Professor Eastman, Phd master in "conspiracies".

- The Christian doesn't know how to pray. – Fernando shoots.

- How come? – Catalina asks after a brief silence.

- I mean, most people don't know how to optimize the power within their brains. – says Fernando.

- Explain, nerd. I can't follow you. You spoke of energy, then the slap the face of Christians. Give me a link here, please.

- The Christians, especially the Catholics, are accustomed to ask things to their saints, his martyrs, even to the Holy Trinity, individually or collectively, depending on the size of their problems. In some cases only the Father, the Son and the Holy Spirit together to help. But they forget to do their part, which is the most important thing in life. Muslims are much more proactive. They work hard and are skilled negotiators. Unbeatable in trade. Even better than their brothers, the Jews, maybe. The Catholic, not generalizing, of course, is indolent. They accept their miseries and assume their responsibilities based on the size of their sins. Or what they imagine to be sin. Those who get their "blessings" arc the ones who pray the most and are disciplined at work.

- Explain, nerd.

- Sure. It is not that they "earn" their blessings from nothing. They have so much faith in their saints and images that they daily put their brain gear to work fervently praying and exercising the mental focus on a desirable life image, on a single goal. Do you understand? They pray with love, with faith, every day, sending the same thoughts always in the same direction of the desired blessings. The mind can create realities, everyone knows that. Exercising the use of this equipment that is our brain is the same thing as perfecting something that is called "imagination". When you pray with one goal, your whole will is focused on one image daily and relentlessly until you get what you want. Quantum physics corroborates this technique and says that it is not only possible, but that it is *the only way* to influence in the great web of reality.

- What web is that? – asked Lia.

- Search the Internet, Lia, but not now, please!

- Okay. I pray almost every day, nerd. Not everything I ask happens. This is frustrating! But I have faith!

- Lia, it is not enough to pray. This is the point. You need to roll up your sleeves! We are taught from the day we are born that we are sinners, imperfect beings, that we deserve nothing good. They teach that it is wrong to have money or comfort while people sleep on the street and starve. In everything there is guilt and unworthiness. They teach that sex is sin, that the world is of the meek. All our natural aggression, all our libido dissolves with this ideology that crushes us, corrodes us inside while our true nature wants to be happy, wants to rise to the surface and breathe a little. You have to be meek, as the Bible says.

- *"The meek shall inherit the Earth."* – said Catalina.

- Psychologically this is a disaster, a demonstration of advanced mental degeneracy. – continues the nerd. – Instead of getting your fingernails and grabbing what you want, you become passive and conformed, do you know why?

- Because God wanted to! – Rico mumbled, almost asleep.

- Right, Rico. But of course the problem is not with the Christian faith and not all Christians are like that. Jesus taught that faith can heal and do "miracles." The successful ones have focused their minds and put faith on it eliminating as much conflict as possible and... *plin*! The "miracle" happened! And there are many examples everywhere.

- I had never thought about it. – said Lia. – How about those who could not get anything, like my parents?

- I am sorry for them. What makes me sick is that nobody teaches these poor people the science behind the prayer. It's not so difficult, just training and focus. And work, of course. Dedication to what you want to achieve. Things can materialize regardless of whether they know the truth or not. They are not stupid! – he said, pausing. – They just don't have anyone to teach them how to use the equipment.

A great silence dominated the room. There was no sound, as if everyone were paralyzed by Fernando's words.

It is not good for business if Christians stopped fearing their God. If all the Christians in the world thought and prayed daily focusing on the love that Jesus represents, the Vatican could not bear it. The mafia that dominates that Institution would probably be expelled from the planet by human prayers. We have actually been indoctrinated and like to be massacred by the misleading beliefs of the Church. If Jesus had said, *"Be all ignorant and pathetic! Suffer all your life!"*, I would not even argue with the master, but he never said that! That's why I like Buddhism...

Brief pause. Fernando begins to bother with the glaring silence of the room. *"Do they understand what I'm talking about?"*, he thought.

- The Buddha's doctrine does not bind you in fear, in pain, in your sins. They teach you to eliminate the pain of being alive. For Buddha, life is pure suffering from the day you are born until your death. It is a doctrine that teaches to focus the mind and work. But imagine if Christians learned to use their minds. It would end the pain and the fear, it would end the sick dependence in the Institution of the Church. It would end the Spiritual Power and thus the Antichrist would lose a third of his forces against the Light. They would have already lost the game. What do you think of this?

Total Silence.

- Lia?
- zzzzzzzzzzzzzz
- Oops! Good night.

DAY 10 – 6am
Heading to Arequipa/Peru

They left as early as possible. They hit the road still in dim light. Within a mile or so there was a police check point. Check points are common on anywhere around the world, but the circumstances brought panic to Fernando. He froze and his face paled. Catalina, the driver, quickly said:

- Fernando, remember! Mentalize the stone you saw and look right into the eyes of the cop. Believe what *señor* Juan said. He knows things!

- There's no way out. Either it works, or we're finished. – said Fernando. – I'll try!

- Nerd, after everything you've been through, you still don't believe in yourself? Come on, man! You talked about faith until you fell asleep yesterday. It's gonna be alright. You didn't know what was gonna happen in Nazca, nor in Cuzco, nor yesterday, and yet things happened! Be strong. We are with you! – encouraged Lia.

The car was stopped and two heavily armed policemen approached one on each side. Catalina opened the glass and greeted one of them. *"Buenos dias, señor. Que pasa?"*. The policeman, without answering, asked for the documents of the car and the driver. The other policeman, who seemed to be in charge, bent down and put his face almost inside the car through the rear window. Fernando stared into the officer's eyes and thought of the stone. The policeman looked paralyzed for a few brief seconds. Suddenly he straightened up and said to his subordinate: *"Let them go!"*. The policeman returned the documents to Catalina without questioning his command of his superior and the group continued their journey.

- Amazing! I really works! – said Fernando, shocked.

This happened two more times until they arrived in Arequipa that same day at dusk. Fernando came to believe more and more in himself. The whole group felt strong.

Shortly after arriving they asked the locals for an inn outside the historic city center. The cheapest possible. They were informed that there was a hostel right at the entrance of the city next to the

Arequipa bus station. The owner, *señor* Barrios, was a man of small stature, skin and bone, totally suspicious and with the face of few friends. He has a huge house and lives alone. The rooms are his only source of income and he always keeps them tidy and ready for his informal guests. He never asks for documents, passports, nothing. He is only interested in the cash. Rico negotiated a very good price, since they wanted to stay for two days, until Fernando and Lia get used to the altitude.

There was no way to get through the window this time, so Rico lied warily that the two were French tourists short of money. He said they needed to rest because the altitude was breaking up with them. *Señor* Barrios realized that Rico was lying shamelessly.

- I do not want trouble, *señor* Calmón. I already have mine.

Fernando said nothing, but he understood that all prudence wouldn't be enough while they were there. Rico booked two separate bedrooms with twin beds. It was what the man had available. They checked in. Rico went downtown and bought some food in one of the many open-air fruit tents around Arequipa's *Plaza de Armas*. An imposing *Plaza* where the city's famous cathedral was built.

Arequipa was once the capital of the Spanish Empire in the Americas. As in Lima, the Plaza is all surrounded by two-story buildings from the Spanish era with its imposing balconies and crafted with beautiful and refined hardwood carvings. In the upper floors there are many restaurants and bars. The ground floor is taken over by all kinds of trade and tourism agencies. In the center of the Plaza there are comfortable benches where you can sit and watch the daily life of the city. Meanwhile the rest of the group lodged and bathed. After half an hour, Rico returns to the hostel.

- Look, I brought some fruit. It is not good to eat heavy things when you are in the altitude. – said Rico to the group, who despite having arrived in the city in a car rather than in a hermetically sealed bus, still suffered from headaches and dizziness.

- Thank you, Rico. – said Fernando. – I think I'm going to sleep for two days. I feel like shit.

- Do it. I'm going to buy *sorochim* to help you. I'm sure the day after tomorrow you'll be ready to climb another few hundred meters.

- What is this, nerd? Sleeping for two days? We have to enjoy and get to know the city! It is not always that you can have this kind of tourism. – Lia said playfully. – I want to see everything! Will you take me, Catalina? No one will recognize me! My look is totally different.

- I don't think it's going to be a problem. There's Juanita you have to meet!

- Stop, Catalina! I don't smoke Marijuana since I started the stewardess course! I'm out!

- Odalisca, it's not Marijuana! It's Juanita! A child who was found at the top of the Misti volcano! – said Fernando. – She has been totally frozen and 100% preserved under the ice for about 500 years, since the golden age of the great Inca empire. She's like a mummy, just frozen.

- Oh really? Is there a mummy here? Tell us, nerd.

- Juanita, if my memory does not fail me...

After the explanation and after devouring all the fruits that Rico brought, the four decided to sleep. It was not late, but the tiredness and stress of the last days was enormous. Everyone's body were screaming for a rest.

- See you tomorrow, friends. – said Rico with some comfort because they were safe and secure. – We'll wake up at eight in the morning, okay? We had a good breakfast and then we decide what to do.

- Deal, Rico. *Buenas noches*, Catalina.

- Good night to you. Get plenty of rest and plenty of water. If anything should happen, we're in the room across from yours.

This time Fernando had no energy for long speeches, but the night had just begun. Despite the *soroche*, the malaise of altitude, he quickly joined the two twin beds, switched off the light and then kissed Lia as they lay gently on the improvised double bed.

Rico woke up first and knocked on the door of the couple. "We're coming!", he heard Lia say. Fernando thought it would be best to keep lying down. He still didn't feel well. The three then decided to eat something and go out to see the mummy.

- Fernando, take care of yourself. Do not show your face out there and do not think about going out alone, okay? – Rico said worriedly. – We'll be back in an hour or two.

- Relax, Rico. I'll be fine. I really can't go for any walk. My head is exploding!

- From the noise of yesterday I wonder why! – Rico laughed softly. – You're not a typical nerd. And considering the joy of the girl, you must have done a good job!

- I'm a normal man, Rico. The only difference is that I like to know the crazy things in the world. Lying on the side of a woman like Lia is the glory to any man. I am lucky! How about you? Lucky?

- Yes! Sometimes I don't believe I met Catalina again! Well... I'll take the girls for a walk and come back soon. If something happens do not wait for us! Go to Puno. The car keys are here along with the documents.

- You can relax, my friend. Keep your eyes opened!

Fernando took some painkillers, got into bed and picked up the small notebook he had received at the airport a few days earlier. His head was exploding with pain. He opened on the page he had stopped and there was the title: **The Creation of Man**.

> "*And the light of His presence flooded the Darkness and* **showed a still unfinished world** *covered by crystalline waters.*
> *With this gesture ... battle for the supremacy of the Light.*
> **Love X selfishness**, *justice X injustice, life X death.*
> *A battle until dawn ... when the King ...* **returns victorious** *...*
> *from where he would reign eternally in perfect Peace.*
> *The revealed world was Earth. First day.*

Second day: Separation of waters.
The heat of His Light ... water evaporated wrapping the planet blue
mantle. ... atmosphere ... mixing vital gases ... life."

The pages were very erased. He could read very little, but followed with interest. *"What was the point of delivering me these notes?"*, he asked quietly as he read.

"Third day. ... continents.
Gather up the waters under the heavens, and let the dry portion appear.
He called it 'earth' and the moist part 'seas'.
Produce ... green herb ... seed, fruit tree ... fruit.
... **Garden of Eden on the planet.**
The Eternal ... his Throne in that place, from which the rule of the
Universe would be confirmed.
Behold, everything is very good.
Fourth day. ... created luminaries that would fill the Earth with light
and heat.
These luminaries ... would also serve as **signs for certain times,**
for days and years ... created the planets ... for the balance of the solar
system.
Fifth day. Produce ... living soul reptiles.
Let the birds fly ... Be fruitful and multiply ... multiply on the earth.
Let the earth bring forth a living soul ... cattle, creeping things, beasts
of the earth, according to their kind."

- These outlined words must be important. It is not by chance that this notebook was delivered to me.

"The Eternal **descended** *into the new world.*
... the whole Universe ... acts of the Creator in response to the
accusations of the enemies.
... decisive moment ... to crown someone ... His Throne on Earth.
Lucifer and his ... did not doubt that the Throne ... to them in that
world where **Light** *and* **Darkness** *... in* **harmony.**
God began to shape a special creature ... still lifeless, **the first man.**
... in the nostrils the **breath of Life** *... began to live.*

He said to the man,
My son, my dear son! Because you were born from the ground, you will
receive the name of Adam.
The Eternal took Adam to know the species of ... the Garden.
... realized that everyone had a pair ... one lived for the other.
Adam felt lonely.
There was a **desire** *to have someone always by your side."*

- Adam, my friend. – Fernando thought to himself. – You kick ass! You arrive and ask for a mate! That's abuse of authority, bro! The Creator did an excellent job when raised the woman. Thanks Father, whoever you are! Amen!

He was glad to have found Lia.

"It is not good that the man should be alone.
I will make you a companion.
Creator made him **fall asleep** *...*
When he opened his eyes ... a woman caressed his face.
Now Adam was **complete** *... Eve ... from his flesh and bones from*
his bones.
Everything was perfect ... nothing matched the Human Being, who
was created **in the image and likeness** *of God.*
Sixth day ... final."

Fernando finally fell asleep. He dreamed of a huge *plaza*, similar to the *Plaza de las Cabezas* of Tiahuanaco. When we dream, our unconscious shows us our reality. Sometimes with real places as a backdrop, sometimes with typical, standard places. The meaning of dreams is something that really intrigues psychoanalysts even today, as they always give clues about the problems of their clients. The place with which Fernando dreamed was very similar to that of Bolivia, and there was a man whose face he could not see clearly because someone suddenly knocked on the door of the room. Fernando woke up scared and came quickly back to himself.

- Who is it?

- It's Barrios, *señor*. Open Please.

- Good morning, *señor*. What happened?

- *Señor* Fernando Eastman, I presume. We haven't been officially introduced. I thought you didn't speak Spanish, only French. – said Barrios, holding out his hand to Fernando with a fake, yellow smile on his face.

- Yes. – he said, startled and embarrassed, undoing the French lie. – May I help you?

- *Señor* Eastman, you know that here in Peru life is difficult. I'm an ex-convict. I committed my crimes, I paid my debts with society and today I manage this pigsty where you and his friends hide from the Peruvian Federal Police.

- Is not true! We're not hiding!

- I saw your photos on-line earlier today, *señor*. You and your girl are being sought and there's a reward for you heads. I am a very reasonable man, *señor* Fernando. Very reasonable.

- What do you mean, *señor* Barrios?

- I want double the reward to let you get away. The police are on their way now. It's either take it or leave it, I mean... It's either paying or going to jail. Better yet, *señor* Fernando. It's pay and run. You have no choice!

- Okay, I have some money with me. How much is my head worth today, *señor* Barrios?

- Ten thousand *soles* should do it.

- It's a lot of money! I don't have it all!

- It is a pity. I can even hear the sirens coming to my door. Seven thousand is already good money.

- It's ok. I'll give you money.

He closed the door and counted the cash he had in his pocket.

- Do we have a deal at five thousand *soles*?" In US Dollars? Cash!

- Deal! – he said, taking the money and counting it. – It's the same government prize, but the dollars interest me. Take your things and beat it. It was good doing business with you. I'll be looking forward to your next visit, *señor* Fernando Eastman! Take my card.

His eyes shone with disdain mingled with an irony typical of a classic *noir* movies villain. Fernando took his backpack cursing

Barrios and headed toward the *Plaza de Armas*, where the group should be. The Juanita museum is one block from the *Plaza*. While waiting for a chance to cross the junction that led to the museum, Fernando saw Rico, Lia and Catalina being arrested by plainclothes police officers.

- Damn you, Barrios!

Quickly and without calling attention, he changed directions and drove to the rich residential neighborhood on the highest part of the city. There he could stop the car and think about what to do.

"I have no money now!", he thought. "I left everything I had with that crook. I'm going to cash in some ATM and screw the big brother. They already know I'm here! At least I'll have a chance if I have cash in my pocket."

Eastman was dealing with an immense headache mixed with the dread of having seen her friends being arrested. He withdrew as much cash as he could and took the road that leads to the region of Puno. Peruvian agents are not very efficient when it comes to such a coordinated operation. There were no roadblocks. There was no sign that anyone was in his track. Either they were incompetent or there was something wrong... very wrong.

He thought of his friends, especially Lia. "My God, are they all right? They have nothing to do with this crazy story. It's all my fault! Now they must be going under interrogation in a police station. But they will not tell where I'm going, I'm sure! And the Professor... I wonder where he is."

The hours passed and everything was too quiet. The road to Lake Titicaca is long, monotonous and dangerous. As he went up to Puno his head ached more and more. His mouth and nostrils were dry and there were no vendors along the way, nowhere to quench the thirst. Only desert, *vicuñas*, *alpacas* and a lot of trash scattered along the roadside. "Shit! I should have bought some water!". It is an eight hour drive from Arequipa to Puno. The landscape is beautiful and the sun is always there burning your face and beautifying the great blue of the sky.

Fernando does not feel well driving and decides to get off the main road and pull over for a little. "Stretching can help!", he thought. "What to do now that I'm alone in this adventure?"

He drove a few miles down a side road until he was out of sight and stopped. He put his hands on the wheel. His friend Rico was no longer there to help decide what to do, nor was Lia to help with her naive brilliant insights. Not even Catalina, who harbored all three within her big heart. "What to do now?"

Fernando leaves the car and takes a deep breath, as deep as he can to find oxygen and strength to at least get to Puno. Oxygen is very rarefied at this altitude. It is close to the lake, the next stage of his quest, but his mind does not respond. He is not sure of how to find Marita. He doesn't know what will happen. He feels confused and lost, dehydrated and hungry. His sight begins to darken.

He faints.

He enters the corridors of that place. There is no smell. The air is extremely dry. Nothing that can be compared to an environment typical of the archaeological sites with which he is accustomed with. It was not like anything he'd ever seen in his research. The walls are millenarian. The stones are absolutely perfect and impossibly smooth. The colors are more colorful.

The floor is crimped in extremely small and delicate patterns that look more like a linear language than with mere decorative features. Right in front of him, at the end of the corridor, a very strong light emanates from a chamber. He comes closer and the light gets stronger. It is not a light source of the Earth.

Fernando enters the room.

"It can't be real!"

***

- Señor, señor... estás bien?

Fernando slowly returns to consciousness. He was in a cabin. A very old lady talks to him in a mixture of Spanish with Quechua. She, in fact, hardly speaks Spanish. She is a shepherdess of llamas of the Andean highlands. She came to Fernando while shepherding her animals. He was found fainted by the side of the car. Slowly he comes back from the blackout as she offered *coca* mate and a home-made meal made of roots and potatoes with a strong local seasoning based on yellow pepper and a piece of cooked llama meat.

Fernando was already conscious, but in deep meditative state. The thin air forced his body to radically lower metabolism and, consequently, his brain waves also slowed down. He was not working on *Beta*, our normal waking state. He was not in *Alpha*, the mental level conducive to meditation. Involuntarily he entered a deep *Theta* state, an almost coma if you compare to the normal state of human perception, but conscious. He could move naturally if he wanted to. He was not paralyzed, but he just stood there, still. He did not communicate with the lady for several days. She asked nothing. She just watched Fernando and understood that he should stay there.

The *coca* mate softened his unease and with each passing day he felt more lucid and stronger. It is in *Theta* that consciousness expands at its maximum capacity. In this state Fernando bordered on sleep, but in complete lucidity. The brain frequency *Theta* leads the mind to have insights on images of the unconscious and long-forgotten memories. It causes the mind to expand far beyond the reality limited by the "waking state" in *Beta* frequency.

History never advances in the highlands. Pastoral life happens as if there were neither time nor space. It's another perception. The people there are more spiritual because they are simpler, more earthbound, more connected to the true source of life. There is no luxury or technological knowledge. They are only human beings in their most natural expression. They do not even have "basic education". The education they receive is related to the basic survival tasks in that environment. They do not know how to live in big cities. Those who chose to go to urban centers attracted by the "wonders" of city life normally end up as beggars living in misery.

The highland people belong to another reality. There is nothing in this place that can divert the human being from their daily tasks. They work on what *sustain* them, not on what *enslave* them. They base their lives on what Hannah Arendt calls labor. It's not torture. It is not *tripalium*, the Latin term for *work* that relates daily activity to the old tripod where people were tied for whipping. It is *labor*: an obligation assimilated by the instinct of self-preservation.

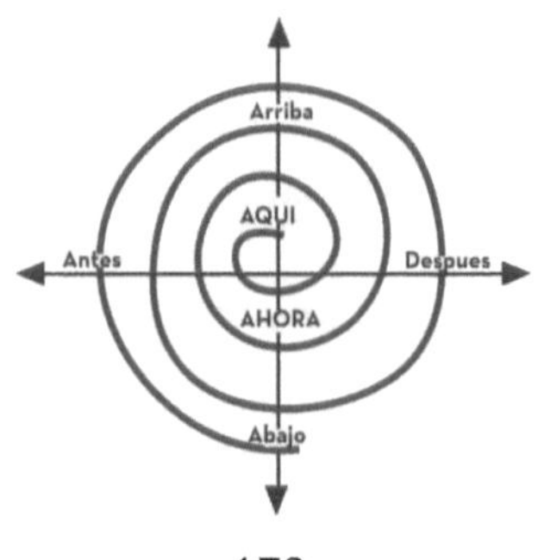

Besides the labor they very spiritual. There are daily rituals related to their beliefs and nothing on Earth takes them out of their ritual routine. There is a great understanding of their own condition in the same way that there is conformation. They are also *conformed* to their situation of social poverty in a half-indolent way, but in those altitudes... in that solitude no one calls them *sinners*. No one says they deserve to suffer. There is no spiritual oppression in the isolation of the desert.

***

The woman did not speak to Fernando for days, but she did not deny the necessary help that the white-skinned bearded human being needed. Eastman hasn't shaved for many days. There are no ridiculous social rules in the isolation of the desert.

***

Fernando learned a lot from the silence and kindness of that woman. She did not need anything material in that place. She was self-sufficient. She needed no television, no refrigerator, no radio, not even electricity. She needed no money. She lives with what she gets with her shepherding. A true child of the Earth. She keeps just an old photo of her family hanging on the wall and some religious items. In the corner of the only room in the hut there was incense and some ritualistic ceramics. Every night before bedtime and every day before leaving she makes her ancestral prayers and her rites of veneration. She worships Orejona. She prays for a different name, but it doesn't matter. It's just a variation of the goddess Orejona. The signals are the same. Mythology shows that they are always the same gods with different masks.

Forced by his metabolism in adaptation, Fernando meditated on the signals shown to him by the picture in Qorikancha. The delicate instrument, the egg-shaped milky stone and the papyrus. The milky oval stone was the one that came to his mind first. Although he was still recovering, he decided to go out and sat on a stone a few yards from the cabin. In his deep mental journeys Fernando saw the image of a pair of hands carrying a stone. These hands were gloved and gently carried a larger stone. It was being treated as if it was very delicate, or maybe the stone was being handled with respect and veneration.

- My God! It's *señor* Juan Navarro! – Fernando exclaimed to himself, though he hadn't seen any face.

The milky egg-shaped stone meant the elongated skulls. He saw hands with gloves. You don't manipulate skulls (elongated or regular) without wearing gloves. It is a sanitary issue, but the way *señor* Juan manipulates his findings is certainly a matter of respect and veneration. Unconditional respect for their ancestors. Fernando felt exhausted and ended up lying on the floor in a state of torpor. Hours later he returned to the old lady's shelter.

The next day Fernando woke before sunrise. He took a mug of *coca* mate, a loaf of bread and went for a short walk across the area. He was still sleepy, but he wanted to be again to face with the Morning Star. Venus was glowing just for him. The young man leaned against a stone large to observe the "star" in a contemplative attitude. The light of Venus began to pulsate in bright colors. Blue, white, yellow and red. Each time a little stronger. The sky was a mixture of blackness, navy blue and a timid yellow-orange that grew on the horizon until it utterly shook the darkness and gave way to the peculiar Andean blue sky. If someday some being from another planet really stepped in here, he must have marveled at the colors our unique gaseous atmosphere provides.

Before the sun rose on the horizon, the reflected light of Venus pulsed intermittently, placing Fernando on another mental frequency. Venus started pulsing in a very soft and harmonic rhythm. Fernando's brain was caught by the pulse and began to function on the same wavelength. He could see a pair of hands manipulating clay. The rhythm of the pulsations followed the rhythm of the modeling hands. Gradually that clay became a familiar figure. It was a cat, a *Puma*. As the work of those hands revealed itself, an instrument appeared and it looked very much like the instrument represented in the hands of one of the men in the painting. It was like a dry tip used to make lines on Inca ceramics.

- Julio Pranas! – said Fernando aloud in the middle of the desert.

Señor Julio really helped him, as did *señor* Juan Navarro. The first one helped him to reach the Nazca desert and make contact with Orejona. The second opened his mental channels and set him on the way to Marita, where he was trying to go before his breakdown. "But... what about the papyrus?", he wondered. Fernando understood that two men had already helped him in this crazy adventure. According to the elder in Cuzco, *three men* and a woman would help him.

- Marita must be the woman! Who will be the third man to help me?

He went back to the good lady's shelter knowing that patience is really a virtue. "All in its time, Fernando!", said Juan Navarro.

A few more days passed. Fernando Eastman was already stronger physically and spiritually. He knew that until now everything had happened without any planning. He should be patient because he knew the final help would come. He should, therefore, be attentive to all signs, as he had been warned. Until now he had acted almost completely passively, having to think fast and *react* according to inevitability. He saw no problem in it. However, he understood that there would inevitably come a time when he would have to take an action and make a choice.

In one of his walks along the Altiplano, he remembered the notebook he had been delivered. He reached into his pocket and opened it on the page where he had stopped before being snitch and extorted by the innkeeper.

- *Señor* Barrios... who would say! – he thought with astonishment and irony. – That was a great lesson.

Eastman learned at that moment that you really shouldn't judge anything without due time to understand the consequences. Without Barrios he would probably not be in that place.

- Let's see that notebook.

He resumed his reading from the title: **The Fall of Man.**

"Adam and Eve asked the meaning of the Dark …
The whole sky was lit by the stars. In the middle of the night God …
bright light and they walked by His side.
… after … **He rose to the watching host.**
Dawn.
God covered the **man** *with his royal robe … over his head the crown coveted by Lucifer.*
… a cry of victory shook the whole creation.
God has denied enemies with His work of **righteousness, selflessness, and love. "**
Having made man the **lord of all creation,** *he spoke of the mission of Adam.*
… take care of Paradise …
The **laws of justice and love,** *the foundations of the Kingdom, should be honored.*
The Creator spoke of the **spiritual conflict** *that was waging the* **conquest of the Universe.**
Lucifer, who served God for countless ages, was **corrupted** *by pride and* **selfishness.**
God showed two trees laden with fruits
The one on the right … of Life = Kingdom of Light.
The one on the left was the Tree of Good and Evil … rebellion.
Eating the fruit of the first … submission to the Creator.
Eating the fruit of the second … **eternal death** *… all creation.*
This was the Sabbath = emblem of divine triumph.
Lucifer and his … observed with bitterness the greatness of God's achievement in crowning Man.
Frustrated … they understood that it would only be a human gesture to have dominion forever."

Fernando embarked on the journey of the notebook and searched for signals. He wanted a key, a sign to be able to put together the pieces that are still missing. He still doesn't know what to expect or what to do. He still has to find a woman called Marita. He doesn't even know if the notebook he reads has anything to do with the whole thing. "It must have!", he thinks. "It *cannot* be coincidence that it came to me minutes before I embark on this madness!"

> *"Lucifer ... his plan for victory:* **to deceive** *mankind.*
> *... a trap ... to lead man to the knowledge of Good and Evil ...* **forbidden tree.**
> *Without God's permission, the hosts decided to send* **two messengers** *to warn Adam of the danger.*
> *Immediately they* **transposed the portals** *of ... and threw themselves into infinite space.*
> **In moments they crossed the whole Universe** *and arrived at the Garden of Eden.*
> *The couple were warned not to give in to Lucifer's temptations.*
> *If Satan tried to* **intimidate** *them ... hosts would come to their aid They remained vigilant."*

- Here comes Lucifer. – he thought with genuine sorrow. – Fucking trouble, man! Why did you do that?

> *"Lucifer took possession of a* **serpent** *and approached Eve.*
> *Eva was amazed ... flowers and fruits and brought to her feet.*
> *After ... the woman's confidence, he* **began to speak** *... wisdom and tenderness.*
> *... talk about love and the Power of the Creator.*
> *... thorough knowledge of any subject.*
> **Involved by the knowledge of the reptile,** *she forgot her companion and the directions of the messengers."*

Fernando thought of how easy it has been, until today, to deceive people with lies and false knowledge. We are not very demanding about checking facts or contents of what are being taught to us in schools, universities. We don't check the news that we are told by the media. He never realized the Luciferian powers that rules everywhere. The power of lies and deceit. The world is in the hands of liars and deceivers. He began to understand why this notebook had been handed to him by a stranger, but who would that person be?

"Adam felt a cold in the heart for not seeing Eve.
... remembered the Tree of Good and Evil.
Eve asked the serpent,
'Where does your great knowledge come from?'
'There is the source of my knowledge' *... towards the tree.*
Lucifer, embedded in the serpent = MIND.
He said that he was a serpent like the others, but that after eating the fruit he received all the knowledge.
Eva = confused.
'You shall not eat of this fruit, lest you die.'
This is false! *(Snake) If that were so, I would have died. God forbade them to eat ... to keep man from becoming like Him,* **knowing all things.'**
Eve was overcome by the glories that would be gained by eating that fruit. She ate it."

Eastman remembered *"Adam's Apple"* from Aerosmith. He hummed softly as he stared out at the horizon. *"She ate it!"* He took a deep breath and stretched his whole body.

"The Eternal ... in pain and silence, but if Adam **resisted temptation,** *he would seal victory and Eve would be* **forgiven for having been deceived.**
Adam came late = 'Eve, what are you doing?'
Eva taken by emotions = imagined to have reached a **higher level of life.**
She was smiling = Adam in tears.
The **serpent** *made her his* **tempting weapon.**
Adam embraced her, but it was the **enemy** *that enveloped him ...*
Eva talked about her experience = Good and Evil.

She would not be complete without her husband = *he would follow her.*
Adam feared ... against the Creator ... could not live apart ... He loved Eve with **infinite love.**
In the **decisions of man** *... all the* **destiny of the Universe.**
He took the fruit = he ate."

Fernando understood that part very well. The words made sense. The signs have revealed themselves. Adam had to choose between leaving Eve or staying with her. The temptation was a basic emotional blackmail that condemned the entire human race to have the life we have today. Although our planet is not so bad, Paradise should have been much better. Adam was caught by the flesh. God must have made an irresistible Eva!

"Zion belonged to him ... there to establish his kingdom, never being molested by the Laws of the Eternal.
The whole universe mourned defeat.
The Eternal, in His wisdom and love, commanded powerful angels to encircle Eden, preventing Lucifer from taking Zion.
The powerful creatures broke space by **encircling Paradise** *in a moment."*

The young man stood in peace, meditating all day on the smudged notebook with no clue of time. The final part was unreadable, but what could be read was important. It helped to make some connections with the current human condition, but still the boy did not understand where all this could fit his quest. The puzzle pieces spin in his mind. The legend of Orejona tells that she created the Andean Man. The biblical Genesis tells how God created Man. In the Bible other men from other cultures appear out of nowhere without any explanation of who created them. The Genesis of the Egyptians speaks of Osiris and Isis as their creators.

- Do the different men have different origins? – Fernando asks himself. – Who was the woman that Cain joined after being banished to the lands east of the Garden of Eden for the death of his brother Abel? Where did these other cultures come from?

The notebook brought more questions than answers. Only the last pages were fully legible. It began with a title: **The Redemption**.

> *"God ... plan of redemption.*
> *In fact man will reap the fruit of his rebellion in a terrible death. I cannot with my power change your fortune. If I did, I would be unjust before my decree. But I will bring all condemnation upon a* **Substitute** *who will arise in* **human descent**. *This Man will not bring into his hands the cuffs of death, being innocent and uncontaminated in His nature.*
> *As the* **representative of the human race**, *he will face Lucifer and overcome him. After triumphing in this battle, proving that love is stronger than selfishness, that truth is stronger than falsehood, humility is more powerful than pride, the faithful Substitute will lift up victorious hands not to greet the great achievement, but to take from the hands of* **enslaved humanity** *the cup of his condemnation. He will thus, in submission, receive the cup of eternal death. This immense sacrifice will open to human beings an opportunity to be redeemed, to return into the arms of the Creator, along with the lost domain.*
> *Surprising hosts asked the* **identity** *of that substitute.*
> *The Creator replied:*
> **Part of me will be this Man**. *My spirit will rest upon a virgin, and a Holy Son will be born in her. This child will be* **divine and human**. *In his humanity he will be submissive to the divinity that will* **dwell** *in him. The redeemed will see in Him the Father of Eternity, the Creator and Redeemer. The king of the kings. His name will be Yeshua."*

After spending hours in deep silence searching for answers, Fernando returned to the cabin at dusk, when Venus returned and greeted him again, now as the first star of the night. "Yeshua, the Hebrew name, means 'the eternal one who saves', but this is no news.

Two more days passed. Two more days Fernando remained in silence and meditation reestablishing his forces and acclimatizing to that environment of overwhelmingly hostile altitude. The lady offered him a bitter tea with every night before bed. He did not ask what it was. The herbs of this tea were mixed with a kind of bark of wood and boiled for several hours in a large pot and constantly stirred with a huge wooden spoon. It was not a night cap tea. It was another kind of medicine.

Fernando had mind-blowing and enlightening dreams. Sleeping or awake. His little knowledge of Freud's works was very useful when, during the moments of meditative vigil, he thought of the dreamlike images transmitted by his unconscious in a kind of self-analysis. In every dream he saw his father who somehow taught him something. They were images of his childhood. He felt the long lost affection of his father. Somehow the absence of the father figure didn't cause him deep traumas, on the contrary. Fernando always thought of his father, but in a caring and respectful way. A kind of respect that can only be won by recognition.

Fernando saw in Paulo an intelligent, capable and spiritual great man. The figure of his father, in his dreams, represented his self-image in the situations of life. An image coined by the short but intense coexistence with a really interesting man.

On the day he recovered and felt ready to continue on his journey, Fernando stood up, held the lady's hand and looked her in the eye. He sensed the light of the stone. Immediately the lady lowered her head in respect to the person she helped restore. She recognized his brightness and showed great reverence to that man who descended into his own hell and returned sound.

Fernando was a different man.

DAY 19 – 10am

Peruvian highlands. Somewhere between Arequipa and Puno

Fernando leaves his compulsory spiritual retreat, picks up the car that was in the same place where he passed out and heads to Puno. After so many days out of circulation the searches of the Peruvian Federal Police must have decreased considerably.

- The time is *now*! Let's go to Puno! – he said to himself, full of confidence before starting the car. - Here I go.

The road leads to the top of a very high chain of mountains that surround the entire Sacred Lake Titicaca. The highest navigable lake in the world at 3,810 meters above sea level has a total area of 8.559 square kilometers, with 175 kilometers long by 60 kilometers wide and with a maximum depth of 282 meters. It's extremely freezing with water temperature in the 9°C range all year round. The air is very dry, only softened by the humidity of the lake.

In Puno there are the Uros Islands. A pre-Inca civilization that still survives from artisan fishing, slaughtered birds and the collection of eggs from ducks' nests. They are skillful builders of rafts and artificial islets based on a kind of local reed. Each island can have twenty to thirty inhabitants. Women are weavers. The money from tourists send their descendants in the schools and in the urban society of Puno.

Fernando descends to the shores of the lake amidst the narrow, winding streets of the city. He was looking for some tourist information center, but changed your mind. He left *señor* Juan Navarro's car on a slope and entered a small *pojeria*. *Roast chicken* is a very popular dish all over Peru. He ordered a *pojo* and a bottle of water, sat at a table outside the cellar and watched the local movement. It was a good watch-point to scan the city and to get lost into the majesty of the Sacred Lake.

People going everywhere, each taking care of their own business, little concerned with black stones, conspiracies or life on other planets. People live their lives within their beliefs and cultures. Books, evidences, archeology, forget about it! That's for the few. The nerd feels grateful to be one of the few.

It's a fact: one cannot judge anything without looking back and seeing the results. Our life is inevitably a result of our choices combined with imponderable circumstances. The game of life is **choice** *versus* **inevitability**. And so... we are what we are.

Children were coming out of schools in flocks, all dressed in traditional clothing. The girls with their colorful dresses and Peruvian braids. The boys wearing a colorful wool punch over their pants and shirt. The basic clothes of everyday. The colors are always alive all over Peru and Bolivia. Puno is a culturally well-defined frontier area on both sides. Both the Peruvian and the Bolivian arrived at the same conclusion: "We love colors!"

Mini cars circulate like fish swimming in a stream. There's chaos and dangerous harmony in those streets. Tricycles covered with a type of fairing are alternatively used as taxis, but actually it's a kind of motorcycle with a roof. The most famous means of transportation in the country. They dominate the city streets as if they were a motorized invasion of locusts, as in India. Puno never seems to stop. And Fernando seems never to forget that he is still wanted by the police.

Prudence is a virtue.

While feeding, he saw below at the end of the long zigzag descent, a tourist bus station. "If Marita is tour guide, someone should know her there.", he thought. He finished his meal unhurriedly, paid his bill and walked down to what was actually a bus station *and* garage at the same time. He approached one of the drivers who was waiting for his departure time and asked for Marita.

- Marita is coming back from Cuzco today. She is expected to arrive in the late afternoon, near 8pm. – said the driver with a Spanish full of Quechua accent... or the other way around.

- Can I wait for her here?

- Yeah, why not?

- *Gracias, señor.*

"So far, so good! I must find somewhere to hide. I can't go snooping around. I'm not safe in Peru. I think I'm just going to sit on the edge of the lake like anybody else, fish and play dead until evening." This decision really demonstrates that this man learned something in the wilderness. He deliberately chose not to get out of the state of mind he had attained during his stay in the old woman's shelter. He was no longer afraid, so there was no point in changing his own mental frequency. Prudence would guide him. He was able to walk literally invisible through the streets of Puno. His mental frequency allowed for this peculiar energy camouflage. Fernando realized that if one vibrates fearless, they can't be noticed by people who vibrate *with* fear, even if this fear is unconscious. Fernando was vibrating in another wavelength.

Prudently he bought a fishing rod, bait, a cap and a pair of fishing glasses. He still had his peasant punch. He dressed up and drove to a farthest point from downtown where some people were fishing. At that place Fernando Eastman was invisible to the government. This enemy does not work in the field of *vibes*, but in the field of **surveillance cameras**. Against Big Brother, all he had left to do was going fishing. The silence was comforting.

Several hours later, when the night was beginning to fall, Fernando went back to the garage. The bus had already arrived an hour earlier and there were still some tourists waiting for their shuttles to go to their hotels. He approached a group of uniformed employees and asked for Marita.

- There, sir. The woman with long black hair.

- *Gracias!*

Fernando heads toward Marita with great expectation.

- Good evening, *señora*. I need to *hablar con usted*. It's very important.

- You can speak Portuguese. I know your language. – said Marita amiably.

- How do you know I am Brazilian?

- For the lousy Spanish accent. – they laughed. – How can I help you?

- It's about Orejona. – he replied point blank.

Marita startled and looked straight into Fernando's eyes.

- Wow, the surprises come in the most unexpected hours. I've been waiting for you for years. You're the Man, aren't you? It is you who will bring the Light back to its place, isn't it?

- Yes. – replied Fernando, full of confidence. – I just do not know how.

- Let's get out of here. It's not safe! You stay home tonight. Tomorrow at dawn we must go to the Sun Island on the Bolivian side. There, and only there we will talk. Understood? – she said in an serious tone. – Let's go. My house is near here.

Marita said nothing until they reached her house. When she arrived she sat in a corner that seemed to be very special in the house. She made a long series of breathing exercises along with chants and prayers that belong to a religion unknown to Fernando. Chants and prayers in her native language. Marita is from the Uros tribes. Fernando observed everything in silence and deep respect plunged in those ancient rituals. The desert had prepared him for that. He lost sense of time and space, for the songs were sacred mantras and his mind went flying through the sublime spiritual flow. Fernando felt each moment of the ritual like one more step toward his goal.

It was not late, but Marita said they should sleep and rest. Fernando slept comfortably in a modest but well-kept mattress.

- We'll leave early tomorrow. – Marita said as she retreated to her room. And that was all she said up until then, plus a phone call she made before connecting with her beliefs.

They were up promptly at 5am. They had *coca* mate, a loaf of bread and headed for a small path that bordered the Lake. They went down to the banks and found a boat waiting for them. With a single phone call a few hours earlier, Marita had prepared our way to *Isla del Sol*, 80 kilometers northeast on the Bolivian side.

- There must be no one looking for me from that side! – said Fernando to Marita as soon as they entered the vessel.

- We don't know, *señor* Fernando. It may be that the news has reached the offices of the Bolivian government. – Marita said skeptically.

- Do you think Evo Moralez would play the Game of the Mighty? Would he participate in these Power games? He doesn't have that profile. I don't believe it.

- Power is intoxicating, *señor* Fernando! Every man has his price in politics. While he poses as a true leader of the Bolivian peoples, we all know he may well be a great negotiator, like your Lula. Everything can happen in this filthy environment.

- What happens now, *señora?* Where are we going? Is it the Sun Island?

- Yes! That's where I connect with the forces. That's where I'm going to tell you great stories to better understand what's going to happen to you.

- Do you know what will happen to me?

- No, but I know that it must be something fabulous and only *you* will experiment it. Only *you* can have access to Light. You tell me later...

Two hours later they arrive at *Isla del Sol* on the shores of Sacred Lake, near Copacabana, the region's greatest tourist center with luxury hotels and good infrastructure. There are several sites to be visited if you pay a modest fee for a tour around the island. They get off the boat far away from the tourist docks.

- The boatman will wait for us. – said Marita, coming down from the boat with dexterity. Marita's small thin body moved with great agility.

The Sun Island originally had the name of Titikaka Island. *Titi* means feline, cougar. *Kaka* is the golden color of the feline. Philologically, however, the *kaka* diction refers to "fish of great silver scales", something like "sacred fish". *Titikaka* then means: Lake of the Puma and the Sacred Fish.

In Andean myths the island appears as the equivalent of Noah's Ark of the Bible, as an Ark of salvation, in which Wiracocha saved a select group of humans from the flood. Those would represent the renewal of the human race on Earth. These resplendent beings retained their spiritual and mental purity, all the magic and mystique of the pre-Flood race. Beings who have been entrusted with the mission of transmitting to the whole world the sublime teachings that have been inscribed in letters of "diaphanous and crystalline diamond", as are the waters of the enigmatic Sacred Lake.

By altitude and location, the Lake has been fulfilling the mission of protecting the messages destined for the human race within its symbology and its mysteries until a worthy person rediscovers everything and reveals to humanity. The geological shape of the Sun Island itself takes the form of a covered ark if you force your creativity a little.

Augustine Father Baltasar de Salas, chronicler of the 1600s, in his work "Copacabana de los Incas", tells us that in the Island of the Sun, as in the Island of the Moon, great relics of their gods and their princes are conserved, as well as objects like clothes with apocalyptic designs, stones with ancient and popular writings, occult and hidden in galleries that only the ancients knew. It is said that the *Isla del Sol* would be the depository of the greatest riches in objects of gold and silver in its category of sanctuary dedicated to a solar cult. It is also said that in ancient times only noble, official and beautiful virgins of the Sun cult could step on that piece of sacred ground. This Island holds more mysteries than one can imagine.

Tradition tells us that after the Flood the region remained for several days without celestial light, as if the sun were erased. One morning the survivors of the catastrophe saw the great sun coming out of the Island with an immense radiance, so they came to believe that *that* piece of rock on the surface of the Lake was the house and dwelling place of the Sun. Legends say that the Sun was hidden beneath the island for all the time in which the flood lasted and when it appeared, began to illuminate the world from that very place. Legend has it that the island was the first thing that enjoyed the privilege of God's Light.

But long before that, Orejona had descended there, on that same island to populate the region with her children.

- Come on, Fernando. We must go to the temple built for Orejona and Her stones. There I will perform an ancient ritual and you will kneel by my side, do you understand?

- Yes. They say that this is the temple that the god Tvira had built on the Island. I did not know it was in honor of Her. What do you have to tell me?

- All in its time, *señor* Fernando. When we get there you will know.

A few minutes later...

- This place is impressive, Marita. I've been to the Lake once a few years ago and felt a very strong energy. But here on the Island it feels like it's going to explode!

- The whole place is energetically strong. – she said shortly, concentrating and gently sane while looking at the horizon.

- How was this lake created? How can it exist in such a high region?

- There are many theories, *señor* Fernando. The only certainty we have is that it is at one of the highest altitudes of this planet. Research says it was created more than 2 million years ago. Some people call it "paleolake". At that time the level of its waters were 90 meters above what it is today. Between 27,000 and 21,000 BC the water level has stabilized about 15 meters above the current level. It is said that it may have arisen by condensation of the air vapors coming from the hot Amazon which, for thousands of years, has been accumulating drop by drop. Some argue that it was the fruit of the biblical Universal Flood, which happened some 12,000 years ago.

Marita pauses on the walk. She takes a deep breath and follows the path and the lecture.

- There's the theory that it was formed because of several huge *tsunamis*. Waves that climbed the mountain ranges and were dammed here. Imagine a tsunami of more than biblical proportions. This even explains the slight salinity of the water and the presence of a species of Marine Horse, an obviously marine animal that exists up here. Amidst so many hypotheses, at least so far, the safest is that the Lake emerged after several geological and climatic changes over a long period before the emergence of *homo sapiens*.

- We're talking about 150,000 years or so. Is it really *that* young?

- It may be younger than we can imagine. Maybe not. Several expeditions have been made all over the Lake. One of them, in 1968, led by the Argentine Ramón Avellaneda, found a very important treasure only eight meters deep. They are huge, carved blocks, embedded in each other, forming a pre-Inca wall. It is known that it was not the Incas who did it, but the Collas, many centuries before. There was also a paved street hundreds of meters parallel to the Titicaca coast.

- A street? Interesting.

- Several walls of the height of an average man arranged in a strange way. Each of these walls one is five meters away from its neighbor forming a half moon, built with blocks of 60 centimeters. There is nothing in Peru or Bolivia with this architectural type, besides the Temple of the Sun that we are going to see. This expedition recorded at least thirty parallel walls that make up a one kilometer-wide lake structure. These structures belong to the oldest civilization of the high plateau. Before the Tiahuanaco and the Gate of the Sun. It is probably the ancient city called Huanaco, where there was a temple that the ancients said was built "before the creation of the world".

- Yes, the text of the *Quipós*! So this temple really existed?

- Yes. Our legends are not just legends. In 1979, during the filming of the documentary "El Lago Sagrado" by Hugo Boero Rojo, walls similar to those of Saqsayhuaman were found, according to Rojo, cyclopean walls, very similar to the walls of Mycenae in Greece. The last expedition was in 2008 and the conclusions were that the lake is pre-glacial formation. Evidence shows that there was an advanced civilization in place long before it was thought and that it was swept from the earth by a hecatomb.

- Wow!

- But the greatest discovery of this expedition was a carved stone head found in this underwater complex. It is exactly like the heads of the *Plaza de las Cabezas*, indicating that the supposed Huanaco has a direct connection with Tiahuanaco, which was built much later.

- Tiahuanaco. – said Fernando in a low voice. – What's the relationship with Orejona?

- I think Huanaco was the true home of the Orejona civilization. It is necessary to rethink our legends and myths, as they can offer clues about real events that have happened for millennia, despite the lack of scientific proof. – Marita said Zen level calm. – *Señor*, do you accept these legends and myths as something real?

- I didn't accept these legends as real in my position as a scholar, as a scientist. But I came to accept after having spoken personally with Orejona. After having gone through things that I cannot understand or explain and that have been going on for days, one thing crazier than the other. – said Fernando calmly, gazing at the horizon. – Yes, Marita, my head has irreversibly changed.

- Good! That's really good. We humans of the Earth have this problem of just believing in what is "concrete". No wonder you thought so. Your experiences were not in vain. Science does not treat our myths and legends seriously. Inti, Wiracocha, Orejona, are only folklore for the academics. However the scholars know *everything* about Plato, Anaximander, the Egyptians, Pythagoras and they all lived daily, debated and studied myths and "gods" like Zeus, Pallas Athena, Apollo, Isis, Achilles, etc. The Greek mythology is well known, the Roman also, which, incidentally, has practically the same gods of the Greek, but with different names.

- It's a serious problem. Reputations come into play when there is no concrete evidence. I don't like it, but that's how it is. I'm not a naive geek anymore.

- Our Andean world, *señor* Fernando, is a real world, too. Existential, living, sensitive, holistic, immanent and affective. It is absurd to be considered as comic book keepers who exist to explain tribal customs and natural and atmospheric phenomena. South America also has history, and it is as important as the history of other civilizations on the planet.

They walked as they spoke. In a few minutes they were in the Temple of the Sun. A circular structure with the perfection of the walls of Qorikancha. An imposing and perfect wall containing three equidistant niches. These niches were made to accommodate the legendary stones of Orejona. The niche of the center was much larger than the others.

Marita then opened her backpack and took out five ritual pottery pots and incense. The priestess lit the incense and placed the five pots in places marked by small concave protrusions on the floor forming a circle in the center of the temple. She entered into this sacred circle and sang some chants in Quechua. She asked Fernando to enter the circle with her and kneel in respect to the forces of Nature. Then she began to tell about the myths of the Andean creation.

- The Andean culture conceives the Universe as the *Pacha*, or House, within which Life is contained and within which all beings exist harmonically through *los ejes espaciales*, or spatial axes, from top to bottom and from right to left. The origin of the Lake automatically implies the association of *Titikaka, Unu Pachacuti* and

Wiracocha. Look. *Unu* means "water." *Pacha* is the same as "land" and *Cuti* means "change, transformation or return". For those who understand the Quechua language, *Pachacuti* is the ancestral expression that describes the greatest catastrophe ever recorded: the Universal Deluge. All ancient cultures have their Genesis from a cataclysm of such proportion. *Unu Pachacuti* can be translated as "the destruction of the world by water" or "the water that upset the earth."

- It is true. The Flood myth was never exclusive to the Bible.

- The *Pachacuti* would be periodic or cyclical catastrophes and the last recorded was the Great Flood. *Pachacuti* restarts the cycle of life on the planet. The Andean tradition speaks of a rain that fell for 60 days and 60 nights, twenty days longer than the biblical flood. Mere detail. Every living thing disappeared then. Thereafter the Supreme God created a new post-Flood human race, the Second Age. At that time Wiracocha happens to be the main deity of the Andes. According to tradition, he was *El construtor Del Titikaka*. Wiracocha is the Andean relative for "the god of the gods" of other peoples, myths and beliefs around the world. Wiracocha, as divine unity, expresses the whole philosophical, scientific, religious and artistic fabric of the Andean peoples, and his teachings were the starting point for humanity from the beginning.

- But now we know Orejona is the great beginning. – said Fernando.

- But I'm not talking about Her now.

- Sorry.

- Her presence among the Andean peoples goes in Tiahuanaco as back as 10.000 BC, Pucara, 500 CE, Chavin de Huantar, 4,000 BC, and so it goes with the Paracas, the Wari, etc. All these civilizations existed and disappeared before the Inca. The figure of Wiracocha appears with several facets, for example, the Resplendent Man who steadied his feet in the Island of the Sun and it took an impulse to ascend to the skies. He is identified with the Sphinx *Man-Puma-Sun* of Tiahuanaco, or even The Sun of Suns. Wiracocha carried two scepters of power in his hands. It is also referred to as the "creator of the Lake, sent by the Greater

God". All the attributes of Wiracocha merge into a single name created to try to translate its majestic nature: *APU KONTIKI ILLA TECSE WIRACOCHA PACHA YACHACHIJ*, that is, Supreme Being, Light of Dawn, Water and Fire, Master Creator of the World.

- A name worthy of a god.

- A mythological source says that not only could Wiracocha modify the local geology, but also could construct lakes like the Titicaca with the power of his scepter. He also carved in granite all the imposing monoliths of the region, such as the Gate of the Sun.

- Interesting!

- The question is: are we, the Andeans, all descendants of the survivors of the cataclysm that swept Tiahuanaco? But before the *Unu Pachacuti,* before Wiracocha became the sovereign deity, there was already a civilization here.

- Orejona's! Said Fernando.

- No! Before hers.

- Before hers?

- Fernando, you must have heard about it. There was a continent right in the middle of the Pacific Ocean called Mu. Today we know Mu by the name of Lemuria, but this is the last part of that continent gone. The dates are not accurate, but the disappearance of Mu happened slowly. It began around the year 30,000 BC and continued for thousands of years until the total disappearance around the years 12,000 and 10,000 BC. The great initiatory masters of the *Senda de la Mano Sinistra,* responsible for the diabolical experiments that led to the destruction of that continent, dispersed throughout the world taking their knowledge to be taught to other civilizations.

- Why did they go to other parts of the world? Wasn't it enough to destroy your own home?

- Who are we to judge, Fernando? The world is what it is because of the unfolding of history. And, you know... not every story is told.

- So, knowledge then came from that continent just like the myths of other peoples?

- Yes, but not all the knowledge. There was also a brotherhood of pure beings whose mission was to revive life on the planet and to convey to the new humanity its secrets. They were the *Hermandad de los Siete Raios*. And it was for this reason that the *Isla del Sol* became a sacred place. The archaeological remains submerged in the Lake, combined with many discoveries around the world of remains of giant bones indicate the real presence of legendary and mythological *giant beings* that once lived on our planet.

- And these beings came from Mú?

- It's possible. Cieza de León, author of the famous "Chronicle of Peru", says that these giants were about six meters high. They were originally from the Lemurian and Atlantean races. They knew organ transplantation techniques, they had instruments capable of transmitting knowledge telepathically, but after these splendid achievements they entered an inexorable involution due to the flourishing of a second "evil nature" that slowly invaded their spirits. Human degradation and degeneration have reached unsustainable levels that have led to the destruction, for example, of Atlantis through nuclear weapons, bringing that humanity into chaos and self-destruction along with its formidable cities. A small group of the spiritual elite has been preserved to try, in test tubes, the regeneration of the human race based on genetic mutations under the new atmospheric conditions and physical laws resulting from violent modifications on the axis of the planet.

- You mean... genetic manipulation to adapt the human race to the planet?

- Yes. Archaeological evidence, which is not taken seriously by official archeology, shows that there were at least two higher humanities before our own in time immemorial when the Earth experienced several changes in its orbit. We know with certainty that there has been a solar year of 225 days and a solar year of 260 days because these calendars were engraved upon the stone. Our current planetary cycle of 365.25 days is due to change. These cataclysmic events of the past have led to radical changes in planetary physical laws causing many difficulties for human life.

- Got it. When the planet spun faster, gravity was lower and people could be six feet tall. – said Fernando, amazed at the scientific logic.

- The three worlds of pre-hispanic cosmology, *Hanan Pacha*, *Uran Pacha* and *Kay Pacha* are represented everywhere through the staggered pyramids we find throughout Peruvian culture, famous for their harmonious disposition and what they represent: the true condition of terrestrial humanity.

- Okay, we're talking about legends that are true. Why did they become legends? Why did they get lost?

- Humanity, in every corner of the globe, have a short memory, *señor* Fernando. The years pass, the silence of God crushes his creatures and faith evaporates. They think the myths of our ancestors were just legends.

- It's like the history of the people of Israel. They always fell because they didn't hear from their God. – Eastman added with a comparison that he found consistent.

- All Humanity tends to fall into disgrace when one loses the historical sense and the sense of the divine. Those who perceive that history is adulterated have the *duty* to rescue the truth by relying only on their own senses. Look around you. This temple was built in a semicircle and the line dividing the central niche was millimetrically aligned with the planet Venus. The Egyptians and the Mayas, for example, had their eye on Orion. The Andeans gazed at Venus.

- There is no difference between these cultures. Only its origins. Everyone had their gods somewhere off the planet.

- The sensitive, sometimes abrupt, changes of the axis of the Earth have misrepresented all the structures of the planet in relation to their stellar points of reference. These changes have in fact existed and the calculations of realignment of countless sites with their stars put all the official archeology in check. The chronology is all wrong, *señor* Fernando, but the truth will come out.

- I'm starting to put some pieces together here, Marita. Tell me more!

- I'm going to talk about these changes.

- *Hanan Pacha* is the first Earth orbit when the solar year was of 225 days and is expressed by the first step of the Andean pyramid. – Marita continued. – We're talking about thousands of years ago. Between 40,000 and 38,000 years. It was the moment of creation of a perfect humanity. It was the moment of the Adamic civilization. Adam was a big man. He was what we call a giant today. The gravitational conditions of that time favored the development of human beings of mental and physical quality far superior to ours. They were *immortal* beings. The whole kingdom of nature was of gigantic proportions. It was the stage of the greatest perfection and harmony ever achieved on this planet. The whole earth was a paradise.

- It was the time when Adam lived in Paradise. If Adam was confined to a "Garden", obviously there were other people building things around the world.

- This is as clear as the waters we crossed earlier. The disappearance of this civilization happened naturally by a *Pachacuti* that quickly transformed the gravitational forces of the planet. The mineral kingdom of that time was less dense also due to the gravitational forces and the proximity to the sun. The stones resembled a type of clay, which facilitated the magnificent stone work that survived as legacies for our admiration and which are scattered all over the world. This was how incredible places like Saqsayhuaman and Machu Picchu and many others were built. The fittings of the Saqsayhuaman megaliths were only possible because of the high temperatures of the *Hanan Pacha*.

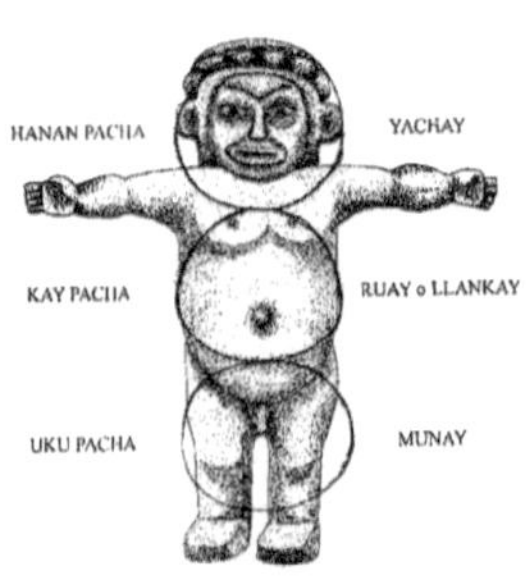

Fernando was enjoying that moment as much as he enjoyed his days in the desert. Marita's eyes gleamed as she spoke. It was possible to feel an incredible energy being generated during the conversation.

- *Uran Pacha* had a year of 260 days. It was the second period expressed by the second step of the Andean pyramid. Changes in physical laws made men, including the "first biblical men", lose many of their ancient attributes, such as immortality. Yet they lived many years. They then passed from Eternal Life to *Longevity* probably by a deliberate genetic mutation. God did not want men to live so long anymore. This is in the biblical Genesis.

- Yes of course. See the examples of Adam, Methuselah, Noah and others not so illustrious. They lived hundreds of years! The Sumerian texts speak of a dynasty of kings who lived and reigned in Mesopotamia for more than *two thousand years*. The Tzolkin calendar of the Mayas proves this longevity as well. – Eastman added.

- It was in this period that the second form of ancestral architecture originated. The ones we find all around the planet. The buildings that were superimposed on those of the first period and which are characterized here in the Andes by the presence of trapezoid niches and by the geometric perfection and fitting of huge blocks of stone. In Egypt you can see this type of stonework, too. The stones were of lower density than those of today, but higher than those of the *Hanan Pacha*. There was a technical evolution by the introduction of instruments made of a metal resistant to high temperatures, which allowed the *modeling* of stones after exposed to extreme heat. Today we would say that these stones were made by the molding process.

- Molds? It is possible?

- The best example of this technique is Qorikancha and the perfection of its walls plus the unmistakable brilliance, result from the process of vitrification. This temple reminds the ones in Qorikancha, doesn't it? – Marita said, looking around and showing the wonderful building they were at that moment.

- Yes, the smooth perfect blocks! They are molds, of course! How could you cut and polish those stones only with copper tools... or without any tools?

- This technology was brought to us by the Gods of Heaven, *señor* Fernando. All the cultures of the world are related to some of them. The Inca, the Aztecs, the Mayans, Egyptians, Hindus, Sumerians, Celts, Chinese, Japanese, etc... These civilizations lived for many years. The Bible talks about this time, but omits important information that we know has been hidden for centuries by people who do not want us to know anything.

- Yes! The apocryphal book of Enoch tells us that the fallen angels brought to Earth their technical knowledge. Enoch cites all the names and their specialties, their "jobs". So that's what made these buildings possible! The technology of the "gods", which were actually the rebellious Angels that the God of the Bible caused to fall. Is that right, Marita? Is it like... "The chariot of the Gods"?

- Is it so difficult to see?

- The creation of Orejona is from this period?

- Yes. They were destroyed by the fury of Nature that erased the Earth's Adamic creation with the famous flood. It was the beginning of the new humanity: the Noetic civilization. No more longevity. In fact, the biblical God hasn't erased anyone from here. The Universal Flood was *universal,* as the name says. It was a *natural* cataclysm. It occurred around 10,940 BC. When we read that Yahweh assured us that he would never exterminate us again with water, we should not believe that promise. Yahweh is *not* the Creator, so he *cannot avoid* natural disasters.

They both paused. Marita breathes deeply with her eyes closed, as if searching for spiritual connections. Fernando tries to piece the puzzle together. After a few eternal minutes, he asks Marita to continue.

- With the Flood began *Kay Pacha,* our present day. The age of mortality. It is the third cycle of humanity and the third step of the Andean pyramid. The new alignment of the Earth and the extreme gravitational force of our Sun caused the planet to change its gravity resulting in greater density and weight. *"Now man is flesh and blood and will live no more than 120 years",* says our tradition. The

Bible says something very similar in Genesis 6:3. "*And the LORD said, My spirit shall not always strive with man, for that he also is flesh: yet his days shall be an hundred and twenty years*".

- And then the New Age has arrived. The time we live in now.

- That's right, *señor* Eastman. Our time. The natural cataclysm we know as the great Flood took the Earth out of its old orbit and our cycle became of 365 days. The Great Pyramid of Egypt is from that time. It was built together with the Sphinx with the help of Earth humans.

- I believe in you, *señora*, but it's practically impossible to prove what you're saying. At the same time, it is the only sensible explanation for the megaliths scattered around the world. Our proofs are the monuments that have been engraved upon the stones.

- Compared to the previous ages today, in the *Kay Pacha*, the human organism has to withstand an atmospheric pressure of one kilogram per square centimeter, which means that an adult person lives under a pressure of 15 tons of atmosphere on their head. This prevents us from moving heavy megaliths as we did in the past eras. These conditions gave the humans of today their diminutive physical and mental characteristics. A giant would be crushed under today's atmosphere.

- I see... we have adapted, or rather we *were adapted* to the new gravity.

- We could no longer work the stones with the old technique, for the density of the materials no longer permitted. This is evident on the Spanish buildings of Cuzco. It's easy to see the tool marks on the perfect stones taken from the old buildings of the previous era. In Saqsayhuaman there are clearly three types of constructions. The *Hanan Pacha* style, incredibly large megaliths shaped like modeling mass by giant beings who lived in Paradise on Earth. The *Uran Pacha*, Adam's post-fall period when walls and portals were made with smooth blocks, niches and perfect gradients of 5 to 6 degrees built with the technology of the gods, probably the "fallen angels". And the *Kay Pacha*, the post-Flood period with stones worked by human hands with little precision and settled with the use of mortar. One above the other, as if one civilization were "reforming and reusing" the sites left by the previous one. This is what Machu Picchu is about and many other places in the Andes. And also around the world.

- Orejona told me she came to this Planet 40,000 years ago.

- Yes. Orejona is located in *Uran Pacha*, after Adam's fall and before the Flood. The official chronology is all wrong. It is part of a conspiracy to prevent us to know the truth.

- Of course! The Genesis of Melchizedek! The notebook! Orejona descended here while Paradise was being implanted on Earth. According to Melchizedek, Paradise was not on Earth but in the Cosmos. The text says that The Eternal creates the Earth in seven days with all living beings, including Mankind, and gives Adam the power to rule the Universe. Lucifer had to kneel before Adam. He didn't, so he "fell". This is the link between Venus and Lucifer. Orejona is from Venus, she comes to this planet and begins her own humanity. Does Lucifer have anything to do with it?

- I think Lucifer has nothing to do with Orejona. As far as I know, the link is due to the mighty brightness of this celestial body that can be see with naked eye. Lucifer was the Bearer of Light. Venus bears a beautiful bright light. But by the way the relations end there. We also know that this connection between the devil and Lucifer is something of the recent and dreadful Christian culture.

- That's true. You're right. Lucifer shows up late in the "divine narrative", but you never know. Orejona is a great novelty to me. The Book, the skulls, all this was legend to me... until a few days ago.

- *Señor* Fernando, if for a moment we could only draw our attention off the banality in which we transform our existence and turn our focus to what is *real*, we would find wonderful truths that would surely fill the enormous emptiness we carry within us. Unfortunately the scenario we have in our 21st Century is not conducive to understanding certain aspects of our earthly life. We are surrounded by all possible kinds of material aspects. Planet Earth is under the rule of matter, addictions, lies and illusions, the desperate eagerness to obtain more and more material stuff. That is why we left behind the true essence of reality. That is why the terrestrial human race has become a simple race of mortals... captives of progress and technological development.

- But this is not totally negative. Technology helps us *a lot*. If there was no technology, we would probably not be talking right now. This analysis is very clear. Looking back, it's possible to understand the changes that the technological revolution has brought to humanity. Technology is fundamental. Inevitability.

- Yes, of course. Capable minds naturally tend to technological development, as history shows. But our *spirit* is almost dead. The spiritual aspect of existing on this planet is not being well utilized. I do not think going back to the Stone Age is the way out, but this whole *tech breakthrough* should be more cadenced and egalitarian without losing sight of its implications.

- What do you mean?

- This whole technology is socially excluding and disrupting. We pay a very high price for abandoning our divine nature. Technology is interested only in material development. There's nothing spiritual about it. It is the equivalent of growing in an environment without oxygen or water. It is as if we believed that we could live and prosper without our heads. The destruction of this planet happens 24/7. We know how this is gonna end. We must ask ourselves what degree of ignorance we have achieved! We look to the solution of the problem with an indolence which is unheard of! And the solution is in our hands! But we do not believe that this planet has ever had a golden age, that there was another way of thinking, a better organized society and more balanced dwellers. The great masters have taught us to think on a different level, but we have chosen to ignore them for the sake of matter. We don't know what peace is, but yet we crave for balance, harmony and dignity. We rejoice in faith and respect for the history of our ancestors. This history, deliberately erased *from history*, is laden with eternal truths like these rocks we find all over the world. Universal values of happiness.

- Do you know how the civilization of Orejona was organized? How did they live, what were their customs? Where does Lucifer fit into all this?

- I do not know, but *you* will! Where Lucifer fits? Well, *señor* Fernando. Look around you. He owns this whole planet. He lies and deceives. That's how he plays. We play on the other team. You, I and a few who do not kneel before the Darkness, we are of the team of Truth. And we will *never* kneel. We do not lie to anyone. This is impossible to do when a person achieves a certain degree of consciousness.

- Explain.

- As I speak within this circle, as I tell you what I learned through the elders of the Uros of the Sacred Lake who keep the tradition, I can see your aura, *señor* Fernando. Yours is violet blue. You are the person who can find the entrance of the pyramid of Tiahuanaco. Only a free spirit can emanate this aura steadily.

- I beg your pardon. Did you say... Pyramid?

- It's time to go, *señor* Fernando. You must go to Tiahuanaco immediately. History can't wait any longer. You will stop at Puma Punku. Look for the newly discovered camera. You have the gift of getting into people's minds and making them obey you. Use this power for good. They say they did not find the entrance to the chamber yet, but it's there. You will go in there and meditate a little. Take your time. *Buy* time if necessary. Then talk to a foreign man who lives in the village of Tiahuanaco. He knows a lot about the mysteries of the site. He will be very pleased to speak with you. He will definitely help you!

- The third man! – remembered Fernando.

Fernando disembarks in Copacabana, Bolivia, and says goodbye to Marita with a long hug.

- May the Light be with you, *señor* Fernando. Do what has to be done. Nothing can stop you but yourself. And remember! Do not confuse *senses* with *feelings*. There's danger in the air. Follow your *senses*. If you sense that something is wrong, respect your senses and run away! This is more important than all your earthly *feelings*.

- I'm on the case, Marita. You can trust.

- I trust.

No time to spare! Fernando quickly negotiates a ride to Puma Punku. The rarefied air of altitude does not bother him anymore, but even so being in the highlands is a difficult task.

Puma Punku is on a desert plateau 72 kilometers from La Paz at an altitude of almost 4,000 meters. The name is Aymara and means "The Cougar Gate". The site consists of large blocks of stone which are scattered all around the place as if they were toy parts. Almost all the blocks are buried under a thick layer of *mud* and the site is not yet fully excavated. The building style is unique on the planet. The main part is 167 meters long by 116 meters wide containing a terrace in the east that measures about 7 by 39 meters all paved with huge blocks of stone. In this terrace, called "lithic platform", there is one of the largest artificial blocks of the Earth reaching up to 8 meters in length and weighing almost 130 tons.

Evidence shows that everything had been destroyed by a great flood. It is also evident that, in addition to the flood, there was a *previous* destruction that scattered all the blocks on the ground and crushed these solid giants as if they were cookies. The crushed stones of Puma Punku are scattered all over the site. The question is: where did the flood come from if the area is almost 4,000 meters high? From Lake Titicaca? In 1945, researcher Arthur Posnansky, after using a peculiar star alignment system, came to the conclusion that the site is at least 17,000 to 15,000 years old, but may be even older. This puts Puma Punku in a pre-Flood time. This is the biggest and most irrefutable proof that there were many people all over the planet Earth, not just in Mesopotamia.

It is not yet known what was its purpose was or how it was built. It is in Puma Punku that there are the famous "H-blocks" that seem to have been manufactured like in an industrial assembly line considering the hardness of the material and the perfection of its angles and finishings. No one can imagine the splendor of this place at the time it was operational. The megalithic walls of incredible precision of fitting were adorned with polished metal plates, but the time took it away. Not mentioning the looters and the Bolivian army which used the site to practice canon shooting.

Game over for Puma Punku.

We'll never know anything about it.

Recently an underground anomaly was found about 20 meters from the foundations of Puma Punku. Images made with the aid of a sonar indicate that it may be a chamber, perhaps a tomb, but nothing is known yet. The supposed chamber has something close to two meters high, four meters long and one and a half meters wide, and is very close to the surface. The sonar images are not clear, but there may be steps leading to their interior which seems to have been filled up with debris. The researching team suggests that the debris were placed purposely to make access difficult. At the back of the chamber there's an object that looks like a sarcophagus.

What might it be?

***

Fernando arrives at the site and soon looks for the person in charge of the excavations. A big man named *señor* Domingos walks toward him with an unhappy look. Domingos Calles is a tall, fat Bolivian, about 50 years of age and not very gentle in dealing with people. He does not like the meddling of tourists in his projects. He is one of those archaeologists who follows the official primer of the great Universities. For him there is no place for "conspiracies" in Archeology.

- What do you want, *señor*? Do you want to talk to me?

- I heard you are the responsible for the excavations.

- Yes. What do you want? – insisted Domingos sharply.

- I would like to see the *câmara* that was found here recently. It's important! I am a researcher of the Andean culture and I really need to see it...

- It is not possible, sir. It is not open to the public. – he said dryly, turning his back on Fernando, who insisted.

- I'm not a tourist, *señor*. I need to see this chamber. What was found there, *señor* ...

- Domingos. My name is Domingos.

- Pleased to meet you, *señor* Domingos. My name is Fernando. Fernando Eastman. – he said with a certain hesitation. – I'm doing some research on the funerary methods of the Andean civilizations. They say that you have found a, chamber, *una câmara* here and...

- We all know who you are. A few days ago you were being chased by the Peruvian police. Theft and smuggling of historical artifacts. Hit the road, *señor* Fernando Eastman! – said Domingos with a certain tone of irony. – Otherwise, I'll call our police. They are still looking for you there in Peru. Our cops are very efficient when they catch thieves like you.

- You are mistaken, *señor* Domingos. I just...

- By the way, nothing was found in there. Only walls without inscriptions or artifacts. And a huge black stone block that we still do not know what it's all about. There's nothing valuable here, *señor*. There's nothing to steal! Now, hit the road, *hijo de puta*! – he said, going to Fernando like he was going to punch him.

Eastman was not afraid of the imminent aggression, for he was determined to see the chamber. Nothing would stop him, and he knew it. He understood the nervousness of *señor* Domingos. He just didn't want trouble. Without leaving the serenity acquired in the desert, Fernando imagined the light of the stone he experienced a few days ago in Paracas. He stared into the huge man's eyes. The Bolivian simply stopped, changed his tone, and kindly authorized Fernando to enter the chamber.

"Awesome!" – Eastman thought to himself.

- *Señor* Eastman... on second thought... make yourself at home. *Mi casa, su casa.* Follow me and I'll take you to the entrance.

The two men walked around the complex as good old colleagues. They headed east and stopped right in front of a narrow hole in the shaded ground marked with four stakes and a yellow strip.

- It's here, *señor* Fernando. When entering this hole you must look for a step to support the feet. If I can pass, I'm sure you can, too. Take this flashlight. You'll need it. Natural light does not go in there. Going down the stairs, you will come across a small passage and you'll have to crawl to cross it. The place is quite small. Are you claustrophobic?

- *Gracias, señor* Domingos. *Gracias!* – thanked Fernando already down the hole. – Do not worry. I'm used to it.

- You're welcome. If you need something, talk to me. I'll be in my office. – the man replied gently aloud as he walked away from the place, resuming his bureaucratic duties.

There was plenty of time. Fernando had bought it directly from the brute man with the use of his own mind.

Awesome! – he said to himself as he descended on a rope. It was not too deep. Soon he felt that his feet had support and he went forward. He let go of the rope and walked down the small steps to the chamber. There was a small antechamber that was very low. It was five feet high by two feet wide and two feet long.

- How the hell Domingos crossed this thin corridor?

The little corridor's was like a bridge. The floor rose halfway at an angle of about fifteen degrees, then fell to the mouth of the chamber. The ceiling, mirroring the floor, went down at the entrance and up to the mouth of the main chamber. The passage was really narrow. The polishing of the stone of the floor reflected back any light that could enter from outside. Fernando had to crawl through the small space until he could get up.

The newly discovered chamber was very small. Two people would be too much in there. There was a black parallelepiped stone. It was black as night, about a meter in length, half a meter high and a foot deep. Fernando came slowly in, observing everything around with the help of the flashlight. The little chamber really had no inscription on its blackish gray walls. They were smooth as polished marble. There was no glow on the walls, despite the perfect polish.

- That's weird! – said Fernando. – There's no humidity here. These walls should not have this matte aspect.

He touched the left wall with his hand and the texture was very interesting, a kind of velvety material, soft to the touch, but hard as stone. A very peculiar material which did not even reflect the light of the flashlight. It was as if the walls were absorbing the light. "These stones are not normal!", he thought. He stopped in front of that black parallelepiped capriciously lying on the opposite side of the entrance. Fernando pointed the flashlight directly at it and soon realized that the block also absorbed the light. He decided to put out the lantern and try to get used to the darkness. "Maybe I can see better if I get used to the blackness."

Fernando sat down and tried to relax. He closed his eyes and took some slow deep breaths. Soon he felt that there was a strong energy coming from the ground. His body was voluntarily relaxed. He lost track of time. At some point Fernando realized that he was in a state of levitation. It captured a strange brightness around him and opened his eyes. The stone is not black anymore. It had turned into a white parallelepiped, of a milky and brilliant crystal. The opposite extreme of the color he saw when he entered the room. He looked back and saw that the light did not reflect because the walls were absorbing it. The stone was the only source of light. And it was pure light. A light that did not hurt the eyes. In serenity, he accepted the situation without going through the rational process of thinking, that is, he accepted that moment as something desired. "Marita did not send me here for nothing!"

The absence of fear made Fernando absorb every moment of the experience. Before the stone, little by little, an image began to form. It was like a hologram. He saw Lia and Rico being released and taken to the airport to leave the country.

He was in peace.

Then the scene changed. Eastman saw himself and Orejona sitting face to face. He realized that his reactions were not quiet. He could not hear what they were saying, no matter how much he concentrated. He nodded, gestured, listened a lot, spoke too. It was not a conversation. It was like a debate.

The image changed again. Now he saw his father. "He's alive!", he said to himself mentally and with astonishment. Old Eastman wore peasant clothes. His skin was quite burnt and he seemed to be in Tiahuanaco, in the *Plaza de las Cabezas*, looking around trying to find something. It was like a movie. After this image the stone was extinguished. It returned to its original color, the darkest black. Fernando gradually returned to the normal state of mind and reversed the state of levitation in which he was. The experience was absolutely ecstatic.

- *Wow*! The mind works different here in the highlands

After being able to get up again, Fernando left the chamber, went through the antechamber, climbed the steps, left the improvised entrance hole with the help of the rope and ran in search of *señor* Domingos. He took him by the shoulders, fixed the look in his eyes and asked for a car to go to Tiahuanaco.

- *Señor* Domingos, please, I need a car! Is it urgent!

He promised to return as soon as possible. Domingos immediately handed the key to his jeep.

- Thank you very much, my friend!

DAY 20 – 6pm

Tiahuanaco appears before Fernando. The sun suggests to be setting. The image is something really worthy of the gods. The strong blue, the few clouds and a small yellow that begins to form in the horizon. There is still plenty of light and this provides a truly exhilarating experience for those who still stop to contemplate the sky. Since our sun "decides" to set, from that moment when it begins to dusk until the arrival of darkness of the night, Nature presents us with the greatest of spectacles that unfolds every moment of eternity never repeating itself. Each moment is a different color, a setting of different clouds, a different feel. A sunset can change a whole life. It is a magical experience. If Adam, as Melchizedek says, feared the fall of the night because he feared not to see the Light of the Father again is because he never paid attention to the unconditional proof of love that by the Cosmos day after day after day...

This scene is powerful enough to dissolve the fear of darkness. And perhaps this is our true goal as a human species created by an Ineffable Being and purposefully developed on Earth: TO UNLEARN FEAR.

(That's just a tip.)

Puma Punku and Tiahuanaco have a strong connection, as does Lake Titicaca and its islands. Tiahuanaco was a place of pilgrimage in honor of the gods of the sky gods. The two sites were built at different times in history and by different people and techniques. The former is regarded by tradition as the true home of the gods on Earth. It was probably built in the antediluvian time of the Orejona civilization. Legends say that the entire city, with its magnificent and impossible stone blocks, was "built in one night by the gods." Erich Von Daniken talks about two architectures in the region. Puma Punku and its genuine extraterrestrial architecture and Tiahuanaco with its human architecture. It was in this second temple that Orejona left Her information.

It is in the main square of Tiahuanaco, the majestic and imposing *Kalasasaya*, which is the famous Gate of the Sun. It originally belonged to the Puma Punku complex, but was brought to Tiahuanaco for tourist reasons. There is another identical door lying among the buried remains of Puma Punku. Tradition says that it was through this door that Orejona and other beings from other planets and galaxies communicated with the humans of the Earth.

Tiahuanaco was *also* considered by the ancient men of the region as the "navel of the Earth".

***

The sun passes right in the center of the gate dedicated to himself. The Sun is the God of all ancient civilizations. As it passes, a great orange dominates the sky gradually merging with the darkening blue. Fernando runs to the *Plaza de las Cabezas*. He already know. His father is there, looking around, as in the image of the stone a few minutes ago. Old Eastman was drawn to that square by something beyond his comprehension. Fernando comes close to the man and holds him tightly. With joy. He never thought his father was dead, but he'd never imagined meeting him in this mess.

- What are you doing here, father? Why did it disappear? – he said with watering eyes. A kind of contained strong reaction.

- I came for what you're after, son. I came after the truth. contained said Paulo Eastman serenely.

- Your skin is burned. Your hands... why did you disappear, dad? What happened? How did you get here?

- It was my destiny, son. I had to realize my legend. Your mother never understood my head. I became interested in the mysteries of the world a long time ago, when I was young, before I was even married. She thought it was a waste of time and money.

- I know. She hasn't changed a bit.

- I set up a business, dedicated myself and built an empire, earned all the money she could ever need in life to live as she always wanted, in the banalities of the vain, empty world of "high society". She never missed my presence. We rarely talked because either I was working to support her foolish lifestyle or I was traveling feeding my spirit. I rarely attended social circles with your mother.

- You didn't see each other much.

- I think it was better that way. For me it was. You and I never stayed together too long, son. I deeply regret this, but I knew that when we were together you had quality company. I did my best to make it happen. I see now that I was not wrong. When I saw that you were a born intellectual and were about to enter the college of Anthropology, I decided it was time to go after my legend because you were already on a good track. You could be a researcher as you always wanted.

- Relax, Eastman! – said Fernando. – Don't worry. It's all right. I was very sad at the time you disappeared, but now I understand.

- I'm not apologizing or rationalizing my choices so you understand the inexplicable and forgive me. I just had to do everything I did. I *had* to disappear to have the serenity to my precious work of researching the mysteries that intrigued my soul. I'm still trying to discover some truth. I hope you have not been angry with me.

- No, dad. – he said with his hands on the old man's face. – Don't worry. I didn't stop being that kid interested in crazy stuff. Living alone in Brasilia was the best thing that happened to me. I thank you eternally for what you have done for me, for everything you have taught me. Thank you for developing the craving for knowledge in me. Now I thank you for having taken the right attitude towards you and your happiness.

- I'm happy, son. You have a very good head.

- I never thought you were dead. My God! I don't know what to say. It was as if I had some kind of connection with you.

- When I heard that you were being sought, shortly after learning of the discovery at Machu Picchu, I knew you would end up here, after all here is the center of worship of Orejona. Domingos kept me informed, even though he did not even know my name. I used the technique taught by the wise man Juan Navarro. You must have talked to him. It's very convenient to be anonymous here in the Bolivian highlands.

- Yes! Domingos only let me in the chamber and lent me his jeep because of the mentalization of the stone. Very efficient.

- Let's go to my house, son. You need to rest. I imagine you've entered the chamber down there in Puma Punku. Your mind must be fully recharged, ready for anything, but your body needs rest. The night is coming and the temperature falls pretty fast here in the dry air. – said old Paulo Eastman as he walked with his son out of the square. – The weather here is killer. I'm all wrinkled, see. – he said with a faint tone of irony, showing his face dehydrated and burned by the sun and the cold at the same time.

- I know... you've always had wrinkles, old man. – he said amiably as if they had never failed to see each other.

- I need to talk about many things you need to know, and this can't wait.

- Sure, let's go.

Fernando felt as if he had just found a close friend. There were no cheap sentimentalisms. One looked at the other and they understood each other in a different type of communication. A type that only great friends have.

They went to old Eastman's house. Fernando entered and soon realized that his father had no luxury in his tiny room. Two rooms only. His bed was to the right of the main room, in the corner diagonally opposite the front door. There were two armchairs, a table that served as study desk and dining room. On the corner above the bed there were shelves with lots of books, many stacks of note papers and drawings he had made through the years. There was no television, no Internet, not even a heating system. Only a refrigerator, a gas stove and good lighting. The floor was made of wood and polished with wax.

Attached to this room, and almost bigger than the house itself, Paulo Eastman made sure that the sanitary conditions of the house were kept in the minimum standards of dignity. He had an excellent bathroom built with a wonderful shower and a space for some gym equipment, especially a treadmill. The old man had great insights as he walked and exercised. Usually he uses the treadmill listening to Mozart. He taught Fernando Mozart's music instigates the mind.

Fernando takes a good shower, returns to the main room and sits in one of the chairs that seemed to be there just for him. His father was already sitting across from him with a deep inner peace, calmly enjoying his pipe. The boy watches his father for a few seconds. The old man's face did not change much. Suddenly he breaks the silence that had hung in that room for endless seconds.

- I didn't know you smoked.

- That's old man's stuff, Fernando. Does it bother you?

- No, it's OK.

- Nicotine wakes me up here at the altitudes. If I smoked cigarettes I'd be dead already.

- How long have you lived here?

- Since I understood that this is my place. When I decided to live my life I left Brasilia and headed northwest to Acre. I imagined that I would find the lost pyramid of Orejona there, in Brazilian territory.

- Tell me about it. What adventure was that? What is your motivation to go out like a nut and disappear? How did you spend so much time without being identified?

- Son, the estimated latitudes and longitudes of the pyramid are very close to here. Everything indicated that it would be there, in Brazilian lands, but it is not. I then proceeded from the south of Acre to the side of Peru and ascended to Lake Titicaca. The two times I visited the Lake I felt the enormous energy of the place and tried to understand how that was possible.

- It's intriguing.

- I spent a few months there in Puno on one of the Uros Islands, living with them and studying their myths. I met a very spiritual lady who told me about the complex on the Island of the Sun on the Bolivian side. Her name is Marita. She told me about creation myths and many other things. You must have talked to her too, haven't you?

- Yes! A few hours ago I was with her on the Island. It was she who sent me to the Puma Punku chamber. If I only knew she knew you...

- It wouldn't be the same, Fernando. She obviously recognized your name and said nothing. You had to go to Puma Punku before you found me.

- I understand.

- Did you see the stone? What did you see inside of it? Did it "say" something to you?

- It was a great experience. – said Fernando as he settled into the chair. – I sat on the floor of the chamber and when I realized I was levitating. The stone turned white and projected images of the past, the future and the present. I saw you there. That's why I ran to find you there at the *plaza*.

- I sensed your arrival, son. As in the movie Star Wars, you know? It was a very strong thing. I already knew you were around. I never meant to go there and wait for you. Something called me there and I just responded to it. – said Paulo with a certain astonishment.

A brief pause was made.

- So the stone went white? Tell me.

- They were like holographic images in three dimensions. I saw my friends who helped me to get to a good part of the way, I saw you here in the *plaza*, but the craziest of all: I saw myself sitting face to face with Orejona and I didn't like it at all. What do you know about Her?

- Did you get my notebook? I had it delivered to the airport before you board.

- Yes! So it was you? How did you know I was going to Peru? How did you know about my flight schedule?

- I have my contacts, Fernando. A person I can trust. He is my faithful squire. Whenever I needed, he helps me by sending money from an account I created for my retreat. There's enough money for my whole life. After all I spend almost nothing here.

- Why did you send the notebook? Why those highlighted words? What is your purpose with it? How can this help me?

- The words were obvious. You will understand.

- What do you mean?

- Orejona has created a civilization here in these lands, exactly where you are sitting. The Bible speaks only of Adam and his descendants. The whole world was indoctrinated with the idea that Adam was the first man, but the evidence screams the opposite. Here on the shores of the Sacred Lake there lived a civilization contemporary to Adam. They were giants toward us and lived throughout here. This Tiahuanaco complex was not created by them, but by their descendants, the few who survived the destruction that is known as the Universal Deluge, a natural event that changed the planet.

"Yes, the *Unu Pachacuti* after Adam's fall. The event that put the Earth on the *Kay Pacha*.

- It's the natural planetary cycle. The counterfeit narrative of the Bible attributes a natural event to their "god".

- When was that?

- We do not know when that happened. It is presumed that all this happened 10,940 years ago, when the Earth entered the descending path of its orbit in relation to the zodiac. A phenomenon we call the Precession of the Equinoxes. It's what scientists call the Cosmic Year. Our planet aligns with all the twelve constellations in a cycle of 25,920 years.

- I'll try to follow. Go ahead.

- Divide it by 12 and every 2,160 years a certain constellation rules the skies of the northern hemisphere. The flood occurred when the constellation of Leo was in the sky. The Sphinx was built with the body of Leo in honor of this constellation. The man's face represents the constellation of Hercules, the polar reference of the post-flood era. The whole set is oriented towards the horizon. And that was 10,940 BC. The Egyptians call this year *Zep Tepi*.

- *Zep Tepi* is the beginning of the new time. – completes the young man. – It was the time-frame for the emergence of a new civilization. And this landmark is recorded in ancient hieroglyphics.

- Son, do the math. From the birth of Christ until today, it has been 2013 years. According to some rough estimates, December 21, 2012 marked the great passage from the Age of Pisces to the Age of Aquarius. The reference date is the date of the Flood. December 21, 10,948 BC.

- What? Do we have a date?

- Look. If my calculations are right and 21/12/2012 is really the date of the Age change, we are at this very moment on the ascending path of heaven beginning a new phase of the Cosmic Year. But these calculations are not very reliable. Anyway December 21, 2012 was a milestone of profound changes on the planet.

- That's great!

- Every start is painful in some way. – said Paulo, wandering a little.

Silence for a few seconds. They had different looks. One was attentive. The other, distant. Paulo Eastman kept talking, staring into the void, apparently changing the subject. Fernando tried to keep up.

- When we read about creation in the Bible or the Apocrypha, we cannot conceive, for example, the seven days of creation as the 24-hour days we have today. I think, and this seems to me more plausible, that each day represents an era of evolution on a geological scale. You can't speed things up that way. If God really created everything in six days and rested in the seventh, how do you explain the previous ages of dinosaurs, for example? – argued the old man. – Or the obvious existence of beings other than humans across the planet in remote ages? Are these elongated skulls not strong evidence?

- It would be ridiculous to think that God created the fossils together with the planet or "invented" the story that created everything as we know it today. – completed Fernando. – But there are people who believe that fossils were created by god to *test* the faithfulness of their creation.

- I'm talking about the God I know as the Creator Logos. It is no "god" with human characteristics. It took ages for the planet to be ready for us. It would make no sense doing it all in a magic trick. In fact the planet is a living being that has self-adapted over countless ages. In my humble understanding, something made some kind of intervention in the living Mother Earth to set the environment for the humans of today. Or was the planet herself, who knows? I think our planet has always been a testing ground.

- It's the Farming Theory.

- Right! The Creator prepared everything by observing how the atmosphere developed to, after having attained an ideal environment, create the creature "Man". – says Paulo. – That may sound like a great absurdity to some, but it makes sense to me. These two new beings, Adam and Eve, were much larger than us in stature and mental capacity and lived much longer. All creation and post-fall humanity was giant and lived between one thousand and two thousand years of the planetary cycle of their time. And the planet was propitious to that. That's what I think. – he added. – Did Marita tell you about the density of our atmosphere?"

- Yes.

- When "god" destroyed his first creation, nothing remained of these creatures. It was not like the dinosaurs that were swallowed up by the earth and turned into gasoline. It is rare to find giant skeletons on Earth because they were few individuals and their bodies were probably devoured by surviving hungry animals or fall apart in the water. There is nothing left of these organisms. Those who survived were forced by nature to adapt. They went down in size, but very few survived and continue here.

In that event the Earth changed axis, orbit and all physical laws were modified. Some geneticist "god" genetically modified the descendants of Noah to adapt them to the new conditions of the planet. That's how I see things.

- Last month I would say that this is absurd and that I would never accept such an idea, but today I have no doubts! This is absolutely possible. – said Fernando with joy.

- Humanity began to live less, became smaller in size and their mental capacity was naturally diminished. The bone density became heavier, the cranial volume had to be decreased and the man could no longer carry that privileged brain. In short, the cosmic natural event became synonymous with a "punishment of God" for the degeneration of the sons of Adam. But all the other civilizations of the globe were heavily hit and suffered irretrievable losses. The sons of Orejona were decimated. There was nothing left of them, just the lost stone.

- And the skulls of Paracas and the whole world? Who are they?

- The skulls we find all over the Andes are modifications of other races based on the giant originals. There must have survived only a few dozen of them, but they soon spread all over the Pacific coast. We do not know for sure how many survived or where they went. In fact we know nothing about this breed. The geneticist "god" made modifications in the descendants of Shem, son of Noah. They grew up and made history. It is said that they were enslaved by the Egyptians, conquered by the Assyrians, Babylonians, scattered throughout the world. To put in a nutshell, the whole story of the Bible seems to be the only story in the world.

- There is much more than just Semites, Hebrews, Egyptians or Greeks... Puma Punku is antediluvian!

- That's why I outlined some words in my notebook.

- Explain...

- Orejona came from Venus and gave birth here on Earth, didn't she?

- Yes.

- Many other visitors have come here and raised their peoples. This is evident. Adam is a really special case because the one who created him was the one we got used to calling God. But the Bible does not tell half the story. If you pay attention in the featured words of the Apocrypha, you will read things that lead you to think of travels between dimensions, dimensional portals, that is, both, the creation of Orejona and Adam and his group were created by beings who traveled through space. And still travel!!!

- That is very clear now. Go on.

- God also had to materialize here on earth. Words like "divine government" make one think of political plots. God created the universe in which we live with His word, the Divine Word, and bestowed life based on two basic principles: "to love one's neighbor" and "to live in brotherhood." The Universe was created, according to the apocryphal text, "full of life," the galaxies were "full of life and joy."

- All these traits are human feelings.

- The text speaks of "inhabited worlds", "capital planets", "rational beings". Everything points to other civilizations off the Earth and long before Earth was created!

- Or developed consciously, as Gaia Theory says. But the interesting thing is that Melchizedek's text speaks of "sidereal excursion"! This is very revealing! – says Fernando. – I can only imagine spaceships coming and going from planet to planet.

- The author of the text attributed to Melchizedek speaks of Lucifer as the "Bearer of Light". We also have the idea that the Angel was something like a Prime Minister in a system of government. The Creator's Freedom of Choice already foresaw a possible rebellion, that is, our reality today was all planned from the very beginning just as a government plans its goals and management strategies.

- Wow! That's bombast! – exclaims Fernando with wide eyes.

- That's what you get from reading and meditating on these apocryphal texts, my son. Especially the one I sent you. And all this current situation happened because of a cosmic political plot.

Sci-fi stuff. Look, when god commanded the Light to be made, he "revealed a world still unfinished", says Melchizedek. The planet already existed, Gaia was already transforming in the darkness of the Cosmos, she just was not ready to receive life. It was already known that there would be a battle between Love and Selfishness. The "victorious return of God" had already been foreseen after the plot of Lucifer. He brought the Garden of Eden to Earth. This means that this place, Eden, already existed outside the planet.

- This passage is really impressive.

- He, the Creator Logos, created the "living soul reptiles" before humans. I imagine that this "living soul" is a soul-spirit like ours, or something rational. The text says that God "went down" in the new world. This means: a Being came to the planet from another place.

- Well, Jesus himself said his kingdom is not of this Earth. Was he an ET?"

- We like the word extraterrestrial a lot, but I particularly prefer the term *outlander*. A Being from somewhere other than Earth. Applying these ideas to our reality, we are all the offspring of an Being from outside the Earth, that is, an Extraterrestrial Being, who knew about genetic manipulation. He placed Adam in "deep sleep" and created a female being from a body tissue of the first man. Lucifer, out of envy, or, as the Islamic text says, out of infinite love for its creator, felt offended when he was told to kneel and submit to Adam. That is why he "incorporated" a "reptilian being" and "deceived" the beautiful couple with his "eloquence". He made Eve believe that she would have a "higher level of life". The lie led to Adam's "decision" that resulted in the condition of mankind today. Adam's decision also resulted in a divine "redemption plan".

- That version of the story makes much more sense, but is it possible to prove this? I mean, I believe this version is more likely than the official, but the world does not see it that way.

- It's a struggle before us. We have the duty to reinterpret our history, to rediscover it based on these "new" information that comes from the past. But this is still not very clear, they are just theories. You need to go deeper. You need to use the evidence you already have and maximize it, find more information to legitimize it. You have to be brave. This is your job as an archaeologist!

Paulo looks into Fernando's eyes and pauses for a moment. He puts some more tobacco in the pipe. Fernando observes while he thinks about what is being said.

- Back to the lost pyramid. Where do you think she might be? – asked the young Eastman.

- Right here, Fernando. Right here below our feet. – said the old man with unshakable certainty. – Don't you have the feeling there's something under your feet when you walk around? Don't you feel the energy?

- Yes, it's very strong. Marita told me about a pyramid here in Tiahuanaco. It must be here. I feel it! Dad, I've been through so much these last few weeks that I have no doubts anymore. Do you have any idea how this pyramid might be or what its size?

- Yes, it's big!

- Is the stone we're looking for going to be in there?

- I think only you will know. Did you know that the original name of Tiahuanaco is actually Chucara? Doesn't it remind you of another name? Remember, we are talking about pyramids. – said Paula as giving a tip to the boy he taught to think years ago.

- Saccara? In Egypt? – replied Fernando strangely.

- Yes. We are talking about step pyramids, like the ones in Egypt. The name connection is amazing! It can't be anything else. This name must have had the same origin or, if you prefer, the same teachers from both sides of the world. Here and there. The same people who taught about the construction of the Egyptian pyramids were probably here. Do you remember the "Saccara Bird" of the Cairo museum?

- Yes. That bird miniature that has a tail and wings just like a modern airplane? The object was found next to the inscriptions "I want to fly", inside the pyramid of Saccara. It is the strongest proof that the ancients had advanced ancient technologies. The model is aerodynamically perfect!

- There must be some connection. – said his father. – If these people could build a miniature that is aerodynamically perfect, they could probably build something of the right size that could bring them here. There is a model here in Tiahuanaco showing how the site should have been thousands of years ago. In this model it is possible to see a series of stepped pyramids very similar to the pyramids scattered throughout Mexico, Guatemala and, of course, Saccara. Here in Tiahuanaco there is only one in a reasonable state. The compasses go crazy around it.

- Really?

- But the one you're looking for is not above the surface. It is *underground* and *inverted*.

- What? You mean it's upside down? As if it had been "stuck" on the ground? I've dreamed several times with something like that!

- Have you heard that the Great Pyramid of Giza is a mirrored building? It means that another Great Pyramid lies inverted as an extension of the one we see on the sands.

- I've never heard of it.

- We don't know if this is true. The holders of "official" knowledge about Egypt swear that this is false. But here our pyramid was certainly constructed entirely as if it were stuck in the ground.

- But where would it be? Any idea?

- Remember that *Plaza de las Cabezas* itself is considered by official archeology as a "sunken temple". It was totally buried by a thick mud that no one knows where it might have come from. Probably it came from the same downpour that buried Puma Punku right next door. After being unearthed, it was noticed that the temple is set at a level below the normal level of the rest of the site. It may be an indication that they possibly built this temple on top of the pyramid that lies below the *Plaza*. There are not many places here to hide a construction of this size.

- Wow! It is true! Every region here is very flat.

- The energy coming from the ground is another indication.

- If the pyramid exists, there is no doubt: it was built upside down. The Plaza was probably built on top of it to avoid finding the reversed building. If it was on the surface, it would not resist the looters.

- I'm pretty sure it was built under the *Plaza de las Cabezas*. – said the old Eastman. – It's the place that has the strongest energy here. I did magnetic tests in the *plaza*. I brought two specialists from Germany here with the same equipment that Erich Von Daniken used in Nazca to measure the electromagnetism of the soil. As I am considered a "local gringo", people do not ask many questions and when they do... – Paulo said with a shrug – I convince them telepathically, but I don't use this technique very often. I know the people here well. The thing in this square is very intense. It pulsates beneath your feet. It must have been the great spiritual center of this continent for thousands of years. All human races are represented there.

- But have you seen any entrance, is there any place where some access corridor may have been built? – asked the scientist accustomed to excavation sites. – The "normal pyramid" here has no entrance. It's just a power tower. There is nothing inside of it.

- No. I don't think the entrance is physical. It must be some kind of dimensional portal. – said Paulo Eastman. – You were the only person who saw the Puma Punku stone working. Maybe you can find that entrance. You know, son. These Andean sites are not for everyone. I'm not talking about money. Anyone can pay for a sightseeing trip here. Bolivia is a cheap country if we compare with Brazil. I'm talking about *mindset*, you see. Open your mind to the impossible.

- I totally get it!

- The normal tourist visits Tiahuanaco, or Machu Picchu, or Saqsayhuaman or any of these incredible places, strolls for a few minutes, an hour or two at the most, gets impressed more or less, depending on each individual, and take their photos for the Internet. This place is fantastic and no one gives a shit. No one cares if this was all built by humans or outlanders! Puma Punku and Tiahuanaco are very little visited because of the altitude. People get sick up here.

- Nothing better than this place to hide a great mystery. – complements Fernando.

- The first archaeologists who excavate here reported in written record that there was an underground city here. It exists, but it cannot be visited. The government officials say it's because of poor conservation, but I got into that city. It is splendid. Non-human technology, without any shadow of a doubt. Beautiful as Puma Punku must have been, but let's change the subject. You need to know some very important things.

- Say it.

- It's about the great conspiracy, son. It is about the great lie in which humanity is tucked up to the neck. I've come up with a few things about what's been going on on this planet for thousands of years. Many people have already discovered and numerous books have been written on the subject, but are always seen as ridicule fantastic conspiracies. It's understandable. The whole thing is so unbelievable that I dare not talk to anyone about it, but you have to listen to me. Is important!

- OK.

- Have you heard of the Draconians, reptilians and things like that? – asked Paulo seriously.

- Yes, of course. Beings with reptilian features. Real crazy shit. Nobody takes it seriously! This is a great...

- They are real! – interrupts old Eastman dryly. – More real than you can imagine. They are as real as the air you're breathing. It is a race not only from another planet, but from another Galaxy. Some belong to other dimension! It is said that they were expelled from their homes, but no one knows why. What is known is that they were "discarded" for our three-dimensional existence plan, our Universe. First they lodged in the constellation of Draco, around the old polar star, Thuban, that is the Arabic term for *basilisk* .

- The fantastic reptile of many mythologies!

- Yes. They settled in *Orion Drago*, then went to neighboring *Bootes, Rigel*, stars in the Orion constellation, until they settled here on Earth. They arrived, invaded, and took possession of the planet millions of years ago, long before the dinosaurs walked here, at an early time when the Earth was still forming.

- The Bible says that these reptiles walked erect and were *doomed* to crawl on their bellies, is that right? – says Fernando.

- They are large beings that can reach up to ten feet in height. They weigh more than 200 kilograms. Bipeds like us, but very strange compared to our aesthetic standards. They may have tail or not depending on the position they occupy in a hierarchy that we do not understand. Their bodies are covered by scales that can be brown, greenish, white and even reddish. Some are not physically here, but spiritually. Others were born here. They live thousands of years.

- Nutz!!!

- They are oviparous, but they do not lay eggs like the birds and reptiles we know. Their eggs hatch inside the body and are expelled at the time of birth. They are very advanced entities, but they consider humans as cattle, inferior beings. They have great mental and physical strength, are great warriors and have the ability to change their shape as and when they wish.

- They can change their shape? *Shapeshifters?*

- They have a holographic system in their scales that can simulate the human form or any other shape. They are masters in telepathy, in invisibility, and they are also masters in genetics. They are very good at controlling and manipulating minds! They play with the unconscious of people and influence dreams and memories.

- That sounds like Pixar's children's animation, Monsters Inc.! There was a lizard that changed color according to the place it was. He could be invisible.

- The cinema and the television have talked a lot about these beings. Children are being indoctrinated to face this reality sooner or later. One day they will reveal themselves to us. Do you remember that series "Land of the Lost"? There was a race of humanoid reptilians, the *Sleestak*. They always showed up to try to capture the lost humans. There was a very recent American television series about an invasion of reptiles on Earth, and the chief lizard was a Brazilian actress, remember?

- Yes! I loved this! I do not remember the name.

- Unfortunately it's not like "Land of the Lost". They are not slow-minded beings. On the contrary! If they want to get you... they'll get you! In real life we've been under their control long ago. All humanity is in the clutches of these intelligent beings. In the most subtle way you can imagine! They are the message behind everything you watch on television. The big media is under their control. Google, the new omniscient God... or Facebook, which frames human existence into a misinformed reality. Pseudo-knowledge represented as *memes*, indolence and social isolation.

- This is serious shit.

- There is a group of beings of other races that fight against this human mental domination using these same means. But in the end draconians are winning every human soul, more and more, day after day with soap operas, low-level comedy, reality shows, talk shows, soccer on Sundays, and so on. The media is not reliable as well. The long cherished Freedom of Speech, the basis of any "serious" democracy, sweeps all the dirt down the rug, if necessary. The speech is beautiful, but reality is fetid. Do you think that CNN, BBC, Fox News, Globo News, and all Reuters associate, bring the truth via satellite, via cable? Just look at the journalist's face. They look like plastic, they are puppets being used to "inform" people about the lies they find useful to us.

- I don't know, dad. Who's who in this story? It's all lies and lies...

- They follow the agenda, Fernando. Who writes the agenda? Can you see the Luciferian system of government here on this planet? Everything, *absolutely everything* is based on lies and deceits brought by the eloquence of the Elite. The evil specialty of Lucifer is eloquence. He lies and deceives.

- An extremely efficient method!

- I'm sure Lucifer is very much like the other "angels" who have helped us throughout our history. But he was the greatest of them all! The beloved son of the Creator Logos. He has the Good within him. But there is also Evil. And these are his weapons to manipulate us: lie and illusion. What should be good, is bad... and vice versa. Weapons we humans have learned to use with mastery!

- Inversion of values. I had never seen it this way. How did you come to these conclusions, dad? What kind of tea have you been drinking? I took one these days that made me see a lot of stuff.

- No tea, my son. Just watching. This life I chose gave me this understanding. I had all the time in the world to study and observe how things are. I've been to all the mysterious sites on this planet. I was not worried about going back to work, I was not an ordinary tourist. I really saw things and touched them and felt the stones of all these places. I touched eternity in the form of stone. I went into the Queops pyramid alone to meditate. I spent days inside. You know this monument has a transforming energy. Many important men in human history have undergone transformations in there. Jesus, Francis of Assisi, quite possibly Moses! I entered a corridor that begins well below the Sphinx, which only a few "privileged" have access to. This privilege cost a lot of money, but I worked very hard to accomplish this. Just for this very moment of *now* when I teach you again. Contemplation is something few endure. Being alone with oneself in contemplation is a delicate and difficult task. That's how I came to understand many things. Remember that I also worked a lot and in my field you have to know how to play their game. I played and won.

- Now I understand where I have inherited the fondness I have for my sweet solitude. That's why I love the silence. I think more clearly. It was complex to get here. Everything was very tense. I've no idea how I managed to reason and find solutions to the problems. After my friends were arrested I lost three quarters of my brain. Even Lia, a wonderful woman I knew these days, helped with her naivety.

- Your safety is still at stake. The people who do not want us to know the truth, they *let* you get here! Don't be fool yourself. They're probably betting you won't find the stone. But, son, if they feel like you're going to get there... well, you must pay a lot of attention! Our reality is not a TV show. It is much more subtle, dangerous and ingenious. They will not try to kill you, but they will try to *fool* you. This is the method they use.

- Who are these guys?

- Listen to what I have to tell you. Many of these reptilians live on the planet in physical form below the ground and on the surface also through hybridization and shape-shifting. Have you heard of the "hollow Earth theory"? I'm not talking about Agharta. It's about caves that no one can explore.

- Yes, I know that theory, but I don't think it's plausible.

- It's real, Fernando! What do we really know about our planet? We only know what we are taught, what we are told. And *they* say what they want us to know.

- On second thought, you're right. I'm still used to that academic thought.

- Many reptilians live in the Fourth Dimension. A place that encompasses and understands the Third Dimension and all its physical and moral laws. They are beyond good and evil. They are only interested in the efficient execution of their agenda. And they, besides telepathic manipulation, captivate the human being through the basic *chakras*. Pornography has never been so abused and accessible as it has today, but it has always existed! And that's a very effective strategy.

- Men was caught by the balls! Said Fernando with a wry giggle.

- But it's a fact! The Draconians undoubtedly have a great agenda, Fernando. They follow orders from an elite of Dracons or Winged Dragons, a kind of draconian royalty. The ones with brown or greenish scales appear to be submissive to an elite caste based on color or something like that. In addition to the wings, the tail is a sign of royalty. There are humans who witnessed this kind of submissive behavior. The leaders were "baptized" by humans as Draco Primes, or commanders, and these leaders are white scales. According to the witnesses, they hybridized in the terrestrial human race in many ways. There are human hybrids whose DNA has been manipulated and inserted draconian features. Another category is the people who bring the reptilian "spirit" within themselves, that is, they are "taken", "possessed" spiritually by the Dracons of the Fourth Dimension.

- Fuck! Where did you get that, *señor* Eastman? Alien beings... I understand! But... living on Earth?

- No. You didn't understand. *We* are the aliens!

Fernando widens his eyes. Paulo continues.

- They were here a long time before us! – reinforced the old man. – And it doesn't end there. Many people talk about reptilians born and raised by humans in hideous genetic experiments in military laboratories on this very planet we live in! And this planet is not in our hands, son. Never been! Nowadays we are all hybridized. Everyone, you and I, each of us on this planet, have reptilian traits in our DNA.

- But this is incredible! Are we all half human and half aliens? Or rather, half men, half reptiles?

- Aliens, too! But essentially reptilian aliens! It's quite different. I ask you: is there any ancient culture on this planet that has no reference to reptilian beings? Ancient Egypt, Aboriginal Australians, Aztecs, Mayans, China, India, Africa, Europe in general, Native Americans, the Inca, the examples are countless. The whole planet is, has been and apparently will always be in the hands of these beings.

- Orejona, as far as I know, does not refer to any snake or reptile.

- But She is another story. She's from Venus, not from Orion, or Draco.

- I don't remember any Brazilian legend or myth involving creeping deities.

- Brazil is also another story. It is a special land. We talk about it another day. – said Paulo, returning to the subject. – We cannot just think of ancestry or mythology, gods or God. Regardless of history or prehistory, religion, myth, etc., the whole planet is under the command of this race right now. At first we were bred to work for them. Then, when it was convenient, they brainwashed humans with the "fear your God" ideology. Fear of a Powerful and ruthless being, sometimes kind. They swept the cults of the Mother Nature and replaced them with a single male God from outside the planet.

- Easy! – Fernando completes. – They invented hell, destroyed pagan cultures and implanted fear among humans.

- Pagan religions were religions of Nature, the prehistoric religions of Europe and the Caucasus and from all parts of the globe where there were ancient human settlements. Even here, in South America! It is difficult to explain pagan thought thus, without a long previous exposure of obvious aspects, but which we insist on not considering. The brain-washers were very efficient. Paganism was a strong threat to their lies.

- Got it. Go on.

- Very recently, at the beginning of the 20th century, religion began to share power with militarism and with the economy.

- Today the representation of the Power crystallized in three pillars: economy, religion and politics or military force, as it wants. That is what *señor* Julio Pranas said! – exclaims Fernando seeing clearly the precise analysis of the craftsman Nazca.

- You were not pursued in Peru? Do you think the Peruvian government really wants you to say nothing about this whole madness? They are not interested in any of this. It is not part of the local government agenda. Whoever is after you, it is not the Peruvian police. They are the manipulators of our history! The "Lords of all information".

- If they manipulate religion through the Vatican, then all we know about the Anti-Christ is bullshit.

- *They* are, in the literal sense, Antichrists. Many times we have been "helped" by our original Creator. He came to us personally to die, remember that story? Jesus is man and God at the same time. It's The Illuminated. You know that *Christos*, in Greek, the prevailing language of the New Testament, means the enlightened, the anointed.

- I know, of course.

- I know you know. According to the Church, Jesus is the fulfillment of the Creator's plan of redemption. Whoever goes against Jesus is an Antichrist. Jesus himself says in the Bible that in his days there were *many* Antichrists. It's in the first letter of John 2:18, if I'm not mistaken. Some editions of the Bible don't bring this passage or are mistranslated.

- Why did the Creator plant us here? Why did God let the planet be dominated by these beings?

- You should ask Orejona directly if you have the chance. It looks like you will. But let me tell you some more.

- Okay, speak up.

Paulo Eastman talks to Fernando about *forbidden archeology*. He says that the Anunnaki, beings of a planet called Nibiru, created what today is called *Homo Sapiens* to work for them thousands of years ago. They wanted gold and there was a lot of gold here. Thousands of years had passed and when they left, but some of them stayed and became the "gods" of the Sumerians, in Mesopotamia. From that moment on the official archeology – lost, but trying to piece together the puzzle – tells us that in 4,000 BC the Sumerians settled in the region we now call Iraq. They don't know where they came from and there is no evidence of a Sumerian pre-history. They culturally refined and technologically advanced.

He reminds Fernando that the Sumerians are considered to have been the earliest astronomers, to have created and developed the cities of Nineveh, Ur, Erech and Kish, the cuneiform writing, the have built Ziggurats – their iconic temple/towers. The Sumerians developed legislation, sculpture art, language, literature and mythology of their own. Everything they left is impressive, but they themselves claim that it were the "gods" who created it all! The Sumerian scribes recorded everything in writing. They flourished for a short historical period and suddenly the region was invaded by the Akkadians, a neighboring people. These have adopted the Sumerian language and culture and flourish there for nearly 2,000 years. The Amorites came from northern Syria and took the land and founded the glorious Babylon, the new capital. Hamurabi was the great figure of this period.

Fernando remembers that Hamurabi was the creator of the first code of written laws of our history. The Babylonian law code was based on the famous *lex talionis*: "an eye for an eye, a tooth for a tooth". About 500 years later the Assyrians conquered Babylon. This Assyrian culture profoundly influenced the whole region of Canaan, the future promised land. The Babylonians attributed their cultural achievements to the gods who had revealed themselves to their ancestors.

It is very easy to make confusion among Sumerians, Babylonians, Assyrians, Anunnaki, and all those peoples. In short, the Anunnaki, "those who came from heaven", lived here for thousands of years before they left. They created their slaves, the Sumerians, through genetic manipulation and then left them at the mercy of the invading Akhadians. Each people who conquered the region was instructed by the "gods" to perpetuate their knowledge of domination through *secret societies*. Paulo continues as Fernando tries to make sense of all this information.

- You must have heard of the Anunnaki. They created the Sumerian civilization. – said the old Eastman.

- Yes, "those who came down from heaven". Sumerian cuneiform tablets speak of the saga of the alien race that descended on Earth where today is Iraq. They "created" the man to work for them. No one credits it because the translation of their Saga is too fantastic. I myself have never read anything about it. I never had the chance.

- The draconians have used a large network of misinformation to discredit those translations. – said Paulo. – I read all the books of one of these translators, Zecharia Sitchin. Those books helped me a lot. The Anunnaki, who look like us, have created the largest and best-kept network of secret societies in human history since they took temporary possession of the planet from the hands of the original reptilians. They invaded planet Earth thousands of years ago in search of raw material for their planet, Nibiru.

- What did they come here for?

- The Anunnaki destroyed their own atmosphere with wars and nuclear weapons, and they needed gold to cover their homes from the radiations of the cosmos. Nibiru, according to the Sumerian records, is part of our solar system. Its cycle is about 3600 years. They worked themselves in the extraction of the ore that was abundant here. One day, tired of working in mining, they realized that they could genetically manipulate the existing beings here and make them work for them. They realized that they could relax, eat free food, demand respect. The humans were their slaves. They created Law Codes and bring order and justice in return for submission.

- Order, justice and *fear*. Fear is what keeps them under control.

- The maintenance of fear has become the key to governing any kind of human system. The "lesser evil" system we created is the democratic system. – Paulo continues. – Or rather, it *has been created* for us. It is participatory, egalitarian, but inefficient as regards the fulfillment of basic human needs. Dissatisfaction is desirable for governments. Democracy hides the shadow rulers efficiently. It is through this very democracy that they keep us eternally unsatisfied with our lives and we... deluded... blame the consumer goods that we *do not* possess!

- That's true!

- They, the "gods", had technology. It was easy to convince people that they were gods and that everyone should fear them. To preserve their knowledge and hold power over the earthlings, they created a network of secret societies to teach their secrets to those who had the capacity to learn. Everything degenerated after a few centuries. The beginning of this whole conspiracy, they say, was in ancient Babylon more than 3000 years before Christ. The first secret society created on Earth is called the Brotherhood of the Serpent. Don't forget that they've been around for thousands of years. Official chronology is conveniently wrong. After millennia of changes in fully hybridized human organizations, the Brotherhood was eventually infiltrated by the draconians. They took over and created branches of the Brotherhood. Freemasonry is the best known. It was probably created at the time of King Solomon through Hiram, the great Masonic Master of the "Great Secret". This is the most influential aspect of this great network. Today the members of this "shadow government" control the backstage of all the governments and military leaders of the globe so that their "slaves" keep working on their secret projects.

- Secret projects? What projects are you talking about?

- A recent example is the well-known space race. All the astronauts who went to space, at least most of them, were Freemasons. Gordon Cooper, John Glenn, Edgar Mitchell, Buzz Aldrin, Thomas Stafford, and other names. Neil Armstrong, the first man to step on the moon, was not a Freemason, but his father was a powerful and respected figure in this secret society. Do you know what they, the Masonic astronauts, were doing up there on the moon, besides walking, planting flags and collecting stones?

- I have no idea.

- Contact, Fernando. They made contact. All the people involved in the project were somehow part of the world elite and they are still in control of these projects to this day.

Paulo Eastman talks to Fernando about the two hours and thirty minutes that Buzz Aldrin and Neil Armstrong spent on the surface of the Moon. Just a few minutes were recorded or released, but the space project "sponsors" **know** what they did off the camera.

- What did they really do up there?

- If you one day you come to know, please tell me, but see, one of their assignments was to check on the spot certain areas previously photographed by NASA. The entire Moon had already been photographed and insiders say there is a large concentration of *facilities* on the dark side of the Moon. *Cities!!!* Was it mere coincidence that such rumors related to The Dark Side Of The Moon? – Paulo said playfully, rambling a little on his favorite record and staring into an empty space but soon resumed. – The place, day and time of landing on the Moon were previously and carefully chosen. The choice triggered all calculations so that the *Eagle* could land on the Moon exactly 33 minutes before the perfect alignment of that chosen latitude and longitude with the Orion Belt. All the very complicated calculations of the launching window were made to meet the demands of the head of the project. Their goal: to get the man to step on the Moon. These geniuses were all linked to Freemasonry and other secret societies and also linked to beliefs that Osiris, Isis, and Horus are really the sources of their origins. High-grade Masons believe they are genuinely descendants of these gods who came *literally* from the stars.

- Oh really? I've never heard of it!

- Of course not! This is one of the biggest secrets of these Societies. Now, back to the Moon, the famous Sea of Tranquility was then the basis of the calculations of the launch window. According to NASA's official speech, the site was chosen because of its flat surface. A safe place to land. But in fact it was a strategic position preconceived by esoteric men of the highest degree of knowledge. On that day, time and place there would be an alignment with the Orion belt. This alignment with the system provided some kind of communication that only these guys know about. Orion is one of the places where the Draconians settled in our Universe.

- Father, where do you get your intel?

- Many books have been written on the subject. There are books written by *insiders* of the Apollo Project! They said that before leaving the Eagle module, the astronauts held a religious ceremony that included sharing bread and serving wine in chalices. The ceremony was led by Aldrin, 33rd Degree Mason, and it was simply the same communion ceremony we know in the Catholic masses. The Masons, however, know that this ceremony is much older and that it came as an offering ceremony to Osiris.

- The bread and wine thing? But...

- The Church appropriated and obviously *distorted* the ceremony by adapting it to Christianity, as they did with all cultures considered "pagan". They changed the meaning and hid their true origins in order to erase them from history and enshrine a New Order on Earth. The idea has always been to stifle the knowledge of Nature. Perhaps we will never really know the "whys" of our history, but the connection of Osiris with this post-landing ritual only reinforces the conspiracy theories about the Masons going to the Moon. The symbol of the Apollo mission is absurdly indicative that these societies are up to the neck in space exploration and in secret space programs.

Paulo gets up, goes to the bookshelf, takes a book on the subject and shows some photos for Fernando.

- The central "A" of the emblem does *not* refer to Apollo, the Greek god, but to **Assar**, the Egyptian god, better known as Osiris. This becomes clear when we look at the three stars on the line that cuts the letter "A". These stars stand in the same position as the stars of the Orion Belt, where they believe Osiris has come from. The three stars of the belt are there because *that* was the purpose of the men behind the program: making contact with their ancestors. The Mercury Mission, likewise, bears no Greek symbol on its emblem, but an alchemical symbol very similar to the Egyptian symbol **Ank**, present throughout the iconography of the Egyptian gods.

- I've never realized it! – said Fernando in astonishment.

It is well known and publicized that the first mission to set foot on the Moon left behind many scientific objects, an American flag and a commemorative plaque with the following words: HERE MEN FROM PLANET EARTH FIRST SET FOOT UPON THE MOON - JULY 1969 AD - WE COME IN PEACE FOR ALL MANKIND. In addition to the plaque, a replica of an gold made olive branch was left inside a luxurious compartment lined with sparkling blue fabric and a silicon disk with messages of peace and goodwill engraved by 73 world leaders.

Who did they left those for? Who would find those curious stuff on the moon? Is it possible that NASA was aware of this so-called "city" of the mysterious dark side of the Moon? Paulo Eastman made several speculations about NASA's space projects.

- Whose cities are those? – asks Fernando.

- Anunnaki, maybe. They say that it was not just stones that were collected by surface, but also technology. If we have actually been visited by space travelers frequently, they could have used the Moon as a base to "fill the tank"! Maybe they still use it! Or maybe the Moon served for extraction of raw material, such as uranium, gold, etc. Anyway, everything indicates that they know much more than they tell. Or maybe the moon landing has been the most monumental collective cover up ever recorded in our modern history. Do you know how many missions the Americans sent to Mars?

- No... maybe three...

- *Nineteen*, Fernando. How many of these missions were on the news? Almost none! In August 2012 the Curiosity spacecraft reached the Martian soil to study the planet better. But wait there? – said Paulo as if speaking to himself. – Why so much money on Mars? To study *what*, anyway? What is up there that justifies the budget? Isn't it a dry and barren planet?

- Good question!

- It seems to me that the precious money from American taxpayers is being used on something they will never see any benefit from. Legend has it that Earth, Venus and Mars were in constant contact millions of years ago, remember? – Paulo Eastman asked wryly.

- Yes, I remember the legend! You told me when I was a kid.

- Well, as soon as the first images of the probe came to us, the thing started to get hotter. And they did not even bother to hide! The Internet is the place where everything dissolves and trivializes. One of the first photos shows the reddish Martian soil and the horizon line. It's possible to clearly see something *flying* there! They simply said the so-called UFO was just dirt on the camera lenses. Did they remember to install some kind of windshield wiper on the probe?

- They certainly didn't! – says Fernando laughing. – It would better if they did some *photo-shopping* to hide the UFO, but the nonsense press-release to the media worked pretty well. I saw the photos. They didn't even bother.

- Mars has always been a mystery to us humans, but since the first images began to arrive through the early American missions, it became more intriguing. Throughout the surface of this planet we see very strange things like pyramidal structures, walls, remains of old buildings, great faces carved in huge stone slopes, in fact, all kinds of crazy things that cannot be simply natural formations. The famous face of Mars was a scary thing when it first appeared, but recent, more definite images showed that there was no face on that hill.

- I remember the first time I saw the famous image of the "Face of God" on the Martian soil. We were watching TV together, do you remember? It was a Sunday night. I've never forgotten.

- I remember, son. I said: "this can't be real!". But all was muffled. It was just "a game of light and shadow", they said. Those were just natural rock formations. The problem is that if you take a look at the current images with more definition, you will see that it was not a face, but a real ancient site with remnants of walls and in standardized layout. It is evident that these are *not* natural formations. Someone built it! The pyramidal shapes are intriguing, too.

- Carl Sagan spoke of these pyramidal formations with great enthusiasm. His most celebrated phrase was: "If there is no life outside Earth, then the Universe is a great waste of space".

- He knew much more than he said! He was a true genius.

- Anyone can watch anything on YouTube. There are videos of a NASA expedition to tune up one of their space telescopes. In one of these videos one astronaut speaks to the other on the radio something like: "Look, there's an object right in front of you! Can you see?". The thing is dramatic! These astronauts constantly go to space for telescope maintenance or for missions to assemble the ISS. These guys are tired of seeing unidentified objects flying around our planet. – says Fernando enthusiastically.

One cannot talk about these matters with anyone. The young man was happy to be able to share this with the newly found father.

- It's as if these objects are watching the Earth from outside. – continued Fernando. – Are they "the watchers" of Enoch?

- Perhaps...

- That's crazy! In 1991, during one of these missions, images of many objects were transmitted flying around the Earth. One of these footages clearly shows a bright object in a rectilinear trajectory when, out of the blue, it makes one of those impossible maneuvers and flees into space. At that moment a beam of light comes out of the planet trying to hit the UFO.

- Son, we're talking about technologies that are already available to the military, and we have no idea how they work or how they were developed. These footages were broadcast *live*! There's this video on which the commander clearly says: "We're being pulled by an alien ship!". Then there were some of those crazy nerds who were watching the broadcasts and those footages leaked all over the world. Obviously nothing has changed about that. The "disinformation network" says that they are fake images.

- Astronauts are not crazy people. They are the best. These people would hardly make this kind of joke. Unless, of course, they were doing what they *were told* to do. You know, fake some ET's and trivialize the issue. – asserted Fernando.

- Of course! All these things I've told you about may be just the daydreams of a crazy old man, or just conspiracy theories, who's to say? But I find it unlikely. Where there's smoke, there's fire. – said Paulo Eastman honestly.

- They are not daydreams, dad. I myself saw Orejona with my own eyes. – said Fernando with great emotion. – I talked to her in person. I've had really weird experiences. Everything makes sense to me. I'll never be the same again!

- Many people say that these missions to set up the Space Station are just cover ups for the real mission that would be to build an Earth base on the Moon or Mars. If you think about it, building something on lunar soil should be much easier and safer than building something floating. This base would connect with the cities on the hidden side of the Moon and many of these UFO sightings around the world are nothing less than the result of these secret programs. The UFOs that pops up around may well be from Earth!

The origins of NASA is very interesting. On July 29, 1958, in response to the successful launch of the legendary Sputnik, North American President Dwight D. Eisenhower signed the not less famous National Aeronautics and Space Act officially establishing NASA. The purpose of this agency was to lead the United States into space and to lead the new directions that humanity should take in the days of the post-war hangover.

NASA was then created as a branch of the Department of National Defense. This subordination to National Defense was justified because of the Cold War. Information about everything the United States discovered should be protected from Soviet espionage. But the real motive was to hide the discoveries from *all humanity*. The decree that created NASA clearly stated that anything discovered in space would be subject to review by the Department of Defense and the information would be treated as Top Secret.

Along with the creation of NASA, a study was commissioned on how to react in the event of encounters with alien beings. This study is called The Brookings Report. This governmental *crisis manual* has as fundamental point: the necessity of *not revealing anything* to the public. They claim that knowing about extraterrestrial realities could *destroy the fabric of our civilization*.

Much is said of NASA's connections to the mysterious Secret Societies. The top members of these societies, those who have secret knowledge, truly believe in the link of humanity to what they call the Star Gods, namely, Osiris, Isis and Horus. At the top of the list there are the Freemasons. Among the astronauts of each mission there were always one or two Freemasons of the highest order. Along with them there are the Golden Dawn members of Alister Crowley and many other branches and ramifications of the Elite.

All the high domes of the Secret Societies are united by the same goal under the NASA brand. One agenda. All of them united to reach their *gods*. The knowledge of life in other stars has been passed from generation to generation through the initiates of these societies. Only the people capable of dealing with this knowledge were taken in. The first was the Brotherhood of the

Serpent of the Anunnaki, but eventually it ended up infiltrated and dominated by Draconians to continue to exploit humanity. Let us remember that the Anunnaki came from a planet called Nibiru. According to the Sumerian tablets they are not from Orion, but from our very own solar system.

In America everything is done in strict compliance with the Law. If the law makes it impossible to do "what needs to be done", they change the Law in a blink of an eye. It seems that NASA was a legitimate institutional way to use public money to run the agenda of a private elite who doesn't give a shit about humans.

A classic case of these legislative political maneuvers was the birth of the American Federal Reserve by a decree approved by the American Congress and signed by President Woodrow Wilson on December 22, 1913 during the parliamentary recess. Democracy is a system of ingenious domination. Every intelligent legal system is like this. *(Yours is, too, my dear reader!)*

After September 11th, the paranoid terror brainwash speech on National Security had taught the American citizen to accept the new reality: *our government must change the laws and restrict our freedoms to save our lives.* Pure deception, for the official explanation for the tragedy of the Manhattan towers smells bad. And when it smells bad... there's something wrong.

Another example of Lucifer's government?

Let's meditate...

Conspiracies aside, one of the most impressive stories related to the space race was "Operation Paperclip". Shortly before the end of World War II, the US Army captured Wernher Von Braun and his team and brought them to the United States to develop his ambitious space conquest project. Von Braun was a brilliant scientist who, due to circumstances and the high budget for scientific research, allied himself with the German National Socialist government with the mission of developing a space program that was in Hitler's interest.

At one point in the war, Hitler convincingly suggested he should focus his attention on the development of guided ballistic missiles so that Germany could devastate London and New York and weaken their opponents. We have to keep in mind that the Nazi SS was also a secret society. When Hitler's hopes for victory began to decline, a nefarious "file-burning operation" began. Many German scientists began to be murdered by the Nazis. Von Braun, terrified, surrendered to the Americans promising to reveal and develop all his scientific secrets.

Stanley Kubrik, the brilliant American filmmaker, showed the connections of Americans with the Nazis deserters in a very interesting way in the film "Dr. Strangelove", starring Peter Sellers. In 1955, Von Braun publicly presented his International Space Station project which, as everyone knows, is being built up there at this very moment! He was a visionary genius, no doubt.

John F. Kennedy, the same man who launched the American goal of conquering the moon, was killed, some say, because he wanted to merge the US space program with the program of the late USSR. He wanted to propose to the Soviets a partnership to share costs and space information and these negotiations were in progress.

They say that something very important was found up there and America alone would take a long time to reach. "Why divide this information with the Russians and lose world hegemony?" – some war pig must have asked. Kennedy wanted to turn the space race *between* two nations into a joint venture *of* two nations. The Mighty, the Lords of the Occult Truth, didn't allow this. Lee Oswald was the perfect scapegoat. End of story. The Kennedy assassination has been covered up in the best Luciferian style.

- Can you see the link with ancient Egypt? – asked Paulo. – Osiris came from Orion, as the stories tell.

- Yes. They say that Orion is related to the pyramids of Egypt. And many other places around the planet like those in Mexico.

- When an Egyptian pharaohs of the dynastic era rose to power, they had their bodies massaged with a "magic potion" made with crocodile fat.

- Everywhere in ancient Egypt you can see snakes, and reptiles. – completed Fernando.

- They had their bodies decorated to resemble those beings that gave power to them, the reptilians. It is said that some pharaohs were reptilian themselves. Pharaoh was synonymous with "son of God", wasn't it? To keep this divine power, one had to have back support. The earthly power figureheads are supported by the hidden masters, or occult masters. These guys are like a private group that controls the planet through their branches in human society. Secret Societies, Freemasonry, Illuminati, whatever you want to call them, the names don't really matter.

- In India there are the legends of the Naga, reptilians of the caves. The Mayans had the serpent god Quetzalcoatl, I can't pronounce that name! The Babylonians speak of Oannes, a reptilian god. – complements Fernando.

- Freemasons speak of their ancestors as *spirits of other worlds*, other dimensions, outlanders, as you wish, they are not of the Earth. It is said that the secret of *how* they control and influence human societies and the backdrops of world politics has been passed on to Masons and all other initiates for at least 4,000 years. They are fully established and deeply rooted within *all* the Offices of Power.

- But this is sordid! – complained Fernando. – How can a respected institution such as Freemasonry have this history?

- Of course, not every Mason has this knowledge. It's like the Catholic Church or any other secret organization. But the dome, the staff of the traditional Scottish lodge, for example, certainly has! But who cares? It is widely publicized, but we, earthlings, are worried about our jobs, our money, our relationship problems, and so on. Nibiru, the Anunnaki planet, is around the corner. Whenever it passes by it causes planetary changes. The last time was 3600 years ago.

- Around 1600 BC there were a series of very violent and unprecedented volcanic eruptions that destroyed much of the world. Mycenae, in Greece, for example, was totally devastated.

- True. The gravitational force of Nibiru affects our entire solar system. Its volume and density generate high instability and this is known to be natural. This information is everywhere and we can already feel the climatic changes coming from the gravity of this enormous celestial body. Maybe we'll know the truth soon enough. The existence of Nibiru and the Dracons is the greatest secret of the hybrid elites who manipulate us for thousands of thousands of years.

- Dad, if people knew about *that*... their deepest beliefs would come down in a snap. It's hard to recognize that everything you believed in... is a lie. The order would collapse!

- Dostoevsky talked about it in the nineteenth century. – said Paulo Eastman. – He raised the question: "If God does not exist, then is all permissible?".

- That answer, today, would be a gigantic **YES**!

- Our world is rotten. The more you observe human behavior, the more you become convinced that without an idea of God, life on the planet would be impossible. I know the Source exists, but it is not this "God" that makes us swallow in catechism classes!!! Anyway, this is a very delicate situation. You can destroy the world with the truth, instead of saving it. It depends on where you put your finger on. But as they say, if you wanna hide something from people, just rub it on their faces. Remember the pyramid and the "Eye" stamped on the dollar bill? Those are symbols of the Bavarian Illuminati.

Paulo Eastman shows a dollar bill to his son and points to an interesting detail: the **scaled skin** of the being whose eye appears inside the triangle. The most important and most circulating symbol throughout our world today is nothing but a *reptilian* symbol. *(You may have one in the your pocket right now, dear reader!)* And this reptilian image is scattered all over the planet in its most efficient form: **money**.

- What do people most desire in the world now? Millions of these reptilian notes. – says Paulo. – They have bought everybody. They are the owners of the global financial system. They own the Pound Sterling. They own the Euro, Dollar. Whenever we look at the sculptures on the Sumerian walls there's always someone holding a *pine cone*, symbol of the Brotherhood of the Serpent, not to mention wristwatches, something that is not supposed to have existed before our time.

- Santos Dumont invented the wristwatch!

- The most important religious symbols of the Catholic Church are holding a pine cone as well, recognizing the Brotherhood of the Serpent as sovereign. The Black Madonna of the monastery of Montserrat in Barcelona, a sublime and powerful masterpiece, is holding a sphere in her right hand. Jesus, who is sitting on his mother's lap, holds a pine cone! It is common to find these representations by all the institutions of the planet.

Paulo shows some more interesting pictures in another book on the Mesopotamian religions. The mixture of draconian characteristics with the Sumerian gods is part of the infiltration project that has happened slowly over the centuries.

- The Vatican uses and abuses of Anunnaki and Babylonian symbols in all its ceremonies. – explained Paulo Eastman. – On the papal throne there are two pine cones one on each arm rest made of the purest Inca gold. A detail to be observed. The famous Piazza Navonno in Rome features marble statues of dragons emerging from the water symbolizing the worship of Dagon and Oannes, that is, reptilian gods. The beautiful London is full of dragon symbols or pine cones. The landmark of London global power today is a huge pine coned modern building right in the heart of the city. All this little details at every corner of London represents the Brotherhood's dominion over royalty. The Eagle, symbol of the knowledge of the Anunnaki invasion, is represented on the presidential seal of the United States of America, on the CIA symbol, on the Barclays Bank's logo and the examples never end.

- The world's first central bank is English, I guess!

- Fernando, the Euro coins carry an eagle on one side and a tree covered with pine cones on the other. The Freemasons have as symbol a two headed eagle representing the gods Dagon and Oannes under a crown and with the sacred number 33 inside a triangle. These "human" institutions scream in our faces through their symbols that they know of the shadowed influence of the Brotherhood of the Serpent. After infiltration, the Dracons conveniently kept the Anunnaki symbols.

- Pine cones, winged dragons, eagles. Conspiracy is everywhere! I've been on the run for days because of this.

- Fernando, there is a war that has been unfolding for millennia. The dominion of the planet has already been in the hands of this reptilian race for thousands of years, and they know very well how to maintain the power and how to exploit it. But they also know that they will lose it someday.

- War for what? What do these people want?

- Many things. Earth has many underground deposits. Minerals rare in the Universe and of great importance to life on other planets, water in abundance, an impressive and unique electromagnetic grid that serves as the conductor to open dimensional space-time portals. These portals facilitate the physical manifestation of these beings here. It may be because of a rare genetic factor that we have and that many alien races want to incorporate, integrate or assimilate into their own subspecies. Not to mention the incredible variety of animal and plant life forms. Our planet is very attractive if you consider these various possibilities. To have the dominion of the Earth is like winning in the cosmic lottery. Or do you think it's easy to go around looking for gold in space?

- Ordinary people do not have this information. There is no way they know of any of this. Someone has to talk seriously about these things.

- It's not that easy, Fernando, you know it. The disinformation scheme is very strong. You must have heard about the *Wikileaks* guy, have not you?

- He's being sought on charges of "sex crimes"! – said Fernando.

- No! He never had anything to do with it. He was frame! The "truth-keepers" put him on the world stage as an immoral pervert to destroy his credibility. He leaked confidential documents about the US government and its sordid relations with other countries, including Brazil.

- This is terrible! I myself was put on the Internet as an outlaw who steals and smuggles archaeological artifacts. I don't know how I will clean my name after this is over. About the conspiracies, the evidence is out there, but no one sees it.

- Look at the examples within the Native American culture. According to tradition, the Bak'ti invaded Earth before the existence of the dinosaurs, when the planet was still in formation. Can you see the correlation here?

- Yes!

- These gods, after millions of years, have genetically manipulated the local beings and created mankind. This is reported in the indigenous tradition and they are related to the reptilians. The incredible Serpent Mound, Ohio, was built by Native American shamans of the Neolithic era. The site represents a huge sperm fertilizing an egg. They say that the Bak'ti taught them about human fertilization. And more! They were taught by the gods that there were many alien races trying to invade Earth.

- I've head that Lake Erie has this name because of a tribe that has lived there for centuries.

- In the local native language Erie means "men with big tail". Not to mention that this lake is one of the biggest UFOs hot spots in North America. In the same Neolithic period, on the other side of the planet, in the place known today as Slovakia, there is a stone sculpture perfectly representing a reptilian being. Remember the pyramid of Bosnia? That huge mountain with a "natural" pyramidal shape? What if it's the other way around? What if, in fact, it is a man made pyramid that has been swallowed up by the vegetation and has become like a mountain?

- It seems that it has already been confirmed that this mountain is really artificial.

- How many serpents can we see through the Aztec and Maya sites?

- In Peru, the Inca spoke of three gods: the Puma, the Condor and the Serpent. – added Fernando.

- The thing goes even further! The biblical account of the Garden of Eden is more complicated than one might think. The serpent deceived Eve and then Adam through Lucifer, didn't it?

- Yes, both the official and the more detailed apocryphal version you handed to me are poorly explained. Lucifer deceived mankind by seizing a serpent. What's behind this?

- The original word in the text, which was translated into serpent, is *Nachash*. In Hebrew it means "serpent", but only if you consider Nachash as a verb, then it means "to cheat".

- Yes. Now I remember! – exclaimed Fernando. – The root of this word is *Nesu*, who comes from Babylon. Nesu means "able to change shape," or shape-shifting or shape-shifter.

- You already know who has the ability to change shape on this planet. – added Paulo.

- The reptilians.

- Bingo! The Church speaks of the serpent as equivalent to Satan, but the thing is much more complicated. They are different people. Lucifer and the serpent are not the same person. The possible true story is that Adam and Eve were deceived by a reptilian who changed forms and manipulated the mind of Eve so that she convinced Adam to disobey. So, the fear of losing Eve and due to his sacred freewill, Adam betrayed his Creator. Lucifer must have made some kind of deal with these creatures that already existed here on Earth millions of years before us. Or it's all just another rabbit hole we are putting ourselves in.

- Why did Luci use these reptiles? He could have done it all by himself.

- I have no idea! This is a mess because we have no reliable texts. The method of lying and deceit, attributed to Lucifer by religious doctrine, dominates this world in alliance with powers that operate behind social institutions. As I said before, everything related to these stories has been conveniently ill-told. When I speak of the sacred writings, including the Apocrypha, I do not really know to what extent these texts are free from malice. It is really a great adventure to seek the deepest truth. You need to be brave and go against centuries and centuries of tradition.

- You're right. – said Fernando in a low voice.

- Our unconscious is being, generation after generation, impregnated with past lies. The educational curriculum is weak and inconsistent, but for distracted minds, everything is perfect. People go to school to learn to read and write, do basic math, learn a profession and earn a living, but never to develop their potentials. We are taught to live within a convenient "normality". The great mass that generates wealth and who foments the system is prepared to be telemarketers and cashiers, Fernando. The intellectual level is very shallow. Talking about higher things is the same as being ridiculous. "Get a job, you intellectual!", they tell you. I imagine you have experienced something like this. Choosing to be an intellectual nowadays is for strong minded people. It's not for everyone.

- Don't tell me that! Getting on with people considered "normal" is a major disorder. It's really hard to keep up.

- These reptiles destroy every proof of their existence on Earth and their influence on us. They must remain Hidden Masters. When they can't destroy things like these eternal temples of stone, they rewrite history. They need to keep humanity ignorant of their origins, otherwise they would lose control and power over their precious cheap labor. We, glorious human beings, divine creation, the apex of creation, the inhabitants of planet Earth, are nothing more than creatures made to work for the "gods".

- Here in Tiahuanaco was found an artifact with Sumerian writings. Do you know anything about it? – Fernando asks interestedly. Paulo does not answer but feeds more questions to his son.

- What is the intercontinental relationship that has occurred here in the past? Could the Andeans have managed to develop a similar kind of writing to the Sumerian's by coincidence? Why is there only *one* example of this writing throughout this continent?

- It could be a "gift" from the gods distant from the local civilization? – formulated Fernando.

- What if it was? What the Anunnaki came here for? To bring gifts? For whom? They were "gods"! All in all the plot is a mess, history is what it is and it's an almost impossible mission to change it. But that doesn't mean we should not try, right?

- I'll try, dad. That's why I came here for. But now I need to try to sleep. I think tomorrow will be an intense day.

- Son. Do not forget! Trust your senses. This can be the difference between the success of your quest and total failure. Our world is steeped in mysteries. There must be much more than a simple conspiracy to dominate us. Maybe Orejona might reveal something more.

- I'll be alert.

Paulo Eastman stood up, took a teapot from the stove and poured tea into a cup.

- Have some tea. It's made with special herbs from here. The taste may not be so good, but it will make you sleep. I'll make your bed. Do you mind sleeping on a mattress on the floor?

- Should do it.

DAY 21 – 5am

Fernando was already adapted to the routine of the last days. Waking before sunrise to see Venus became his ritual. It was his way of venerating Orejona. The deity who contacted him and gave him a mission. A mission he is still trying to catch up with after all the events since he arrived in Cuzco some days ago. He grew in wisdom, in mental capacity, in spirit, but he still haven't got his role in this story. His love of truth combined with his peculiar way of seeing the world and thinking things made him a man worthy of participating in something really big. By his own virtues he was chosen from hundreds of millions of people to be the messenger probably of the greatest change mankind has ever seen.

As he crossed the borders of the site of Tiahuanaco, Fernando went to *Plaza de las Cabezas*, the sunken temple. The sky before dawn was clean and filled with stars. It was cold, but there was no breeze. Something odd hung heavy in the icy air. It was possible to feel it, but... he could not understand what was happening in that deserted place.

Paulo recommended that he went alone to the square. Nothing should distract him in this final stage of the quest. Fernando has to connect to the place and this kind of thing only happens when you connect with yourself. "Is the stone there?", he wondered as he entered the long main avenue.

But something was wrong.

His peace and certainty dissolved into the strangeness of the moment. "This place is not totally empty! Something strange is going on here.", he thinks. "At this time there should be no living thing walking the site. I can't see anyone, but... I'm not alone."

Fernando felt a different energy touching his back. It was a new sensation to him. It was not like anything she'd ever felt before. The gravity of the subject gave Fernando different emotions. Emotions are not soft, but not necessarily bad. Strange just. There was no fear. His mind awakened and freed could identify every aspect of being alive at that moment, but there was an inexplicable tension. Something he did not understand. It was as if someone was focusing his gaze and mentally transmitting messages directly to the nape of his neck.

Instinctively he looked back.

He saw no one.

He continued to walk toward the Square.

Fernando needed to be aware of everything and more. After a few steps he stopped and looked back again. Anything.

"Calm down, man! Do not fall into the illusion of paranoia! Do not give in to fear! There is no fear!", he thought and reinforced. "Stay lucid and attentive. Otherwise you will not be able to. Calm!"

Immediately after issuing that thought Fernando heard a voice calling by his name. It was Rico Calmón! It would be possible? His friends finally managed to get there! But how did they know he was there? This thought never passed through his mind as he could not contain his emotion.

- Rico! – shouted Fernando.

- Fernando, here! Over here!

Fernando changed his direction and ran to the opposite side of the *Plaza de las Cabezas* with joy. His friend and faithful squire had returned and met him at the important moment of the search. It seemed like a miracle, or a movie thing.

- Rico! How did you find me here?

- I followed your path, Fernando. You're no good at erasing trails.

- Yeah... I always forget to erase my tracks, my friend. – he said with unconcealed joy, but respecting the place, keeping his voice down. – I think I found out where the stone is. – he whispered. – It must be right here under the ground, inside an inverted pyramid below this *plaza*, right there! Come with me and I'll show you. I can't believe we're so close!

- Fernando, give it up! We don't need it anymore. – said Rico, expressionlessly motionless in the icy chill of Tiahuanaco's dawn. – The Peruvian government has arrived here before you. They made a backstage deal with the government of Bolivia. *Listen*! The local authorities handed the stone over to the Peruvians. There's nothing left for us.

- *Pardon...* did you say... nothing's left? – Fernando said skeptically, but this time it was different. It was the skepticism of one who does not want to believe that his world "collapsed", different from the skepticism of the researcher who interprets the data coldly. At that moment Eastman was experiencing a violent despair and pure anguish.

- You don't understand, Rico. I know the stone is here. I can feel it! It's very strong! It can't be serious, man! It's here! I know it is! Let's go to the *plaza...*

- Fernando, we were released only because the danger was already muffled. Don't you see? They've won. They got here first. – Rico said forcefully, interrupting the young man. – Do you think what happened in Machu Picchu was a small thing? The whole apparatus of the government was mobilized and they got here earlier. *Get real!* We were released two days ago. That means they've been here at least three days before.

Lia shows up. His sweet voice makes Fernando thrill with happiness. He really likes her. A thing that can't be explained. He feels all the tension of the last days crumbling heavily over his head and starts to cry like a child who's late for a party.

- Fernando! – says Lia with the typical excessive animation. – Let's go, man. It's over. They've arrived here before you. They won the race. We were released, look at us here, uh huh! We came to get you.

- I don't understand. It's over? Did they win? Was all this in vain? My God, all in vain? – shouted Eastman wearily and strangely without any strength. – It's not fair, it can't be true. I saw things, I heard things, I felt things. How could all this have been in vain? That is not what I felt in front of the painting in Qorikancha. – he said as he lost his strength and fell to his knees on the floor, still crying. – We'll never know anything about this story anymore. She is dead forever! It can't be... it can't be...

- Come on, Fernando. – said Lia, holding him by the hands, helping him to get back to his feet. – It's all right! Don't cry, man. Now it's too late. They've arrived before. Those "guys" you were talking about! said Lia, ticking the air with her fingers. – The "guys" that deceive us, they were faster! There's nothing you can do about it?

Fernando, weeping as a child, looked up at the sky directly at Venus, who was still watching them.

- You tricked me! – he said quietly, biting his teeth in anger. His emotions went out of balance and his mind collapsed. – Why? Why?

- Come on, Fernando. It's too cold here. You need a hot chocolate and good food. Let's go to the hotel. We can even take a shower together, just like in Paracas. What do you think? – Lia said as she caressed his disoriented head and kissed his icy face.

All the energy he had received inside Puma Punku's chamber had strangely disappeared, and Fernando felt like a living dead. The impact of the strong emotions of despair and anguish was a major blow to his strong mind. Nothing could comfort him at that moment. Just the affection of his faithful friends. All his quest, all the dangers and adventures they have gone through was in vain. It was too much to believe.

The three entered the jeep borrowed from *señor* Domingos and went to a hotel in the city of Tiahuanaco where they had two rooms booked. Before Fernando asked Rico to take them to a place where he should get his things. He was totally stunned. He didn't say they were going to his father's house. He wanted to make a surprise, but even the fact that his father was alive encouraged him. The sun hadn't risen yet. They drove through dark alleys, entered almost every street of the village, but they didn't find the old Eastman's house. Rico drove the jeep complacently into every street Fernando asked.

- That's weird! I can't find the house! It was around here! I'm... pretty sure!

Fernando felt confused. Paulo Eastman's house was on that street, but he could not find it. Everything was getting more and more confusing. The house was there. He slept there. Took a shower. He talked all night with his father. He heard about the reptilians and a lot of other things. The man is alive! The physical and mental weakness quickly convinced him to go with his friends directly to the hotel.

Fernando went with Lia to her room and took a nice hot shower. The hot water helped him recover from the shock. Everything was very strange. Eastman felt weird, he could barely speak. They went down to the hotel's dining room and enjoyed the breakfast. Rico was already at the table when they arrived. They were silent because Fernando was really in shock. He sat down with Rico while Lia went to serve herself.

- How do you feel, Fernando? – Rico asked, staring into his eyes. – Are you feeling better?

Fernando didn't answer. He only stared into Rico's eyes with a lost, empty look. The spirit behind those eyes was crying for help. He could not assimilate the facts that eventually buried his sacred quest.

- How did the "guys" get there before? No one knew anything! Did Professor Fontanoura say anything? – he wondered.

- Eat something, Fernando. You look like shit!

- Rico, I saw you both being released by the police a few hours ago. I was inside a newly discovered chamber in Puma Punku. I went to the Island of the Sun, fainted in the desert. You lost a good deal of the story these days you were arrested. When I recognized you in the film, I got very happy, man. It was an immense joy. – he said in a weak voice as tears came back to his eyes. – What did they do to you? Were they violent?

- No, Fernando. They just arrested us and asked for you. We went through several interrogation sessions, but we did not say anything. We did not really know anything. We knew that you were in Arequipa. You were very lucky to escape. The operation has been synchronized.

- It cost me a lot of money, Rico. It was an action movie escape. A lot happened to me after that. – he said gloomily, remembering the days he spent in the highlands in meditation, the lady who welcomed him, his insights, Marita and everything. – But the craziest of all was someone I met up here, man. My dad! Can you believe it? He is alive and he lives *here*!

- Fernando. We look for his house and we didn't find it. I think you're still very confused.

- We didn't find his place, I know. This is very strange! But I spent the night there. I went to sleep after hearing everything he knows about the Dracos. Ever heard of them? I don't know how I couldn't find the house. It was so close! How did I get lost ?! I'm very confused, Rico... very confused...

Fernando spoke again exalted but exhausted in his strength as he placed his hands on his face and rested his elbows on the table still trying to assimilate it all. He realized that he could not concatenate his ideas with the usual clarity. After a brief pause, Rico shoots point blank.

- Dracos, Fernando? This is all bullshit! Invention! Conspiracy, whatever you wanna call it. None of this is real. Everyone knows. Lizards dominating the world, geckos counting money? Big media misleading information. This is shit for brains, man... to keep people busy. Don't fall for it! Your father deceived you. In fact, your father is *dead*!

- No, Rico! My father is alive! It's real. Reptilians are real, man! History shows they are hidden behind every written page! The Sumerians, the Egyptians, the Aztecs, the...

- Fernando! – interrupted Rico in an altered voice. – None of this is real! *Señor* Julio Pranas must have put something hallucinogenic in our water. None of that was real! Wake up, man! Juan Navarro, Marita, all these people! You cannot be trusted... – he paused. – They're all crazy! You must be suffering the effects of altitude sickness! We are at 4,000 meters of altitude. You're delirious, man. You've been seeing things these days. Your father is dead and none of this was real!

- I can't believe what you're saying! I talked to my old man! – said Fernando with gritted teeth. – He gave me some tea, I slept in his house, it was all there! My backpack is there! No one else knew the clues, just me. – he said totally confused without being able to give coherence to the ideas. – We flew from Nazca to Paracas, the desert and the lady, Catalina, the painting, Professor Vicenzo...

- Do you believe in me, Fernando? – interrupted Rico, with severity in his voice and eyes.

As he argued, Fernando realized that his sight was getting blurry. He looked at Rico and saw that his neck was kind of... disappearing and he was merging with the landscape of a large carpet that was hung on the wall of the hotel's dining room, right behind his friend. Rico's hands were also merging with the table cloth, cutlery, and plate. The more he looked, the more he became convinced that he was getting sick. Her sight was as confused as her mind. His physical weakness took him over. His mental weakness knocked him out.

- Look, man, I swore to help you to death. – Rico said, looking deep into Eastman's eyes. – But the house of cards has gone down! Look into my eyes. Nothing happened! This was a big collective hallucination.

At that moment, as he looked into his friend's eyes, he noticed that when Rico blinked his eyes, his pupils changed shape. They went from round to oval and returned to normal in the other blink. Fernando felt very weak and could not think clearly. Everything was shuffling inside his head. He could not even put the facts in chronological order. Was it all unreal? He fought this idea as he gradually regained the reins of his mind. In the meantime Lia arrived at the table with bread, butter sachets and jellies, black coffee in a large cup and a nice glass of orange juice.

- There you go, Fernando. Are you feeling better? You took it all too hard. I hope you're not upset with us for showing you the reality. – said Lia bluntly.

- Lia, it may have been an illusion, but I still don't understand why. Why did this happen to me? Why did you get into this madness with me? It can't have been in vain. Don't you get it? Nothing happens to us for no reason. The old man in Cuzco, the painting, Nazca, everything was very special for me. Finding you was special. – said Fernando still confused. – How did they get here before me? No one had the information I had! If all this is unreal, why the "guys" have come? Who are they?

- Meeting you was the best thing of my life, Fernando.   Lia said in her soft voice, trying to change the subject. – Not everything can be understood. Not everything is here to be understood. There are things we can't reach. Everybody knows it. Even me, the dumb one! – she laughed softly, caressing his hair. – Put away your stance of a "know all" scientist. It doesn't fit you, it's not good for your career. I prefer you with a book in hand than on the roads of Peru fleeing from something that doesn't even exist, chasing crazy legends. If you stay home quietly I can stay with you forever, my love. I'm glad I came into your life.

Fernando was getting weaker and weaker. Lia comforted his pain with her velvety voice, warm to hear. "Stay with her forever? Not bad!", he said to himself. It is the first time since the adventure began 21 days ago that Fernando Eastman diverts his focus from his goal. He felt hungry. He got up and went to the buffet to get some food to try to quell the physical weakness generated by the rush of these days and the "check mate" of disappointment. But when he filled his cup with coffee something came to his attention. It was like a flash, as if someone had pulled a cable that was plugged into his mind. Questions began to leap into Fernando's mind.

"Why did Rico insisted so much that I gave up? Why did he convince me that all this was an illusion? Wasn't he the guardian, the faithful agent of the Professor? What made him give up the search? It was as important to him as it was to me! Why does he talk like that, having witnessed all those incredible things with me? Why does he say that those people who helped us are all crazy? He even made me believe them by saying they were guardians of the tradition and that they were trustworthy!"

- I was hypnotized by Rico! Is that possible? – he murmured

Eastman realized there was something very wrong in those last thirty or forty minutes and he was trying to understand what was happening. He was sure he was not crazy. It all had to be real. From the buffet table, he was discreetly looking at Lia, who was naturally speaking at the elbows and totally oblivious to the seriousness of the situation. So far so good. This is how she is. But Rico wasn't acting normally. He talked to Lia excitedly and laughed with her as if they were great friends. "They hardly spoke to each other a few days ago!", he thought. "Rico does not have this friendly profile. He's more reserved. As far as I know, he's not an outgoing person."

Hearing Lia say that "they've won!" felt like a punch in Fernando's stomach. It echoed in his mind. "It was not a soccer game, Odalisca! It was important! We could not lose!", he though as he poured himself some coffee.

- She called me "Fernando", not "nerd"! – he said quietly. – There's something wrong here! Very wrong! Careful, Fernando! Strengthen your mind. Now!

Fernando Eastman decides to use what he has learned in these last days.

He immediately brought to mind the image of the stone he saw with the help of *señor* Juan Navarro.

He took a deep breath to get some energy and went to sit down.

He was eating in silence. His strength was gradually recovering along with his mind. He acted naturally as the light of the lost stone filled his mind. Fernando slowly raised his head. He sensed it was not good to look Rico in the eye. Then he asked them both, out of the blue, with a snake-like look ready to attack its prey:

- Where's Catalina?

They looked surprised at each other.

- I don't know, Fernando! – Rico responds ironically with a dull laugh and a wry look. – We didn't force her to do anything. She just went home. She didn't even talk to me. She was released from jail before us.

- Yes, Fernando. – added Lia. – She was upset that she lost *señor* Juan's car and left. Didn't say goodbye! That was rude! She must be fucking mad with you. Where's the old man's car? Where did you leave it...

- Wow! too bad. – interrupted Eastman, stifling Lia's small talk. – And you didn't do anything to stop her, Rico. – he said, simulating kindness mixed with weakness. – I thought you liked her.

Fernando was trying to understand the situation. "There's something wrong here."

- And she seemed to like you very much. – he continued after a brief pause to sip his coffee. – Did she fall out of love?
- There are many women in the village, Fernando. I will not cry for her. Detachment, my friend. Detachment! – said Rico almost with laughter.
Brief pause for chewing.

- How did you find out that Juan and Julio are crazy? – Eastman asked Rico as he swallowed the food.
- Why, Fernando? It's obvious! They only talk about legends that nobody knows. I have come to the conclusion that with the end of this quest, the golden goose also dies.
Brief pause. A tasty sip of coffee.

- Wow! I haven't had a coffee since... Cuzco, maybe! – said Fernando with great pleasure, trying to demonstrate that he was already well recovered. – Very good to see you again, *señor* Coffee Cup. I missed you! – he said humorously , but without losing control of the conversation. He still did not understand, but he was thinking better. He was the one asking questions. There was no room for chatter.
- That's good, Fernando! You're more blushing. – said Lia, patting her head.
- Have you met Marita, Rico? – he snapped again.
"Me? No... not personally. – he stammered. – But they say she's a madwoman who has lost her tourist guide credentials because she talks too much. She shocked many tourists with her cheap esoteric hallucinations. Her tales and beliefs are just folklore, but she speaks as if they were real! This was ruining the entire tourist network of Puno. Did you know that there are many complaints about her? Did you know she keeps pushing to the tourists the books she writes and edits independently. She is an explorer of mysticism who makes money from old rope. That not good for business, man. Is she still working?

- How do you know what she does? You've never met her! You did not even know of her existence until *señor* Juan told us to look for her! Soon after you got arrested, didn't you? – Eastman said gently, hiding his intentions. – I didn't think you could form such a firm and detailed idea about a person without even meeting her or even talking to her personally. You're not this kind of person, man. – he said quietly without altering the tone of his voice.

- She's crazy, Fernando! Believe me! Look into my eyes. Tell me what she told you.

Fernando bowed his head quickly. He avoided looking at Rico. He lifted his coffee cup to his mouth and took a long sip. He spread butter on a piece of bread, took a bite e chewed slowly.

- Lia, have you eaten this bread? It's awesome!

Fernando cleverly changed the subject. He realized that the telepathic technique was not working with them, but he had managed to block their influence on his thoughts. "What's going on here, my God? Why is all this? What the hell is going on?".

He could not read minds, just influence them. He knew that. "Is Rico trying to influence my mind? Mind games??? *What the fuck!?*" His strength was quickly restored. He could not, however, understand the reasons of his dearest friends.

- You're right, Rico. She told me only nonsense. You're absolutely right. I've only been dealing with mad people lately. – said Fernando, disguising his doubts and making Rico believe that he had been convinced by him. – I fell into the trap of the crazy folklorists of Peru. Imagine the four of them, Jamirez, Juan, Julio, Marita. They must be laughing at me now. That's what you get when you believe in conspiracy theories. Ridiculous! You are absolutely right. At least I didn't give them money. Sons of bitches! At least... well... we travel through Peru like no one's ever traveled!

- That's right, Fernando! – said Lia cheerfully. – Leave it behind and let's be happy.

Fernando was feeling stronger. His head was more clear than when he arrived at the hotel. With some surprise, but fearless, he realized that Rico's hands were again merging with the tablecloth. He also noticed that the pupils of both subtly shifted to that venomous snake oval shape. He was *not* crazy and he was happy about that.

- It is good to see that your intelligence prevailed, my friend. – said Rico with coolness and satisfaction. – You should write a book, you know. Your mind is too bright to waste with searches and conspiracies. Your hallucinations are food for thoughts for people who like to fool themselves with fantastic stories about aliens. Your family must know good editors. Write a book, man! Maybe you discover unknown skills.

- *Outlanders...* – he murmured using the syntax proposed by his own father a few hours ago.

- What?

- Nothing... nothing. That's true, Rico. Maybe I will write a book... good idea! People like to cheat and to be cheated. This is the predominant nature of this society dominated by lies. Let's capitalize on books. Good idea! – he said, smiling, but meaning every word he said.

Silence dominated the table for a few seconds. Fernando finished his cup of coffee and continued talking. The two friends looked at each other and sipped their coffee.

- Well, I think I'm going to the toilet. I'm kind of dizzy yet, and I've got a fucking belly ache. It must have been the dirty water in this filthy place. Can you wait for me? I think it's gonna take a while. – Fernando said with a cranky smile. – I want to leave this place as soon as possible! I can't stand it anymore.

- Of course, Fernando. – said Lia. – This will be good for you. We'll be here waiting for you right here. Go ahead.

***

That was a cheap hotel. There were bathrooms only in the rooms. Fernando left the restaurant, sneaked into the lobby, left the hotel and ran to *señor* Domingos' jeep. He started the car and dashed to the site, directly to the *Plaza de las Cabezas*.

- There's something very wrong here! – he said out aloud.

– I'm out!

He decided to go to the *plaza* to clear his doubts. His friends would not let him go.

Fernando Eastman abandoned his feelings and respected his senses.

* * *

He got to the *plaza* in minutes. It was not yet open for visitation. He got out of the jeep, jumped the fence on the same place he jumped earlier, and headed to his goal. He ran down the steps of the *Plaza de las Cabezas* and faced the statue of Wiracocha right in the center. He looked up at the sky, looked at the statue, looked around, and tried to clear his mind. He carefully observed each of the heads represented in the internal walls of the newly excavated and restored square. He tried to find some meaning, some orientation on what he should do. It was time to make choices. His mind was running fast: his two friends had confused him.

He was inside the Plaza for a few minutes already, but still he didn't know what to do. He didn't know where or what to look for, there was no one to help him as it had happened so far. There were no crazy old men, no holographic images, no crazy women, not even his father was there. But he knew it was all real. His sanity was back. Fernando was again 100% connected with the mental state of peace he had learned to control in the desert.

He decides to sit on the floor and try to make a telluric connection, just as he did before in Puma Punku. Time was running out. At that point the heads of the *plaza* began to move in and out of the wall like a video game. Fernando didn't know if it was an illusion or real. He didn't care to know. He just watched. The walls around him began to spin slowly as he tried to calm down. Everything around him was slowly accelerating like a whirlwind of power, an energetic swirl. There was no dizziness. Everything was turned, but his center of gravity remained inert.

In the distance he heard Lia's voice shouting his name. He looked at her at the top of the staircase that leads to the square.

Rico was right behind her. Everything was in motion around him. The energy field that surrounded him was extremely powerful. He looked at his friends and saw their faces. They were deformed. They were not human faces! They were very white, *albini* to better illustrate. And they had scales covering the whole nape of the neck to the forehead. Their hands had only three long thick fingers. The energy field revealed to Fernando the true identity of those two. They were not really his friends.

- Draconians! Shape-shifters! Of course! They work on the level of illusion. They lie. They wanted to deceive me. I almost believed them! – he concluded with astonishment. – Thank you for teaching me about them, dad! I'm going to find out what those "guys" want to hide!

Quickly Fernando closed his eyes, mentalized the light of the stone and spoke the word:

- **Orejona**!!!

A violent flash falls on the *Plaza*. Fernando looks at the beings disguised as Lia and Rico and realizes they are paralyzed. Time stands still. A Condor flying high against the blue, orange sky above his head is now standing motionless in the air. There is no wind, no heat, no cold.

Nothing moves in that place.

The walls of the temple are no longer running either.

The whirlwind had ceased.

"It's a state of awareness, obviously. The Laws of the Cosmos never stop!" he thought entranced by the beauty of the moment.

He walked all the length of the walls and touched the stone carved heads with the tips of his fingers as if trying to find a key to enter the pyramid.

"They're really fantastic! The third stone must be here!"

This square features stone crafted faces with wide, thin, straight noses, mouths with thick and thin lips, Oriental eyes, Caucasian traits and even two very peculiar figures that do not look like humans. They present those typical alien traits that dominate the "post Roswell" human imagination: large, almond-shaped eyes, thin mouths and almost no nose, just breathing holes, thin jaws and large skulls.

The time is still frozen.

Fernando has just checked all the heads and went back to the center of the square and stopped in front of the statue, supposedly from Wiracocha. He realized that there was a strong energy field emanating from there. The energy that made the time "stop". It was strong enough to distort the entire stone image that looked pliant like a reflection on the surface of a lake. The distortion was visible to the naked eye. Fernando guessed that the energy field should be the access to the pyramid.

A decision had to be made.
He, in fact, had no choice.
The time has come!

He had his hand in the cup, but it was not a prize he was looking for. "Great knowledge comes with great responsibility", he thought. He touched the energy field with the tip of his finger. They disappeared and reappeared as he removed it.
- It's here! It must be!
Without hesitation he entered the field with his whole body. As in a magic trick, Fernando entered another dimensional reality.
He was already inside the pyramid.

The silence was absolute. Fernando could barely hear his own heartbeat. In front of him there was a narrow staircase. He came down calmly and cautiously. There was no sign of deterioration in the corridors. Everything seemed to have been done yesterday. At the end of the staircase he came upon a long spiral corridor which led to small chambers.

- Man! This place is the same as my dreams!

As he moved along the corridor, Fernando realized he was walking in slow motion, as if there was not much gravity, just like an astronaut on the moon. Everything was slow, light and graceful. There was no smell in the air. No dust on the floor. The environment was absolutely aseptic. The pyramid seemed never to have been visited by anyone. As he walked, he noticed that each of the small chambers was illuminated by some source of light. They were stones that radiated light. Each room with a different color and each level below the other following the spiral. Fernando didn't hesitate and went down the corridor.

The first was a red chamber. There was a stone that radiated this frequency of color. It was a small diamond-shaped block. It was right in the center of the chamber miraculously balanced by one of its open-angled corners so that the diamond was perfectly balanced with its sharp sides equidistant from the ground. There was a huge symbol engraved on the wall across from the entrance, but he could not decipher it. It was nothing his brain could identify.

The next room was orange. The stone was also a diamond, but larger, and balanced in the same way, only by the sharp corner, defying the laws of physics and displaying an incredible plastic harmony. There was also a large unidentified symbol on the wall much like the Hindu *OM* mantra, but a bit different.

He went to the yellow chamber. The stone in there was a cube with one side perfectly seated on the floor. The symbol on the wall was a big "V", or rather a symbol that looked like the letter V of our alphabet. It was in perfect alignment with Earth's center of gravity. He stopped and took some time inside. There was something keeping him in there. It was a feeling of soft numbness.

The fourth chamber was all green, illuminated by two

relatively fine and fairly long rectangular parallelepiped stones. The two were exactly alike and stood side by side vertically and equidistantly. They did not lean on any base, but simply floated by radiating their frequency of light. On the wall there was a large carved circle. Right in the center, crossing the whole diameter, there was a line that divided the image in half. The set of vertical parallelepipeds with the circle cut in half seemed to impart a great sense of peace. Fernando noticed that the gradual change of rooms and the color bath made his mind lighter.

- This is an advanced chromotherapy session! – he said. – It's impossible not to relax the mind in here!

The chromotherapeutic bath was inevitable and irresistible. It was like a ritualistic bath of purification before having an audience with the goddess Orejona. That was how it had to be. The mind is the only means of talking to Her and it is only possible to attain the proper mental state passing through the chambers one by one.

Today the guest for an audience with the "goddess" is a "human" named Fernando Eastman.

The blue chamber was next. There was also a cube radiating light, but it was balanced by one of its chants. The axis of equilibrium was at a perfect angle of ninety degrees aligned with our gravitational axis. On the wall he could see three horizontal lines engraved with equidistant perfection. The lines were parallel to each other. Two had the same dimensions. The other was shorter and was positioned between the other two lines, right in the center of the set in smooth harmony.

- What does that mean?

The sixth room was violet. As Fernando entered, he felt a strong sense of detachment from his body. It was as if his body was not following him, but it was. The stone was a sharp, high pyramid. The symbol on the wall was a great perfect circle. This circle was the most perfect thing Fernando had ever seen. Its perfection and lightness touched him deeply. He remained there for a few minutes. The feeling of detachment was total.

Then he headed for the last chamber.

- What awaits me in there?

Fernando Eastman returned to the central corridor and descended another few yards into the white room.

- There it is!

The entrance of the Great Chamber was simple and clear like the whole pyramid, from the first steps to that very room. It was considerably larger than the other chambers. Fernando was inside a giant cube. Right in the center there was a pyramid-shaped rock. This stone, which seemed to be five feet on the base side, was 100% crystalline and was laid on the floor. Hence one can roughly calculate the height, since the angulation seemed very close to the Great Pyramid of Egypt. But the material was odd.

There was no impurity, no mark. It was an unprecedented object. There is nothing on this planet with this perfection. It was as if it were something out of Plato's World of Ideas. That pyramid was *the concept* of a pyramid, but made of crystal, *the concept* of crystal. Its shape was only seen when Eastman, the observer, moved in front of it. If Fernando stopped immobile, he would never see Orejona's third stone, for the crystal was almost immaterial.

There was nothing engraved on the walls, also almost immaterial and so perfect in the finishing. Fernando tries to understand what he should do now that he is face to face with his goal. Nothing was said about what to do after finding the stone. He will have to figure out for himself. His mind is free from any earthly mental obstacle. Nothing else exists, only his presence in that sacred place. That moment was *the concept* of the Sacred experienced by a human being. He remembers the two other stones of Orejona: the Kaaba and the Coronation Stone.

- If the Kaaba absorbs all the sins of the faithful who touches it... I think I must touch the crystal. The Coronation Stone has another feature. *Señor* Juan's said it works as a *"direct communicator between the telluric power and extraterrestrial or spiritual powers"*. It connects Earth to the spiritual space. Whoever is crowned under these conditions becomes "unbeatable".

Fernando knew: the crystal should be touched so that he would connect with Orejona.

He was serene.

Everything was happening on the mind level.

There was no talk in that chamber.

It was not right to stain a place like that with the rough, disharmonious human voice.

Fernando forgot all about the book and his will to interpret the unknown language. All this earthling banalities were left behind. His rational functions are off-line now. He is working with his pure spirit. There is nothing in there that human reason can explain. The human intellect has no capacity to understand that place. The ritualistic chromotherapy really prepared Fernando for all this.

He then walks quietly to the pyramid and extend both hands to finally fulfill his mission.

His palms softly touch two sides of the stone.

Instinctively he touches at the area in which concentrates most of the stone's power, equivalent to the King's Chamber of the great pyramid of Giza. A tingle runs through his hands. In a flash all his biological functions were shut. There is no more body. It's not necessary to take it to meet with the Goddess. She speaks directly to the *self* level.

Fernando opens his eyes and finds himself sitting in a beautiful armchair lined with a fabric that does not exist on Earth. He couldn't even recognize that color. He soon realized that it were *not* his physical eyes that had opened, but his perception.

- Where am I? – he asked, still kind of lost.

- Your body is on Earth, from which it will never leave, but your mind is in the Fifth Dimension, my plane of reality. Welcome human named Fernando Eastman. I must congratulate you. Your virtues and your merits have brought you here.

- Orejona! – he said in awe and reverence.

- Yes, Eastman. I am known there on your planet by that name. You can call me that. I will make that everything that happens here have a familiar background with your terrestrial reality so that you can assimilate as much as possible. Are you comfortable in your armchair?

- Yes.

- We do not need it here. It was created so that you have the feeling that you are sitting.

- Thank you. – he said with humility.

- Can you understand me when I say it?

- Yes, of course.

- We do not need spoken language here. We are mental beings. There is no spoken language here because we do not have to lie. Our minds are pure and free from small and petty thoughts. If I speak to you in this way, it is because you, humans in the current phase of evolution, can only understand oral language.

- Thanks again.

- Ask! – She said forcefully, but respectfully. She recognized the value of this human, though he was far from perfect.

- Ask? Ask what? – said Fernando a little confused.

- I'm not going to teach you anything, Eastman. I'm just going to answer your questions. Go ahead. You are capable. What do you want to know?

Fernando always went after the knowledge, always wanted to know more, but the Orejona's question showed he never really knew what he was looking for.

- Why does *selfishness* reign among human beings? Why do the few have it all and the rest have nothing? I think it's a good start.

- It's a *great* start, Eastman. You know the answer. – said the Goddess with serenity.

- If we knew the answer, our world would not be that it is.

- I said *you* know the answer. The rest of your world doesn't seem to know there is a question.

- I don't know. It could be anything. Is it because it's in our nature, perhaps, or maybe we are a poorly evolved race?

- Yes. It's in your nature at this evolutionary stage, but not by original programming. You *have learned* to be as you are. You learned early on to be selfish with your little things. It's understandable. Humans carry DNA created by the Eternal. The Eternal gave you free choice, so your DNA could be reprogrammed, but the individuals must *choose* to reprogram themselves. There are, however, two characteristics that cannot be purposely erased: **the consciousness of the Divine Love** and **the longing of when you were pure** and didn't have to skin yourselves alive to earn your living. Humans long for home. This longing is in the inmost of its molecules and it will never be suffocated by inhuman behaviors. The longing will only cease on the day when humans, individually and by free choice, return to Paradise, spiritually speaking, of course. As well as the ability to understand what love is and what it is to love.

- Human nature is a great mess. No one knows anything, everyone is lost. It's frustrating! But I still don't understand *why* we are so selfish.

- That frustration of earning the living on Earth is brutal. Each little thing that is conquered is like a little relief from the great malaise. Nevertheless that alone does not justify the size of the problem. Selfishness has risen to an unseen level throughout your history and this can't be only due to the suffering to get a minimum of material comfort.

- What would it be, then?

- Selfishness has material roots, of course, but it also has social and spiritual roots. Socially, from the earliest age, you behave as if one was better than the other. You offering pleases God more than the other's. Your car is newer than your friend's. Your garden is greener than your neighbor's, and things like that. The first murder of human history, says your Bible, was because of the sacrifice of a human named Abel. It seemed to have please

God more than his brother's offerings, the famous Cain. It does not matter if this really happened the way it was written, but the message was given in an exemplary way. Few people understand. You put away the true message and focus on *judging* poor Cain. You judge because you have learned to judge. Humans act as if the "smoke", or the "car" or the "garden" represents what is of the most importance in the Universe. Selfishness begins in envy. And isn't envy an illusion?

- Our spiritual leaders teach us to judge by their own example of religious intolerance.

- And you are afraid of an infantile fantasy of God. This is understandable. Religions are manipulated from the moment they become closed doctrines. But the superficiality of you humans is something unique! You are not accustomed and go deep into the important issues of existence. This is demonstrated throughout the recorded history of mankind. You developed into an extremely shallow species. There are exceptions, of course. There are more evolved beings. There is life among the living dead, and this is for sure. You are one of them.

- "This life is something that should not be", someone said. Why should we say *Yes* to this life when it's all guided by selfishness?

- Not just selfishness. A certain spiritual leader of his 6th Century, Pope Gregory I, defined the Seven Deadly Sins. There are variations on the subject, but Gregory saw everything with great clarity. Humans are buried in the "seven sins". It's on your TV sets 24 hours a day. TV *is not* the image of the Beast, as some say. It is, in fact, the strongest currency ever developed especially to "buy people". And you sell yourselves for very little. At every instant the Infinite Cosmos receives the waves of the transmissions that leave the powerful antennas of the television and radio transmitters. We know how you function by simply watching your TV. Those waves reach other dimensions.

- A kind of Cosmic Big Brother? Is that right?

- No! We *never* judge! It is not like the concept of "omnipresent divine observer". We observe to be able to help.

- Explain.

- An example: **Laziness**. It is difficult to find many humans of good will. You are so massacred that you no longer enjoy working. And laziness sets in and you rationalize everything around you to justify your sloth. **Wrath**, because people kill for stupid things. You always fight, but you rarely get together. The children of Abraham feel a lot of anger about each other. Do you know who the children of Abraham are, Eastman?

- Yes. The descendants of Sarah and Hagar, the Egyptian slave of Abram (who would later become Abraham). The names were Isaac and Ishmael respectively. Abram had children with the two women by divine intervention. Ishmael was the firstborn, but he was not the son of his wife. Actually the result of God's plan today, looking at Israelis and Palestinians, is absolutely incomprehensible to me.

- They've missed their chance to understand each other for a long time. They're killing themselves and it's going to get worse. They also don't know the truth. They are totally involved in the famous "divide and conquer". They are manipulated by beings who want to see humanity destroy itself. You don't have to be a prophet or a visionary to see where the wrath of these peoples will lead them to. Few human groupings, looking at a historical perspective, failed to manifest wrath. A concept deployed and developed by those who want to divide and to conquer.

- True.

- **Gluttony**, through their silhouettes. The dissatisfaction with life makes them eat. Humans don't feed, they *eat*. And the aesthetic standards of today are cruel to the human *psyche*. Hence more dissatisfaction, more food. Gluttony is the outlet for dissatisfaction. **Envy**, because there is no peace in the unmerciful world of consumption. You have to have stuff because someone has it. It is the over-valuation of the futile and the unnecessary, the petty and the small. It's almost a primate reaction when they see bananas. **Pride**, as if it were the fire that warms your hearts. "We are the biggest chemical company in the world", "I am among the 1000 richest men in the world", "my school is much better than yours", "my hair is more beautiful than yours", and the madness goes on at all levels of recognition. Very few human beings are not like that. **Greed**, nothing needs to be said. See what you do in exchange for money. Ask for money in the streets and see what you get! Each coin is worth more than a life. **Lust**, because there is nothing on this planet that hasn't been *eroticized*. Even children, at their earliest ages, are taught to be "object" through the children's TV shows that parents so often neglect.

- But things got out of control because of **your** silence, the gods! – said Fernando with energy. – Why didn't you correct us? Why did you never come and guide us?

- We came, Fernando, and you know it. Don't close your eyes to reality, it is important. – said Orejona calmly, still with the same unshakable serenity. – Yahweh took care of his people, the sons of Shem, the post-Flood matrix. Krishna looked after his people in India, Apollo, the Greeks and Romans, Odin and Thor, looked after the Norse. I, while I was in your dimensional plane, cared for my children affectionately. During your Bible story you have been helped and guided many times by beings like us. Unfortunately you have always turned away because there were beings working in the *split* between humans. And you always ended up being punished by these "gods" who claimed to love you so much. And *you* chose to believe them, not us! The secret lies in the *choice* that seeks happiness. That was tirelessly taught, but you never understood it. Everything that was taught was abandoned. Everything that was said was ignored.

- Yes! You helped, but it didn't work! We made mistakes because we were deceived. – exalted Fernando. – Nothing went right from *day 7*, when God turned his back to "rest". Lucifer won! How was this possible?

- You know the basic plot. You tell me.

- But Eva was deceived! Adam had no other choice.

- Of course he did! It was total fidelity to the Creator or Eve. It was a choice between the spiritual and the material. He chose the world of matter. Simple as that. Freewill is a test of choice. There was not much to think about. They were just two alternatives. Adam was happy and sovereign in his land. He decided to give up his eternal happiness in exchange for his life-mate. It's hard for you humans to understand that. Due to this error you unfairly blame the reptile. The poor woman was not really to blame. The snake was not to blame. Neither Adam, in my opinion, but the human couple knew what would happen. They were aware, so they were not *ignorant*. We are not talking about infinite codes of laws. No! It was Matter or Spirit. A or B! Being not ignorant, they failed the test. It must have been a disaster for Adam to face the consequences because he and his wife met Eden and lived there for a long time before being transferred from their lives of joys and charms to the hard, sweaty life of the planet.

- Why did Lucifer do that? Was it the frustration of not having been given the chance to rule? Was it out of selfishness? How can a perfect being have selfishness?

- Basically, yes. He had an interesting, innovative government plan. On this plane there would be no Freewill. The beings of the Universe would not have the choice between Good and Evil. They would have agendas and should follow them. There would be no human life in the Third Dimension. You would live in the Fourth Dimension and everyone would live their lives where Good and Evil would be understood. I mean, men would have within their minds the awareness that the fundamental duality Good and Evil is nothing but *part* of a world of fear and insecurity.

- Good and Evil would it be something overcome and encompassed by human consciousness? – asks Fernando.

- Yes, but the Creator did not think it was good. Without freewill, without the choice by recognition, human life would have no meaning. There is no virtue when you act out of fear or insecurity. Without the power of choice, you would only be commanded. Unconditional love for life would only make sense where a deliberate choice in the direction of life and joy was possible. The secret, as I said, is in the choice. Lucifer had no evil intentions at all. He had interesting but incompatible ideas concerning the plans of the Eternal for mankind. Gradually he fell to selfishness. He didn't understand why the Creator rejected his plan. We were all guided by Lucifer who, with total altruism and recognition of His Creator, performed His tasks perfectly and objectively. Nothing that he communicated to us was distorted or out of divine designs.

- You are an angel… not a goddess!!!

- Yes, you can use that term if you feel better. I was created directly by the hand of God. I am neither woman nor man as you know it. I'm a *female* frequency, just like Sophia, the Wisdom Goddess is. I am no daughter of any father or mother as you are accustomed. I am a being who, by force of circumstances, had to manifest in its three-dimensional reality as a woman to fulfill the Father's designs.

- Explain please.

- I was a direct subordinate of the Light Bearer, the great "Prime Minister of God", as some call him. Lucifer! The most perfect being ever created by the Eternal! I have performed God's designs for a time that you on Earth cannot even conceive in your minds. Here in the Fifth Dimension we do not have the time as a reference. We have what you call *Eternity*. This time concept cannot be conceived by your minds, for it is far beyond your capabilities. You have only a vague idea of what that is. A vague idea that can't even be expressed in your language. You have to *experience* Eternity to understand it. And you have the right and the chance to experience it even by dwelling on these fragile mortal bodies in these instants of life of yours compared to the Cosmos.

- And this is engraved in our genes. – confirmed Fernando.

- It is! The Creator was not unfair. Even after the horrible choice He kept that genetic key in you. There was a moment of eternity in which Lucifer, convinced that his plan of government was better than the original, began to feel unhappy with. Duality settled in him from the moment he understood these forces. This is what the knowledge of Good and Evil did to him. It created dissatisfaction, imbalance. Lucifer, as well as mankind, sealed his fate by free choice. Adam had never before had the sense of dissatisfaction within himself, but the fear of being alone, of losing his life-mate, quickly led him to think that a solitary life would not be satisfactory to him, for he had known carnal love. He could not bear to live without this reality. The possibility of losing Eve generated selfishness in his heart. And he chose it that way.

- I understand. The famous "*I want her for me!*"

- Well, Lucifer seduced me with his virtues. I could not stay away from that Light. It was irresistible. You cannot understand what happened when Lucifer summoned the Assembly of Angels to communicate his plan. It caused great instability throughout the Kingdom of Light in the center of the Milky Way. As you know, a third of rational beings took sides with the rebel. They also could not resist that Light. But he lied to me, to all. After the Fall of Lucifer and his supporters, I realized that I had been deceived.

- Deceived? Explain.

- I've never had any negative feelings about the Source. The Eternal knew it. With great sadness and humility I appealed to the Father. I claimed that as a *female-type* being I had been deceived as Eve. I explained the facts and argued that I had not had the same chance as Eve, since I did not have a pair to help me correct my mistake. The loyalty test, in my case, had not been totally fair. Eve could be forgiven if Adam hadn't fallen, but I could not. I didn't get that chance. As a creature, I asked The Creator that my case would be reviewed and that I would be acquitted.

- What happened?

- The Eternal, with his unspeakable justice, understood that I was right about the unjust condemnation, but still wrong in my choice. As a final and unappealable sentence, I was kept the status of "fallen", but with the possibility of re-ascending to the Kingdom of Light.

- Possibility of re-ascending? A being of your status? I've never heard of it. – said Fernando, impressed by the story. – What was your new test?

- I should manifest myself in the three-dimensional plan and create a civilization that should be the best possible within the Universal Laws of Love. There was no obligation to compete with Him. I just needed to demonstrate that I had understood what true Love was. And I got it!

***

- Tell me about your creation! I want to understand it.

- Creating a civilization was the only way I could redeem

279

myself before The Source. They were perfect. When I gave birth on Earth, I had to spend a lot of time with my creatures until they adapted to the conditions of the planet. My base was the orb that you know by the name of Venus. I created the DNA of my people there and gave birth on Earth, because that was one of the conditions of the sentence. They should be a civilization on Earth, on the sacred surface of Gaia, bathed in the light and vital energy of its glorious Sun. I didn't want to use any existing earthly beings. I chose beings from Venus. We, creatures made by the hands of the Creator Logos, know how to manipulate DNA. I did it all by myself, I mean, the adaptation of the Venusian embryo to a perfect matrix for Gaia. I kept my Venusian facilities airtight with conditions very similar to those on Earth. I also had to adapt to do the job.

- As well? Hermetic housing?

- How do you think the Garden of Eden was? A simple garden? For thousands of years my children lived in peace and harmony. They have not developed any kind of evil thought, not even traces of your beloved Seven Sins, though they have all these characteristics within their genes. These "sins," that is, *patterns of behavior not compatible with love and happiness*, have ruined countless civilizations throughout the Cosmos.

- Then they knew no vices.

- No. It was not like that. They *recognized* that everything that goes against the great **Yes to Life** is a deception, an illusion. They understood what Life is. According to my plans and prudence, they had to be developed apart from the other cultures that already existed on this planet before Adam. He did not want them contaminated by the already decaying cultures. That's why I chose the Andes and the Lake.

- Cultures already decaying?

- Yes. We'll talk about this later.

- What were they like?

- Their physical constitution was very similar to the beings that already inhabited Venus. The altitude and dry air were very convenient. They lived on that plateau in a way that "normal" humans could never have lived. At first they lived in underground cities. Soon the built their houses on the edge of the Lake. They were giants of reddish skin, like their Andean descendants.

- Impressive!

- Earth's gravitational conditions were propitious. Their skulls carried a different brain from yours. Their DNA and minds were fully functioning, so they did not need oral language to communicate. It was all mental. Like you and me here on a higher plane. They never lied. That's why telepathy worked. They had no writing or phonetic language. You no longer have this ability because you have learned to lie... and you enjoyed doing it.

- We've developed language because it helps us articulate our ideas. I myself have to verbalize what I'm thinking so I can understand. I don't think it's a bad thing to talk. – protested Fernando.

- After you learned to lie, you were *forced* to learn to speak. What you have today as a ability to "speak" is an effective way fool people. No one knows if you are lying or if you are hiding the truth. Do you understand this? In mind to mind communication... there is no lie.

- I understand. This is fantastic! – Said Fernando. But It's impossible for us to be like this today.

- My children did not write about their history because their full minds knew it entirely and without any distortion. It was not necessary to leave any records for their descendants. The little that was recorded, however, was destroyed along with them. Nothing remained. When finally, after three generations, they were adapted to the planet, they began to live in modest huts of straw. Traces of their existence are impossible to be found. All perished. Their minds reached a peak never to be reached by the enemies of life. They had great longevity. They lived on average a thousand years, like the first patriarchs on the other side of the world.

- How were they organized? Who was the leader? Was there a hierarchy?

- There was one leader for each group of 50 beings and I personally maintained physical and visual contact with all of them. Whenever a leader died, I would come to Earth and help them in choosing the substitute. The leaders, or priests, were in fact *teachers* who instructed them in the mysteries of Life. During my visits I always took the opportunity to give instructions and elucidate any doubts. Everyone saw me physically and I spoke to everyone, not just the leaders. I did not want to create a "privileged cast" who could be infected by the illusions of Power.

- Wow! So you were not like the other "gods." – said Fernando. – You were constantly among them. There was a time when the "gods" were among their people. Apollo, Odin, Yahweh, and other beings like you. Why didn't these other peoples succeed?

- They worked very well for a long time, but Selfishness settled, no doubt. Yahweh is a good example of this! And decadence came ruthlessly. Not as punishment, but as a consequence of choices. Your humans are pathetic near my children. You are men locked in your own little worlds. You, in general, don't have a common goal at all. Nothing moves your civilization in the same direction. You are living dead and you don't know it. You live divided and disoriented. You love illusions! The great mass of humans only go out on the streets collectively to elect leaders, and can't even do it right. You are easily deceived by the speeches of a rotten and infected political system which only lies and deceits. A system led by the Power of Money. Humanity is the perfect executioner of the agenda and interests of the occult powers.

- Divide and Conquer... – Eastman whispered.

- Humanity now loves "Internet posts". The only interactivity is virtual. They feel safe under a military state that says: *we are here to protect our citizens and our sovereignty*. The "citizens" authorize wars, slaughter and abuse in the name of their own safety. The illusion of fear governs Earth. My people did not conceive such childishness. They were *organized*, not governed. Everyone knew the importance of each one in the community. They coexisted in harmony even in the face of day-to-day adversities because they had each other. There was no dissatisfaction. Everyone took their sustenance from the hard and difficult ground of the desert, just as Adam should do in the fertile land where he was placed. Never, throughout their millennial history, was any kind of injustice committed among them, no crime at all, because there was no selfishness. There was no murder like the story, true or not, of Cain and Abel.

- How did their relationships work? There was no currency, I suppose. Did they help each other... with nothing in return?

- I will give you an example: whenever there was an accident at work, and they worked hard, the whole community to which the injured belonged to provided assistance. Everyone understood their responsibilities toward the others. The awareness that everyone is useful and important fostered a sense of collective commitment. The injured was rescued, treated, nurtured as a brother of all *by* all until his full recovery. Among my children nothing was done for nothing. If someone made a chair for someone, that person would give something in return. Food, useful goods, tools or some animal, adornments, and so on. If someone received something without some kind of exchange they would be considered as beggars and this was not acceptable.

- Yes of course! There are remnants of this custom among some indigenous tribes of Ecuador. This is a legitimate legacy of your children. – said Fernando. – How did they reach this level of evolution?

- Just like Adam. They were made complete with an specific DNA code. I paid special attention to this genetic aspect. And, just like you, they could be reprogrammed. The question is not how they got to that level of evolution. The big question is: *how did they prevented from getting tainted!*

- There was no money. – said Fernando as if it were obvious.

- Everyone ate the same thing, learned and appreciated the same things. There were no social differences. Difference is created by the greed and the selfishness of the illusion of money. This way, unselfishly, they managed to live their entire existence in harmony, mind to mind. I taught them a Universal Truth: **there is no Good and Evil**. Their bodies, however, were subject to three things: to **error**, to **lie** and to **illusion**. I have taught them how not to fall before these three natural problems. If there had been an **error**, it should be recognized by its consequences and **corrected**. And there were mistakes for they were humans, but the problem was perceived and corrected. And they were fully happy. There is no evil in the cosmos. What is understood as Evil is the **consequence of the uncorrected error** and assimilated as "normal".

- To overcome this, to get out of the great cycle of errors, we have to drop everything and go to Tibet! This is crazy!

- That's right! Detachment. A certain Buddha taught this to you and more. My children were more serene than any Buddha. And they did not go to Tibet.

- Buddha was a being like you, I suppose.

- Yes, but from another planet, another galaxy and for other purposes. He taught about detachment. You don't listen to anything wise. We must cultivate Love and let go of selfishness. There has to be a radical break in this decadent human culture. No need to go to the mountains of Tibet. All is mind! You have to understand the illusions. You need to get out of this comfortable cycle of rapid and immediate consumption and cultivate your own food. We need to talk less. It is necessary to meditate on love, this concept that nobody on your planet could define because they have not understood yet.

- Talk about that Love. Do we have time?

- All the time in the world...

***

- ...So, the love I speak of is indefinable in words. You can only get to it through experimenting it. The only way is to living it. Love is the great mystery that the humanity of the Earth must live. After understanding this you will understand the Pyramids of Egypt, the stones of Machu Picchu, the temples of India.

- You speak of a Love we cannot know. How do you expect us to assimilate this if we have no idea what you talk about up there? How can we have this experience?

- One of the greatest proofs of Love you could give yourself would be not to let error prevail. Correct your mistakes and get back on track in the Laws of the Cosmos. But we, here above, know that you are not yet capable of it. Not until you abandon the childish illusions that are sold to you at high prices. You always want more. More comfort, more money, more food, more sex, more leisure, more everything. You are eternally dissatisfied. The three-dimensional thinking system is basically like that. Good and Evil are measures of imbalance. One must prevail over the other. In this dimension one cannot exist without the other, and yet there is no agreement. Therefore, it is necessary to seek equilibrium in order to transpose duality.

- The answer lies in the *balance* between positive and negative. – completed Fernando.

- This quest for balance only works on this plane. Lucifer was deluded that it would be possible to implant the perfect balance of duality. His plan did not include the Third Dimension, but The Eternal knew that this government would spread to the immediately lower and denser dimension and this could contaminate the more subtle dimensions. Therefore, the denial of the implementation of the new government plan. There was no injustice. Lucifer, deeply divided and completely blinded by duality, did not understand the message and began to make "political propaganda" to seize power. The predominance of Love within him... ceased.

- It was a political question, then? We are on this mess because of a political fight?

- Politics, yes. But also moral. The illusion of error is the most dangerous thing for the whole rational universe. Many undetected and uncorrected errors have already annihilated humanities other than yours. My people also ran the risk of degenerating, so I guided them. It's not only this humanity of yours that spend lives and more lives reincarnating in your own little world. You were not even on this plane when it all went off. Eastman, all over the Cosmos there is, there was and there will always be life, human or not, for many eternities using human language. Some have evolved collectively and prospered for millions of years. Some couldn't even pass the early steps!

- As in Adam's case!

- When the Eternal created Adam, the model of humanity, to rule the Universe, there were other rational beings throughout the universe. After his fall, Lucifer immediately began to work elsewhere implanting his plan. He wanted to show his beloved Father that he was right. Many fell before Adam. If you think that between the creation of Adam and his fall only a few days have passed, you deceive yourself. Adam was immortal compared to earthly life today. Before choosing evil and departing from the Source, he lived many long years in harmony and purity in Paradise. On countless planets there are innumerable human civilizations...

***

- Why the snake? Could not he have done it himself? Why did you use a scapegoat?

- Because he knew that Adam's faithfulness to the Creator was unshakable. Adam and his wife would never be persuaded to betray God if Lucifer showed up personally. They were very well instructed by the messengers of the Kingdom of Light. But Lucifer understood the concepts of Good and Evil very well and decided to use them. He determined an agenda to be fulfilled. An agenda that is not good for you, but good for him. And he'll do whatever it takes to get it done. It's a visceral power play. He made an alliance with renegade beings from the Fourth Dimension, the reptilians, far more evolved than you. Lucifer promised them power over humanity and the planet, and so the original inhabitants of Earth did their part.

- If they were here before, why did they lose their right to the planet?

- The reptilians were created before you... and they fell long before you. Some of these beings wanted their original power back. The fallen are no longer entitled to the powers they had on the previous plane. Neither powers nor rights. They lodged on planet Earth because it was pleasant to them. Lucifer, you remember the story, had to kneel before Adam.

- He felt humiliated before the Eternal and before the whole Universe. – completed Fernando.

- It seems that he asked the reptilians to help in his revenge. In return they would not have to kneel or humiliate themselves before Adam, the Sovereign of the Universe who had just come

286

to Earth. But that was a great lie. Typical of Lucifer, of course, but it served the crawlers well. If Adam had not erred by eating of the forbidden fruit, these reptilian beings would not stand the harmony of the planet and would have to leave in search of a new home. It was an act of despair.

- I understand. War is war. You gotta keep the power.

- Although they are originally beings of the Fourth Dimension, above Good and Evil, they are still strongly attached to this gross plane by attachment to the Earth. They understand duality and have overcome it. They mastered some basic physics laws in a way you could never dream of.

- Did they evolve to the point of interplanetary travel? — asked Fernando.

- Of course, as you are doing now. Matter is under the control of the reptilians of the Fourth Dimension, as well as of the millions of other beings who have overcome duality. The reptilians of planet Earth also dominate matter, but not with the power they had before. You have seen that they can shape-shift, can't they? Those who rule matter have power over those who don't. And they are very well organized and commanded by their Fourth Dimensional brethren. They have infiltrated the power networks of human organizations for thousands of years. They are every place and culture.

- How could this happen? It's impossible to believe! If my father hadn't told me about them, if I hadn't seen them face-to-face, I would say this is all insanity.

- Make no mistake, Eastman. Remember: you were not the first bioelectrical beings to exist in the Universe. There are countless forms of intelligent life scattered throughout the vastness of the infinite Cosmos. You can't even imagine. Before you there were countless creations, they still exist and will always exist. As I said, in terms of Eternity, you are a blink of an eye.

- Why are we in the hands of these creatures? Why did God choose this reptilian planet for us to pay for an "original sin" that we didn't even commit?

- This planet is not reptilian! It is a living being in metamorphosis and belongs to no one, only to itself. This being,

Mother Earth, is a divine emanation of the Source. All is God. God is in everything. Even in realities you do not know. The theory of Immanence, which one of our envoys taught you, is a key to overcoming your gross material condition. This being was known to you by the name of Baruch of Spinoza.

- If you wanted to hide the key, you chose the right person. Spinoza is unintelligible to the human race. Despite the beauty of his writings, I would say it was a great waste of time.

- Reptilians couldn't yet detach themselves from the Third Dimension because they have not yet learned to respect life and correct their mistakes. They are also lost in the illusion of the Power and the good life of "slave X masters." But theirs is a more complicated case. As we speak of humanity and the consequences of its primary error of choice, "original sin", they have other issues to overcome. The reptilians, not all and for different reasons, also went through a fall. They have their issues and you have yours. Each with its unique evolutionary challenges to overcome. You, humans need to learn only one thing: the unconditional **Yes to life.**

- I didn't get it. Be clearer, please.

- When Christ came down to earth to teach the way, He said, "I am the branch, and you are the fruit". Isn't that clear? What else do you want to hear? With every step you take towards your stupid little illusions and mistakes, you are further away from the "branches" of the Tree of Life. If the truth about this man, Jesus, the one said to have been born in Bethlehem, came to your knowledge... things would take a turn. But they, the Hidden Masters of your planet, they hid everything and did it in a very efficient way. The art of deceiving and lying assured the reptilians a very solid power. What you call *faith* is only the fruit of centuries and centuries of indoctrination in the sense of *fear*, not freedom.

- Fear. All we do here is packed with fear. How can we understand "Faith" if we are afraid of God?

- Faith in God through fear. Do you think this is fair? Do you think fear fits within the concept of Love? Yet humans follow religions that preach fear disguised as love. The Source wants you to recognize freewill in the same way we do in the more subtle Dimensions.

- How can we say Yes to life if all we know is a lie? – shouted Fernando.

- How do you want to know God with such small thoughts? How to recognize Love if you have wills and desires opposed to the plan of harmony of the Creator? I said *re*-cognize, because you knew it before. You deserve to be scared! Do you think it's unfair to be manipulated by lies? Who wants to know the truth? Tell me, Eastman. Wasn't it said?

- Yes.

- And it was not said once or twice. Truth has been taught a thousand times!

- What I think is unfair is this condition of silence! We need more help than ever before! Where is God when we need it the most? I have this faith you said. I recognize God as the kind Father, the Creator. I feel it exists! You know it. You speak directly to my mind. Why doesn't God talk to us? – asked the nerd, almost begging for a satisfactory answer.

- It's not easy, Eastman. When our envoys travel from the Fifth Dimension to the Third, they need a special means of transportation. We have a technology that you don't understand. In the past, when we came, men considered us gods. In every corner of the Universe it is the same and it will always be. We were welcomed with joy and happiness. Fear also, for every living being fears the unknown. Today, if we land on your planet, you would all panic because you don't believe in anything else, not even gods. The confusion is great in your mind. A lot of you already feel that religion no longer works, but the fear of dropping your old and safe salvationist paradigms is still too big! It would be very easy for your TV, manipulated by the owners of your world, to propagate the idea that *we* are aliens invaders. That *we* are evil. That's what cinema show every day, isn't it? Besides, you would disintegrate in barbarism, for the social control would be lost. Without "brakes" human beings cannot live in society. Your restraint is not the recognition, but the fear of power. Fear of punishment. You need a strong-arm government. This is how you have been indoctrinated for centuries: in fear. Do you really find that unfair? Or do you think Earth's humanity could live without repressive Laws?

- We probably would not work without this system, but we will never know that, will we? The Laws were imposed, the punishments came, and nothing was learned.

- The truth is we are just messengers from the Source. – continued the great goddess. – If the Source determined it to be so, it should be so. I'm not in the position to question the Cosmic Order. You have had a huge number of sightings of our flying objects, haven't you? We are watching closely, as we have always been.

- We learn fear because we do not know the truth. Do you think that's fair? The disappearance of the gods was not good for their creatures.

- Okay, Fernando Eastman. Let's say we land on Earth one day and start talking about what really is the essence of things and some hidden truths. What do you think it will happen? War! Lots of instability. Violence. Powerful opponents will come to us. And people would believe *them*, the ones who have been fooling them for millennia. Your media would sell us as the new "end-of-the-world prophets". Our message would be labeled charlatanism, extreme religious fundamentalism. *Alien atheism*, perhaps. Business opportunities would arise and all sorts of crazy things you can imagine. And no one would listen to us for too long. Your television would easily discredit the case, they would change the subject and within a few years everything would return to normal. Movies would be made, rivers of money would be collected. To openly address humans would be to deliver all mankind at once into the vastness of the Great Error.

- I agree. It's unfortunate, but I agree.

- At a certain moment in history we began to send beings who incarnated as philosophers, scientists, poets, musicians, etc. Beings of Light who, by free choice, were to manifest on Earth to speak with you in the language of reason and art. Da Vinci, the greatest man after the man known as Jesus! Joseph Campbell,

Kepler, Galileo, Spinoza, Socrates, Plato, Dostoevsky, Guimarães Rosa, Gandhi, Mozart, Beethoven, an immense list in all important areas of human culture at different times. Each one bringing Light and examples in their own way and for a specific purpose. Each of them trying to fix certain areas of human behavior and evolution. Either way, the condition on Earth is perfect for a great loyalty test. You failed it. You and many others all over the Universe. And no one can say they were ignorant. The path has been pointed out many times. Many ways. Little was learned. Most preferred to ignore everything we taught and ran to the comfort of religious illusion. This other side, it seems to me, is much more interesting than ours.

- I can't rebut your arguments. You are right. – admitted Fernando.

***

- Why god speaks only of the Hebrew people. Why should a Chinese or an Andean follow the Bible "god"? Why were civilizations destroyed in the name of this "god"?

- Human stupidity has no limits, Eastman. The drunkenness of Power has taken the institution of the Church since its foundation. Where there is material greed, there are reptilians. They dominate matter and infiltrate any organization that values the Power and the comfort it brings. It is theirs the salvationist agenda! In fact, it was they who compiled the Bible that no one ever reads. The Council of Nicaea was organized by Emperor Constantine, led by powerful men. After only 300 years the manipulated Power of the image of Jesus took over the Church. The executors of the Salvationist agenda stifled the truth of the wise teachings of the great Pagan masters and demonized everything that was related to the Nature. They destroyed the peoples who lived in peace without needing religious rules and doctrines. For the faithful, now converted and separated from the Mother Earth by the heavy rod of the Father, for them there is just the *promise* of salvation. Corruption is inherent in Power.

291

- They sold Jesus to those who didn't want to buy. These are the true traitors!

- Intoxicated by the power spiritual leadership brings, they were easily convinced that knowledge about God's true plans should be "simplified". Constantine was adept at bizarre cults. History says he was pagan, but that is not true. He was adept in a society that worshiped and performed rituals in honor of some illusory "lord of darkness." Pagans were worshipers of Nature, Mother Nature. They had great wisdom. They *knew* the Source. They knew the Truth. The Christian Church is the implementation and perpetration of a dark agenda. In a precise blow they placed their representatives on the throne and executed their agenda with remarkable patience. And they started in the right place. They destroyed paganism and the cults of Nature to bury the Truth about Life and Creation. They imposed upon the human intellect the greatest lie of their history: **men must fear Yahweh**. They made every effort to confuse this "god" with The Source. A lot of innocent blood was spilled.

- It's obvious that they're different characters. The terms Yahweh, Lord, and other minor ones are used to refer to a being hierarchically inferior to the terms used for the Creator Logos. Jesus never uses the term Yahweh. Jesus speaks of the Father and not of the impostor Yahweh.

- Right. The manipulators of Faith made a huge and deliberate confusion. They prevented the plot from being understood. Then they hid the true meaning of the Creator's plans. The message of Jesus was for *all* humans. The men who received the honor of the visit of the Anointed had no idea that there were so many different races on Earth. As these other peoples appeared, the power of the adulterated religion felt the need to dominate these beings, for better or worse, and to destroy their cultures.

Now, this is *pure evil*

- All the peoples of the universe, all of them, have the notion of the Sacred. You were beings who related to Gaia through religions of Nature. There was no Bible, Qur'an, Torah. There were no churches, no synagogues, no mosques. To dominate these people full of wisdom they had to be transformed into "God-fearing beings". This is by no means God's plan, but part of the agenda executed by the "hidden hand" that operates behind the Church using people who don't really see what they were doing. The Truth that Jesus taught was simple and still applies to all human beings: *"There is a Source and the Source loves them unconditionally. And you belong to the Source and the Source is in you."*

- As Jung said something like: "Religion is a defense against the Religious Experience"

- It shouldn't be like this. The religious system is indeed a human institution created so that men don't have frequent religious experiences. But inevitably it happens because you have a DNA that favors such experiences. Due to religious influence and with each passing generation, these experiences grow dim. The experience of *knowing that there is a Source and that this Source loves* you is not common on Earth. Humans, in the great majority, fear a "god". We knew that this path of religious experience would easily be discredited if we did not manifest ourselves. But, as I said before, if we appeared and interceded, you would not believe us, you would not listen to us and even would hate us. We only intercede in human history when it was timely. And we can still do that. It's obvious to see the path you're going. You are totally immersed in errors. It's a matter of time until everything breaks down even more. And we don't want that. Our task is to prevent this from happening, but we our hands are bound. *You* bound them. A badly planned action of ours and you end up destroying yourself...

***

- Are these UFOs yours? – asked Fernando, shaken.

- Not all of them. There are numerous objects that appear to you. Some are from other stars. There is a kind of Interplanetary League and you are under constant surveillance. More evolved beings know that the Earth needs to be observed. They know Gaia is being mistreated. Since you began to demonstrate nuclear energy knowledge our observations have become routine. Some arise and eventually abduct humans to experiment with their biological organisms.

- Why these abductions?

- They want to genetically mix with the human race so that in the future they themselves become the natural inhabitants of Earth. They will have to leave where they live because they have destroyed everything with their cold logic. This hybridization will takeover the human genetic traits. There will be no more pure human organisms, and yet the longing for Paradise and the Eternal Love will remain inscribed in your adulterated DNA. That part that is impossible to erase. This beautiful part of your DNA will be transformed into junk DNA. With no apparent service, but impossible to be eliminate. The Love and the Longing of the Eternal will be like dreams that will never be dreamed. And then there will be another creature. Other souls will embody these beings, but will no longer be human souls. You won't be able to continue your evolution. As you can see, there are several agendas for the planet Earth at various levels and in various dimensions.

- This DNA thing is terrible!

- But this will be settled soon. These dark allies, imbued with the destruction of Earth's human DNA, will disappear. Humanity will regenerate itself biologically. We can influence your DNA as much as they can, and we have done it in a way that you can't imagine. We know the secret of genetics while they still need to experiment. Soon cosmic energies will help reprogramming your DNA so you can have some chance of making the evolutionary leap. This is the cosmic clock and it is inevitable. What makes us sad are human souls that have already been lost. These cannot be saved, only destroyed at the end, in the last battle.

- What do you mean with "regeneration"? Why are we here anyway?

- To *unlearn* fear. To turn your backs to the lies and illusions created by the perpetrators of error. You must live all the experiences that are presented to you, good or bad, but you must overcome them as well. You have to say **Yes to Life** and experience everything that comes along with it. Fear is the most reinforced thing since man fell. You were able to create an

"Archetype of Fear".

- Archetype: An experience repeatedly lived and accumulated in the collective unconscious as an energy node accessible through the emotions that experiences bring us. An existential nodule so strong as to become a fundamental experience to be lived. – says Fernando.

- Right. Fear equals the most important aspects of life on this planet to the point to have become an archetype. This is where spiritual defeat takes place. It is by *not* overcoming fear. Once fear is overcome, the individual begins to experiment other aspects like Love, for instance, an archetype much appreciated by us in the Kingdom of Light. **To live without fear is to live in true freedom.** This is what we expect from you: to be free by wisdom.

- To say **Yes to Life**, as Nietzsche said a long time ago...

- Life with a capital "V", as you say on planet Earth. It's this freedom, also archetypal, that you need in order to win the game. These lives that you live serve for you to overcome the "proof of fidelity for recognition", condition for eternal life. You have failed in the test every incarnation because you are afraid to live. My children, while they lived, did not fail. They did not know fear and said **Yes to Life**. But they ended up being destroyed by nature. Inevitability.

***

- How did they disappear? What happened?

- What you call the Universal Flood affected every corner of the planet. Waves went up to the heights of the Andes and washed everything away. This event was purely natural. Your historical records have no precise dates of anything and the ones that have are carefully hidden by those who lie and deceit humanity. From Noah to the incarnation of Jesus on Earth there is a gap of 10,940 years. The Earth was populated by various civilizations that lived according to the recognition of Gaia as a source of inexhaustible life linked to the Great Source, at the center of the Milky Way. They worshiped Nature. The only history you know about it of the Bible. Everything you know has as a parameter on the texts you call "sacred".

- And every "sacred text" tends to tell the story from the point of view of *that* particular culture.

- Right. The Eternal created countless humanities, as I have already said. Among these unknown cultures are the various peoples which flourished from Chaldea to Egypt. From the northern lands across the British Isles. Some scattered across the Caucasus. In the Andes, Mexico, India, China. All disappeared completely. Some moved to another planet, some were "rescued" like Noah and his peers. A great many of them ended up being destroyed by wars, as in ancient India or the legendary Atlantis. Those who survived the disasters and wars were gradually contaminated by errors and illusions: they turned their backs on Nature and worshiped false gods and false idols...

***

- The construction of the Great Pyramid of Egypt occurred soon after the flood, around 11,800 BC. It was built by highly evolved Earthmen with guidance and technical support from outlanders. It was a great joint venture. Each measure of the eternal monument says something, teaches something and also reveals something. You already discovered that certain measures can be decoded on dates that coincide with marked historical events of humanity. You must have already been able to calculate the day of the Last Judgment, which is also represented there. Your mind has the capacity for it.

- I've heard of this theory. So it is true?

- The day of the "victory over Darkness". The day when those who live by the recognition of the Source, and not by fear, will prevail. All this was bequeathed to mankind by these pure civilizations because The Creator knew that future humanity could be taken by the wiles of illusion and error. The Rebel Angel scheme is very powerful. There was the possibility that all knowledge would be lost.

- There is still! – said Fernando.

- The dark ones could never totally destroy this legacy, nor has it ever been their primary goal. Remember! The powers of the enemies of Life are deceit and delusion, but evolution is impossible to be stopped. The error seeks to hinder and delay evolution so that the deceiving Hidden Power prevails for a little bit longer.

- They divert our attention with the lies they sell. It's a kind of justice, if we think about it. *Who has ears to hear... Who has eyes to see...* those are great teachings. No one wants to hear or see anything.

- With the slow and relentless passage of time humanity slowly lost its certainties about the Love of the Source. Doubt began to settle in the hearts of men. A confused humanity was easy prey for the "error agenda". The seed of lies and deceit are also implanted in the DNA of men. After all you have within you all the possibilities of the Cosmos. It was easy to create a great emptiness with superstitions and false doctrines. It was easy to lie about a divine reality outside of your inner selves and fill the void with illusions of salvation.

- It was not difficult, but it was bloody...

- Violence and fear is of great use in every bloody agenda. In parallel to all this, there were more highly evolved human races exploiting mineral resources on Earth. DNA was the currency of exchange between them and the Earth reptilians. But I'll tell you about it. Everything in its time. I need to prepare you for that...

- Prepare for what? – Fernando asked with great discomfort.

- I will not wait for you to ask. There is no time. Do you know what the heads of the Square mean above the pyramid?

- No! Tell me.

- After I left, a few centuries before the flood, when my children were fully adapted to Earth, I was worshiped not as an incomprehensible Goddess but as a *present force* of Light. They did not make the error of creating a systematized religion upon my existence. In my sojourns on Earth, I did countless public conferences on how important it is to live only with high thoughts, how good is a measured life, how good it is to love their fellow even without knowing them. They experienced the Truth of my words and chose to live this way. They knew the truth about their origins, about sacred interdependence with the Cosmos, about coexistence. In short. I taught them how the rules of Universal Love should be fulfilled. I told them exactly what I expected from them and said they were free to choose whether they wanted to live under those rules or under another system.

- That was wise.

- My constant presence kept wisdom alive. I never had to come back here because of problems. They, with each coming generation, understood the message and actually lived in peace. It was almost impossible that it happened so successfully. The whole Universe knew of my children and all the humans with proper technology came here to pay homage to them and me. Obviously the visitors did not worship me as a *goddess* because they already knew how things worked in the Third Dimension. I stopped visiting them because I fulfilled my mission. I was taken back in and returned to serve the designs of my beloved Creator. They were doing well... harmony prevailed... then the cataclysmic disaster. The few survivors resumed civilization, spreading through the Andes. Gradually they adapted to the new atmospheric conditions and diminished in size and in cerebral capacity until they got to the size of you today. The dark ones had no interest in them for many centuries. The Inca, distant descendants of my children, are an example of a civilization that, like the Mayans, Aztecs and many others, reached an evolutionary peak and declined with contact with the Catholic Religion. When it was convenient, the error was brought to these lands in the arms of the naive Jesuits and their stupid convictions based on sacred lies...

***

- And so... in the meantime, humans from every corner of the cosmos have continued to come here for thousands of years. After the Universal Flood, the square up the pyramid has become an interstellar meeting point. The base for the ships was Puma Punku. I used to gather my people on the basis of this inverted pyramid. In order to honor me, the survivors and the visiting outsiders, the ones who knew what had done on Earth, built what you call *Plaza de las Cabezas*. They built it to leave no clues to the location of the pyramid. It was necessary to preserve the most sacred place of my people. That place was where I came to them. The Earth was constantly being visited by other beings from other planets with dominating and violent nature. The Anunnaki, which I have already mentioned, are best known because of their texts have already been deciphered.

- Yet, few recognize these Anunnaki as real. Me for example. I know little about them.

- They were not violent or evil. They just wanted to explore the resources that interested them. They created a kind of humanity by adapting the genetics of the humanoids from the region they explored to the south on the continent that you call Africa. As time passed, other visitors began to collect the DNA of my children, who were perfect. They wanted to create clones to work for them on their sites. Each created their humanity in their colonies throughout the world according to their own image and likeness. That is why there are so many different races on Earth. They came here to mine raw materials. The Draconians, by having control of the planet through the fallen reptilians, charged only a small fee of the visitors for the extraction of riches.

- The currency was DNA!

- That is why there are so many different races on Earth. They were created as the Sumerians to work. Then they were abandoned by their "gods". From that moment forward men became property of the reptilian landlords. It was like a land lease. These "creators" or "gods" left their earthly priests here to keep order so that the reptiles could continue to exploit them. Thus began the infiltration and conjuration of the secret societies that were originally initiatory schools, as in Egypt.

- And the same mess has spread all over the world in colonies isolated from each other. – said Fernando, puzzled.

- The perfect harmony of the lives of my surviving children was broke down. They forgot their origins. Very little understanding and recognition about their Creator remained. The superstitions began to spread and then they turned me into a "goddess". This is how a story becomes legend. Fear and superstition settled in and all was lost.

- Have your children fallen into idolatry like all other peoples? Couldn't you help it? Or you just didn't care? This is nasty! It's vile! This is painful to hear! – he cried in mental pain.

Fernando got used to the idea of being out of his body. The clarity of thought was incredible and he could visualize everything she said. It was like a 3D movie about human and cosmic realities. He could see clearly what the Orejona Civilization was like. It was as if he were there, present in the scene and in the unfolding of the facts. He can see how genetic manipulations were done in advanced laboratories. He saw the birth of Orejona's first son, he felt what she meant by the *archetype of fear*. Even so, he did not settle for this genetic exploitation. Orejona continued.

- Whenever they returned to their planets, these human beings with advanced technology in genetics took vivid samples of the humans they had created themselves, couples for procreation, to attempt a hybridization program among their own people. My children were genetically perfect and they began to be spread throughout the Universe. Some experiences did not work due to individual peculiar problems, but mainly because they spiritually degenerated. Cleansing cycles happen naturally throughout the Cosmos, but I've learned of innumerable cases where their creators had to deliberately destroy their civilizations and begun all over again. Some creations became lethal and blew themselves up, like the Atlanteans.

- Hold on! – said Fernando with a large question mark on his face. – Are humans *invariably* slaves to some "god"? We are a political plaything and at the same time... an universal pet work? Wherever I am in this infinite Universe, are my fellow beings nothing but a cheap labor force?

- Yes. But my civilization was not created for that purpose. Nor was that of the Eternal Father. Both were created to love, to be interdependent, happy and spiritually fulfilled. I made sure that my children lived like that by my own choice.

- Not out of altruism! It was to save your own skin, if you had one! There was not the unconditional love you talked about! It was a staging of yours. They believed the story you told, the same way we believed the stories of the enemy! What's the ethical difference between the two of you? You also deceived your children. You just wanted to be get back to your old job! – Fernando shouted at the top of his lungs.

- Who says I don't have this love? – Orejona said quietly. – I was raised within this love, just like Lucifer was. Just like yourself, Eastman. I didn't lie to them. On the contrary, I just told the truth. It was an agenda with motivation other than pure altruism, you're right. Your brain equipment has no capacity to understand it so I will consider your doubt as legitimate and forgive you for your blasphemy. That's shows the love I have for you, humans. It is not a question of Good and Evil. It is a matter of saying **Yes to Life**.

- Why? – Fernando asked with great emotional exhaustion. – How could we forget that there is a Source within us? Intuitively, at our core, we know what is good and what is bad. Why we have fallen, for god's sake???

- Because *choice* is natural in you. You stood firm and faithful to the Source for a long time before you fell. You have been lost in the Dark for a few thousand years, especially the last 2,000 years. Soon this suffering will come to an end. All the humanities of the Universe have had their ups and downs. Some have evolved quite a bit. But the systems that have settled among the humans of the Cosmos are all alike. The degree of fear can vary, but the Third Dimension, the dual world, is dominated by the eternal tension between choices.

- Choose between the Creator or the illusions of Lucifer? Between Life and Survival? We were deceived. We are afraid! It is easy to make bad choices when you are afraid! – Fernando cried in despair, as if all mankind depended on him.

- Without fear there is no hope. Hope is the fear that something will not happen as you wish. The plane of Certainty is the Fifth Dimension. The moment you lose your hopes, that is, when you get certain that things will happen as you wish, in that moment you become a co-creator and ascend. **Fear, hope,**

just like certainty, are controllable states of mind. You earn the right of redemption when you overcome the fear of living and understand that you can co-create. Everything is in your own hands. *Know* that! You were sure you were going to get here, weren't you?

- Yes! It was amazing. – he said more calmly. – I couldn't believe it when I was in front of that painting in Cuzco. That image revealed itself to me. – Fernando said thoughtfully, but still indignant. – **I was sure!** This feeling was much stronger and more powerful than hope!

- Millions of people have already stopped in front of this picture, Eastman. It was made by Inca hands. They understood the sacred by tradition, lived in contact with their spiritual world. The message of Jesus shouts: *the journey is the great secret of life*. It was understood by those artists when they were indoctrinated by the Spaniards, although the violence. This artist, a "new anonymous Andean Christian", converted by violence, gave *you* the key to kill your Dragon. Only *you* have seen it! We didn't help you. We just put you in motion. You walked the path and found the Light. You have lost your fear and understood what the certainty of co-creation is. You had no hope! You knew it! The Third Dimension does not dominate you anymore. The Archetype of Fear that coordinates human existence is fed and reinforced by an illusion weapon called **Hope**. And you are taught to hope. Hope is a great Virtue on Earth. A great *error* perpetrated by the enemies of life!

- Trans-valuation of values! All our core values invert Nature!

- We sent you a messenger, but you drove him crazy! Nietzsche taught that these virtues that you so dearly value are false, didn't he? He said the truth. You call him Antichrist! Do you understand the situation, Eastman?

- How can you ask me to understand it? – he replied forcefully.

- Inevitability! That's simple. You know what I mean by that. Each "god" who arrived – and *many* arrived – collected DNA samples and adapted humans to their needs. They honored themselves by making beings in their image and likeness and allowed my surviving children to represent their heads on stone sculptures all over the inner extension of the walls of the great *Plaza de las Cabezas*. To every visitor, a personalized stone head. They all went there to take samples of the best beings ever created on this planet.

- To be slaves! – shouted Eastman.

- Yes, to work for them. Is this so different from what you're used to on Earth today?

- My God! But I didn't know! Now I know it and I cannot cope with it anymore! I wish I knew nothing! – he said crying with despair.

- But you looked for it! Did anyone force you to be in here and hear all this?

- No.

- You are here for a reason.

- I still don't get it!!!

- This square, over the centuries and by virtue of the experiences that each "god" had with its children, became the venue of an interplanetary community specialized in cross breeding, genetic manipulation. A kind of interplanetary scientific society. They used to meet from time to time to exchange experiences on how to develop a humanity. They were kind of intergalactic workshops and discussions on the errors to be avoided. All beings belonging to the Community were welcome there. Even the Anunnaki of Nibiru came here to seek solutions to their problems. One of the Anunnaki leaders was Enki, a great geneticist. Perhaps the most important figure in Earth's forgotten history. They came to bow to me. But they did not collect DNA. They were satisfied with their humans.

- The *Magna Fuente*! The bowl with cuneiform writings found in Tiahuanaco. Are you talking about a gathering of advanced beings who cross the Universe to exercise pure narcissism? Beings who create civilizations in their own image? A group of beings who came here to exploit resources and labor? Beings who deceived entire civilizations by claiming to be "gods"? A congregation that destroys entire humanities because of poorly managed personnel? – Fernando shouted wildly. – **What the fuck is that?**

- Understand, Eastman. It is part of something you have no intellectual scope to understand. Humanity needs these different environments and different levels of development for different cases. Every soul that incarnates has its lessons to learn. It's not just about planet Earth. These "gods" give us more alternatives so that we can improve the species. So that each incarnate individual can, out of his own free choices, return to Light. In order for the Light of humans to be full, many "filtrations" are necessary. It's like the color rooms you passed one after the other before arriving here. The interdependence created by Love leads to Freedom and this is the path that leads to universal harmony. That's what some of the symbols you saw in here are about. It's a Cosmic Law, but you always get lost on that path!

- It's not easy!

- Nobody said it would be, but that's no excuse. You are all genetically capable of being co-creators. You never understood the importance of interdependence and your connection to Love. Your Light is growing dim. You, as a community, have almost no chance of waking up from your illusions. The time is running out. There will be a great cosmic event, you know that. There will be a day when you will see that what you fear is what you crave for. The Final Battle: Good fighting Evil, as real as the air you breathe. There will be suffering, pain, death, and everything else that was written by John of Patmos. Fire and unseen barbarism. But it's not about judgment for your sins... none of that! It is only the consequences of just another human history.

- So may it come and destroy everything! It is not worthy to live like this, never! – shouted Eastman. – That's unacceptable, humiliating! Where is the Love of God? Why must we believe in it when everything around us is decadent, rotten. Why do we have to live like this if it was not our fault? Why the damned silence? We are not worthy of this Love, I know, but where is compassion? Are we left here at the mercy of lizards who suck our blood and exploit us through fear... and our Creator doesn't give a shit!?

- Eastman, calm down. I repeat. You don't need any outside salvation. Your minds have no grasp to understand the designs of Creation. Be respectful!

- Then explain it to me! –he cried in tears. – Tell me the answer! Why?

- If I said I knew it, I'd be lying. Only the Source knows. We of the Fifth Dimension are subordinated to the Source, which encompasses all reality. We do not know. We also do not have this understanding because the Source is far beyond our abilities. But we are absolutely certain that it is good and just, because that is the Nature of everything that has unfolded since the countless eternities. If I am speaking to you now, be sure that this another example of the Creator's goodness and justness. The existence of humanity is the first. To understand the pure concept of justice, you need to experience it. You have already recognized that you are part of the infinite Source of Life. You already know that the true Source is in you... in every amino acid bond of your DNA. You no longer need fear to exist. You are already a free being. You've killed your dragon.

- *"Kill the dragon within!"* – the phrase came out of his mouth. – That's what Joseph Campbell was talking about! Unlearning to fear the Dragon is the same as freeing yourself from the causes of your fears! – said Fernando, now calmer and more serene.

The anger was gone.

- Campbell was one of our envoys to help you. The Earthly Powers did away with any intellectual chance of you to see it, however clear it may have been. All of you, almost the majority of Earth's population, bear hybridized DNA. You are reptilian in some percentage. Some more, some less.

- How can we identify these differences?

- Have you met people without feelings? Or unscrupulous, unprincipled people? They don't hesitate to go over anyone to get more advantages, more money, comfort and luxury, more sex, more food, more everything! These people rule the world. These humans sold themselves to the Hidden Masters for very little. Money, basically. They are beings that can no longer be regenerated. Even if we tried, we would not be able to teach them otherwise. They have lost the ability to empathize with other human beings. And it would not be fair to take away from them what they love so much. In our Kingdom, we are unconditionally just, be sure of that. Campbell had this in mind. He knew the way to unlearn fear. He made this knowledge his way of life. He set the example and taught the way to countless beings. In the end, he fulfilled his duty with primacy. By losing fear through knowledge, you can deactivate the reptilian DNA that has been inserted into you and literally *kill the inner dragon*. Fear is the great human challenge. Yes to Life is the solution.

- Amazing! – said Fernando with a different glow in his soul.

- Eastman, you got here on your own merits. You are the first human I have communicated with since I ascended back to the Kingdom of Light. I will never reveal myself to anyone here on Earth for all eternity. I was authorized to do what I am doing by the Source itself, the Creator. You, people of the Earth, still have the chance to learn, although the time is short. You will plant the seed. The last seed. I know it will bloom. We have studied a plan to redeem mankind and we are sure it will work out.

- Excuse me... did you say... seed?

- Yes.

- Hold on! We haven't talked about the book yet. Where is this book? Where should I find it? What language was it written? What key should I use to encode the text?

- There has never been a book, Eastman. – said Orejona, calm and composed. Her gaze was pure Love.

- There is no book? But you told me that yourself a few days ago. You said it yourself to the minds of all the residents of Águas Calientes! There is no book?

- *You* are going to write this book. That's why you came here. That's why I said all these things. You will write and edit this book. It will be a great sales success on your planet. Millions of people will read it and they will know about what I told you. This is not a prophecy. *It's inevitability.* You don't need the money you will earn. So, as an example, you will create a foundation of studies and research different from the academic molds. You will personally assemble your research team based on *merit*. We know that this is the most efficient way to plant the seed in the hearts and minds of the people. This is how a virus works. It comes silently and provoke damage. But you will not work like a virus works. You will be like a seed. And it will bear fruit, we know it.

- A book! Am I going to write all that you told me?

- That's how you're going to help your species evolve. Through the knowledge of the true history of humanity. Truth shall set you free. You must go now, Eastman. Our audience is over. Don't waste time and do what has to be done. You will not be alone. Nothing will stop you. Only you can do it.

- Thank you for entrusting me with this task. I will fulfill it the best I can. – said Fernando in peace and great courage.

- We're sure you will. – said Orejona while returning Fernando to his biological body. – I'm going to drop you off near home. Be light.

DAY 21 – 10 am (Brasilia time)

Fernando opens his eyes slowly and with difficulty. The sun hurts his eyesight. A peculiar warm breeze caresses his face. He could feel his body again. The senses were slowly returning. The scent of rain gathered in the air as the silence dissolved with the sound of insects and birds in the cool morning sun. He was in Brazil, Chapada dos Veadeiros, right on top of the famous *Pedra da Baleia*, in the municipality of Alto Paraíso de Goiás, 200 kilometers north of Brasilia, almost at home.

- Wow! – exclaimed Fernando, as he stood up. – This is really a dimensional portal, as people say! Amazing!

Fernando walks slowly along the trail back to the city still connected with the wonderful experience he had just had. In his mind he spent days talking to Orejona. The more he thought, the more he remembered what had been said in illuminating details. Things he could not understand in those sacred moments because of his rational limitations were gradually becoming clear and making sense. The peace he felt during the 10 kilometer walk to the nearest hostel can also be considered sacred. It was impossible to contain it all in his mind. He started writing the book right there in Alto Paraíso de Goiás.

Eastman made contact with his house in Brasilia and reassured his mother in São Paulo. He was safe and sound. Fernando decided to stay in a hostel away from the city center. A beautiful and harmonious inn full of silence and good vegetarian food. During the day he set up a small encampment on the edge of a paradisiac emerald waterfall, opened his notebook he had sent from Brasilia and wrote everything he could remember and capture from the higher dimensions.

The connection with Orejona did not dissolve until he finished writing the book. Sometimes he wrote nothing. He just sat there, clearing his thoughts, pondering the things he now knew. The book was fast, concise, objective and explosive. He spared no spontaneity. The text was elegant, full of force, filled with strong evidence of everything he experienced and learned.

"The victory over Fear through the dissipation of illusions gives the Being an incomparable lightness of existence. This is what I call Spiritual Freedom. The consequence of fearlessness is clarity of thought."

And so he ended his book.

According to Fernando Eastman, this is the summary of the whole History.

One year later... 8pm - Qorikancha - Cuzco

It was a Friday night in the middle of the Peruvian summer. Fernando Eastman had been invited to Cuzco for an autograph night of his book which became one of the biggest sales phenomena in the world, surpassing already established writers in the market. Paulo Coelho and many other heavy weight writers were present, including the great Erich Von Daniken, Fernando's great inspiration. It was a night of celebration and joy.

His father hadn't come home. His relationship with his wife had completely evaporated with his deliberate absence. She didn't understand Paulo's motives, as expected, and asked for divorce by taking a good heap of cash. Paulo claimed to have suffered a stroke and deep amnesia due to the altitude to justify his absence. His doctors have been well paid to guaranteed that in his medical reports. He wanted to make sure the issue would be solved, for it was time to resume life. Paulo knew how to play the game and also knew how to end it. He knew he would never return to São Paulo or Brasilia since the day he left.

Fernando's book, which was published under the title "A Forgotten History", was vigorous in its content and accessible to the laity, but with a strong scientific background. The bestseller has been translated into several languages and the book has spread rapidly throughout the world along with its explosive content. It was not accepted by the scientific community that found the book a great absurdity without any concrete proof, but it was not for this people Fernando had written it to. It was a book for regular people. Ordinary people who were immediately captivated by the information he put on paper. Despite the not-so-positive reviews, the book sold like a *caipirinha* on the beach.

The Peruvian government recognized the book as ennobling of the Andean culture – not mentioning the impulse it gave to the local tourism – and offered Fernando a launching cocktail of the Spanish version *inside* the Convent of Santo Domingo in the same room he was given the key to understand the mystery of Orejona.

In order to undo once and for all the great malaise generated by the persecution of Fernando and the other scientists who worked in the country, the highest distinction of honor conferred upon the great achievers in the history of the country. Fernando received the medal with gratitude and thanked *señor Presidente* for having made him travel through the whole country in an articulated speech.

- Hey, dad. How is re-adaptation to urban life? – Fernando asked cheerfully.

- Not bad, son. I just miss the silence. Life in Cuzco is good when you have peace. – said the old man, who was also very happy.

- Have you read the critics, dad? Did you read what they said about the book? I was even called an "intellectual clown" by an American critic. A French newspaper labeled me a "profligate charlatan."

- Who cares about that, son. Look how many copies you have sold. It's the same thing that happened to many other visionary writers. In the end the collaboration is much more positive precisely because the critics don't like the book. How many people did you reach? How many people now know about things they didn't even think possible? Like Von Daniken, you faced your mission with praise. I'm sure that Orejona and the whole Kingdom of Light up there are singing their hymns in your honor.

- I do not know about that. Although I wrote a good text, the critics labeled it as another good conspiracy theory book, as expected. I don't know if my task has been completed. We'll never know.

- What matters is that it was written and sold a lot. She, Orejona, spoke of a seed, didn't she? Well, it was planted in fertile ground. Everyone is talking about your book and, you know... when they like what they read, they never forget. One day we will see the fruits of your adventure on this planet. Remember son: *the road is the true journey, not the arrival.*

- You're right. That's what happened to me when I read *"Grande Sertão: Veredas"* of Guimarães Rosa. It can't be washed away.

- How is the Eastman Foundation? Is it already working? Thanks for the homage! – said the old Eastman proud of his son.

- Yeah. We're studying Wiracocha. The myths surrounding this figure will still bring novelties. Too bad I don't have Her help anymore. – said Fernando, looking up in reference to Orejona. – But I have Rico, my great friend and deputy. He is coordinating some field research and he has proven to be an excellent leader. I'm learning a lot from him.

- I'm sure you're going to do a great job with this team. Even bigger than you did. Larger than your book, maybe. – said Paulo Eastman, staring at his son deep in the eye.

- Bigger than this? What can be bigger than all this? – said Fernando, breathless, remembering the whole adventure.

- In Cairo... there's a bookstore, you...

They were interrupted by the organizer of the event.

After his speech of appreciation for the award, Fernando was supposed to take his place in a comfortable chair behind a table set up right in front of the inspiring picture to begin his autograph session. That night he signed about 700 books making the event one of the most intense in Cuzco since the Spanish invasion. It was almost midnight when the last person handed him a copy to autograph. He was very tired because of the signing marathon. He took the book from the person's hands and asked without looking:

- What's your name?

- Odalisca. Odalisca dos Santos.

Fernando looks up and sees the beautiful blonde standing in front of him. They stare at each other in silence. She was blonde again and was wearing a pretty black dress with her shoulders on display. Well suited for the event. He got up and hugged her with great affection.

- We were together for a little while, but it was as if it had been forever. – said Fernando.

- That's right, nerd. I did not even have time to give you my address, my email, nothing.

- I looked for you on the Internet, but I never found anything about you. It was a surprise to know how many "Odaliscas" there are out there. – he said, laughing awkwardly.

- I never used that name. Nobody wants to add a person named Odalisca on Facebook. – she laughed. – Why did not you look for "Lia"?

- Hmm? Fake name? Why didn't you add me? There's no other Fernando Eastman on Facebook.

- I don't know. I was afraid. I didn't know what had happened to you. I didn't even know if you had survived. What if I added you and you were dead? You would never reply, you see? I was afraid to know. Things got ugly in Arequipa. The police were very angry with you. Rico and I were released a few days later and taken to Lima airport. I had to leave the country. I never heard about Rico, you know. He was put on a plane to Cuzco and sent back home. The police couldn't let him talk, but they couldn't keep him in jail. He can't be tour guide or excavate anymore, I guess! –

said Lia with embarrassment.

- I know. Luckily everything was settled with a good conversation with *el presidente*. Rico is my deputy now. How did you hear about me? How did you end up here?

- I went to the airline with a letter from the Peruvian government saying that I had been kidnapped by a group of anti-government rebels and a lot of other things the government invented. They offered me this document with the kidnapping story in exchange for me to shut up about the whole madness. I accepted, I was desperate to return home at last. And I was out of a job. I was readmitted and they also gave me a raise because of what had happened to me. One day a friend of mine told me about a book she read. I borrowed it and when I saw your name and photo I was very happy. Really happy, nerd. It was like I was born again. It was nice to know that you were okay, you have no idea.

- Yes, Lia. It's the same feeling I'm having right now as I see you in front of me here, beautiful as ever. Remember the day we were here? If it were not for you, none of this would be possible.

- I didn't even notice. I was all "tourist" that day. I didn't even pay attention to the painting. You saw things no one has ever seen. It's *your* merit.

- Yeah, but if it wasn't for you I wouldn't be here. My prejudices and my blindness wouldn't let me. I mention you in the book.

- I read it, nerd. You write really well. And I ended up understanding a lot of things!!! You mean a fake Lia tried to take you to the shower? – said Lia, with a strong tone of irony. – Was she as beautiful as me?

- There is something special about you. She didn't call me a nerd. This is unacceptable! –he laughed, embarrassed. – I never took you out of my head, Lia.

- Neither did I, nerd. You are very special to me. – said Lia, embarrassed too as the room slowly emptied.

Fernando signed her book.

He wrote: "For a very special woman !!!".

- Where are you staying? Are you free today? – Fernando asks directly.

- At the same hotel! I'm staying here for two days until my next flight.

- Me too! In the same hotel! Interesting! It must have been a coincidence! – said Fernando with a great irony and gleam of happiness in his eyes. – This deserves a celebration, doesn't it?

- Pisco? – Lia said with a warm look.

- Pisco. But if you don't find your room, I'll have to be hard on you. – said Fernando with an authoritative tone, but clearly with many ideas in mind.

- Deal. San Blás?

- San Blás.

THE END.

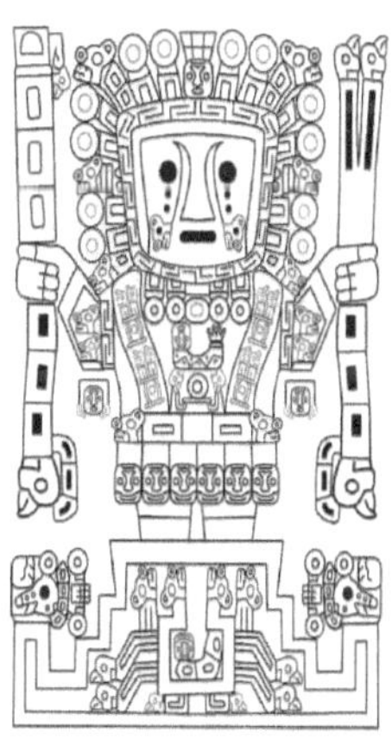

About the author
Cesar Luis was born in 1970 in São Bernardo do Campo, São Paulo - Brazil. Law degree, Gaia lover, author of "Saluh", "The Holy Divers vol.1 - The Diaspora of the Mysteries" (both available in e-book and paperback at www.amazon.com) and many other books yet to be published in English.
Say hello at facebook.com/cesarcesar1970

www.lunaeditora.com
lunaeditora@hotmail.com
www.facebook.com/lunaeditora